TIED *to the* TRACKS

TIED *to the* TRACKS

ROSINA LIPPI

G. P. Putnam's Sons
New York

G. P. PUTNAM'S SONS
Publishers Since 1838
Published by the Penguin Group
Penguin Group (USA) Inc., 375 Hudson Street, New York, New York 10014, USA ·
Penguin Group (Canada), 90 Eglinton Avenue East, Suite 700, Toronto, Ontario M4P
2Y3, Canada (a division of Pearson Penguin Canada Inc.) · Penguin Books Ltd, 80
Strand, London WC2R 0RL, England · Penguin Ireland, 25 St Stephen's Green,
Dublin 2, Ireland (a division of Penguin Books Ltd) · Penguin Group (Australia),
250 Camberwell Road, Camberwell, Victoria 3124, Australia (a division of Pearson
Australia Group Pty Ltd) · Penguin Books India Pvt Ltd, 11 Community Centre,
Panchsheel Park, New Delhi–110 017, India · Penguin Group (NZ), Cnr Airborne
and Rosedale Roads, Albany, Auckland 1310, New Zealand (a division of Pearson New
Zealand Ltd) · Penguin Books (South Africa) (Pty) Ltd, 24 Sturdee Avenue,
Rosebank, Johannesburg 2196, South Africa

Penguin Books Ltd, Registered Offices:
80 Strand, London WC2R 0RL, England

Library of Congress Cataloging-in-Publication Data

Lippi, Rosina, date.
Tied to the tracks / Rosina Lippi.
p.   cm.
ISBN 0-399-15349-7
1. African American women authors—Fiction.   2. Documentary films—Production
and direction—Fiction.   3. Women motion picture producers and directors—Fiction.
4. Georgia—Fiction.   I. Title.
PS3562.I5795T54   2006   2005053939
813'.54—dc22

Printed in the United States of America
1   3   5   7   9   10   8   6   4   2

BOOK DESIGN BY AMANDA DEWEY

For Bill, who makes all the difference

Happiness is the china shop; love is the bull.

· ONE ·

Summer in Georgia, sweet and ripe and heavy with heat at a quarter to nine in the morning. In the window of a redbrick building awash in early-morning light, the figure of a man. Tall, broad of shoulder, rumpled short, dark hair, blue eyes. Framed by oak and ivy he looked like an advertisement from a glossy magazine. Elegant, self-assured, unapproachable.

It's only John Grant, Lydia told herself. *Lucy Ogilvie's oldest boy. You've known him all your life.* And still he seemed as alien and remote as a face on a television screen. John Grant had connections, money, looks, education, position, authority; he had a beautiful fiancée who was his social equal, and on top of all that, he was the new chair of the English department at Ogilvie College.

It had been a stupid idea to make an appointment to see him. She was thinking of turning around when he caught sight of her.

"Lydia?"

A smile broke out on his face. A real smile, one that made the skin around his blue eyes crinkle, but more than that: it made him look real. His voice was deep and a little hoarse and his tone—the word came to mind and she couldn't dismiss it out of hand—sincere.

"Come on up, coffee's on and time's a-wasting."

The office was a mess. Stacks of boxes everywhere, books in wobbling towers in front of empty bookshelves, a cascade of binders. He held the door for her and she stepped over a small mountain of manuscripts bound with rubber bands to get to the couch. The whole time he talked, asking questions and sometimes answering them himself, but his manner was easy and his tone friendly. He might have spent half his life in the North with his father's people, but John Grant sounded like Georgia to her, and more than that, he had things to say and he wasn't afraid to share them. He was in the middle of a story of lost boxes and wayward moving vans when he interrupted himself to hold out a cup in her direction.

"Milk? Sugar?"

Lydia, against all inclination and training, told him the truth: she liked both, in quantity. This didn't seem to faze him at all, he just loaded up the cup and then brought it over to hand to her. And then John Grant pulled out a white bakery bag, transparent with butter and smelling of browned sugar. "Have a cinnamon roll," he said. "They're still warm."

Lydia studied his face closely, but found no trace of mockery. She had this idea—and very strange it was, too—that she could sit here and devour a couple thousand calories and he wouldn't take any real note of it.

"So," he said when she had told him she'd already had breakfast, "what made you decide on Ogilvie College?"

She said the first thing that came into her head. "Probably the same things that brought you back here after so many years."

That made him laugh out loud. He stood up and went to the window. "This is the best place on earth," he said. "It gets under your skin."

Lydia said, "So why did you leave?"

He turned back to her. "Because I had to earn the right to come back to stay. That's how it works in academics. Now what about you? Why Ogilvie?"

"Because of the reputation of the creative-writing program. I want to work with Miss Zula."

He was leaning against the wall, his arms crossed. "Okay, that's what you write down on an application. What's the real reason?"

Lydia considered lying, and then told the truth. "Because I'm afraid to leave home."

He thought about that for a minute. "My advice is, take advantage of this place while you're here, you'll forget about being scared. Now, you wanted to talk about your schedule, do I have that right?"

Lydia said, "Maybe I should make an appointment to talk to an adviser about this, you're busy." One last opportunity for him to get rid of her, send her to somebody, anybody else. One last chance for him to be dismissive, to be dismissed.

John Grant said, "Nah, you're here, and I might as well jump right in. You got a copy of that schedule with you?"

On his first full day in his new job as chair of the Ogilvie College English department, John Grant kept going to the window to remind himself that he was really here, settling into an office that might well be his for the rest of his working life. A thought that would disturb some men, but one he found greatly satisfying, even comforting.

Lydia Montgomery was just leaving the building, headed toward town. She stopped to talk to two kids sitting on a bench, gesturing over her shoulder toward this very window. Students would start trickling in, now that word was out. John wondered if these two would come see him. Metal glinted from lips and eyebrows and nostrils, as though they were armored knights ready to do battle. They looked vaguely familiar, but he couldn't place either of them. Her T-shirt read Rehab Is for Quitters, and his, Metallica. They would be good kids to have in a literature class, willing to ask hard questions and look beyond the words on the page.

Then an elderly woman came around a corner, erect of posture in spite of the cane she used, her face shadowed by the broad brim of a straw hat. A small dog trotted beside her, perky and watchful.

Lydia and the kids on the bench went very still as the old woman turned toward the library. Then they all relaxed visibly and John Grant, just as relieved to have escaped Miss Zula Bragg's notice, retreated back into his new office. He had no business staring out of windows anyway, not with so much work to do. Standing in the middle of a canyon of moving boxes, he contemplated where he had landed, and realized two things.

First, a single summer was hardly enough to get settled into this job before the fall semester began; and second, he had help. This office would be orderly and organized within two days and he could get down to work, because as the chair of the largest department on campus he had an executive assistant and a secretarial staff. Of course he also had 19 full- and part-time faculty members, 120 undergraduate majors and 20 graduate students—all of whom he wanted to meet with—six unstaffed courses, and a disaster of a schedule to fix. He went out into the reception area.

"Rob?"

The woman behind the desk had teeth of an unnatural pure white, very small and very sharp.

"I'm covering the desk for him, Dr. Grant."

She fawned; there was no other word for it. It was distracting, and might even fool a man who hadn't grown up around southern women like her: a cross between Lucrezia Borgia and the Avon Lady. Bone and blood, with sugar on top.

John meant to smile. He wanted to smile, but the urge to retreat was so strong that the best he could produce was a quiver at the corner of his mouth.

He said, "Call me John." It was easier than explaining, yet again, why he didn't like being called "doctor."

"Oh, I couldn't." She raised her hands to ward off the suggestion and then leaned forward to whisper. "Not in the *office*."

A battle for another day, then. John said, "Where is Rob?"

"He's out on an errand. But don't worry, I'm under strict orders to make sure you get to your meeting in time. I saw Lydia Montgomery leaving just a minute ago. In't it a pity?"

He could walk away, just extricate himself from the conversation, but this was a test of sorts. He said, "I don't see any cause for pity. She's here on a full merit scholarship, her writing samples are stellar, she's got excellent plans for her education. She's on her way to England to attend an invitation-only seminar for the summer. I'd say she's got a bright future ahead of her."

John looked Patty-Cake directly in the eye, daring her to drag out a coded phrase: *and her with such a sweet disposition;* or, *her mama is a big woman, too;* or, *in't it lucky she's got other gifts.*

After an uneasy moment while Patty-Cake sat with a frozen half smile on her face, John said, "I better get myself organized. No calls, please." He stepped backward. "Thank you, Miss Walker."

She said, "Dr. Grant, you know everybody around here calls me Patty-Cake. Except Caroline, of course, she calls me Aunt Patty-Cake. You could call me Aunt Patty-Cake if you like, seeing as how we're going to be related and all? Why—"

"Excuse me."

She stopped in midsentence and blinked at him.

"I've got some things to go over before the meeting."

All those white teeth. He showed her his own, and then retreated, contemplating the mysteries of genetics and the one thing that might keep him from actually marrying Caroline Rose. Tall, elegant, quiet Caroline Rose, a medievalist of international standing, was related to Patty-Cake Walker by blood.

John closed the door firmly behind himself.

"You look like Saint George after his first run at the dragon."

John let out an undignified yelp. His brother was sitting behind the desk, leaning back with his hands behind his head.

He said, "Shit, you scared me. I locked that door, I know I did."

"Shhhhh. Patty-Cake will hear you." Rob held up the key to the private entrance between two fingers. "A good executive assistant knows where all the keys are hidden."

"A good executive assistant doesn't hide from the office staff," John said.

Rob began to sort through a pile of mail. "And yet, here I sit, shaking in my boots."

John flopped down on the ratty green velvet couch. It was his favorite piece of furniture in the office: as big as a boat and lumpy in all the right places. He sorted through the pillows, rejected one painted with the likeness of Robert E. Lee and another with Elvis embroidered in beads. He finally found what he was looking for, a pillow that made no aesthetic or political or historical statements, and pulled it over his face.

Rob said, "She's been grilling me about you, has our Patty-Cake. And so has everybody else I've come across, from the janitor to the gardeners."

"You knew that would happen. I'm an outsider."

Rob snorted at that. "You're Lucy Ogilvie's firstborn son, that's what makes you so interesting."

John couldn't argue that point. Their mother had been born an Ogilvie, a great-great-great-granddaughter of one of the two brothers who had founded the town and the university itself. Lucy Ogilvie might have married a Yankee with the unfortunate last name of Grant, but she had brought her boys home to spend every summer right here. Then Rob had done the right thing and settled in Ogilvie, although he had found a way to do it that confounded every reasonable expectation. Now that John had followed that good example and turned his back on the North, there was real hope for the Grant boys.

"What Patty-Cake wanted to know," Rob went on, "is if y'all have decided on whether or not to settle down at Old Roses once you get married, because then you'll need a decorator, and Patty-Cake—"

"Christ," John said, burrowing deeper into the couch. "The woman is relentless."

Rob came over to drop a pile of folders on his chest.

"I told her you were the big, strong silent type who left all those little details to the bride and her four capable sisters."

"Good strategy." When he had made a bundle of the files he said, "What is all this, anyway?"

"For your meeting with the regents. You go from seeing the dean of student life directly to your lunch meeting. Your briefcase is by the door."

John pulled himself up out of the depths of the couch. "I love it when you talk executive. Faculty club?"

Rob said, "The regents never eat at the faculty club. Thomasina's. And come right back after," he added, making herding gestures toward the door. "You've got a one o'clock with the registrar."

"Hey," John said, "I got here three months early specifically to avoid a panic. Why the rush?"

Rob snorted. "All these years in academia, you should know the way things work. Where there's a free slot in any schedule, a meeting will be created to fill it. Nature abhors a vacuum and all that."

"In other words, I've landed in a black hole."

"You wouldn't be happy any other way," Rob said, opening the door. "And you know it."

Patty-Cake Walker stood there, and just beyond her, Miss Zula Bragg and her dog. Miss Zula, who had once seemed the tallest woman in the world, had begun to fold in on herself with age, but the expression in her eyes was as alarmingly astute as ever.

"Miss Zula," John said, sure that his voice must crack, "what a nice—"

"John," said the old woman. "A word, if you please. Louie." She pointed with her cane, and the dog trotted into the office ahead of her.

Patty-Cake said, "Dr. Grant, I tried to tell Miss Zula that you have an important meeting—"

"Not that important. Come in, Miss Zula, please. Rob, would you get some tea and call the dean to reschedule? Thank you, Ms. Walker, that will be all."

Patty-Cake drew in a sharp breath but she slipped away without protest, Rob just behind her. That left John alone with a seventy-five-year-old woman who had once been the bane of his existence, and who promised to take up that role again, now that he had come back to Ogilvie.

She said, "You've gone and thrown your little brother to the lions, John."

John pulled out one of the deep leather chairs for her. "Rob can take care of himself. I was planning to come by to see you this afternoon. I haven't been here forty-eight hours yet."

Miss Zula ignored the chair and walked to the couch, where she settled herself with her gloved hands folded over the head of her cane. Louie jumped up beside her. He had one blue eye and one brown and a companionable way about him. Miss Zula's dogs always did; she would no more tolerate a surly dog than she would a whining undergraduate.

For a long moment she studied John. Silence was her usual response to excuses; it was amazing how a remorseful student would respond to it by digging himself deeper and deeper into a hole. It was an excellent trick, one of many John had borrowed from Miss Zula to good effect in his own teaching career. But he wasn't a student anymore, and he couldn't let himself be intimidated by her, not if he wanted to make a success of this job. That meant working with Miss Zula, who had never found the right moment to retire from teaching, although her doctor—who happened to be her nephew—was constantly after her to do just that.

She said, "Bubba's waiting for you, is he?" Miss Zula was the only person John knew who dared to call the head of the board of regents by his boyhood nickname.

"I'm not concerned," John said.

Miss Zula snorted softly. "You're as bad a liar now as you were as a boy, John Grant. Of course you're worried. You have to go in there and tell them that I don't want anything to do with their party."

John's eyes strayed to the posters pinned to the board behind the couch and just above her head. There were ten of them, one of which would be chosen as the official announcement for next spring's celebration. The undergraduates had already come up with their own name for it: the Bragg Bash. A hundred fifty years for the university was not nearly as interesting as the fact that next June would be the fiftieth anniversary of Zula Bragg's graduation from Ogilvie. Its first black woman graduate, its brightest star, the recipient of every literary prize ever given, this elderly black woman with beetle-dark eyes. In her flowered dress and straw hat and white gloves she looked more the part of a church organist, but she had produced some of the country's greatest literature.

The Regents were so busy contemplating the media attention, the free publicity, and the bump-up to the endowment that they had forgotten to reckon with Miss Zula's dislike of fuss.

"It's the nature of the beast," John said. "I disappoint them, and they cut my budget. Sometimes the order is reversed."

She pushed out an irritated breath, her brow drawn down to a deep V. "Do you think you got this job because they have the idea you know how to deal with me?"

John laughed at that. "Not even the regents are that blind, Miss Zula. You'll do exactly what you want. You always have. And I got this job on my merits."

"But why did you want it to start with, that's the question." She was looking at him closely, her eyes slightly narrowed, as if with enough effort she could see into his head.

"People keep asking me that," John said. "I don't get it. Why shouldn't I want to be here? I've got family and friends in Ogilvie, I like the town, and I love the college. I think I can do some good things for this department. I like the students."

"And there's Caroline." Miss Zula wasn't smiling.

"And there's Caroline," John agreed. "I'm thirty-six, you know. It's about time I settled down."

"You sound like Patty-Cake Walker," Miss Zula said. "Life isn't a cake recipe, John. Following the rules somebody else sets out for you won't get you any prizes."

"Why, Miss Zula," John said, grinning. "You know I'm not about to pay Patty-Cake any mind, not with you close by to advise me."

She flapped her handkerchief at him, but there was a smile at the corner of her mouth. "Don't talk nonsense. Now, what are you going to tell Bubba about his anniversary party?"

John considered. He had one card left to play, and his time was limited.

He said, "I'll tell him you're not willing to take part, but I hope you'll reconsider. A fiftieth anniversary shouldn't be ignored, Miss Zula. It would be rude."

Her chin trembled, and then something surprising happened: she giggled. Miss Zula giggled like a young girl, and then she laughed.

"You just cost me five dollars, John Grant. Maddie was right, and I was wrong." She slapped her knee and bent forward, her shoulders shaking. She took out a handkerchief to wipe her eyes and Louie sat up straight and wagged his tail.

"Give Bubba what he wants, then. They can put my name up on their poster if it means so much to them."

John held himself very still. "You mean it?"

She gave him a severe look. "I never say a thing I don't mean, you know that. Now, if you had spouted a lot of nonsense about doing the right thing for this old pile of bricks"—she gestured around herself—"then I would have said no, and I would have meant that, you can count on it. I'm not an old table to be auctioned off to the curious. But you didn't trot out those sorry excuses. Rude." She laughed again.

John said, "I have this feeling there's another shoe about to drop, directly on my head."

"Perceptive as always." She put her handkerchief away and settled her hands on the head of the cane again. "Let me be clear. I will give a reading, as requested. I will attend the ceremony and the dinner and even the reception—"

"But you don't want the documentary."

She fixed him with her most severe stare.

"Pardon me," he said. "I interrupted."

"You most certainly did. All those years among the Yankees has had a detrimental effect on your manners, John. I did warn your mama."

"I am sincerely sorry."

Her mouth twitched. "Under certain conditions I will allow the filming of a documentary."

John waited, trying to look interested but not particularly worried. It was the documentary that had caused the rift between the board of regents and their prize alumna to start with. They fantasized about film festivals and Oscars; Miss Zula had rejected the idea of a strange crew of discourteous men with cameras following her throughout her day.

She said, "I don't like that Simmons fellow, and I won't have him."

"Film people are often single-minded, Miss Zula. I know you two got off to a bad start, but he's won a great many—" He saw her expression and stopped.

"Prizes don't impress me," she said, holding herself very erect. "And neither do his films. Sentimental twaddle and overextended metaphors. And Louie didn't like him."

Louie raised his head and let out a single low bark of agreement.

From the purse that always hung from her right arm she drew out an envelope. "If the board will agree to hire the film company that made this documentary, then I will allow them the access they need."

There were a hundred questions he might have asked, but he knew from experience that she would answer none of them.

"It's called *L&N 1915*," Miss Zula said.

"L&N. The old Louisville and Nashville Railroad?"

"Yes," she said shortly.

"But—"

"I'm not here to tell you the story, John. Watch the documentary and you'll understand why I want this particular film company." She leaned forward. "I have done some research. I have consulted friends and colleagues who are knowledgeable."

"And this documentary was recommended to you."

"It was. In the highest terms. It is thorough and thoughtful and there's a sharp edge to it that is missing in most of what I looked at."

"Edge." The word came out in a croak.

"Yes. I believe I can trust these people not to romanticize me. I won't be presented to the world as a quaint old colored lady who scribbles. If the board will agree to this—and by that I mean, if they will offer reasonable terms to the film company—you may go ahead with your plans."

John took the envelope she was holding out to him, and then he helped her to her feet.

"I'll expect a call from you later today with the details. I want to see the contract you offer them before it's made, and I would like it to happen quickly. If it is to happen at all."

John looked down into the small face, the bright eyes, and saw a deep satisfaction there. Miss Zula might have lost five dollars to her sister today, but she had won some other wager, one she wasn't telling him about. The real wager.

He said, "Gambling is your only vice, Miss Zula, but it does have a grip on you."

That earned him another smile, a mysterious one. She patted his arm.

"Maddie asked me to invite you for supper on Sunday. You may bring Caroline Rose." She cast him a sharp glance that said *if you must.*

He had seen that look a few times from Miss Zula, most particularly when she returned a piece of work to him that she considered less than his best effort.

"Miss Zula, why don't you like Caroline?"

She pursed her lips at him. "Don't be ridiculous, John. Caroline is my goddaughter, of course I like her. I love her dearly."

That was a relief, but only a little one. There was something else Miss Zula was not saying, and would not say, no matter how he thought to ask.

At the open door she paused to wave off Rob and his tea. She said, "You boys be sure to give your mama and your stepdaddy my love when you next talk to them on the telephone. And don't forget supper on Sunday. You come along, too, Rob, and bring that pretty little wife of yours."

Caroline and Kai together at the table; that was one kind of problem, but there was a bigger one, and John held it in his hand. A square envelope exactly the size to hold a DVD case, with a label in one corner. The logo showed stylized railway ties in black and white and in scarlet script: Tied to the Tracks Productions. Hoboken, New Jersey.

"John?" Rob looked from the envelope to his brother and back again. "You look like Miss Zula took a bite out of you. What is it?"

"Nothing much," John said. "Just the end of the world as I know it."

· TWO ·

Tied to the Tracks. Independent. Full-service documentary film & videogra-
phy, digital storytelling. *L&N 1915* (full-length doc) Finalist, International
Documentary Film Festival, Stockholm; Honorable Mention, Orson Welles
Film Festival; Judges' Choice Award, IG Film Festival. Angeline Mangiamele
(producer, writer, editor), Rivera Rosenblum (photographer, editor),
Anthony Russo (photographer, sound).

1221 Washington Street, Hoboken, NJ. info@tiedtothetracks.com
"Young Blood on the Rise: Ten Independents to Watch"
www.indieindie.com

In many ways this particular summer morning at Tied to the Tracks
was nothing unusual. Angie had seen it all before: the air
conditioner on strike, the telephone company ready to cut off service, and
the reserves of everything from paper clips to videotape alarmingly low.
That was the way most small documentary film companies operated: short
on everything but panic and adrenaline.

And dedication, Angie reminded herself. It would take that much and
more to get them through this oddest of days.

They were, all three of them, in the office at ten o'clock in the morning.
Tony was here because he had been sleeping in the storage room since his
latest girlfriend kicked him out; at almost fifty he preferred the discomfort of
an old army cot to showing up on his mother's doorstep. Rivera was another
matter. Angie couldn't remember the last time Rivera had been out of bed
so early, but there she was, kneeling in front of the ancient fax machine like
a supplicant before the pope.

"Come on," Tony whispered. "Come on, come on, come on."

"I'm gonna faint," Rivera said. She ran her hands over the slick black veil of her hair, grasped the sides of her head, and rocked it. Rivera Rosenblum, who had the looks and bearing of a Cleopatra, was wiggling like a puppy.

"Oh, please. You've never fainted in your life," Angie said.

"We've never been this hungry before."

Angie looked at the damp, crumpled cover sheet in her fist and realized that she wasn't handling this any better than her partners. The phone call late yesterday afternoon from the office of the president of Ogilvie College had been brief and to the point, but she hadn't quite been able to believe it. Not until the fax machine had sputtered to life right on schedule and the pages began to appear, black on white.

Rivera had her face right up to the machine now and she was reading out loud.

"The board of regents of Ogilvie College . . ."

"Ogilvie, Ogilvie, Ogilvie," chanted Tony. His long, thin face, normally pale, was flushed with color, and the shock of black hair stood up in spikes. The jitter in his hands said he needed a cigarette, but for the moment adrenaline was holding him steady.

Rivera read: ". . . join me in extending this invitation . . . pleased to offer . . ."

Tony burst into the air like a startled pigeon, both fists pumping the air. *"Yeeeee-ha!"* Then he grabbed Rivera and they began a crazy polka, bumping into tables and knocking over chairs.

Angie caught the page as it cleared the fax machine. Her eyes ran down the smeared print.

"It's such a huge commitment."

She might have pulled out a gun for the reaction she got. Tony and Rivera stopped in mid-spin. They exchanged a look that was not lost on her, and then Rivera marched over and took the sheet out of Angie's hand. It was at times like these that Angie noticed that she was more than a head shorter than Rivera, who had played center on Smith's basketball team.

"We're doing it."

"Well, of course," Angie began, but Rivera cut her off as she took the next sheet from the fax machine.

"This is *Zula Bragg* we're talking about. The elusive. The ungettable. Complete access—"

"Sufficient access, it says here. Don't go overboard."

"It's national exposure. It's artistic control."

Tony thrust his face so close that their noses almost touched. "It's real money."

Rivera said, "We can't pass this up because you don't want to run into an old boyfriend."

Tony pulled up short. "Boyfriend?"

Angie took the next page from the machine and turned her back on him to read.

"Now you're looking for loopholes," Rivera said.

"No, I'm looking at the budget. It's . . . generous."

Tony leaned over her shoulder, his eyes running down the page. "Oh, man," he said in a low voice. "Oh, man. Who ponies up that kind of money?"

The chair of the English department could pony up that kind of money. But the time wasn't right to bring up John Grant, so Angie kept that thought to herself. She said "The endowment? Rich alums? It doesn't matter to us where it comes from." She kept her eyes on the paper, but even so she could feel Rivera's attention fixing on her.

"We've been waiting for an opportunity like this forever. We can't pass this up."

Angie forced herself to hold Rivera's gaze. She said, "Of course we can't. Of course we'll do this."

Rivera narrowed her eyes and then made up her mind to believe Angie. "Good."

"Good?" Tony echoed. "It's fucking great." And he grabbed her for another polka around the room, leaving the details to Angie.

That's what Angie did: she took care of the details, she kept things going, she talked suppliers into another month's credit, the clients into seeing things Rivera's way. Tony Russo did camera work and sound, Rivera Rosenblum directed and edited, and Angie did a little of everything, from writing the script and lending another pair of eyes to the editing process, to balancing the books. She was the practical one, lacking the urge to polka, or even to be unreservedly happy about this change in fortune. And after three unfunded grant proposals and a year made notable by the fact that even wedding work wasn't coming their way, "miracle" was the only word that came to mind.

And now, according to the words on the page in front of her, she would be talking to John Ogilvie Grant, chair of the English department, about the arrangements for a long stay in Ogilvie, Georgia. Starting as soon as they could get there.

Rivera looked up from the fax. "We could teach, too, if we wanted. In the fall semester. They've got film theory for you and introduction to digital filmmaking for me. Or the other way around, but I don't think Ogilvie undergraduates are ready for my film theories."

"We'll be done shooting by September," Angie said. "And we can come back here to do the editing."

"We aren't going to get footage of her in the classroom?" Rivera's tone made it clear that this wasn't really a question but the opening salvo in a battle.

"And they've got an editing suite—" Tony began, and then stopped, entranced by what he was reading. He thrust the fax sheet under her nose. "We can't rush out of there, Ang. It would be the death of us if we took shortcuts on this one."

Angie shot him her sharpest look. "You mope, when have you ever known me to take a shortcut?"

"So we won't be back here in September," Tony said. "Admit it."

One thing Angie prided herself on was knowing how to pick her battles, and this one, she could see very clearly, was well and truly lost. She nodded. "Okay."

Rivera did a shimmy that made her earrings dance while Tony rushed to the windows. He leaned out over Washington Street and bellowed. "So long, Hoboken!"

Rivera touched Angie on the wrist and she jumped. "Angie, Zula Bragg asked for us."

"She did," Angie agreed.

"So what's the problem?"

"No problem," Angie said, producing her biggest, brightest, falsest smile. "Not a problem in sight."

Tied to the Tracks was located in a warren of small rooms over An Apple a Day, the diner that belonged to Angie's parents. The advantages of this arrangement were substantial: they paid rent only in those months when they had the money to do so, and food was always available in abundance. The disadvantages were small by comparison. Ten-gallon cans of tomatoes stacked in every corner, boxes of pasta, crates of eggplant: these were things she could live with. Angie repeated that to herself as she went downstairs an hour later, hoping to slip out without being noticed. At least for now; at least until the signed contract was in the mail.

"Give it up, Angie," her father's voice boomed as she opened the door to the street. "I got your lunch plate right here waiting for you."

They all turned to look at her. The regulars along the counter, her mother at the cash register, her aunt Bambina picking up an order at the window, three dozen other faces she saw pretty much every day of her life. Angie went to eat the lunch her father had dished up for her.

Tommy Mangiamele was a long twist of a man with a shock of white hair neatly plastered to his head from a middle part, a great hooked nose, and liquid brown eyes that missed very little of what went on around him. He slid into the booth across from his daughter and put his coffee cup in front of himself.

"So what's all the dancing around? I thought the ceiling was going to come down on our heads. Bad for business, noise like that." He wiggled his eyebrows to make sure she wasn't taking him seriously.

"Call Ma over," Angie said. "I don't want to have to tell the story twice."

He leaned toward her, talking out of the side of his mouth while he scanned the restaurant. "Go on, give me a hint. I'll keep it a secret from her as long as you want. You got a job?"

"Yup," Angie said, examining a forkful of chicken. "That's it. Gotta go see the lawyer about the contract, go make copies, stop at the post office. So I'll come back later and give you all the details, how's that?"

He was eyeing her now suspiciously. "You going to see that Edsel guy?"

"Ford, Dad. His name is Ford."

Her father waved a hand. "Ford, Edsel, Chevrolet. What I want to know is, who names a kid after a car?"

Angie's mother slid into the booth next to him, nudged him with an elbow. "Rich people with no taste name their kids all kind a crazy things. But he's a good boy, Tommy, leave him be. Angeline, did you even look in the mirror this morning? And you got gravy on your chin. Here, let me." She leaned across the table.

"Fran, the kids got new work," Tommy said as his wife and daughter wrangled over the napkin.

"Nice job keeping that secret," Angie said, grinning in spite of herself. "Gotta go."

At heart, Hoboken was a small town. There might be a tumbling stream of stockbrokers, artists, and nostalgia buffs who settled for a year and then moved along, but for the most part Hoboken was still the same place it had been before the money showed up with the bulldozers and the renovation bug. Angie had grown up here, gone to college across the river in Manhattan, and come back again. She had never lived anywhere else. She knew everybody, everybody knew her.

She couldn't wait to get away, and the key to that was in the contract tucked under her arm.

John Grant. John Ogilvie Grant, to be precise. She had asked him once why he bothered to sign all three names and he had looked at her with those blue eyes and told her: he had made a promise to his grandmother.

And that was secret of his success. John's particular talent was dealing with people by giving in on the points that didn't really matter to him and negotiating his way on the important stuff. Southern charm with a veneer that came from old Manhattan money and the Ivy League. Tall, broad of shoulder, sandy brown hair, big hands, deep voice, deeper laugh. Deadly.

She caught a glimpse of herself in a window, small and quick, a little too round, jeans and a T-shirt, her hair a jumble down her back. She had been growing it for five years and had no plans to cut it. Had had no plans; if this thing with the Bragg documentary actually happened—please God—she'd have to rethink that.

Someday soon she would open a door and he would be there, and she would have to hold out her hand and smile and be adult.

It would probably be best to cut her hair.

The law offices were two small rooms above Mrs. Romero's shoe store. Angie ran up the stairs and into the outer office. She nodded to Marlene, who was typing so fast that her purple nails clattered on the keys like castanets. Marlene squinted at Angie from the cloud of smoke that surrounded her head, wiggled her cigarette in greeting, and turned back to the computer screen as Angie knocked on the inner office door and went in.

Ford looked up from the papers in front of him and smiled. He had an endearing smile, sweet and willing, and she warmed to it every time. They had dated for a little while, until Angie faced the fact that the best she would ever be able to say about Ford was that she liked him just fine.

He said, "I thought you'd be here a half hour ago. Lasagna?"

"Chicken and gravy," Angie said, tossing the envelope onto his desk.

"That's right," he said. "It's Wednesday." He slipped the sheets out and made a fan of them on the desk. "So this is it, huh? The big offer?"

"That's it," Angie agreed as she fell into a chair. "If there's something wrong with this contract, Rivera and Tony will slit my throat. So tell me it's all good, please."

"They signed it already," Ford said, vaguely disapproving.

"Hope springs eternal. I'm supposed to send it off right away if everything's in order."

A half hour later Ford cleared his throat and Angie, who had been sure she would never sleep again, bolted up out of a dozy daydream.

"Somebody down there in Georgia must love you," Ford said.

Angie jumped. "What is that supposed to mean?"

Ford couldn't have looked more startled if she had slapped him. "It looks good," he said. "They used the Guild contract and didn't mess with it. Credits, residuals, it's all here."

Angie relaxed back into the chair, trying for nonchalant and coming no closer than embarrassed. "It's solid?"

His eyes were still moving back and forth on the page. "Looks like it," Ford said. "Nobody down there is trying to screw you, at least not at first reading."

"Pardon me?" she said faintly.

"Contractually," Ford said, flustered now and confused, too, and why shouldn't he be; she might as well just admit what was going on. John Grant had materialized out of her past, just as she had always feared he might. John Ogilvie Grant: the biggest mistake and the best summer of her life. Angie closed her eyes and shook her head, willing it to clear and not getting very far at all.

She called the office to give Rivera and Tony the good news, heard the beginnings of a party in the background, and made excuses having to do with the unreliability of the fax machine and a decent printer. At the copy shop she could use a computer to write the cover letter and then fax the damn thing off, before she thought better of the whole business.

Except writing the letter wasn't going to be all that easy.

Dear Dr. Grant.

No, he hated to be called "doctor" and it was stupid to pretend they were strangers.

Dear Professor Grant. Dear Mr. Grant. Dear John.

Better address the letter to the President, pretend she had overlooked the bit about communicating with the English department. Angie put it together in her head as she trudged down Washington. *We are very pleased to accept your offer. Signed hard copy to follow by mail.* Succinct, businesslike, but not unfriendly. Couldn't go wrong there. Why was it then that a different letter kept writing itself in her head?

Dear John. We need the work. We'll do a good job and deal with Miss Zula. I'll go out of my way to avoid you if you'll do the same, and why is it you aren't married yet?

Of course, he might be. She tried to imagine that, and failed. She could see him as many things: chair of a department, dean, president. But not married, not yet. It wasn't in his plans.

He had charted the perfect career for himself. Ogilvie as an undergrad, advanced degrees at Brown and Harvard, a year at Cambridge, assistant professor at Columbia, promotion and tenure and then five years as a tenured professor at Princeton. Now back to Ogilvie. A lifetime ambition, and one he had never been able to explain to her, not so that she understood. Because he didn't understand it himself.

You can always tell the chair of an English department, he told her once. *It'll be the person who runs the slowest.* But he had gone to Ogilvie of his own free will, she knew that without being told: it was impossible to imagine him doing anything that he didn't want to do. With some exceptions.

Better not to think about John Grant in her bed, but memories couldn't be erased, not even if she wanted to. Which she didn't. And that was the heart of the problem.

They had watched each other for a whole academic year, September to May.

Angie first saw John Grant crossing Waverly Place; he caught her attention because, she told herself, he was a new face in the familiar river of students and staff and faculty. She soon realized two things: first, that she saw him most often around the English department building on certain days of the week, and second, that he was watching her, too.

There was nothing she could do about needing to pass that particular corner every day. It was on a straight line between the apartment she shared with Rivera and the film center. And anyway, she lectured herself, why should she? She saw thousands of faces every day, about half of them men. Some of those men looked at her; sometimes she looked back. She had had a fair share of men in her life, and would have more.

She could simply stop one day and ask him if he wanted to go for coffee. Except she didn't, but neither could she keep herself from looking for him, and when she did find him, he was looking right back at her.

Not a month after it all started Rivera caught on. She was at first mystified that Angie, who had never been shy, should hang back. Then she decided to take the matter into her own hands. In short order Rivera had established that John Grant wasn't new faculty at all, but a visiting professor who came downtown from Columbia three days a week to teach a course on Whitman's New York. Straight and unattached.

"Good for him," Angie said, keeping her eyes on the script in her lap.

Rivera said, "The only question is, which one of you will give in and make the first move."

"Not me," Angie said. "Not this time. It's too corny for words, falling for a professor from afar."

"Sometimes corny is what you need," Rivera said.

"No, what I need is very simple, and I get that from Scott."

To which Rivera snorted. She didn't think much of Scott, a grad student in comp lit who was too quiet and too predictable for Rivera's tastes. Angie liked having Scott around for just those reasons.

The problem was, there was no avoiding John Grant. The very idea of him was everywhere, floating in the air, unavoidable. Total strangers seemed intent on sharing things Angie couldn't possibly need to know. Waiting in line at Starbucks, she heard undergraduates discussing ways to run into him, what might interest him, if it would be a good idea to try to get into one of his courses uptown, if it was true that he was one of the *Grant* Grants and lived in twenty rooms on Morningside.

"He rows every morning," one of them said.

"Should have gone out for crew," said her friend.

But Angie didn't have to hatch plots; wherever she went she ran into John Grant, and soon he was featuring in many of her dreams.

"It's redirected anxiety," she told Rivera when they were in the editing lab together. "Easier than worrying about what comes next." Neither of them had gone on the job market, sticking to their early plans to stay independent. The hard part was watching the other people in their class flinging themselves out into the world, accepting jobs with Lucasfilm and PBS. Of course she had to find something else to obsess about, Angie told herself, and a man she would never talk to was just the ticket.

By January they were saying hello, holding glances a little too long, each of them calculating the next step, the potential gain and the complications. Scott called and she found herself making excuses.

John Grant was faculty; she was a grad student. Angie had nothing to do with his department, but it was touchy, these days, professors and students, no matter the details. That excuse made Rivera laugh out loud. She wasn't one for rules when it came to basic human instincts.

"There he is," she would say in an exaggerated whisper, elbowing her. "Your guy."

Rivera described herself as part English, part Jewish, part Puerto Rican, part Mohawk, and all nose. She could smell attraction on the skin; she said it reminded her of apricots cooking.

On the day they finished the last of their class work—nineteen years of schooling, done and over forevermore—Angie and Rivera sat out on the roof of their apartment building on West Eighth Street and drank red wine. There were three different parties going on in the building across the street, one on each floor. It was more entertaining than television, which felt like work.

Rivera matched up people from one party with people from another, man on man, woman on man, woman on woman.

"Those two," Rivera said. And: "Those three." She picked out somebody for herself, a young black woman wearing what looked like a Chanel suit. Rivera considered it her mission in life to wean women from their preoccupation with penetration.

"Go on over," Angie encouraged her.

"Soon," Rivera promised. "Oh, no, look at that." A tall, awkward type with a very, very short woman, both of them wobbly drunk. "That won't last a week, but the sex will be interesting."

Angie laughed so hard that she almost choked on her wine, and while Rivera was pounding on her back they both caught sight of John Grant, talking to the Chanel suit.

"Your guy, my girl," Rivera said. "Let's go."

Angie wasn't drunk but she wasn't quite sober, either. Otherwise she might not have done it, followed Rivera across the street and up the stairs. She walked right up to John Grant, her blood pounding in her ears.

He was wearing an immaculate white shirt with long sleeves folded to just below the elbow, black jeans, and a day's worth of beard. She had to tilt her head back to look him in the eyes: blue, with creases at the corners. He gave her a flashbulb smile, blinding, electric; she felt the shock of it slide up her back.

"You've been watching me," she said.

"Oh yeah. It's what I do."

He had deep voice and a very southern accent, something Angie hadn't noticed in passing, and never anticipated. The surprise of it robbed her of what she was going to say next.

He leaned toward her. "It was your hair first caught my eye."

She touched it: untamable, best ignored.

In the noisy room he leaned closer still. "It's beautiful."

Angie smelled the beer on his breath, and other things: curry, a hint of ginger. Food was something she could always talk about.

"You went out for Indian," Angie said sadly. More than a little drunk now, but it had less to do with alcohol than with the way he was looking at her.

"Come on, Angeline," he said, taking her elbow. "We'll get you something to eat."

"You know my name," she said, letting herself be directed.

"You don't know mine?" He drew back to look, challenging her: she could try coy, or they could get right to it.

"John Grant. Columbia English Department. Straight and unattached. Except for—" She looked for the Chanel suit and saw her in the kitchen with Rivera, both of them laughing.

"Gloria. Just a colleague," he said, and steered her toward the door.

They sat across from each other at a small table covered with dishes: lamb vindaloo, chicken tikka, a great milky bowl of cucumbers in yogurt, curried potatoes. Angie had an appetite, and food was the right distraction just now.

They talked easily. She told him about her thesis project, the short documentary she had put together about the Armenian population in the Bronx, the company she and Rivera wanted to start up. Her family over the river in Hoboken, the diner.

"Mangiamele," he said. "Apple eater."

She glanced up at him over the rim of her cup. "You speak Italian?"

It turned out he had spent a year in Italy as an undergraduate, but the stories he liked to tell, the ones that made his face open up, had to do with his family. He had a brother in law school who made a career out of flaunting expectations, a whole town of relatives in Georgia and another, aging contingent on the Upper West Side, but he was closer to his mother's people down south. The apartment building he lived in on Morningside had been in his father's family since 1910. The fact that he had accepted a tenured position at Princeton starting in the fall slipped out sideways when she asked him if he thought of moving back to Georgia.

And all the while they kept falling into short silences, looking at each other and smiling. Never talking about the months they had just spent circling each other; not needing to.

Then she had enough of food and of waiting, too.

"Rivera says—"

"Rivera?"

"My roommate. My friend. With the"—she swirled her hand around her head—"embroidered headscarf?"

"With Gloria in the kitchen."

"Yes, that's the one. Rivera says we've got a month at most, but it will be good while it lasts."

He was trying not to smile. "What leads Rivera to such a hasty conclusion?"

Angie was flustered now and felt the first throb of remorse. "Probably she was overly optimistic."

That was the first time she saw a particular look come into his eyes, a narrowing that meant he had plans. Her hand was on the table and he picked it up, pressed her fingers to his own wrist. Muscular forearms—*should have gone out for crew*—and cool skin; she felt herself jerk. She said, "Your pulse is racing."

"Oh, yeah. I got the Kentucky Derby going on."

That flashbulb of a smile; she had to look away.

On the street in front of the restaurant he caught her hand again, pressed her up against the wall to take her pulse, and then he kissed her. Ivy League and old money, but he was good at it. Angie kissed him back, and meant it.

They walked back to Angie's apartment on West Eighth Street, no sign of Rivera or Gloria of the Chanel suit, and thank God; Angie had never been so nervous or so sure. But still she went first thing to the refrigerator and stood in its cold light, one arm on the open door, feeling him behind her and afraid to turn around. Gooseflesh on her back and arms and the insides of her thighs.

"What are you doing?" he asked.

"Genuflecting in front of the leftovers. It's an Italian thing. Want something to drink?" She took a can of beer and turned to touch his cheek with it. He started and covered her hand with his own, moved the can to her throat and down.

"Ah," she said, and he kissed her there, up against the overfilled refrigerator, the smells of salami and Gorgonzola and very ripe peaches rising around them. The cold can pressed to her collarbone, and his mouth, warm and soft and knowing.

That was the start of it.

At Jin-Woo's Copy Hop she wrote the two-sentence cover letter to the university president and watched the pages of the initialed and signed contract go through the fax machine while Ramon told her about his latest idea for a movie: *Die Hard* meets *Priscilla, Queen of the Desert.*

"Woman hires a hit man—she's tired of her husband screwing around, you see it? But a chick shows up, a hit woman. Then she turns out to be a man after all. A transvestite. So the rich lady, she's all confused because she's got the hots for another woman, and then she finds out she's a he anyway." Ramon's tattoos glowed in the fluorescent lights. "I'm thinking Penelope Cruz."

"As the transvestite?" Angie could usually coax a smile out of Ramon, but today he was wound up in fame and fortune. He frowned at her lack of vision.

"It's been done," she told him. "*Victor/Victoria, The Crying Game.*"

Ramon leaned across the counter, muscles in his shoulders rolling. "Angie," he said. "Listen to me, girl. You going to grab a good thing when you see it, or let this one get away from you too?"

There's the question, Angie thought as she went back to the computers to write the harder letter.

She could do this by computer, but she wanted more control. One click and e-mail was gone into the ether, as absolute and remorseless as the spoken word. The letter she could carry around in her pocket until the right moment came, and then even once it was in the mailbox she might be able to get it back; she knew all the letter carriers.

. . . we understand from President Bray's letter that time is of the essence, and so we will be arriving in Ogilvie toward the end of next week . . .

She went through it step by step, answering every question she could anticipate, working hard to strike the right tone: cooperative, thorough, detached. At the end she hesitated.

We look forward to this opportunity to work with Miss Zula.

Her fingers hesitated above the keys while she listened to the sentence humming in her mind. *For whatever role you may have played in bringing this work our way, many thanks.*

It was a statement and a question, too. The real question, the one she had been pushing away since the first hint of what was coming her way, that phone call from Georgia. What she wanted to know but could not ask was, Who was it who had given Zula Bragg their work to look at? All the way back to the office, Angie tried to get that question out of her head, and failed.

· THREE ·

Zula McGuffin Bragg was born in Ogilvie, Georgia, on April 2, 1930, the first daughter and second child of Martin Bragg, a music teacher, and Luisa McGuffin McCleod Bragg, a graduate of Bethune-Cookman College. In 1948 Ms. Bragg was the first African-American to be admitted to Ogilvie College. After graduating magna cum laude in 1952 she taught English at Ogilvie's Colored High School. Her first novel, *Magpie*, was published by Knopf in 1955 when she was twenty-five. In 1958 she was awarded the Pulitzer Prize for a series of essays on voting rights in the South. In 1961 she received a master of arts degree from Columbia University and accepted a position on the faculty of the English department at Ogilvie College, where she is still active. Ms. Bragg has published more than fifty short stories, three books of collected essays, and six novels. Her work has been translated into twenty-three languages. Her novel *Catch Can* won both the Pulitzer Prize and the National Book Award. She has twice been shortlisted for the Nobel Prize. Ms. Bragg lives in Ogilvie, Georgia, in the house where she was born.

The Dictionary of Southern Women Writers of Color

J ust when John was beginning to hope that dinner at Miss Zula's might turn out all right after all, she pointed her sharpest gaze at him and asked the one question he was hoping to avoid.

"Did you watch that documentary, John?"

All faces turned to him. "Yes, ma'am, I did. Miss Maddie, might I have a little more of your fried chicken?"

"Of course you may. Caroline, will you please eat, child? I swear, you've got to stand up twice to throw a shadow."

Kai said, "Documentary?" and that was the beginning of the end.

John's sister-in-law was Japanese. She had been in the States for ten years but her curiosity about things American was unquenchable. Kai Watanabe also had a doctorate in math, which meant that her curiosity was bolstered by an unflinching logic that she applied indiscriminately, whether or not the subject matter could bear that burden. On top of that, Kai was married to Rob Grant, who delighted in her apparent compulsion to say exactly what she thought and ask the questions that everybody was thinking but nobody else dared to put into words. Together at any traditionally southern table, Kai Watanabe and Rob Grant constituted a cultural revolution.

Worst of all, Kai was the only person who could throw Caroline off balance. John had seen it happen a half dozen times and it still surprised him; he had yet to find an explanation that made any sense. Caroline, who could face down the nastiest of critics in open debate at a conference panel, seemed to fall apart when Kai Watanabe's attention turned in her direction.

Now Kai's perfectly shaped face was lifted up to John's. "What documentary?"

"Miss Zula gave it to me. Done by the company that's coming down to do the filming. And, yes, Caroline and I have watched it together."

"And?" Kai said, her fork poised. "Did you like it, Caroline?"

Caroline cleared her throat very gently, which meant she was irritated by Kai's questions but was struggling not to show it.

"Yes, I did."

Kai's fork hovered still. "Why?"

"What documentary is this we're talking about?" Miss Maddie said. "Is it the one about the opera singers?"

"Lord, no," said Miss Zula. "It's the one about the old L&N Railroad."

"Oh, yes," Miss Maddie said. "About the Shortt children going off to Berea College." She turned to Miss Zula. "Who sent that to you, sister? Was it somebody from one of those northern schools?"

As far as Miss Maddie was concerned, no institution north of Princeton had any claim to her attention, and she refused to remember their names.

"That's right," Miss Zula said, smiling at Kai.

Miss Maddie warmed to her story. "A poor farming family in . . . where was it now?"

"Virginia," said Miss Zula, who was watching the table with undisguised pleasure. No doubt she would write a short story about this. Miss Maddie collected postcards, and Miss Zula conversations.

"Virginia," Miss Maddie nodded happily. "Subsistence farmers, the very poorest, but hardworking? Oh, my. And they managed to send all five of their girls and three of the boys off to Berea College. The boys all studied to be teachers and the girls all became nurses. Every last one of them. The first one in 1915, if you can imagine such a thing. One after the other they got on the train and off they went."

"Yes," said John. "Even the one who shouldn't have gone."

"Now, that's true." She wiggled a little in her chair, a sign John recognized. Miss Maddie was settling in for a good long discussion, but at the other end of the table, Miss Zula had made other plans.

She said, "What did you think of the documentary, Caroline?"

John got a sudden trace of Caroline's perfume, which meant that she had begun to perspire, a rare thing.

"It might have been melodramatic," Caroline said. "But it wasn't handled that way at all. I thought it was very good."

"Please explain," Kai said.

Caroline's smile was brittle. "Well. Let me see—the script was good, excellent cinematography, a compelling and insightful accounting of a socioeconomic anomaly . . ." Her voice trailed off. She knew how stilted she sounded, or at least John hoped she did.

"A good story?" Kai asked.

"Well, yes." Caroline's irritation was rising as surely as her color. "I suppose that would be one way to put it." She sent Miss Zula a sidelong glance.

"Good," Kai said, her English clear and precise. "I would like to see it."

Later John said, "She's like a kitten, Caroline. You dangle yarn in front of her, of course she's going to want to play."

They were sitting in John's car, parked at the curb in front of Old Roses, where Caroline lived with her mother.

"Kai Watanabe is more like a tiger than a kitten," Caroline said. Her hand strayed toward the door handle. "I suppose I had best learn how to deal with her, and the sooner the better."

That was one of the things about Caroline that John liked best. She was uncomplicated in the ways that mattered most, logical where she might have been reactionary, calm at all costs. He had known her only by sight when they were children, but then last year she had come to Princeton to give a paper just about the same time he had accepted the Ogilvie offer, and they had had a lot to talk about. John had been taken in by what had seemed to him an odd combination of southern soft and academic sharp.

John ran a finger down her arm, the skin cool and pale, her elbow a perfect right angle. "Do you want me to come in?"

She smiled at him. "Harriet and Eunice are coming over in a half hour to look at bridal magazines with me."

John sat back. "What, just the two of them?"

"The others will be by later."

When John thought of Caroline's four older sisters it was always as a unit, one he thought of as the Army of the Thoroughly Married. Not happily married, all of them, but determined to draft new inductees nevertheless. Caroline went along with it because she loved them but also, John believed, because she actually liked all the wedding fuss. Not that she could admit that, even to herself, and it would have shocked her if he told her that he found this pocket of sentimentality a reassuring thing.

"These planning meetings mean a lot to my sisters, you know."

"I've got paperwork to take care of, anyway." He rubbed the bridge of his nose. "The film people and all that."

"Just as well," she said. Then she leaned forward suddenly and kissed him. "Call me later."

The English department was deserted, quiet, and cool in the hot of the day, and John closed himself in his office and fell onto the couch to watch the shadows of the trees play on the far wall.

There was a television and DVD player on a portable stand between the windows, and the remote, usually so difficult to locate, was digging into his hindquarters. He shifted, and the television burped and buzzed and came to life.

He really didn't need to watch the damn documentary again. There was nothing productive to be gained by it. The contract was signed, the deal was done; Angeline Mangiamele was on her way here, along with Rivera Rosenblum—there was a name out of his past, one that made him smile in spite of himself—and this Tony Russo. Whoever that was. Maybe Angie's husband, or boyfriend. She couldn't have stayed alone, not for five years. Surely not.

Except the documentary really was good, better than good; more than he had let himself hope for.

On the television screen a clip of old film showed a train moving across a winter landscape in grainy black and white. And then the voice, the one he didn't need to hear again, not just now.

John got up and went to his desk, where he found a piece of bright pink paper with Patty-Cake's handwriting: office assignments for the visiting faculty, and the paperwork for the payroll office, and the question she seemed to ask him twice a day: Would Ms. Mangiamele and Ms. Rosenblum be teaching the fall courses they had been offered? If not, they'd have to start looking for somebody else.

John made himself sit down behind the desk to take care of the housing request, the one he had started to work on three days ago and hadn't been able to finish past question ten.

In order to best match available housing with visiting faculty, we would appreciate as much detail as can be provided on the visitor's family and any special needs to be taken into consideration.

The things John knew about Angie Mangiamele could hardly be written on a form for a clerk in the housing office to read. Especially as that clerk might well turn out to be Harriet Darling, Caroline's oldest sister.

She snores, he could write that, and no doubt she could share a few colorful facts about him, too. But if this was going to work—and it had to work—he would have to find a way to put all those little things out of his head and start fresh.

From the television came the soft deep lilt of Virginia and in counterpoint a more familiar voice, slightly husky, carefully modulated and still New Jersey. She disliked her accent, or had, back then. Maybe she had learned to appreciate it; maybe they couldn't afford to hire a professional voice-over actor. In fact, she sounded as if she had a little bit of a cold when she recorded the narration.

Prone to upper respiratory infections. That was something to write, and: *Hates going to the doctor. Hates letting anybody do anything for her. Does her own taxes, paints her own walls. Cuts her own hair.*

He pushed away from the desk and went to look out the window, imagined Angie down there walking under the cherry trees. She was coming, and he couldn't stop it. She would make friends in the town; in a week everybody would know her name. It was her particular gift, making people open up. He had seen her following an irascible old mailman around for days until she had soaked up everything he had to teach her about a neighborhood she was interested in filming. No doubt he still sent her Christmas cards. No doubt she answered them.

The truth was, he didn't want to stop what was coming, and there was the hardest truth at all, one he could hardly admit to himself or even to his brother, who had given him a particular look when he found out who it was that owned Tied to the Tracks.

At the very least, he had to tell Caroline, and soon.

He thought of Miss Maddie's small, kind face, the light in her eyes when she talked about the documentary. Thought of his own silence, when he should have spoken up. The things he meant to say were simple: *It's a brilliant piece of work. She's come so far, she has the eye.* If he could give her nothing else, he must give her that much, respect for the work she did, for the work she would be here to do.

From the television set came another voice, strong and sure but with an old woman's gentle wobble.

"Nobody asked me," she was saying. "My turn came and I had to climb up into that train. Sometimes I thought about just lying down in front of it, instead."

John looked out over the empty campus. Then he turned back to the form on his desk. On it he wrote: *Please contact these persons directly for answers to these questions.*

And while you're at it, he might have written, *could you ask Angie what actually happened five years ago this Labor Day?*

Because while John had what seemed like almost perfect recall when it came to that summer before he left Columbia for Princeton, the last few days—the last days he had spent with Angie Mangiamele—were a complete mystery to him.

From the television came the sound of a train whistle, long and plaintive.

A month of very good, two months of excellent, and then it all seemed to fall apart in the course of a disaster of a weekend.

He had come up to her door at a trot, his overnight bag bumping against his leg, calculating traffic and distance in his head and whether or not they would make the train, and what it would mean if they didn't—his grandfather would hold it against him all weekend if they showed up late—and rapped on the door even as it was swinging open.

It wasn't the first time the sight of Angie Mangiamele had robbed him of words. Angie asleep in the first light of day was enough to do it, Angie in a temper or scrubbing the sink or scowling at the pages of a book. He had it bad, no question about it, and so here they were, after weeks of discussion, on their way out to meet what was left of his father's family, and when was the last time he had done that?

But the sight of Angie in the doorway made it clear that he had miscalculated, and badly.

She touched a tentative finger to her hair. The hair that had first caught his attention, lifting in the wind, twirling with a life force of its own, perpetually tangled, wild, enchanted hair. Sometime between this morning and now she had cut it all off into a short shag. And if that didn't make a clear enough statement—even in his shock, he understood that she was trying to tell him something that he was too dense to have picked up on his own—she had dyed it blue, too.

If he hadn't been running late, he told himself later, if he hadn't been thinking about his grandfather, he would have handled it better. He would have said, *Where's your suitcase*, or *Let's move, we're going to miss the train*, or even *That's a particularly stunning shade of cobalt*, but none of those things had come to him. He had stood in front of her in the narrow hallway where—this is the way he would always remember it—he had had her up against the wall on more than one occasion, unable to stop long enough even to unlock the door—and opened his mouth to say the wrong thing.

"Oh, no."

The tremble of her jaw gave it all away, though he didn't realize it at that moment. It would be months before he could think about that afternoon with anything approaching objectivity, when it would finally occur to him that Angie had set him up. And by then it was too late.

John got up and left his office abruptly. The sound of Angie's voice came from the TV speakers to follow him down the hall.

· FOUR ·

Ogilvie, Georgia. Pop: 3,400. Est: 1820 by General Joshua Ogilvie (born 1780, Savannah), philosopher, historian, slave owner, and hero of the War of 1812. While many small southern towns went bankrupt in the sixties, Ogilvie survived and prospered, thanks primarily to its major employer, Ogilvie College, a private liberal arts university of international standing. Located on the Seaboard Coastline Railway between Savannah, Georgia, and Jacksonville, Florida, the town is a popular destination for tourists who come to see the beautifully maintained Victorian, Georgian, and Greek Revival homes along University Parkway, the wealth of specialty and antique shops on Main Street, and the many acres of gardens and parks. The town's Independence Day Jubilee and New Year's Pageant are counted among the most elaborate, well organized, and worth seeing in the South.

A New History of the Oldest Coastal Towns

I t's like a terrarium," Tony yelled. "Only bigger."
"You mean a jungle," Rivera yelled back.
The van's air-conditioning had whimpered and died as soon as they crossed the Mason-Dixon line, and they had been shouting over road noise and wind ever since.

"No, I mean a terrarium. The place looks like it's been manicured." Tony waved his arms to indicate the entirety of the city of Ogilvie spread out before them, which did look, Angie had to agree, like a lovingly kept garden perched in the oxbow of a river that ran toward the sea. Roofs and steeples poked up here and there but overall it was hard to make out much at all.

Rivera said, "It's only an hour to Savannah by train."

"Hey, winkie," Angie said. "We aren't even there yet, hold it with the big city withdrawal, okay?"

Tony said, "I wouldn't exactly call Savannah a big city, but it'll have to do. How far is it to Jacksonville, anyway?"

Rivera poked him in the shoulder and he yelped.

"I was just asking."

"For Christ's sake," Rivera said. "There's a whole campus of co-eds and professors and staff."

"But not until September," Tony said. Then he sat up a little straighter. "Somebody was telling me that Julia Roberts is from around here."

Angie let Rivera handle that, as her concern about the suspicious sounds coming from the van's transmission was escalating quickly. She consulted the directions she had taped to the visor and turned onto University Parkway.

Tony wound Rivera up to the point of spontaneous combustion while Angie tried to concentrate on the directions she had downloaded off the Internet. The Parkway was as wide as a four-lane highway with an island of trees and shrubs running down the median strip. Houses stood far back from the street overshadowed by palm trees and oaks draped with moss. A carriage house roof was all but lost in a great mass of vines covered with bright orange-red flowers; Angie saw box hedges sculpted into the shape of urns and dogs; a pale pink stucco house surrounded by rose gardens. The air was different down here: wetter, heavier, hotter, and filled with smells that settled on the tongue. Sugary flowery smells and sharper, herby ones, green things growing and rotting, river water.

Rivera had been nursing her irritation for the last ten minutes and it erupted quite suddenly. "And if Julia Roberts did come from Ogilvie, what then? A shrine in front of her birthplace?"

"Maybe she'll come visiting at Christmas. Southerners are big on family."

"Cliché number eighty-seven," Rivera said. "If you speed it up you might make a hundred before we get where we're going."

"Too late," Angie said, pulling up to the redbrick security kiosk at the main gates of the university. "We're here."

A wisp of steam rose from the hood, snakelike. "And not a minute too soon."

According to the guard, the director of housing was waiting for them in her office rather than at the English department. That piece of news was so welcome that Angie couldn't even find it in herself to worry about the van, which they left in the kiosk parking lot, twitching like a dog with fleas.

"Five on a Friday afternoon in the summer," Angie said aloud, because she liked the sound of it. Unlikely that there would be anybody around.

"Sure is quiet," Tony said.

"As the grave," Rivera agreed.

Just visible to the far right between the trees were glimpses of another street, this one lined with stores. "I think that's Main Street," Angie said.

"Let's go look." Rivera would have jogged off, but Angie caught her elbow and turned her back toward the building in front of them.

"One mountain at a time." She looked at the sheet of paper in her hand. "This particular mountain is called Harriet Darling, and she's behind that door."

It's the very nicest house we've got and it's so convenient, we thought since y'all will be working together it made sense to have you share? I think you'll be comfortable . . ."

Over Harriet Darling's big head of hair Angie caught Rivera's look: she was mesmerized by the patter, horrified and fascinated, and completely at a loss.

Tony, on the other hand, had latched onto Harriet and was doing everything in his power to encourage her.

". . . the extra bedroom in case y'all have company coming for the holidays . . ."

"Do you have a big family yourself, Mrs. Darling?"

She turned her whole body toward him. "Why, yes I do, Mr. Russo. I've got three boys. Tab Junior, Larry, and my baby, Joey? My sisters—there are five of us Rose girls—my maiden name is Rose, did I mention that?—every one of them has three boys, except Caroline. She's the baby, but she's getting married—" She stopped so suddenly that Rivera would have run into her if Tony hadn't put out a restraining hand.

"I do hope I've got the right keys here. Ivy House it should say on the tag, but I've left my reading— Mr. Russo, would you be so kind?"

When Tony assured her that she had the right keys and Harriet had set off again, Rivera hung back. She took Angie's arm and squeezed it hard enough to make her yelp.

"He'll get us tossed out of here before we've shot anything," she said.

Angie watched Tony, his head inclined toward Harriet's puffed and sculpted hair. There was a familiar expression on his face: Tony on the scent.

Angie said, "She's married."

Rivera smirked. "Exactly. May I remind you—"

"Please don't." Angie pushed out a long sigh. "I'll talk to him."

It turned out that Ivy House really was the best Ogilvie had to offer. Ten big rooms, including a kitchen the size of Angie's apartment in Hoboken, and attached to it was a screened porch that looked over a back lawn that stretched all the way to the river. There were five bedrooms, a basement, two bathrooms with big old-fashioned bathtubs. It had been reserved for a math professor from Vienna with a wife and four children.

"But the poor man took a heart attack two weeks ago and the doctors don't want him to travel?" Harriet was leaning against the kitchen counter as she told Tony the story of how Tied to the Tracks had come into possession of Ivy House. "I wish him well, I surely do, but let me tell you we were in a quandary about where to put y'all. If it wasn't rude I'd have to send him a thank-you note for staying away."

"There's a banana tree," Rivera called from the screened porch. "In the backyard. A banana tree, and a palm."

It was all very southern, which delighted Tony and Rivera both. Lemon and pecan trees, Spanish moss on the oaks that lined the river, ceiling fans.

"What about scuppernongs?" Tony asked Harriet Darling. "I've always wondered. What is a scuppernong, exactly?"

Angie took the bedroom at the very top of the house. It had two deep window seats that provided a view of the campus. It had ancient wallpaper of young ladies in hoop skirts with pink parasols and bead-board wainscoting. It had an air conditioner the size of a small refrigerator that hummed sweetly and belched a long, cold stream of air.

For the last week Angie had been too busy to do much thinking; she should have fallen asleep without any trouble at all, and yet she sat wide awake, her feet tucked under her on the window seat. She could hear Rivera and Tony downstairs, arguing while they finished unloading the van, a duty she was exempt from as she had packed it to start with.

Outside her windows Ogilvie was so still, though she had opened the window to listen. In the distance she heard the sound of a radio tuned to a talk show, the voices indistinct, cajoling, indignant, amused. At two in the morning Hoboken was as alive—more alive, sometimes—than it was at noon; here it was full dark at ten. Somewhere out in that dark John Grant was reading or watching television or talking on the telephone.

The best thing would be to get right to work. Get set up, start blocking out a shooting schedule, lining up people to interview, places to visit, get acquainted with the facilities on campus, go grocery shopping. After two or three days of running full out, then it would be time to see Miss Zula, and after that was taken care of, John Grant.

Then she would be able to smile at him and shake his hand and say something just friendly enough to set his mind at rest. She was here for the work, and nothing else. Given a few days, she would figure out a way to tell him that. She might even come to believe it herself.

· FIVE ·

Ogilvie Bugle
NEWS ABOUT TOWN

Mr. Harmond Ogilvie, Chairman of the Ogilvie College Board of Regents, tells us that the university has brought a company of three documentary filmmakers to town for an extended stay. Angeline Mangiamele, Rivera Rosenblum, and Anthony Russo of Tied to the Tracks Films (Hoboken, NJ) are newly arrived to begin production of a film about the life and work of our own Miss Zula Bragg. They will be staying at Ivy House, and working out of offices in the English department on campus. The Regents ask that the good citizens of Ogilvie extend every courtesy to our guests and cooperate with them as they go about their work. If you have a story or memory about Miss Zula you'd like to share, please stop by the public library and write it down in the memory book the filmmakers have made available for that purpose, or contact them at Ivy House.

B y noon on Sunday Angie had ticked off most of the to-do items on the long list she had written Friday night: they had unpacked and stocked the kitchen, found their offices and the film and video editing suite—Tony was still slightly in shock, and Angie had rarely seen Rivera so enthusiastic—and met the neighbors. The van had been resuscitated by a mechanic named Carlos who seemed pretty much unfazable, and they were ready for the first, all-important meeting with Zula Bragg on Monday morning. Sunday afternoon they would spend at a birthday party for Miss Junie Rose, an invitation issued by her eldest daughter, Harriet Rose Darling, and accepted by Tony for all of them. Angie was wondering if she could plead exhaustion when the doorbell rang.

Tony, shaken for once out of his usual languor, raced upstairs with Rivera just behind him.

"Miss Zula is here," he said. "She just dropped by." He pushed both hands through his hair so it stood on end.

"She's got a half dozen relatives with her," Rivera said. "It's like oral exams all over again. What if they don't approve of us? Can they fire us?"

"Calm down, winkie," Angie said. "That won't happen. Miss Zula just wants to establish who's in charge; that's good, in a way. This isn't the way we planned it, but it'll be okay." She took a deep breath and forced a smile. "Give me your first impression."

Rivera closed her eyes and then opened them. "Daunting. Regal. Inscrutable."

Angie nodded. "We expected that, right? And we're up for it. We better call and make apologies about the birthday party."

"Not necessary," said Tony. "Miss Zula and Miss Maddie are on their way there, too, they said so."

The Braggs had come from church, the women in dresses and hats, the men in suits, their shoes highly polished. Zula Bragg was a small, strongly built woman with a willing smile, but her eyes missed nothing at all. If she meant to put Angie on guard, then her sister Maddie was there to offset that effect. Miss Maddie might have been Zula's twin in body and face, but she was the kind of older woman who clucked and petted and cooed and most probably never said a bad word about anyone. She had brought them an applesauce cake, which was a relief, as they had nothing to offer visitors but beer, coffee, cold pizza, and a half pack of stale Oreos.

The rest of the Bragg contingent was made up of three nephews, the sons of Zula and Maddie's elder brother, who had died in Korea—and two grand-nieces in their thirties. Martin Bragg was a minister, Joseph an accountant, and Calvin was a physician. All three were big men, barrel shaped with high foreheads and deep-set eyes. The two women, both Calvin Bragg's daughters, issued a long list of invitations: to dinner, church, tours of the campus and town and countryside, while their uncles hummed agreement and encouragement. Through it all Angie felt Dr. Bragg's sharp gaze observing, weighing, and coming to conclusions. It was best to turn the tables in a situation like this, so Angie produced her brightest smile for him.

"Do you have any specific questions for us, Dr. Bragg?"

He looked not so much surprised as satisfied. "As a matter of fact," he said, "we do." He had the deepest voice and the most melodious southern accent, so that the overall effect was almost magical. Rivera caught her eye, and Angie knew they were wondering the same thing: whether they might be able to talk Dr. Bragg into narrating some part of the documentary. The idea was so intriguing that she almost missed what he had to say.

He was asking, "My brothers and I have been wondering, what exactly were you thinking when you named your company Tied to the Tracks? Has it got to do with the old films, or is there some deeper meaning?"

"I hope you can answer that in two sentences or less," said his daughter Marilee. "Because once these three get to talking about books you had best hunker down for a while. And we have got to get going."

"Now, child, we can spare a few more minutes," said Miss Maddie. "And besides, I want to hear the answer to this, too."

They were all looking at her, but Miss Zula's gaze was the sharpest, and Angie had a sudden and uncomfortable flashback to school.

"Well," she said slowly, "our view of things is that everybody finds themselves tied to the tracks at some point or another, and that's where the story is. We tell stories."

"Ah," said Reverend Bragg. He sent a satisfied look to his brothers. "Didn't I say? They've updated Tolstoy's unhappy families to suit the vagaries of the digital age."

"I didn't hear her say anything about Tolstoy," said Joseph, looking affronted. "You are up to your usual tricks."

"Our Calvin," said Martin, "is a veritable compendium of logical fallacies."

Tony let out a hiccup of a laugh, and the three men looked at him.

"I could listen to you talk all day," Tony said, holding out his hands. "Really. My uncles argue about baseball statistics and sausage."

"Be that as it may," Miss Zula said, "you boys will have to come back another time to argue literary theory." She used her cane to lever herself to a standing position, giving one of her nephews a look that said she did not want, and would not welcome, his help. "Miss Junie asked me to come by early, and you know how she is before a party."

"I hope you will come back," Rivera said. "I'd like to hear more of this."

"She means it," Tony added. "If it's a debate you want, Rivera is your girl."

On the way out Marilee and Anthea Bragg pulled Angie aside.

"Auntie Zula is a lot stronger than Daddy gives her credit for," said Marilee. "I happen to know that for a fact, as I've been her physician for the last six months, since Daddy cut back on his practice."

"They're just protective," added Marilee. "But the good Lord never put a woman more capable of speaking her mind on this earth. You make Auntie unhappy or push her too hard and you'll hear about it."

Miss Maddie patted Angie on the cheek and smiled. "Aren't those boys something? I blame Zula for reading philosophy to them when they were still in diapers. Logical fallacies." She gave a delighted laugh. "Don't you be worrying about our nephews. They do like to growl but they don't hardly ever bite. Now, I'm looking forward to Junie Rose's birthday party. I expect to see y'all there, and so does Zula."

Caroline said, "You can't spend the entire weekend working." And: "It will be fun."

Neither of those things was strictly true, but there was another fact, a bigger one that John didn't have to hear her say. Junie Rose's seventy-fifth birthday party wasn't something a man could just stay away from. Not if he wanted to stay on good terms with the Rose girls and the rest of the population of Ogilvie, most especially Miss Zula Bragg, who was Junie Rose's closest friend.

Mostly John didn't mind these kind of family parties and hadn't been worried about this one until he picked up Caroline from her wedding dress fitting. For the entire ten-minute drive, she had anticipated disaster in vivid detail.

". . . a nice cardigan, the kind she likes, pink. The card's right here for you to sign."

John put the car in park and turned to her. "I got her a card, and a present. You don't have to do my shopping for me, you know."

Caroline blinked at him. "You got Mama a present?"

"And a card."

He watched her face as pleasant surprise gave way to worry. "What ever did you get her?"

"Just wait and see." John leaned forward and wiped an imaginary bread crumb from the corner of Caroline's mouth, felt her startle and then relax. She had a slow smile, even a timid one, and it was hard work coaxing one out of her.

She started to say something, and then her gaze fixed on an old Chevy parked at an angle in the driveway.

"Uncle Bruce is here."

"I would guess so," John said. "It's his sister's birthday, after all."

"You're not hearing me," said Caroline. "Uncle Bruce and the boys. Here, together."

"Oh," said John. "Well, lead on. I'm prepared for anything."

Established in the shade in the gardens at Old Roses with her third glass of wine, Angie concluded that the Roses would have made an interesting subject on their own if Tied to the Tracks didn't already have Miss Zula to deal with.

Old Roses was a huge Victorian-era house of brick and stucco surrounded by live oaks, azaleas, and magnolia trees. The garden, as large as it was, seemed hardly big enough to contain the entire Rose clan. In addition to cousins and friends, Harriet Darling and three of her four sisters were here with their families. The husbands grazed the far end of the lawn, where a grill sat on a concrete apron; the sisters had retired to the opposite end of the garden, where they had a good view of what their sons and husbands were up to, although it seemed the pile of bridal magazines on the table between them had most of their attention.

Angie was content to watch. She raised her wineglass—empty again—to Tony, who saluted and then went back to his viewfinder. He was wandering around the property with cameras slung around his neck and a cigarette hanging from the corner of his mouth, too involved in work for once to get into trouble. And still Angie had the idea that when the stills were developed a large proportion would turn out to feature Harriet Darling, who was holding up a full-color spread of a wedding cake frosted with purple roses for her sisters to see.

Far more important than Tony and his cameras was the fact that Rivera was sitting a few yards away between Miss Zula and Miss Junie in the middle of a crowd of older women, her sleek dark head swiveling back and forth. Old ladies liked Rivera; she was just irreverent enough to keep them on their toes, but her interest in their stories was real.

Angie found herself so completely relaxed that she might have gone to sleep right there with a plate of food on one knee and her glass on the other, but one of the grandsons was walking toward her in a way that brought junior high school socials to mind. He ducked his head and looked back over his shoulder at the men around the grill. When he came to a stop in front of Angie she thought for sure he was going to ask her to dance. He was about sixteen, tall for his age and awkward with it, a scattering of pimples on his forehead but with a bright look about him.

"Miss Angie?" he said. "I'm Markus Holmes, Eunice's oldest boy?"

His eyes skittered in the direction of the picnic tables and back again. Angie shook the hand he offered and asked him to sit down, a question he seemed to overhear. Then he turned his smile on her, and she could see that he had resolved to ignore his cousins and the teasing that would come his way.

"I was just wondering, will you be shooting digital video or film for your documentary?"

"Digital for the most part," Angie said. "Some film for texture, but mostly high-definition video. You interested in filmmaking?"

"Yes, ma'am."

It was going to take some time to get used to the *ma'am*, but there was no help for it; she might as well object to palmetto bugs and magnolias. And Angie liked the kid right away, in part because he went to such trouble not to brag as he told her about what he had been working on. For his age he had a lot of experience, most of it through the local-access television station.

"Channel twelve, right?" Angie said. "I saw a little of one of the programs last night, political talk."

"That's Scoot Sloan's show," Markus said. "*The Right Side of Ogilvie*, it's called. You should come down to the station sometime, have a look around."

He peeked at her to see how well she took to southern circumlocution, and he looked so eager and shy all at once that Angie was thoroughly charmed.

She said, "I'd like to see what you've done. Maybe you could bring a tape by the media studio this week."

"I'd like that," he said, looking her full in the face for the first time.

"Do you want to sit down?" She patted the chair beside her again, but he stepped backward.

"No, thank you, ma'am. There was just one other thing I wanted to ask you about. You know that memory book you put out, the one for people to write in about Miss Zula?"

"At the library," Angie said.

"Well, what I wanted to tell you was, I've got this idea that the book's not going to do you much good where you've put it."

He was so serious that Angie was a little taken aback. "Why is that?"

"Because of Miss Annie. The librarian? She's got a bad case of the curiosities, and everybody knows it. You couldn't write anything down in that book without Miss Annie right behind you, like white on rice. And then she'll talk about it."

"Ah." Angie thought for a moment. "You have a better idea where to put the book?"

"Yes, ma'am, I do. There's only one place in town where everybody goes, and that's the Piggly Wiggly. Wouldn't nobody be watching, either, when folks want to spend a few minutes writing. Not if you put it over by the recycling bins?" He glanced over to the men around the barbecue grill and then cleared his throat. "I work there, at the Piggly Wiggly, bagging? I could keep an eye on it for you, make sure the younger kids don't get up to mischief. If you want. Just an idea."

"A good one," Angie said. "Thank you."

He backed away, scratching his chin distractedly. "Well, it was sure nice talking to you."

"Markus, if you have any other ideas, I hope you won't keep them to yourself. And come by with one of your tapes this week. I'm in the studio most afternoons."

He gave her a real grin, shy and sweet.

"Hey, Markus! If you're through flirting, move your skinny butt. Father Bruce is here."

An older man wearing a roman collar had appeared on the porch with a large bundle in his arms, and boys were running toward him from all directions. Markus gave her one last apologetic glance and trotted off to join the rest of Junie Rose's twelve grandsons—the youngest seven, the oldest close to twenty.

"Oh, Lordie," called one of the ladies in the circle around Miss Junie. "What's Bruce up to this time?"

Angie sat up straighter. She had heard stories about the local priest and had put him on her list of people to interview, but the last place she had thought to run into him was at Miss Junie Rose's birthday party. And yet, there he was, a slight man of more than sixty and less than eighty in an old soutane that was more gray than black, lopsided eyeglasses with lenses the size of silver dollars, and a halo of pure white hair standing straight up around a pink scalp. He looked like an elf up to mischief.

"Bruce means well, but he does work those grandnephews of his up into a frenzy."

A woman sat down in the empty chair next to Angie. She had the kind of blinding white smile usually found on movie screens, a mass of too-red hair, and her nails and lipstick were the alarming orange of traffic cones. Like all the women Angie had seen thus far, she was as carefully dressed as she was groomed. She wore a dress of deep blue silk with a wide lace collar, bone white leather shoes and matching purse, and heavy gold jewelry on her wrists and fingers and ears. She might have stepped out of a Talbot's catalog. Not for the first time Angie wished she had dug something better than a shapeless yellow sundress out of her closet.

"I'm Patty-Cake Walker. Miss Junie's husband, Bob Lee, was my half brother? I'll bet your head is just spinning trying to keep us all straight."

"It is a little confusing," Angie agreed. "Father Callahan is Miss Junie's brother?"

"He is. You don't see the resemblance now, but when they were younger, lots of folks took them for twins. Or so I'm told."

Angie said, "I didn't think there were many Catholics in this part of the country."

"Mostly you're right," she said, smoothing out her skirt. "But I believe Ogilvie must have the biggest Catholic congregation in all of Georgia." She put a hand on her chest, fingers spread wide. "Not my people and not my husband's, either, you understand—the Roses and the Walkers have been worshipping at Ogilvie Methodist since it opened its doors way back before the War Between the States."

"Is that the little church on Decatur Road?"

"No, you're thinking of Turn Around Circle. They're Presbyterians, but Low Church, if you know what I mean. I've got cousins who worship there."

The first rule of effective field research was letting people talk without interrupting them unless the conversation lagged. Now there was nothing to do but settle down and let the monologue runs its course.

"The closest I personally come to the Church of Rome is my half brother Bob Lee?" Patty-Cake was saying. "He was supposed to marry one of the Stillwater girls, but then Miss Junie caught his eye, and that was that. It was a big deal back then, let me tell you, marrying outside your faith." She pursed her mouth as if to stop herself from saying any more.

"Look there, that's Connie Yaeger. Now, in't that dress just the prettiest thing? And those bright colors draw attention away from her less fortunate features. Connie's been teaching eighth grade at Our Lady of Divine Mercy for just about ever. " She pushed out an irritated sigh. "I guess you could say that Bob Lee running off to marry an Irish Catholic girl made us the first truly integrated family in this part of Georgia. And Junie brought her girls up proper Catholics, too. Naturally having a priest for a brother made that a lot easier."

Patty-Cake leaned forward and Angie got a blast of flowery scent that billowed up out of her powdered cleavage.

"You and I are going to be working together. I'm the senior secretary in the English department? You probably don't realize this, but there's a lot to running a big department like that. I've got a staff of one full-time secretary and two part-time girls, plus work-study students. But in the summer I handle it all on my own. The faculty never show their faces, which just between you and me is just fine. They are a pesky lot during the school year, always needing something. I'm the keeper of the keys, to use an old-fashioned phrase. Why, a body can't get hold of a paper clip unless I say so, and I'm careful with the resources that are put in my care. There's a lot of responsibility on my shoulders."

"I'm sure there is," Angie said solemnly.

"You come and see me tomorrow and I'll get you all set up," Patty-Cake finished. "We're going to get to know each other real well. And bring the other two along with you, now." Her gaze shifted in Rivera's direction and her smile sharpened just a little more. "Why, look at that girl," she said. "You'd think she grew up right here in Ogilvie."

Rivera was telling a story. Miss Junie had covered her face with her hands and her shoulders were shaking with laughter. Miss Zula rocked back and forth and fanned herself with one hand. Miss Maddie looked slightly confused, but delighted with the company.

"Now, tell me," Patty-Cake said. "Did you two young ladies leave your boyfriends up north, or should I start introducing you around? There are some fine young men in Ogilvie who would be pleased to make your acquaintance. And you're not getting any younger, now, are you?"

Angie opened her mouth to attempt some kind of answer that would cause the least complications, but a commotion from the other side of the lawn saved her.

"Bull's-eye!" shouted a boy's voice, and at that the men who had gathered around picnic tables and the grill moved off toward the porch.

"Oh, Lordie," said Patty-Cake, brushing at her skirt as she stood up. "Bruce has gone and given those boys bows and arrows. I don't know if he'll ever learn. And now the men are going to get into it. There will be tears before bedtime, you mark my words. And there's your cameraman, taking photographs of the whole thing."

Tony had appeared from around the side of the house. He had the Nikon out and he was dancing back and forth, the Tony ballet, Rivera called it, when he liked what he was seeing in his viewfinder. Of course it would be far better if he were shooting over here—Miss Zula's laughter was worth a few frames at least—but Angie and Rivera had learned to trust Tony's instincts about where to point a camera.

Then the crowd opened up a bit and Angie saw the youngest of the grandsons, a little boy with a round potbelly, a head of streaky blond curls, and a fat strawberry of a mouth. He stood on a chair aiming an arrow at a bull's-eye set up on an easel at the other end of the veranda, all his concentration on the target. Angie doubted he even heard all the men shouting directions and encouragement at him, while the women for their part shouted warnings. As Angie stood up to get a better look, John Grant came around the corner.

Patty-Cake said, "There they are finally, my niece Caroline and Dr. Grant—the department chair? Her fiancé." Those words were still hanging in the air when the arrow left the bow with a twang that could be heard all the way across the garden.

John's face, familiar and strange and beautiful. How could she have forgotten that face? The answer was, of course, that she had not. She had forgotten nothing at all. In that split second when he met her eye, Angie saw that same flash of recognition, even as Patty-Cake's words ordered themselves in her mind to add up to an understanding of another kind: too late.

Somebody screamed. John, who looked down at the blossom of blood on his neatly creased trousers, made no sound that Angie heard. He touched the arrow embedded in his upper left thigh, not quite center, tilted his head as if trying to make out a whispering voice, and then fell over, gracefully, elegantly, into the arms of the woman he was going to marry.

"Len!" Somebody shouted. "Front and center!"

"It's a good thing Eunice married a doctor," breathed Patty-Cake, her hands fluttering around her face. "I don't suppose we'll ever have one of these birthday parties without making a trip to the emergency room."

· SIX ·

I have lived in Ogilvie long enough to know that nobody will have the nerve to bring up the subject of Miss Louisa, who was Miss Zula's mother, and so I suppose it's up to me. I don't hold much with modern psychology and prying into personal matters, but in this case I do believe you must know the mother to understand the children, all three of whom I watched grow up. There's an old saying, spare the rod, spoil the child, and Miss Louisa lived by it. Her rod was made of hard words, which any caring person can tell you may leave a scar worse than any slap.

Your Name: Sister Ellen Mary. I am Father Bruce's housekeeper, and you may find me at the rectory at Our Lady of Divine Mercy. Though if you'd like to talk to me, you had best be quick about it. I am ninety years old and wait daily for the Good Lord to tap me on the shoulder.

By the end of their first full week in Ogilvie, Angie had established a routine: up long before Rivera and Tony ever stirred, she went down to the screened porch that overlooked the garden and the river, where she waited on an ancient black-and-white-striped couch until the coffee was ready. Then she took her cup with her to the riverfront and sat in the cool of the morning, planning her day, making lists in her head, and contemplating running away.

It had been a surprisingly productive week for the simple reason that she was spending most of her day and her night, too, working.

"This is good stuff." Rivera was looking at Angie's binder when she said this, the one she carried with her everywhere on a shoot. There were three full pages of notes from her talk with Sister Ellen Mary at the rectory, all about Miss Zula's family history and her mother. Rivera made a notation of her own. "I didn't think you'd been out of the house long enough to do an interview, Mangiamele." She looked up with a grin. "If you get this much done without distractions, we have to find a way to put John Grant back in the hospital, once he gets out."

"He's not in the hospital," Angie said, "and you know it."

"Well, then he's in hiding," Rivera said. "So the small-town rumor mill is going full tilt. The latest is that he got blood poisoning and they had to take his leg off. Hey," she said, holding up a hand, palm out. "I'm just the messenger."

"And where did you hear this?" Angie asked. "At the quilt shop?"

"Fat Quarters is the source of all knowledge," Rivera agreed. "I do hear interesting things from the men on the Liars' Bench outside the barbershop, but I've come to the conclusion that Pearl's shop is better."

Rivera had been cultivating a number of leads in the community, primary among them the middle three Rose girls. Pearl, it turned out, owned the quilting shop. A whole army of women came to Fat Quarters whenever they could spare an hour to work on whatever project they had going, and Pearl Rose was the queen of all that.

"So what's the buzz?"

"While I was there, Pearl told them all about what happened to John, and then when she turned her back, everybody tried to figure out what she really meant but was too embarrassed to say directly."

"Maybe you should be hanging out at the Hound Dog. Tony was down there yesterday and heard that John lost a testicle."

Rivera said, "They've got better-looking women at Fat Quarters. Which you'd know if you'd take a break. Come into town with me today, we'll stop by the Piggly Wiggly. Miss Maddie does a lot of her shopping there, you know. There's a world of wisdom in watching her pick out peaches."

"I'll put it on the list," said Angie. And, a little wistfully: "I wish some of Miss Maddie would rub off on you. You shouldn't be spreading rumors. Bad juju."

"You are such a fake," Rivera said, laughing. "You'd go crazy wondering if you didn't have us to bring you the news. He's fine, you know. Eunice says so."

"So are you best friends now with all the Rose girls?"

"According to Eunice," Rivera repeated, pointedly ignoring Angie's tone, "John only needed three stitches, no infection. It was way too close for comfort, but no lasting damage."

"Good for John," Angie said.

Rivera said, "Good for Caroline Rose." And laughed again at the small, tight smile that was all the answer Angie could summon.

Angie thought a lot about Caroline Rose, for reasons she didn't want to examine too closely. Caroline was tall, elegant, silver blond, immaculately groomed and dressed. She had turned out to be not only John's fiancée and colleague but Miss Zula's unofficial assistant in all things. There was no avoiding her, and, worse luck, no way to dislike her, either.

Early in the morning of another day that promised to be scorching hot, Angie sat by the river and contemplated the vagaries of fate that had brought her to this place at this particular point in time, when John was about to get married. Angie crossed her arms over her upraised knees and rested her forehead on the cool skin of her forearms and thought about the fix she was in. The truth was, she would have paid pretty much any price to get back her peace of mind and a few hours of sound sleep. It was becoming increasingly obvious that she'd have to take the first step, find John, and lay down some ground rules, get things said and out of the way.

If she only knew what to say. If only he didn't have better things to be thinking about just now than a neurotic, obsessive ex-girlfriend. An arrow to the crotch, for one, and his upcoming wedding, for another.

"Angie?"

The odd thing was, she must have finally drifted off to sleep sitting in the sun, because she was dreaming about Caroline Rose, who seemed to be floating across the lawn toward her.

Angie righted herself so quickly that a sharp, sudden pain shot up her back.

"I didn't mean to startle you," Caroline said, looking as uncertain and embarrassed as Angie felt. "And I realize that it's very early to be calling, but I do have a good reason. May I?"

"Sure." Angie moved to the far end of the bench, wondering just how much of an ass she was about to make of herself and what she would say if Caroline Rose raised those topics Angie least wanted to talk about. She looked toward the house and sent a silent plea to Rivera. *Come rescue me.*

"Miss Zula and Miss Maddie sent me," said Caroline. "To see if you'd like to come by for breakfast."

"Breakfast?" Angie echoed. A spark of professional interest overrode her discomfort. All week they had been waiting for this first invitation to the little house on Magnolia Street, and here it was.

"It's a tradition, once a month," Caroline was explaining. "The goddaughters' breakfast. Miss Zula is my godmother and Miss Maddie is my sister Harriet's godmother. Once in a while they invite someone else to join us." Her hands fluttered up out of her lap and then fell again. "All women, of course."

"Of course," Angie echoed. All women meant no John Grant, which was a good thing just now. She said, "Look, tell me honestly. Will Miss Zula be insulted if I send my regrets?"

Caroline looked distinctly surprised at such a suggestion. "It's very hard to insult Miss Zula if you're being honest," she said. "Miss Maddie is another matter, of course. She does love to cook for folks."

"Then I'd be happy to," Angie said, resigned. "I'll just get my shoes."

Caroline's gaze jumped toward the house and back again. "The invitation was for both of you. Would Rivera be interested, do you think?"

"If I can get her out of bed," Angie said. "Let me—"

"There's John," said Caroline.

Angie went very still. "John?"

"John," echoed Caroline. She pointed with her chin. "Just there."

Full of dread, Angie turned toward the river and took it in: the graceful bend of the willows, the sun on the water, and the sweep of oars as the single scull came into view. John Grant, tousle-headed, as though he had gone directly from bed to the river, his skin flushed with sun and exercise. The perfect shoulders and arms clenching and relaxing in an easy rhythm and then his face coming up, turned toward them. In the distance a train whistle blew, long and plaintive.

Hysterical laughter, Angie told herself firmly, would be a mistake.

Later, John would try to reconstruct for himself how things could go so wrong in the space of a few seconds. A week's worth of planning, all gone in that single sweep of the oars that had brought him around the bend in the river. His first time on the water since the regrettable incident at Junie Rose's birthday party. He had been feeling good, and settled, and glad of the morning until he looked up and saw them there: Angie Mangiamele and Caroline Rose standing side by side. It was a sight to put a better man than John Grant off his stroke, but at least the river was running fast. Just as quickly as they had come into view they were gone.

Angie Mangiamele in shorts and a faded, shapeless Nirvana T-shirt that was ten years old at least. He knew this because it had been faded and old when he first saw it, hanging on the bedpost in the tiny bedroom of her apartment near NYU. He still remembered how it smelled.

It had seemed so straightforward, in the last few days of self-imposed house arrest. He had written it out for himself, the things he would say. Just as soon as he fully recovered he would knock on Angie's office door, and initiate the conversation they obviously had to have. They were both adults, after all, and reasonable people. A few ground rules and they would be able to interact in public without problems.

On another list he made an outline of the things he would tell Caroline, who was the most reasonable and rational of human beings. Just a few facts, put in perspective, and that would be the end of the matter.

Except, of course, he had never imagined that Angie would still own that T-shirt, or what the sight of it might do to him, the memories it could drag up. Such as what Angie smelled like, in the early morning. Angie in the morning. He had not put that on his list, and that, he realized, was a serious flaw in his reasoning.

Rivera had fallen in love with the house on Magnolia Street where the Bragg sisters lived at first drive-by, and was so eager to see the inside of it that she got out of bed without complaint. In Caroline's car she asked one question after another about the street and the houses on the street, small and neat, a working neighborhood with swing sets in the yards and vegetable gardens. Caroline, animated, answered her questions and volunteered a spontaneous genealogy, naming Miss Zula's neighbors, many of whom were Bragg cousins. Marilee Bragg, who had come to visit them their first weekend in Ogilvie, waved to them from a front porch littered with toys.

"It's like Hoboken," Rivera said. "Angie's got more than fifty blood relatives on one block."

"Doesn't look anything like this," Angie said.

The man pruning roses in the garden across the street raised a hand and touched his brow in greeting as they got out of the car.

"Wait, let me guess," Rivera said. "Second cousin three times removed."

"No, that's Mr. Jackson. He runs the power plant at the university, but he's protective of Miss Zula and Miss Maddie. Everyone in the neighborhood is. And there's Thomasina Chance, do you see there, the woman in the vegetable garden? She owns the restaurant across from campus." The next few minutes were taken up with a discussion of local restaurants, but Angie didn't catch much of it; she was too busy sketching a rough map of the neighborhood and writing down names.

The Braggs' house was set back in a small garden in the full flush of summer, heavy with blossom, alive with bees. There were sunflowers and beans on trellises and young tomato plants tied to stakes with lengths of old nylon stocking. Louie slept in a patch of sunshine, opening one eye to appraise the young women and then snuffling himself back to sleep.

At least Rivera's mind was on business. She stood at the gate with one hand pressed to her mouth and the other to her heart, a pose that meant she was seeing camera angles. This was about work, after all. Angie repeated that to herself as they went up on the little porch. There was a brass plaque on the wall that read MAGNOLIA HOUSE 1880. Below that, a small typewritten card had been tacked into place.

By order of her physician, Miss Bragg may no longer entertain unannounced visitors seeking autographs. Do not ring the bell. Dr. Calvin Bragg.

In neat, slightly wavering handwriting the word please had been inserted before the last, rather abrupt directive.

"Oh, this is going to be good," Rivera said.

Miss Maddie set an old-fashioned breakfast table, one covered with a flowered tablecloth and crowded with heavy, thick plates and platters. Delighted, Rivera helped herself to flapjacks and eggs and bacon and ham and drizzled syrup over the whole.

"I do like to see a girl with an appetite," said Miss Maddie. "Won't you have one of these muffins Caroline made for us? She's the best cook in Ogilvie, is our Caroline."

"You are the sweetest thing," Caroline said, blushing. "But far too kind."

Angie found herself next to Miss Zula, who seemed content to watch and listen as Rivera and Miss Maddie and Caroline carried on a disjointed but energetic conversation about ham.

With her silver-blond hair and long pale neck, Caroline worked like crystal wine goblet among jelly-jar glasses, but she was clearly at home here and very much at ease. She moved around the kitchen as if she had spent many hours there—to refill the coffeepot, to fetch Miss Maddie her handkerchief—and kept up with her part of the conversation.

She was saying, "Mama's planning on going up to the lake tomorrow."

"Are you planning on going up, Caroline? Or are you too busy with wedding plans?" Miss Maddie was small and plump, with perfectly rounded cheeks, but she had a rich voice and a way of speaking that would be welcome in any National Public Radio broadcast booth, not in spite of, but precisely for, her accent.

There was a small silence while Caroline wiped her mouth with her napkin, which was odd, because as far as Angie could tell from her plate, she hadn't eaten anything at all.

"Maybe for a little while," she said. "If Mama needs me."

Rivera, who considered the only real sacrifice she was making this summer her regular trips down the Jersey shore, wanted to know more about the lake, how far it was, who went there. Miss Maddie and Caroline let themselves be drawn into that discussion while Angie turned back to Miss Zula.

"How long have you known Miss Junie?" Angie asked.

The small, round face stilled in a way that meant nothing, yet, to Angie, but it did make her curious.

"Junie Maddox and I matriculated at Ogilvie together and graduated on the same day. We taught high school English, both of us, starting in the fall of 1952. Not at the same school, not in those days, but we often worked on our lesson plans together. And then she married Bob Lee Rose and gave up teaching."

And that, Angie realized, was the smallest part of the story, and all Miss Zula was willing to tell just now. Along her spine she got a flutter of nerves, the sign that she had stumbled, unexpectedly, onto something important.

She was just about to say that straight out when the door opened and Harriet came in.

"Well, now. Finally," said Miss Zula. "Harriet Rose Darling, you are late again."

"I lost track," Harriet said, leaning over to kiss the old woman on the cheek.

"We'll see to it they put as much on your gravestone," said Miss Zula as she patted Harriet's cheek. "'Here lies Harriet. She had no idea it was so late.'"

"What was it, dear?" asked Miss Maddie, holding up her cheek in turn. "Those fractious boys of yours?"

"No," said Harriet as she fell into a chair. "It was Tab."

"How is dear Tab?" Maddie asked.

Harriet seemed to be considering an answer while she helped herself to eggs. Then she said in the languid way of a woman who has been praying for the same thing every day for many years without satisfaction, "Why, it would be best if Tab would just die."

"Harriet," said Caroline.

"What?" Harriet said. "It's true. I mean it with all my heart."

Rivera, unable to contain herself any longer, let out a burst of laughter.

Angie had eaten more than she meant to but found that she was oddly comfortable, given the events of the early morning and the fact that Caroline Rose was sitting across from her at the table. The conversation flowed along from the wayward ways of boys and men, to the new dress Junie Rose was having made for Caroline's wedding, to the benefit auction at the church, to the cost of printing posters, which brought Rivera to the subject of the English department photocopier, and Patty-Cake Walker, who had given Tied to the Tracks a monthly allowance of twenty-five copies.

"Bring that to Rob's attention," said Caroline. "He'll deal with Patty-Cake."

"Patty-Cake and her copy machine," said Miss Zula, her mouth pressing hard. "As proud as a dog with two tails."

"More like a witch with a familiar," said Harriet.

Miss Maddie said, "I swear, I've heard more stories. It's just unnatural, a woman carrying on about a machine like that. I suppose if her Wayne hadn't walked in front of that bus she'd have more important things to keep her busy."

"She did hover over Wayne, but then he gave her reason enough," Harriet agreed. "That reminds me. Patty-Cake has been after her nephew Win Walker to ask you out."

Miss Maddie said, "That young man with the tattoo on his bald spot?"

"No," said Miss Zula. "You're thinking of Walker Winfield, who's a deacon at Church of Christ. Win Walker goes to First Baptist."

"Win Walker and Walker Winfield?" asked Angie.

"Double first cousins," said Harriet. "Jean Winfield married Jackson Walker and they named their first son Winfield Walker. Then Jackson's sister—Sue Ann Walker?—married Jean's brother Joe Bob and they named their firstborn Walker Winfield. Except they don't resemble each other, not one bit. Win got all the looks but all Walker got was religion. And a bald spot, which he went and got tattooed one time when he was struggling with the angel, I suppose."

Rivera pressed a fist to her mouth and then smiled anyway. "What exactly does Walker have tattooed on his bald spot?"

Miss Maddie turned to her sister. "What was it now? Praise Jesus? Wait, no, I remember. Jesus Saves."

Rivera said, "Maybe Win has got some good tattoos, you'll have to let us know, Angie."

Angie resisted the urge to stick her tongue out at Rivera and reached instead for another piece of toast.

"Where does Patty-Cake fit into all this?" she asked.

Miss Maddie got a thoughtful look on her face. "If I recall, her Wayne was half brother to Jackson on their daddy's side." Then she let out a small, very musical laugh. "You'll have to stay in Ogilvie a lot longer than a school year if you've got a mind to learn all the family connections."

"It was just Patty-Cake I was wondering about," said Angie. "As she's taking such an interest in my love life."

Harriet said, "Rivera, I'd guess Patty-Cake has already got some young man picked out for you, too."

Miss Maddie's bird-bright eyes flashed behind her glasses. "Now, won't that be nice, don't you think? With the Independence Day Jubilee coming up and all." She turned her face toward Rivera. "We celebrate the Fourth of July in a big way here in Ogilvie."

"What Miss Maddie in't telling you," said Harriet, "is that she's been head of the Jubilee committee since just about ever. Why, there wouldn't be a Jubilee without her."

Miss Maddie started to protest, but Harriet held up a hand and carried on. "There's a barbecue and games, and in the evening there's the picnic basket auction and dance. Of course you have to have a ticket to be a Basket Girl, but I bet Miss Maddie could see to that."

"I might could," Miss Maddie said. "Now, Rivera, tell us. You got somebody you want to invite down from the city? A boyfriend you might want to show around Ogilvie?"

Angie slid down a little further in her chair, resigning herself to the idea that this conversation, long overdue, would take place at this particular breakfast table with two elderly women.

Rivera looked up from her orange juice, her expression innocent, friendly, vaguely agreeable, and shrugged.

"A girlfriend, maybe," she said. "I'm gay."

"How nice for you," Miss Maddie said. Harriet hiccupped and put three fingers to her mouth as if to hold it shut. Miss Zula handed her another napkin.

"She means she's a lesbian," Caroline said to Miss Maddie. "Harriet, drink something before you choke."

"I understood her, Caroline," said Miss Maddie. "I watch HBO. Are you a lesbian, too, Angeline?"

Harriet hiccupped again, but it would take a lot more than a few blushes to upset Rivera, who was enjoying herself without reservation.

"No," said Angie. "I can't claim that honor."

Harriet said, "But I thought lesbians go around in pairs?"

"Nuns go around in pairs," said Miss Maddie, brightly. "And those polite young Mormon missionaries who dress so neatly."

"To answer your question," Rivera said to Harriet, "as far as I know there's no rule in the lesbian handbook that says we have to go around in pairs. But I'll check with the governing board, if you like."

"Close your mouth, Harriet," said Miss Zula. "You look simpleminded sitting there showing off your bridgework. Rivera is teasing you, and you're embarrassing Caroline."

"Well, there's nothing new about that," said Harriet, touching her napkin to her mouth. "I've made a career out of embarrassing my little sisters.

All four of them overachievers, what's left for me but bad behavior? I might not be sophisticated, but she loves me just the same, don't you, baby?"

Caroline said, "If you try not to insult anybody else this morning, yes."

Rivera said, "Tell us more about this nephew Patty-Cake has dug up for Angie. Maybe he'll have more luck getting her out of the house than Tony and I have been having."

"You don't have a young man?" asked Miss Maddie, turning to Angie.

"There's someone I date now and then, back home."

"Five years of nothing serious," added Rivera, and gave Angie a wide-eyed, not quite so innocent look.

"Five years!" Harriet said. "If you don't want the man, honey, my advice is to throw him back in and get yourself some fresh bait."

Miss Maddie held her napkin up to her face when she laughed. "You are terrible, Harriet."

"Tell the truth and shame the devil," said Harriet.

"I'm very busy with the film company," said Angie. "I've got no complaints."

"But you're such a young woman," said Miss Maddie. "It's a shame if you don't enjoy yourself a little while you're here. Don't you think, sister?"

Miss Zula produced one of her rare smiles. "Certainly. We'll have to see what we can do."

At that moment, struck by the strange turn in the conversation, by Caroline Rose's expectant but sober look, and most of all by the expression on Miss Zula's face, a flash of understanding struck Angie: They had come, finally, to the place Miss Zula had meant them to be. She was going to raise the subject of John Grant, and then there would be nothing to do but tell the story. Angie looked around the table at each woman in turn, and then caught Rivera's eye.

To Harriet she said, "Tell Patty-Cake I'd be happy to make her nephew's acquaintance. I'm looking forward to it."

You've got to give the old woman credit," Rivera said later. "She's got style."

"So did Machiavelli," said Angie.

They had insisted on walking back simply because Angie didn't want to sit in the same car with Caroline Rose, not just yet. Not until she had some answers, starting with the most obvious one: who exactly knew about the summer she had spent with John Grant five years ago.

Of course the only person who could tell her that was John himself. She thought of him on the river, and her pace slowed for as long as it took her to banish that image yet again.

They crossed the old wooden footbridge over the river and paused to look down into the water. Angie said, "You don't think—" She stopped herself.

"No," said Rivera.

"No what?" Angie said. "I wish you'd stop answering questions before I ask them."

"No, Miss Zula didn't get us down here to play matchmaker for John Grant and you."

"How would she even know about that?" Angie said, exasperated.

"Don't ask me," Rivera said. "But she knows. I could see it on her face, and so could you. Maybe she was watching you at the birthday party when John took that arrow. Your face gave a lot away."

Angie pushed away from the bridge rail. "I'm going into town," she said. "I've got to get this cleared up before there's real trouble."

"Sure," said Rivera. "Don't you want to know where he lives?"

Angie closed her eyes, counted to three, and then she nodded. She stayed that way while Rivera gave her directions, and didn't move until she was finished.

"You sure this is a good idea?" Rivera asked.

Angie felt herself flushing. "You got a better one? Never mind, don't answer that."

She was off the bridge and walking fast when Rivera called after her.

"Tell him hello from me!"

The looks Angie got as she walked through town were mostly friendly or curious; a few people said hello and looked like they would have gladly stopped to talk. Any other time she would have done that, but just now she couldn't afford to. If she let herself be distracted, if she stopped to think, she'd lose her resolve.

One plate-glass window after another reminded her that she wasn't wearing makeup, that she had tied her hair back with a rubber band, and that the shirt she was wearing over jeans had a rip in the pocket. She was overdressed for the weather but underdressed if she compared herself to the other women her age who passed her on the street.

She had never been able to manufacture any real interest in fashion, and rarely remembered to look in the mirror. The good clothes she had brought with her to Ogilvie were basic: a dark dress for formal wear; a lighter, dressier one that she had worn to every wedding she had attended for the last three years; a single sundress; a straight black skirt; and a good white silk blouse. She couldn't remember the last time she had bought anything new. When there was extra money she bought another lens for her Nikon or put something aside toward new equipment.

She had never worried much about this particular failing until John had come along. John, who wore expensive clothes so casually and so well. He had an eye for line and color and he never asked, as other men sometimes had, if his shirt matched his pants. More than that, he had never, not once, said a word to her about her clothes, good or bad; he never seemed disappointed in what she wore, although she herself felt at a disadvantage walking down the street next to him. He was elegant and beautiful and strong, and next to him she often felt like a puppy that needed grooming.

Angie thought of going home to change, or at least finding a store where she could buy a cap or scarf or something to cover her hair, but then she had no money on her, even if any of the shops along this part of Main Street would offer something so mundane.

The merchants of Ogilvie, it was clear, catered to tourists who came for day trips from Savannah and to the wealthy parents of its undergraduates. She passed Thomasina's, which seemed to be doing a brisk brunch business; an artisan jeweler; a crowded café-bakery; a clothing boutique with a linen sheath in the window that glimmered in the light. It was made for a long, thin woman who had no bust and no hips, and Angie would have looked like a sack of potatoes in it, which was beside the point: she couldn't afford a dress like that, and she had no place to wear it. It was an elegant dress, for cocktail parties at the dean's house or an evening in Savannah at the theater. An Audrey Hepburn, a Jackie Kennedy, a Caroline Rose kind of dress.

Next came a shop called Shards, which advertised itself with a scattering of paper-thin china teacups over a tumble of black velvet in its single window. *We buy antique china, porcelain, and glassware* was written in fine calligraphy on a small card in the window, and under that: *Constance Rose Shaw, Proprietor. Appraisals by appointment only.* The Rose sisters might have the unruliest sons in all of southeast Georgia, but they were good at other things. Next to Shards was an antique shop, Re-Runs (Eunice Rose Holmes, Proprietor), and beyond that, Fat Quarters (Pearl Rose McCarthy). Connie, Eunice, and Pearl monopolized a full half of the choicest block on Main Street, directly across from campus.

Angie passed a real estate office and an old-fashioned drugstore with large colored-glass vials in the window and then came to Ogilvie Books. A banner spanned the full length of the window: OGILVIE CELEBRATES FIFTY YEARS OF DIVERSITY.

Every book Miss Zula had written was here, in first and more modern editions, many of the jackets sporting silver or gold embossed medallions for one literary prize or another, a galaxy of small stars. Angie wondered if Tony had already been here to shoot stills. The truth was he probably had been, but she should have been with him, making contacts and setting up interviews. Instead she had been hiding in Ivy House. That would have to change.

In the middle of the display of books was a photo of a very young Zula in a cap and gown, accepting a diploma from a portly man. A newspaper article dated 1952, matted and framed, stood beside it on a carved oak easel. The headline was still dark and clear: "Ogilvie College Awards Diploma to Local Negro Woman."

"What a difference fifty years make, eh?"

Angie jumped, a hand pressed to her heart, and then stepped back against the window.

"Rob."

Rob Grant, a younger, darker, and more easygoing version of his brother, had never been one to stand on formalities. He kissed her on the cheek and gave her a hug that smelled of the bakery bag he held in one hand, yeast and dark sugars and cinnamon.

"Angie, I was wondering when I'd run into you. Don't you look good."

"So do you. So you ended up back in Ogilvie after all."

"Where else, for one of Lucy Ogilvie's boys? And Kai—my wife?—Kai is on the math faculty here."

"I heard that someplace. You look happy."

"I gave up on the law and I married well. What's not to be happy? Hey." He held up the bakery bag. "I'm on my way home for a late breakfast. Kai wants to meet you, and there's coffee on. Unless you've already had breakfast?"

"I ate with Miss Zula and Maddie."

Rob raised an eyebrow. "The Rose girls' monthly goddaughter breakfast? Miss Zula must like you. So are you coming?"

His eyes were brown while John's were blue, and Angie remembered quite suddenly playing poker with the two of them on a rainy Sunday afternoon. He had been in law school then, and she had liked him tremendously. He was the only good thing to remember about that particular weekend, and she had the idea that he might actually understand, if she were to tell him what she was about to do.

She said, "I am on my way to find John. There are some things I need to talk to him about."

"In that case"—he took her elbow—"you'll have to come along. We share the house with him . . ." His voice trailed away.

Angie gave him her best, clearest, most intense smile. "Until he gets married. It's okay, Rob."

"Until we find a place of our own," Rob said, but he gave her an appraising look that said he might have given up the law, but still understood a great deal about the way people lied to themselves, and others.

It was a ten-minute walk, long enough for Rob to give her his personalized, highly suspect history of the neighborhood and for Angie to begin to panic. He was in the middle of an anecdote that involved the adolescent Grant boys, a tire swing, a six-pack of beer, and somebody called Louanne who was now the chief of police, when Angie stopped just where she was.

Rob looked at her expectantly. "Rethinking?"

She nodded.

"You know," he said slowly, "I live there, too. You're welcome in my home anytime."

"You think he won't want to see me." If she could have snatched the words out of the air, she would have done that.

"Oh, he wants to see you," Rob said. "As much as you want to see him."

She hiccupped a laugh, started to say something that was a lie, and stopped herself.

"I never took you for a coward," said Rob Grant.

Angie hesitated a moment, and then caught up with him. After a while she said, "Do you mind very much having to move out?"

Rob shrugged. "I thought I would, but it turns out that looking for a house with Kai is an experience not to be missed. And John would never really be happy anyplace else. Something the Rose girls have yet to figure out, as they are still trying to talk him into moving into Old Roses."

"Old Roses?"

"The family place. You were there for Miss Junie's birthday. The occasion of the wayward arrow? The Rose girls have got it in their heads that Caroline should stay there for good and keep an eye on Miss Junie."

"And what does Caroline want?"

Rob stopped short, a thoughtful look on his face. "You know, I don't think I've ever heard her say one way or the other. It's mostly her sisters who talk about it."

Angie thought of Caroline Rose at Miss Zula's table, and how she had disappeared from the conversation as soon as Harriet had come in.

She said, "Miss Zula asked Caroline to work with me and Rivera. She said Caroline is the best source of information about the town, next to her mother."

After a while Rob said, "It's true that Caroline is one of those people who's good at listening, so she hears a lot." He gestured with his chin. "Here we are. It's not Old Roses, but it's where my mother grew up and we're all fond of it."

Set back in a garden was a pale yellow two-story house. The windows were tall and narrow, with white woodwork and shutters, and a deep porch spanned the entire width of the house. The garden was in full bloom with flowers Angie couldn't name, and more flowers bloomed in pots along the edge of the porch and between chairs piled with cushions. And, inevitably, there was John Grant sitting on the brickwork step, looking directly at her.

He had just come off the river. His skin was still flushed with exercise, water glistening in his short hair, his skin damp. Sweat was shining on his bare shoulders and in the hollow of his throat and on his legs, and Angie understood one thing: she should never, ever, have come.

SEVEN

I am going to say this straight out: I don't think it's proper to be digging around in matters that don't concern you and that you can't understand because you are, forgive my bluntness, Yankees. I don't know what the university was thinking, inviting you all to come pry in our business, and I have written them a letter saying just that. The past is past. Leave it be.

Your name: none of your business.

I have a story you might want to hear about the summer of 1973, when my second cousin Anita Bryant came to visit. It has got nothing to do with Miss Zula but it's a good story anyway.

Your name: Howard Stillwater. I own Stillwater Used Cars, and can be found there six days a week from seven in the morning 'til six at night. When you get ready to replace that pitiful excuse for a vehicle you drove down here, come and see me, I'll do you up right.

It made perfect sense, John Grant told himself, that his brother would take it upon himself to force this reunion. Suddenly the wound on his upper thigh, mostly healed, began to itch. He pulled the towel from around his neck and laid it over his lap while he watched Rob cross Lee Street with Angie beside him, and he tried to think what he could possibly say to her, given the mood she was in.

It was not something he could forget in five years or fifty, the way Angie Mangiamele's face gave away her temper. The only comfort, and it was a small one, was that she wasn't wearing the old Nirvana T-shirt she had had on this morning when he saw her by the river. She had changed into a different, equally familiar shirt, two sizes too big, an old Hawaiian print with a tear in the pocket. The T-shirt, he imagined, she had left hanging on the post of her bed.

John closed his eyes and leaned forward, forearms propped on his knees, hands hanging.

"A little early for a nap, isn't it?"

"Rob, I think I hear your wife calling you."

When he opened his eyes she was there, five feet away. Her hair had grown out again, a coiling mass that reached halfway down her back, dark brown with hints of red in the light. There were some new things—a scar at the corner of her mouth, another piercing in her right ear—but mostly she was still Angie, unforgettable. She was looking at Rob, who had a hand on her shoulder.

"I know when I'm not wanted. We'll be waiting on the back porch."

She gave him a tight nod and a tighter smile, and then he was gone, but not before he threw John a particular look, the one that said he had doubts about his big brother's ability to handle the situation.

There was a moment's silence filled in by the sound of a lawnmower's ineffective sputter and, more insistent, birdsong. John was thinking that Rob was right, he had no chance in the world of handling this situation, when Angie spoke.

"Is that a mockingbird?" She was looking up into the oak tree.

John shifted a little. "A thrush, I think."

"A thrush. I've been meaning to go to the library to find a tape on birdsong. So I know what I'm hearing. And a book on flowers." She was looking at the garden, no doubt because she didn't want to look at him. The shadows moved over her face and neck and touched her shirt and the strong hands and the faded jeans. He was glad she stood so far away, and frustrated by it, too, which was ridiculous, which was insupportable.

He said, "Did you stop by just to say hello?"

And saw that he had made the first mistake, as he knew he must, and he always did, with this woman. The color climbed in her face.

"Am I intruding?"

"No," he said, quietly. "No, you're not. I'm glad to see you."

She produced a small, dry laugh. "I just wanted to ask you a couple questions."

John studied his hands where they gripped his knees, white knuckled. He stood up. "Best we go inside, then."

She took a step backward. "Afraid I'm going to embarrass you?"

He sat down again. "Can we call a truce before we get started?"

"I didn't know we were at war."

John forced himself to take a few deep breaths. "Of course not. Go ahead with your questions."

She said, "Does Miss Zula know that you and I used to date?"

He had expected something very different, and at first could hardly make sense of the question.

"Date?"

"Date, yes. You do remember."

"Of course I remember. I'm just not sure I'd use that word. I don't know how she would know. I never mentioned it to her. Why?"

Angie's mouth pursed itself. "And Caroline Rose? Have you mentioned it to her?"

John held on to her gaze, though it cost him a great deal. "I haven't raised the subject yet."

"Why not?"

John heard the screen door open behind him. Angie's face told him that it wasn't Rob standing there.

"Let me introduce you to my sister-in-law," John said. "I may have been slow to bring Caroline up to date, but there's no keeping secrets from Kai."

The house was just exactly what Angie expected. Solid old furniture, simple, elegant, comfortable. Not a pile of paper in sight, or a book out of place. A few small watercolors, an antique map in a gilded frame, a sampler: Jane Ogilvie 1825. No photos, not of his parents or grandparents or anyone else. Nor would she find them anywhere else in the house.

When she took him home to Hoboken the first time, John had spent a lot of time going over what Tommy Apples liked to call the family shrine, a whole wall full of photographs, some more than a hundred years old. John had been sincerely interested in Angie's family, but could not be bothered with the artifacts of his own.

This comfortable, well-used, strictly kept house was much like an expensive hotel room. It was one of the things that she had only begun to understand about John, this way he went about constructing a world for himself free of conflict and unpleasant memories, and it was immediately familiar.

On the other hand, Rob's wife took her by surprise. Kai Watanabe looked like a teenage boy's geisha fantasy, but presented herself like the theoretical mathematician she was. Small and slender with a long veil of shining black hair, she came at Angie so directly and with so much undisguised curiosity that only two choices presented themselves: to be affronted or charmed. The fact that Kai's smile was as honest and unassuming as her gaze made the choice easier.

On the screened rear porch, Angie stood at the old oak table that had been set for a late breakfast and tried to sound regretful.

"I've eaten, but thank you."

"Sit," said John, and pointed at a chair.

"How rude," said Rob.

"Me?" said John and Angie together.

"Both of you," said Rob. "Have coffee at least, Angie. Kai will think you don't like her."

"Don't listen to him," said Kai, holding out a coffee cup. "He is teasing. You will like me and I will like you and now that's settled."

Her English was excellent, save for a distinct and unusual rhythm. To Angie's ear it sounded as though Kai had learned British English that was now giving way to her husband's slow Georgia drawl.

She sat down, and then John sat down across from her with his back to the wall.

The immediate problem, as far as John was concerned, was not the fact that Angie Mangiamele was sitting at his breakfast table with a barely disguised scowl on her face. As odd as it was to have her here, and as disturbing as this discussion promised to be, there was a bigger issue, and that was the fact that Caroline and all of her sisters would be here in an hour for one of their planning meetings. What he didn't want, what he couldn't afford, was to add the subject of Angie to flower arrangements and discussions about color schemes.

"Isn't this cozy," said Rob, looking around the table with true and undisguised pleasure. He put a sticky bun the size of a wagon wheel on his plate. "How is your filming coming along, Angie?"

Angie sat very straight with both hands wrapped around her coffee cup. She was pale, and there were shadows under her deep-set eyes. John counted the tines on his fork.

"We aren't actually shooting yet," Angie said. "There's a lot of prep work to do. As far as Miss Zula is concerned, there are a few mysteries to solve."

"Mysteries?" Kai's small, neat head turned, and the veil of her hair swung with it.

"Yes. The biggest mystery is why Miss Zula seems set on throwing Caroline Rose and me together. Any idea why that might be, John?"

Kai put her hands flat on the table to either side of her plate. "I like her," she said to Rob. "She asks good questions. Do you play poker, Angie?"

"Don't answer that, Angie. My wife is a card-counting shark."

"I could teach you to throw craps," Angie said to Kai, and in spite of the seriousness of the situation and his growing uneasiness, John had to smile at the idea of these two women at a craps table.

She said, "And about questions, the thing is, I keep asking them until I get answers. John?"

A small V-shape crease had appeared between Angie's brows. It was true that she wouldn't stop asking; her persistence was one of the things that made her good at her work.

"Maybe you should ask Miss Zula directly," John said. "I can't read the woman's mind."

"I can," said Rob.

John sent his brother an irritated look, but Rob was unconcerned.

"Well, then," said Angie. "Enlighten me."

"It's simple. Miss Zula's main joy in life is throwing people who interest her together, just to see what happens. A year down the line there'll be a new short story in *The New Yorker* or *Harper's*, unless you and Caroline disappoint her by getting along."

"I like Caroline just fine," said Angie. "You're saying that while we're filming Miss Zula, she'll be taking notes on us?"

Rob said, "That's not it, exactly. She does get most of her stories from watching people, but she's not likely to make it obvious enough to identify you."

"Unless you're Button Ogilvie," said Kai.

"Zula hasn't buttoned anybody for years," said John. "You'd really have to be on her bad side to get that kind of attention."

"I'll bite," said Angie. "Who is Button Ogilvie, and what did she do of such great significance that she's been transformed into a verb by Zula Bragg?"

"It's an old family feud," said Rob. "Button Ogilvie is big on revisionist history, and Miss Zula finally struck back by writing Button into a novel—"

"Miss Callie," said Angie, and a look of understanding came over her face, her eyes bright as she put things together and then filed them away for further reference. "Miss Callie is Button Ogilvie? Oh, it must have been fun, when *Sweet-Bitter* came out. Who else has been buttoned? I'm interested."

"Nobody still living," said John. "These days you won't really recognize any of her characters as real people."

Kai gave a high, hooting laugh. "I recognized John," she said. "She called him Harvey Carson and he ran a family shoe factory in Mississippi."

Very calmly John said, "Harvey Carson was not based on me."

Angie sat up straighter, looking disturbingly pleased with the turn in the conversation, and with Kai. "*Dollar Short*, right? Came out two years ago? Of course you're Harvey Carson," she said to John. "First son of the local gentry sets up the ideal life for himself and discovers perfection is overrated. Or maybe you haven't got to that last part yet?" She took a swallow of coffee and looked at him over the rim of the cup.

John met her gaze and felt the shock of it before he looked away again, this time at Kai. "I am not Harvey Carson. Harvey Carson falls in love with his sister's husband. Are you saying I'm gay and don't know it?"

Kai lifted a shoulder. "Angie would be a better person to ask, I think."

"No," Angie said calmly. "He's not gay. But he might be in love with his brother's wife."

John felt himself flushing. "Hell no. Sorry, Kai, but no."

Kai smiled. "I am not offended. Are you offended, Rob? Your brother isn't in love with me."

Rob winked at Angie. "I always had better taste. And anyway, that's the story where the sister is too weak to stand up for her husband when he needs her most. Obviously not me and Kai. So you're free and clear, John, you can't be Harvey."

"Great. Now can we change the subject?" John asked.

Kai said, "I have a question," and the knot in John's gut pulled tighter. But then there was no harm in Kai and a great deal of kindness, and he liked her for her own sake as much as for Rob's.

He said, "You always do, darlin'. What is it?"

"I would like to know why your relationship with Angie failed."

He heard himself draw in a sharp breath. Angie blinked in surprise.

"And here I was just thinking what a good sister-in-law you've been to me. Sorry, but I can't answer that question."

Kai's gaze shifted to Angie and he added: "And neither can Angeline."

"I can't?" said Angie.

"You choose not to."

"I do?"

"Here we go," said Rob, reaching for more coffee.

Angie put down her cup and crossed her arms so that her hands rested on her shoulders, and she gave him a long, considering look. "I'd like to hear what you have to say about this, Harvey."

"Oh, good," said Kai cheerfully. "I also."

"Me, too," said Rob.

"You see?" said Kai. "We all want to hear."

"Rob was correcting your English," said John. "'Me too' instead of 'I also.' He was giving you the more colloquial usage."

"No I wasn't," Rob said. "I do want to hear."

John took a breath, looked from Kai's intense expression to Rob's amused one, weighed the possibility of further evasion, and gave in. "Our relationship ended because Angie felt our goals and priorities were too different."

"Now see," Angie said, "I'd say it had more to do with the fact that I dyed my hair blue to go meet your grandfather Grant."

John studied the crumbs on his plate before he let himself look up. "The color of your hair was—is—irrelevant. That was just your way of forcing a confrontation."

To Kai, Angie said, "I just didn't fit in. His grandfather Grant hated me."

"But I didn't." John said it clearly and saw Angie jerk, ever so slightly. Which gave him more satisfaction than he deserved, or could explain to himself.

Rob said, "In all fairness, Angie, the old man hated just about everybody, our mother included."

"How is Lucy?" Angie asked John. She had met John's mother only once, but it had been memorable.

"Fine. She's fine." He shot Rob a sharp look, but Kai missed the significance of that. She said, "She is remarried. Again."

"Really?" Angie said. "How many times is that?"

"Four," said John.

"Five, counting our father," added Rob. "If you want to know my theory—"

"Please don't," said John.

"—it all started as a way to irritate Grandfather Grant after Daddy flew his plane into the sea, but then Lucy got into the serial marriage habit and she hasn't been able to break it."

"I think your grandfather would not have liked Lucy no matter what," said Kai thoughtfully. To Angie she said, "He took Rob out of his will when we got married."

"And then he died," said Rob. "That'll teach him."

"I didn't know about your grandfather," Angie said. Her mouth worked as if she were tasting something unpleasant. "I'm sorry for your loss."

"Don't be," Rob said. "We aren't. Or I'm not. I can't speak for John—who got the building on Morningside and the house on Long Island, by the way."

"I sold the Long Island house," John said.

Angie was looking at John, but for the moment he couldn't meet her eye. He was too busy fighting back a swell of irritation with Rob and himself, too, for this irresistible urge to provide Angie with information that she clearly did not want.

Her attention was fixed on him, her eyes so dark and so brilliant that it looked, just for that moment, as if she were about to cry. Which was his imagination, because he had never known a woman less inclined to tears, unless it was Kai. Or his own mother.

Very slowly she said, "Jay, you still won't admit you were angry about my hair."

"Jay?" Kai looked between them. "I have never heard you called this before."

"And you never will," John said. "Angie's always renaming people—" He paused before the rest of the thought forced its way into words: Angie renamed only the people she cared about. He cleared his throat. "She calls her father Apples and her mother Peaches. She calls her close friends *winkie* when she's feeling good about them and *mope* when she's not. How is your mother, Angie?"

"Fine," Angie said, and Kai said, "Winkie?"

To Angie, John said, "I admit your timing was bad, Angie. But that's all I'll admit."

"Harvey, give it up. You were angry and, oddly enough, you're still angry."

"This is all ancient history. And if I have any say in the matter, if I've got to have a nickname, I'd like to stick with Jay."

Kai said, "John does not like to show anger, it is true. In this, he and Caroline are well matched."

It was rare that Kai pushed him so hard that John was in danger of losing his composure, but now it took everything in him to control his tone. He said, "I don't want to talk about Caroline."

Angie's gaze hadn't left his face. "But that's where all this started. I wanted to know if Caroline has been told about our ancient history. Which she hasn't."

"She doesn't know?" Rob sat up straight.

Kai, oblivious as she could be at times, smiled. "Do you think she will be angry at you? Is that why you haven't told her?"

John said, "Now I'm a obsessive closeted homosexual afraid of anger, confrontation, and women."

"Named Harvey," said Kai cheerfully.

The doorbell rang, but John couldn't bring himself to look away from Angie, who had come back into his life to wreak havoc, and was making excellent progress. He let Rob leave the table to answer the doorbell while he held Angie's gaze, because it would have been cowardly to look away, and because there was something in her voice he didn't understand, quite, or even want to understand.

Angie pressed the fingers of both hands to her mouth and then drew them down to her chin. "I think we've established that you're not gay."

"As you have cause to know," he said, quietly.

She said, just as quietly, "But the rest of it fits. As I have cause to know."

Kai said, "So those are the reasons your relationship failed?"

"No," said Angie, her voice wavering. She managed a smile. "Those aren't the reasons. Excuse me, would you, Kai? It's been good to meet you, but we seem to be going in circles here, and I have work to do."

Angie was so intent on making it to the front door before John caught up with her—she heard him push his chair back when she was halfway through the kitchen—that she turned into the hall without looking and bumped into Rob, who stepped sideways and collided, full force, with Patty-Cake Walker, whose arms were full of huge wallpaper sample books that cascaded across the floor, flapping like a flock of mute and uncoordinated geese.

Then John ran into Angie, and she lost her tenuous balance and would have fallen if he hadn't caught her by the elbow. She heard herself gasp, and she heard him draw in breath, and then she was free again—absolutely free again, unattached, alone—and standing, breathing heavily, between Patty-Cake Walker and John Grant. Rob was on the floor, gathering the wallpaper books into a pile.

Angie knew her face was red with embarrassment, but John looked far worse, like a teenager who had just been caught on the couch with a fast girl. Patty-Cake was looking back and forth between them with a sharp, uneasy smile that said she was seeing things she didn't like.

"Hello, Mrs. Walker," Angie said. "And good-bye. I was just on my way out."

Patty-Cake smoothed her hair. "Am I early, John? I'm supposed to be meeting the Rose girls here. Don't let me chase you off, Angie, I'm sure Caroline would be so pleased to see you again."

"You're not early," John said, opening the door for Angie. "They're late, as usual. Thanks for coming by, Angie." He managed a grim smile, which was more than Angie could do. She nodded at Rob, and slipped out the door.

· Eight ·

Miss Zula wasn't ever a beauty and she is still wearing dresses she must have bought in 1963, but she is dignified and distinguished. By all accounts she is an excellent teacher. I cannot speak to her stories, as I have never read one.

Your name: Corrine Stillwater (Mrs. Howard). If you would like to talk to me, you may find me at home, looking after my family. I am also chairlady of the local chapter of the Daughters of the Confederacy.

I've made some resolutions," Angie told Rivera the next morning. "First, I'm not hiding out in this house anymore."

Rivera pushed her hair out of her eyes. "Well, good. You've got to see about Tony. I've got a bad feeling about him."

"I'll corner him and get some answers," Angie said. And then: "Who is it?"

River scowled at her. "Harriet Darling, of course. Harriet Darling with the husband who should just *die*." Rivera had perfected Harriet's accent and mannerisms in record short time. She sent Angie a sideways glance. "I warned you."

"How far has it gone?"

"You'll have to ask him that," Rivera said. "But you'd best go up and catch him right now. Take coffee with you."

Except Tony wasn't in his room, which was pleasantly rumpled and strewn with rolls of film and camera lenses, odd papers, and pieces of clothing. If Tony Russo wasn't in his own bed at seven in the morning, he was in somebody else's. Angie just hoped it wasn't Harriet Darling's.

The rest of the day turned out to be just as frustrating. The office Angie had been assigned in the English department turned out to be without working air-conditioning or telephone—though she remembered both things being there when she had first looked in, over a week ago—and there was no sign of the computer she had been promised. The office was empty of everything but two straight-backed chairs and an old metal desk that looked distinctly out of place against the walnut wainscoting. The top of the desk was covered with something sticky, and all the drawers were firmly locked. With the first glimmerings of a serious headache already making themselves felt, Angie went to find Patty-Cake Walker.

She was barricaded behind a highly polished oak desk the size of a small pool table, the great overturned bowl of lacquered hair unruffled by the breeze from the air-conditioning duct, which might have come off a jet plane.

"Now look who's here," Patty-Cake said with a stiff smile. "Dr. Grant isn't in quite yet, and neither is Rob."

Angie managed to look surprised. "That works out just fine, because I wasn't looking for either of them," she said. "But I do have a few questions for you."

"You shy thing." Patty-Cake tilted her head and produced what Angie thought was meant to be a teasing expression. "You and Dr. Grant used to know each other up there in New York, and you never said a word."

"Because," Angie said evenly, "it was a long time ago." It was never good to hold back anger, her father would say, and here was the proof: her headache ratcheted up a notch.

"Five years a long time?" Patty-Cake wagged her head from side to side. "I guess I'm getting old."

"I guess you are."

The silence between them sparked. Angie cursed herself roundly, took a deep breath, and managed a smile she hoped might be interpreted as conciliatory.

She said, "There's no telephone in my office, and the air-conditioning is either turned off or broken." Then she evoked all the magical phrases due any keeper of the keys: *Don't want to be a bother* and *If it isn't too much trouble* and *I would be thankful if.* She ended with the computer, and decided to leave the locked desk drawers for the next battle.

Patty-Cake tapped a finger on her desk, her smile very white, and bone brittle. "There was a fan in that office. Now, what do you suppose could have happened to it? Maybe the janitor took it off to be rewired. I'll have to look into that, just as soon as I can."

Angie said, "And the phone?"

Patty-Cake had already half turned away. "I'll put in a work order. In the meantime, you've got one of those cute little cell phones, don't you?"

Later, listening to Angie's reconstruction of this first, lost skirmish in what promised to be a long and messy war, Rivera shook her head. "Run for the hills."

"Do you think this is about—"

"John? Most definitely. You practically forced him to tell Caroline about you—"

"You think?"

"Well, of course he did. What choice did he have after Patty-Cake walked in on you? And then Caroline told her sisters, and the Rose girls got on the drums—there was high drama down at Fat Quarters, let me tell you—and now Patty-Cake sees you as a threat to her bid for campus domination by means of her niece's marriage."

They were sitting on the grass in the golden light of the early evening. Angie, who had skipped lunch and was making up for it with a second beer, was finding it hard to worry about much at all.

Angie pressed the cold beer bottle to her cheek. "It was perfectly innocent."

Rivera made a grand gesture, one long hand revolving through the air in a corkscrew motion. "Angeline, my love. Two points. First, where you and John Grant are concerned, nothing is innocent. Anybody who sees you standing next to each other knows that. And second, Patty-Cake might be many things, but she's got a good nose. Watch yourself. Unless you want to call in the big guns."

"John?"

Rivera, whose mother was administrative assistant to the mayor of Hoboken, shook her head with great solemnity. "Rob," she said. "It'll be Rob who writes her job evaluations. Of course, that would be a declaration of war, and you'd end up on the sisterhood's ten-most-loathed list. You'll have to sign an affidavit to get a paper clip in any and every office across the country."

Angie considered. "Do you think administrative assistants take courses in military tactics?"

"That's classified," Rivera said. "Though my guess is that it's administrative assistants who teach those courses."

"The sisterhood," Angie said, burping softly.

"The source of all real power," Rivera agreed.

"Now what?"

Rivera rolled over on her stomach and waved her bare feet in the air. "Well, first you've got to put your requests in writing. Of course she'll ignore the first memo and misplace the second one. The third time you copy it to Rob, and then she'll start to move. Slowly, of course."

"I could go buy a fan," Angie said thoughtfully. "And I do have a cell phone. If it weren't for the computer I could just steer clear of her."

"You're forgetting about the copy machine."

Angie began to giggle, partly because beer on an empty stomach made her head buzz and partly because of the absurdity of the situation. Then she remembered Tony, who still hadn't showed his face, and the fact that Rivera hadn't seen him, either, all day long.

"What if Tony doesn't come home again tonight?"

"Then I go looking for him tomorrow," Rivera said. "And I make him understand the error of his ways."

"We never should have come down here," Angie said, putting an arm across her face.

"I'm glad you did," said a familiar voice.

Caroline Rose had come up behind them. She was wearing a pink linen sleeveless blouse, white jeans, and a friendly smile.

"Well, hello there," Rivera said. "You look like a strawberry parfait, pink and white." To Angie she said, "I forgot to say, we're going out for dinner. You want to come along? We can get Caroline to advise us on how to handle—"

"I'm not feeling very good," Angie said, quite truthfully; suddenly she wished she had never picked up the second bottle of beer.

"Who needs handling?" Caroline asked, looking vaguely interested.

"Your aunt Patty-Cake," said Rivera, ignoring the threatening look Angie threw her. "She's making things difficult for Angie in the office."

Caroline's cheeks turned the same color as her blouse "Oh, dear," she said, her soft voice taking on a bit of an edge. "The copy machine?"

"And the telephone and the air-conditioning," said Rivera.

"Really—" began Angie, but Caroline cut her off.

"I was afraid that might happen," she said. "Never you mind, Angie. I'll take care of it first thing tomorrow."

There were many things Angie might have said, but to carry this conversation any further might mean that it would swing back toward the subject of John Grant, something she wanted to avoid. Angie caught Rivera's eye and sent a small, silent, prayerful message, which Rivera caught like the experienced ballplayer she was.

"I'm hungry," she said, getting up from the ground and brushing grass off her rear. "Let's go, Pinkie."

"You sure you won't come along?" Caroline asked Angie, hesitating.

"You two go on without me." She tried for a pitiful expression, but feared that she was no better than Caroline at hiding her relief.

At eight the next morning Angie found Rob Grant setting up a laptop computer in her office. Over his shoulder he said, "Caroline called me last night and filled me in. She talked to Patty-Cake, too, so you don't have to worry about a counterstrike."

There was a standing fan by the windows and a smaller one on the desk, right next to a telephone.

"Telephone is working," he said, following her gaze. "Computer, too. Your Internet log-in information and your PIN code for the copy machine are in the top drawer. Which is open. And the physical plant people should be here later today to look at the air-conditioning. The fans will help until they sort it out.""

Angie put her bag on the desktop. "That was kind of Caroline," she said. "And it's good of you, too. Thanks."

"Nothing to it," Rob said. "Any other tall orders this morning?"

"Yes," Angie said. "You can find Tony for me. He hasn't come back to the house for two nights."

"Tony is in the editing suite," Rob said. "He was there when I got in."

"You are a whiz at this stuff," Angie said. "Excuse me while I go dismember him, would you?"

"Angie?"

She turned back at the door. He was looking at her as if she had broken out in an unusual rash, one he had never seen before. Then he moved his shoulders in a small, tight shrug, and shook his head.

"I just wanted to say that John is going to be away for the next week."

"Okay," Angie said slowly. "And?"

"Thought you might want to know," Rob said. He stood up and worked his shoulders again.

Angie started to turn away again when he said, "Caroline isn't going, though."

She paused for a moment, one hand on the door, and then stepped backward into the room. When she turned around, Rob was looking at her with great seriousness.

"What are you trying to say?"

He lifted a shoulder. "I don't know anything more than what I just told you. John is going to New York to work in the archives for a week, and Caroline is staying here. No other change in plans that I know of."

"None of this," Angie said, trying to get hold of her temper and not quite succeeding, "is any of my business."

"Maybe it isn't," Rob said, unflustered. He glanced out the window.

Angie thought of what it would mean to challenge that *maybe*: the discussion that would follow, the history that would be dredged up, again.

"Pardon me," Angie said. "I had better go find Tony before he disappears."

"Too late," said Rob. "There he goes."

"Oh, shit." Angie flopped down in the desk chair. "This week isn't starting well."

"Relax a little," Rob said, touching her shoulder as he went to the door. "This is the South, darlin'. Things don't move so fast down here."

Contrary to expectations after such a questionable start, the week went very well. It may have had something to do with the fact that John was away or that Patty-Cake had been brought to heel, but mostly Angie was thankful to Miss Zula, who took a liking to Tony Russo, and laid claim to him and his time.

Hoboken and Manhattan were crowded with women who had tried and failed to tie Tony down, but Miss Zula had some advantages. The first was her age; the second was the fact that while she appreciated his dry and usually sarcastic humor, she would not be distracted by it.

It was Tony Miss Zula called in the evenings to discuss how much time she was willing to spend with them the next day, and to what end. As a result, Tony's nighttime wanderings slowed down, which was a relief to Angie, but gave Rivera the idea that Miss Zula was orchestrating Harriet Darling's social life behind the scenes.

If that was true, Angie could only be thankful. For the first time since the fax machine had whirred to life those few weeks ago, she began to relax and remember why she liked what she did.

They began to shoot for short periods, going with Miss Zula to the university library, to pick up shoes she had left to be reheeled, into the garden while she pulled weeds and set out chipped saucers full of beer for slugs, to her office when she had appointments. The people who came to see her ranged from the university president to the sixteen-year-old son of an old friend who was unsure about whether he wanted to go to college or become an electrician.

Miss Zula's mornings were spent writing, so Angie used this time to begin her work in the town, where everybody knew the Bragg sisters and had some story about them or the family that—Angie was told with great seriousness—certainly had to be included in the documentary, if that Tony Russo fellow wanted to come by with his cameras. In a matter of days she filled two notebooks with names and anecdotes and newspaper clippings pressed on her by the helpful citizens of Ogilvie. She had a growing collection of bad snapshots of Miss Zula with well-known faces, among them Coretta Scott King, Bobby Kennedy, and a dozen different men and women who had Nobels, Faulkners, and Pulitzers to their names.

It would take another two weeks at least until she started hearing the stories that interested her most, the things people weren't likely to say to a stranger but might tell a friendly young woman who came around a second or third time to take ice tea on the porch. But it was a start, and a good one.

Angie spent a lot of time organizing her notes and writing lists of things to look up at the town library, which had a better collection of local history books than the university holdings. There were people she needed to seek out, and questions for Miss Zula or, more and more often as the week went on, for Caroline, who was just as helpful as Miss Zula had claimed she would be.

They saw a lot of Caroline. She stayed near when they filmed, suggested people to talk to, and made herself particularly valuable by providing introductions that otherwise would have been impossible. She did all of this quietly and competently, and nothing seemed to ruffle her except being brought into the center of attention.

Angie found herself liking Caroline, which surprised her and unsettled her, too. The only thing more surprising was the fact that Tony didn't seem to like her very much.

"You know the old saying," he told Angie one evening after Caroline had spent the afternoon with them. "'Keep your friends close and your enemies closer.'"

Rivera reached across the table and smacked him on the back of the head with the flat of her hand.

"Hey!" He scowled and scooted his chair out of her range.

"Give the woman a break," Rivera said. "Maybe she's just glad to get away from those sisters of hers. Paint samples and dish patterns and flower arrangements—*feh*." She flicked her fingers.

Tony rubbed the back of his head. "Christ, Rivera, you got mitts on you like a quarterback."

Angie was bothered by Tony's tone and expression, and so she asked outright. "Why don't you like Caroline?"

"That's obvious," Rivera said. "Harriet Darling. Caroline got between Tony and her sister."

His head came up slowly and he gave Rivera a hard look. Then he got up from the table, patted his shirt pocket to locate his cigarettes, and walked out of the kitchen.

"Well, hell," Rivera put back her head and examined the ceiling. "Guess I pushed too hard."

"I'd say so."

Angie yawned. "Let's just hope he doesn't go get himself shot by Tab Darling in order to prove a point."

"I wonder what Caroline said to Harriet. That would have been an interesting scene."

"Maybe it was Miss Zula," Angie said. "In which case it really would have been worth shooting."

"Oh, that's a picture," Rivera said. "Miss Zula telling Harriet Darling to keep it in her pants." She gave an uncharacteristic giggle and then pressed her hands to her eyes in a gesture that struck Angie as sad.

"Hey," she said. She resisted the urge to get up. "What is it?"

Rivera shook her head, shook it again more forcefully, and then forced a smile. "All work and no play."

Tony came through the screen door trailing a cloud of cigarette smoke. "Just what I was thinking," he said. "Come on, Rivera, let's go to down to the Hound Dog."

Rivera brightened. "That's the first good suggestion you've made today. Maybe we'll get lucky."

"And if we don't, we can comfort each other," Tony said.

There were many things to like about Tony, but at the moment the two most important were quite clear to Angie: he never held a grudge against a friend, and second, he loved Rivera with a cheerfully unrequited passion that was content with wordplay and celibacy.

She got up and hugged him, her arms around his middle. "I might take you up on that someday, you know," she said into his chest.

"Anytime, honey." Tony winked at Angie over Rivera's dark head. "Just say the word."

With the house to herself Angie found that she was unexpectedly lonely. After a short hesitation she called her parents, bracing herself for impact as she punched in the numbers.

She said, "Is that Tommy Apples?"

"Ang! What the hell! I was just telling your ma, she's disappeared into a swamp someplace. It's been a month since you called."

"It's been less than a week, Dad."

"And the mail we forwarded to you came back undeliverable, 'No such person.'"

"It did?" Angie lowered herself into the rocker on the porch to watch the fireflies bumbling around the garden. "Did Ma have the right address?"

"Sure she did, she got it off the sheet you left. What kind of nutty place are they running down there, mail can't even find you?"

"I'll look into it," Angie said, thinking of her mail cubby in the English department, that rectangle that had been empty every day since she got here, and then of Patty-Cake Walker and her smile. No counterstrike, indeed.

Her father was saying: "So, your aunt Bambina wants to know if you met that Jesse Jackson yet. She's always had a thing for that man, you know. Like a girl with a crush on a priest."

In the background there was a snort of dissent, and then the phone was dropped and picked up again.

"Don't listen to him," said Fran Mangiamele. "So, have you?"

"What? Met Jesse Jackson? He lives in Chicago, Ma."

"What do I care about Jesse Jackson? I'm asking you"—her mother paused dramatically—"about John." And then, into the silence: "John Grant."

"I know who you mean," Angie said.

"Well?"

"I told you already, Ma. He's here, he's getting married, end of story."

"What's she saying?" boomed her father.

"For Christ's sake, Tommy, go get on the extension."

"I like this phone better. What'd she say?"

"She says he's marrying somebody else." To Angie, her mother said: "It's a solid thing, this engagement?"

"Ma," Angie said wearily, "you want me to break up his relationship?"

"It's not the worst idea," said Fran. "It's how I got your father, you know. He was going to marry Loretta D'Oro. You remember? We used to call her Goldy, she came in for breakfast every day until her husband took a heart attack and she quit working the counter at the Korean grocery. Your father was going to marry her, until I made him think different."

"That's not true!" shouted Tommy Apples. "Never!"

"Oh, it's true. You ask Bambina, she'll tell you."

The phone changed hands abruptly, and her father said, "You paying toll charges to hash over old gossip, or do you want to tell us something interesting? What's the old lady like, anyway?"

"Wait," yelled Fran. "I'll get on the extension."

A half hour later, Angie put down the telephone and felt it ring, immediately, under her hand.

"Ma, what?" she said.

There was a long pause, and then Caroline Rose's soft voice said, "Am I interrupting something?"

"Oh," said Angie. "Sorry, I thought you were my mother. No, you're not interrupting."

There was a small, uncomfortable silence while Angie realized that she had never spoken to Caroline on the phone before. Then: "Can I help you with something, or did you want to talk to Rivera? Because," she went on, almost babbling, "she's not here just now."

Caroline cleared her throat. "That's all right," she said. "I'm happy to talk to you."

Angie bit her lip and wondered if southern custom required that she respond in kind, but then Caroline had launched into what sounded like a rehearsed speech.

"Miss Zula asked me to call. Tomorrow afternoon she's going to Savannah to see an old friend. Miss Zula has told you about Miss Anabel?"

"Her high school teacher," Angie said. "Yes."

It turned out, as Caroline had called to say, that Miss Zula went to Savannah once a month to visit Miss Anabel, always by train, and this time she was inviting Tied to the Tracks to come along. If all went well and Miss Anabel didn't change her mind, Tony would be allowed to film and they could interview the old lady.

"One more thing, while we're on the phone," Caroline said, and Angie's heart lurched into her throat.

"I have been meaning to apologize to you about my aunt Patty-Cake's behavior. She is sometimes a little too protective."

"She has no cause to be," Angie said. "I'm no threat to anybody."

Caroline said, "Of course you're not. But you're very pretty and successful and sure of yourself, and you and John—" She paused. "Patty-Cake does have a suspicious nature, but I don't. I wanted you to know that."

"Well, good," Angie said, and wondered why she was vaguely offended instead of relieved.

Later, unable to sleep, she came back down to the kitchen and began to make notes for the next day's shooting. She was agitated and couldn't say why, except that Caroline Rose didn't have a suspicious nature, and thought she was pretty. Which made no sense at all; none of that should matter. What mattered was tomorrow, and the work she needed to do to get ready.

A moth bumped softly against the window screen, and from down the block came a very satisfied postcoital tomcat screech. Angie listened to the scratch of her pen on paper, and contemplated Miss Zula's devious mind.

In the morning Angie found Tony in the kitchen when she came downstairs. He was trying to get the filter into the coffeemaker, one eye screwed shut. The other, red-rimmed, jerked fitfully. She took the filter out of his hand and shooed him away.

"I take it you're just coming in," Angie said. "Where's Rivera?"

"She got lucky," Tony said. "Really lucky. Luckier than me, at any rate."

"Looking for love in all the wrong places?"

"Oh, I got some," Tony said, yawning. "You know that blond woman with the chipped tooth who checks out at the Piggly Wiggly? DeeDee."

"I do," Angie said with great seriousness. "I do know DeeDee."

"Well." He slumped into a chair and ran his fingers through his hair until it stood up. "My Piggly Wiggly days are over."

"What was it this time?" Angie asked.

Tony put back his head to study the ceiling. "Day-of-the-week thongs."

She considered for a moment, and then decided that Tony needed no coddling. "This from a man who owns not one but two pairs of Home-of-the-Whopper boxer shorts. No good ever came from looking into a woman's underwear drawer, you mope."

Tony's mouth twitched. He yawned again, loudly, but he was smiling. "Time for bed. We aren't shooting anything important, are we?"

"I'm afraid we are," Angie said. "We're getting on a train for Savannah at exactly a quarter to one this afternoon, with Miss Zula. To go visit a retired high school teacher. If you've got to sleep you'd best get to it, and I'd forget the coffee."

Tony groaned, heaved himself out of his chair, and headed for the stairs. Over his shoulder he said, "You've got a cruel streak, Mangiamele. Someday it will come back to bite you on the ass. Someday very soon."

When Rivera had neither showed her face nor answered her cell phone by eleven, Angie roused Tony out of bed and pointed him toward the shower. Then she stood outside the door and shouted questions at him.

It turned out he remembered very little about the woman Rivera had left the bar with: dark-haired, lots of makeup, nervous laugh. "Your average closeted lesbian," he said when he came out of the bathroom with a towel around his middle, water running down his face and chest. "Or at least she was last night. Today, who knows?"

He leaned over to look at his face in the oval mirror over the dresser, pulled down an eyelid with a thumb. "Christ," he said balefully. "No wonder I can't get laid."

"Didn't get her name?" Angie asked again, in desperation.

"Meg," he said patiently, rubbing his bristled cheeks. "But I don't know her last name. We can do this without Rivera, you know."

Outside, the first rumbling of a storm echoed in the distance.

"Of course we can," Angie said. "No problem at all."

NINE

Ogilvie Bugle

NEWS ABOUT TOWN

Mayor Smith and the Jubilee Committee ask us to remind everybody that the Fourth of July is just four days away. The final organizational meeting will take place in the public room at the library tomorrow at seven p.m., and will be broadcast live on OP-TV, channel 12. The official schedule is available online at www.ogilviejubilee.org, at any of the stores on Main Street, the Piggy Wiggly, and the library. Entry forms for the 5K walk/run, the chili cook-off, baking contests and parade floats must be turned in by noon tomorrow at the library. The editorial staff of the *Bugle* reminds y'all that Miss Annie doesn't look kindly on lollygaggers.

The flight from Atlanta to Savannah was one John had taken so many times that it made no more impression than getting in the car to drive to the store for milk. An hour in the air was just long enough to gather his thoughts and give himself another talking-to.

He was good at making plans and sticking to them, but like so many other things in his life this summer, a simple plane trip was turning into something else, and quite abruptly. Within five minutes in the air, the weather had turned from threatening to bad, and the man in the seat next to him—a dignified, calm grandfatherly type in a three-piece summer-weight suit—had gone the color of his shirt. Trembling, he asked John in an embarrassed whisper if he could hold his hand.

"I'm about to shake myself right to death," said the old man, who introduced himself as Bob Beales. "Even if this plane doesn't go down. I am that scared."

John was trying to think of something comforting to say when a flash of lightning lit up the small cabin and the plane lurched. He held out his hand in a fist and the old man grabbed it, his fingers slightly swollen and red at the knuckle. The hands of a man who had worked hard all his life, who did not ask for help lightly. John was not reminded, not in the least, of his own father or of the one grandfather he had known.

"Don't tell me how safe it is to fly," said Bob Beales.

As John's own father had died in a small plane, he wasn't likely to say any such thing. He said, "I'm too worried about losing my lunch all over your suit to do much talking."

The old man let out a squawk of a laugh and then yelped with the next lurch. His grip on John's hand tightened.

"Tell me why you're going to Savannah," John said. "Maybe that will distract us both."

"I'm going to Savannah," said Bob Beales, "because my wife of forty-six years is there visiting her brother, and I couldn't stand not having her in my bed even one more day."

The plane did a half roll in one direction and then the other. John's stomach lurched into his throat, and he used his free hand to fumble for the airsickness bag while the old man continued talking.

". . . some of those years were a little thin, truth be told, but I have never wanted anybody else, and if I die today," he said in a hoarse whisper, "I'll have no regrets, not a one. And that will have to do for a prayer, because I've got nothing else to say to my maker."

Just as suddenly as the weather had gotten rough, it settled. There was a fraught silence in the cabin and then a woman called out, "Thank you, Jesus. Can I get a drink?"

"Just a few bumps, folks," came the pilot's voice through the speakers overhead. "All's well."

John drew in a deep breath and held it until he was sure he was back in control of his stomach. Bob Beales let go of his hand.

"I apologize for my rambling," he said, drawing his dignity back around himself. "And thank you kindly for your understanding and assistance."

"What's your wife's name?" John asked, and Bob Beales smiled, pleased, thankful, at ease again.

"Josie," he said. "Her name is Josie. Do you have a woman in your life?"

John ran a hand over his face. "I do," he said. And then stopped, because for a single instant he had forgotten the name of the woman he was about to marry.

Miss Anabel turned out to be one of the more difficult people Angie had ever tried to interview. Far from the placid, chair-bound old lady she had imagined, Anabel Spate moved around her tiny house like a whirlwind, dispensing information and questions of her own at an alarming speed.

"My students," she said, pointing to a row of photographs that lined the staircase. "You'll find Miss Zula Bragg in the very first one, there. The bright-eyed young woman who looks to be cooking up some kind of trouble." And she was gone again, in the direction of the kitchen. Angie and Tony went to look at the photographs.

A group of seven high-school-aged girls, Miss Zula standing in the back row next to Miss Maddie, both of them wearing simple dresses with starched collars. Printed at the bottom of the photo were the words: *Our Lady of Divine Mercy, Ogilvie, Ga., Freshman Class, June 1945.*

Tony's eyes moved over the photograph. He said, "I thought schools down here were segregated until the sixties, at least."

"They were indeed," said Miss Zula, who was standing in the doorway. "But Divine Mercy is a Catholic school, and back then the principal was a man of some backbone. And it was wartime, things were a little looser."

Miss Zula came up to stand on Angie's other side. "There's Miss Junie, and her twin sister, Alma. Alma married Harmond Ogilvie the June we graduated and died of a burst appendix not a month later. His mama told him it was God's judgment. A boy whose family worshipped at Episcopal Christ Church and sat down to Sunday dinner with the governor should never have thought to marry a Catholic."

"How did old Harmond take that piece of wisdom?" Tony asked.

"Bubba—that's the name he went by in those days—married Button Preston a year later, and made his mama proud."

"This is Harmond Ogilvie, the chair of the board of regents?"

"And Button Preston, who is president of the Junior League, like her mama before her."

"Ogilvie is a small town," Angie said.

"And don't you ever forget it," said Miss Zula.

Tony was moving along the row of photos. He stopped suddenly in front of a group portrait. There were nuns in full habit, their faces framed by white wimples, two priests, and a half dozen laypeople, most of them male.

"The younger priest looks familiar," said Angie, studying the photo.

"I'm not surprised," said Miss Zula. "That's Miss Junie's uncle, Father Liam."

"Come on over here and eat, would you?" said Miss Anabel. "This humidity is playing havoc with my meringue."

There were many questions Angie wanted to ask Miss Anabel, few of which she got a chance to put to the fierce old lady, who immediately took charge of the conversation. "Zula," she said, "tell me again why Caroline didn't come along. And where is this Rivera Rosenblum I've heard so much about?"

"Junie needed a ride to her house at the lake," said Miss Zula. "And of course Caroline took her."

"Rivera was detained," Angie said. "She'll be sorry to have missed this visit." It was the truth, so she could meet Miss Anabel's watery blue gaze with complete ease.

"Now, that's too bad," said Miss Anabel. "Maybe she'll come sometime on her own. And what about Louie?"

Miss Zula put down her teacup. "I didn't bring Louie because he makes you sneeze."

Tony grinned at Angie as he spooned strawberry jam on his plate. He had a sweet tooth, and no objection to putting off work if the older women were set on a long visit.

Miss Anabel said, "He's the best dog you've ever had."

"You say that about every dog of mine," said Miss Zula. "But he still makes you sneeze."

"So does sunlight," said Miss Anabel, scowling. "And I don't let that keep me from stepping out of doors. Miss Mangiamele, why aren't you married, a pretty young woman like you?"

Angie inhaled a mouthful of iced tea. While Tony was thumping her on the back, she saw that Miss Anabel was watching her almost as closely as Miss Zula.

"Pardon me?" she croaked.

"I believe you heard my question. I asked why you aren't married. Unless you consider the question impertinent?" Miss Anabel held out a plate of cookies to Tony.

"Yes. No." Angie pressed her napkin to her mouth for a moment. "Why does anybody stay single? It's just the way things are."

"But you must be close to thirty?"

"I'm twenty-eight. Women marry late these days, if they marry at all. I believe Caroline Rose must be at least thirty-five."

A light came into Miss Anabel's eyes, one that Angie recognized. She had grown up with old Italian women who enjoyed a good argument.

"So you haven't met the right person?" Miss Anabel said.

"Define 'right.'"

Miss Anabel let out a cawing laugh. "What about you, Mr. Russo?"

"I've got one, too. A backbone."

"You've got to be fifty, and you still haven't married."

"True on both counts." Tony leaned back in his chair and crossed his arms.

"Well," said Miss Anabel, "Miss Mangiamele there is a bright young woman. She's quite pretty though she doesn't dress well, and she's single."

Tony had always been a good poker player, unflappable. He raised an eyebrow in her direction.

"Angie, hey. Want to get married?"

"No," Angie said, swallowing a hysterical laugh. "Well, not to you."

"That's settled," Tony said placidly.

"So you don't rule out the idea of marriage."

"No, Miss Anabel," said Angie. "I don't rule it out."

To Tony Miss Anabel said, "Miss Mangiamele isn't the only available young woman of your acquaintance. Surely."

"I know a lot of women," Tony said. "Of all ages and marital states. But I was inoculated against marriage long ago. At my father's knee."

Without missing a beat Miss Anabel said, "Is that why you prefer to spend your time with married women?"

Tony narrowed his eyes at her. "I guess that must be it."

"Well, then," said Miss Anabel brightly. "Since I've asked my questions, you can go ahead and get out your camera and ask yours. Now that we understand one another."

Tony and Angie took a taxi back to the train station without Miss Zula, whose habit it was to spend the night in Savannah and do some shopping on Saturday morning before she took the train home to Ogilvie by herself. She neither needed nor wanted company.

"It's like an outdoor shower," Tony said, peering out into the rain. Great sheets of it, warm as new milk. "And here I was planning on hanging around for a while, see what Savannah has to offer." His cell phone rang.

"Don't let a little water stop you," Angie said as he fumbled his phone out of his pocket. "I can get back to Ogilvie on my own."

Then he held up the phone for her to see the caller ID and flipped it open.

"Rivera, baby, sweetheart, darling, you owe me one. What's up?"

Angie reached for the phone but he pushed her hand away.

"Oh, yeah, good shoot. Excellent. Wild old lady, you would have liked her—"

"You mope, let me talk to her," Angie said, and he shook his head at her.

"—except now we'll have to figure out whether we want to out Miss Zula for national distribution. . . . You did not."

To Angie he said, "She says she already knew that Miss Zula was a lesbian."

"She doesn't know any such thing," Angie said, and took the phone from him. To Rivera she said, "You don't know any such thing, and neither do we. And we aren't going to deal with this, not unless Miss Zula specifically asks us to."

Rivera's voice was harsh with static, but she was amused. "She takes a documentary film crew to meet Miss Anabel, what do you think she was doing?"

"No," Angie said, "we will not move on this, not yet. Probably not ever."

"Coward," said Tony.

"Wimp," said Rivera.

"I'm being cautious," Angie said. "Somebody has to be."

"Caution," snorted Tony dismissively. He scowled at the rain. "I'm going to throw it to the wind and go explore Savannah." He leaned over and kissed Angie on the cheek, and then yelled into the cell phone, "Bye, Riv," and snapped the lid shut, to Angie's considerable annoyance.

They were stopped at a red light and he put his hand on the door handle, watching her face.

"Be back by Monday," she said. "We have to get ready for Tuesday's shoot."

"Tuesday?"

"The Fourth of July," Angie said. "Independence Day, the Jubilee. Fireworks, parade, picnic. Pay attention, winkie. We're here to make a documentary, remember?"

He saluted as the cab moved away.

John made the five-thirty train to Ogilvie, which was only fair of fate, given the reason he was taking the train at all. He propelled himself up the steps and into the last car just as the train started to move, to find that it was almost full, of course; it was the middle of the rush hour.

"John!" called a familiar voice. Harriet Darling was waving at him from the far end of the car, an armful of charm bracelets jangling. Across from her Pearl craned her head around and smiled, waving him on. He hesitated, not knowing what to pray for. He wasn't much in the mood for an hour in the company of Caroline's sisters, but if all four of them were on this train, he'd have to go find someplace else to sit. In another car. In another state.

He made his way down the aisle saying hello now and then to people he knew, most of them looking as ragged and wet and worn-out as he felt. Then he saw that only one of the four seats in the group was free. The third was occupied by Angeline Mangiamele, her lap full of camera bags.

"Well, my goodness," said Pearl, getting up to scoot over into the empty seat. She was wearing a patchwork jacket, elaborately beaded and embellished, that jingled as she moved. "Don't you look a mess. I thought you took your car to the airport?"

"Nice to see you, too," John said, trying not to look at Angie. "My car is on its way to the dealership," he said. "Hooked to the back of a tow truck. And no comments about foreign cars. Please."

"Well, that's a shame," said Harriet, but her smile said she was delighted with this turn of events. "You just settle down there, John, and rest yourself. Pearl and I have been shopping, for your wedding, no less."

"Angie," said John. "How are you? Did these two drag you along shopping?"

Pearl said, "She's got more sense than that. Angie there was interviewing Miss Anabel. Imagine." To Angie she said: "I'll bet those two old ladies talked your ear off, didn't they, now? Harriet, do you suppose we'll get like that in our old age, telling the same story over and over?"

"She didn't repeat herself to me," said Angie. John could see that she was irritated, that she had liked Miss Anabel and liked Miss Zula and was impatient with Pearl and Harriet, which was surely understandable; each of them was nice enough on their own, but together they were too much even for Caroline. But Angie was holding back, whether out of courtesy or for his sake, he couldn't tell.

Harriet was telling Pearl that most certainly they'd live to be as old as Miss Zula and Miss Anabel—hadn't the woman who read the tarot cards for them last time they were in New Orleans told them so?

"Didn't that woman have a gift?" Pearl said.

"I swear," Harriet said, "it was almost like listening to the voice of God talking to me directly." She placed her hand on her breast.

"I wish God would talk to me directly," said Pearl. "I've got some questions I'd like to ask him."

If it weren't for the fact that Angie was sitting across from him, John thought he might have been able to drift off to sleep, so familiar was the cadence of the conversation, Harriet's voice and Pearl's moving back and forth, the lilt to the ends of their sentences that turned everything into a question, the way they drew in a sharp breath that meant an emphatic yes. But Angie was right there, and she was listening to them, taking notes in her head, the way she did when her curiosity was aroused.

"God only ever talked to me directly once," Harriet said, sounding wistful.

"He did?" Angie sat up straight. Her expression was interested, intrigued, totally serious, as she would be with anyone she was interviewing. John had seen her like this before, with Miss Zula most recently but also back in Manhattan, that lost summer, when he had gone with her while she worked on a short film for a homeless shelter that needed promotional material for fund-raising. She talked to drunks and addicts and street vendors, to mounted policemen and sidewalk artists, and every one of them opened up to her, just as Harriet was opening up now, wiggling a little in her seat in anticipation of telling her story. John found that he was vaguely interested himself.

"He surely did," Harriet said. She put her hand on Angie's arm. "This was back when I was expecting Joey, my youngest boy? I wasn't no more than three months pregnant at the time, and I was sitting in the parlor reading the new *Cosmo* when a voice came right down from the heavens to me. And God said—I remember exactly—he said, 'He will die in the seventh month.'" She paused, her eyes large and round, waiting for Angie to laugh, maybe, or to tell her that such a thing was impossible. It was what people usually did when Harriet told one of her stories, but Angie only nodded.

"Go on," she said.

"Well," said Harriet, "at first I was so upset, can you imagine? I thought he meant the *baby*. But then Joey was born that May without much fuss at all—"

"You had such easy labors," Pearl said with a sniff.

"—and I got to thinking, and it occurred to me that maybe God was talking about Tab? My husband? So I waited right through to the end of July, but Tab never did die. Now every year when July comes around I get my hopes all up, but come first of August, there's Tab sitting across from me at the breakfast table pouring skim milk on his Wheaties." She paused. "I still don't know what the good Lord was trying to tell me."

John closed his eyes in the hope that it would keep him from laughing out loud, but curiosity got the better of him, and he opened one of them to see a thoughtful look on Angie's face.

She said, "Harriet, if you dislike Tab so much, why don't you divorce him?"

"Why, I'm surprised at you," Pearl said, drawing back a little. "You know Roman Catholics don't get divorced. Once the knot is tied, it's tied good and tight." She shot John a look that was impossible to misinterpret: it said, *Marry my sister and you marry all of us.* What it didn't say, what she didn't think to say even with Angie Mangiamele sitting right there, was *Behave yourself.* Because they knew him, reliable and trustworthy and predictable John Grant.

The Rose girls were as sure of him as they were of all the men they had married: Tab Darling and Pete McCarthy and George Shaw and Len Holmes. The Rose boys, as they were called sometimes when none of them was within hearing, not so much out of respect but because George was still built like the quarterback he had been in college, and Pete was a serious weight lifter.

"And anyway," said Harriet. "Money's tight, what with Tab Junior at college and all." She let out a soft sigh, and then she smiled. "But tomorrow is the first of July, and I am ever hopeful."

TEN ·

The way Angie ended giving John a ride home was simple: neither his brother nor Caroline Rose answered when he called, and Pearl's husband, Pete McCarthy, who had come to pick up the Rose girls with two of his sons in the car, had no more room. And so Angie and John walked through the parking lot toward the Tied to the Tracks van, Angie weighed down with camera equipment and John with his suitcase and briefcase. They said next to nothing, but the early-evening air—cool and clean after the storm—was electric enough to make the hair on the back of her neck stand up.

It wasn't until she had started the van and pulled out of the parking lot that she realized that he wasn't embarrassed but angry, which was a rarity; in her experience, John was able to turn off anger as he would a spigot. It was one of the things that she had liked least about him, his ability to shut down in the face of an argument. Except this time she wasn't sure, exactly, what or who had made him mad.

Two blocks of silence were enough, and so she said it. "They asked me to sit with them, you know. It wasn't my idea."

She saw him startle out of his thoughts, and then struggle to gain his composure.

"What?"

"If you're worried about me sitting with Caroline's sisters, it wasn't my idea."

"Why would I care?" he said.

"You shouldn't," Angie said, biting back the rest of what she might have said. She turned onto Lee Street and stopped the van in front of his house, and then turned to him.

She said, "On a purely professional matter, I need to talk to you about Miss Zula and the documentary."

John opened the door of the van with a snap and got out, dragging his suitcase behind him.

"Did you hear me?" Angie said.

"I heard you." He was looking at her with such open hostility that she felt her pulse jump in her throat. But she was Fran Mangiamele's daughter, and she had never backed down from a surly man in her life, so she leaned toward the open door.

"Wake up, John," she said. "This is business. I need to talk to you about Miss Zula."

He blinked at her. "Come into the house if you want to talk." Then he closed the door with a bang, and walked off.

She sat there for five minutes, debating with herself, watching him move through the house. A window opened, and then another. She imagined him turning on the ceiling fans, looking through the pile of mail, listening to the telephone messages. There would be one from Rob, explaining where he and Kai had gone for the weekend, up to Hilton Head or to one of the lakes. There would be another message from Caroline. She imagined him standing there listening to Caroline talk, her voice a little rough and still lilting, all Georgia. She would be telling him about her drive up to Lake Louise with her mother, how the storm had slowed them down, that she would be back later tonight or tomorrow, that she had missed him and was sorry not to be there to welcome him home.

Angie put the van in drive, and headed for Ivy House.

. . .

The phone was ringing when she came in by way of the back porch. The first sign that Rivera was in a difficult mood was the fact that the air was thick with cooking smells: peppers, onions, cilantro, wild oregano, garlic, cumin. Even more alarming: Rivera lay stretched out on the old couch, the ringing phone balanced on her stomach.

"Staring at it won't make it stop," Angie said.

"I didn't know there were any of these old phones left," Rivera said. "The ones you can't unplug."

At that moment the phone went silent.

Rivera said, "Reverend Win called."

"Reverend Win?"

"Reverend Win Walker," Rivera assured her. "Patty-Cake's nephew, you remember. Called to invite you to the Jubilee."

"Actually I was trying to forget. He called himself Reverend Win?"

"No. But I like the sound of it."

Angie said, "There were two of them she earmarked for us, weren't there? One was a cop and the other one was a preacher of some kind."

"This one sounded like a preacher."

Angie gave up. "Okay. So what did you tell him?"

"That we'd be working all day."

"Bless you." Angie sat down on the floor.

"That's what he said. Just after he offered to carry around your camera equipment all the livelong day."

"He did not."

"A persistent guy, is Reverend Win."

Angie pushed out a great sigh. "Okay, well. I'll deal with that when I have to."

"So talk to me," Rivera said, stretching so that the phone wobbled. "How'd it go today?"

Angie picked up the glass of wine sitting on the floor next to the couch and drained it in two long gulps.

"That well, huh." Rivera yawned. "So what's the big deal? Miss Zula has a lifelong companion. With all the gossip that goes on in the publishing world, I can't believe it's much of a secret."

"You think it wouldn't be big news down at Mount Olive or the ladies' auxiliary?" Angie said.

Rivera inclined her head. "Okay, yeah. I see your point."

"Do you think the board of regents would have wanted a documentary about her life, if they had known?"

"Okay," Rivera said pointedly. "I got it."

Angie said, "I tried to talk to John about it." And then, when Rivera shot her a look, she added: "He was on the train back from Savannah."

"Why would you want to talk to John Grant about this?" Rivera said, truly mystified. "I'd have a hard time thinking of a man worse at reading women."

There was little to argue about there, though Angie found herself irritated, whether at Rivera's casually damning assessment of John Grant's failings or at John himself, she wasn't quite sure.

Rivera said, "Miss Zula took you to call on her, didn't she? Without any prompting, obviously because she wanted you there. The only thing to do is to talk to her about it directly. My guess is that we play the whole thing down, and people will draw their own conclusions. But she'll have an opinion."

"Oh, sure," Angie said. "I'm looking forward to that conversation."

The phone began to ring again.

"Why not just turn the machine on?" Angie asked, pouring more wine into Rivera's glass.

"Because," Rivera said, "when I got home there were thirty-three hang-ups on it."

"That many. Okay, but maybe they weren't for you. It could have been DeeDee."

Rivera turned her head to look at Angie. "You mean Tony actually went home with DeeDee last night?"

Angie sat down on the chair across from the couch and took a swallow of wine. "I don't know about the 'home' part. He's hiding out in Savannah, which should tell you something. I wouldn't be surprised if we don't see him until Monday morning."

The phone stopped ringing and started again immediately. Rivera put back her head and howled at the ceiling.

"So what is it with Meg?" Angie said.

"She's a weeper," Rivera said. "A high-maintenance weeper. I need at least a day to recover before I deal with her."

"Okay," said Angie, gritting her teeth against the ringing of the telephone. "But it might not be Meg. Maybe it's Miss Maddie. Maybe it's Caroline. Maybe it's DeeDee, in which case you can have the pleasure of ratting out Tony. That will put you in a better mood."

For a moment she thought Rivera had gone to sleep, which was actually possible; she had known Rivera to nap while a jackhammer took apart the pavement directly below her window.

"Fuck it." Rivera picked up the phone and barked a hello. Angie hoped, in that moment, that it wasn't Weepy Meg.

Rivera's scowl cleared. She listened, her eyebrows drawn together in a sharp V.

"Okay," she said, and hung up. "John is on his way over."

Angie inhaled a mouthful of wine. When she had stopped coughing she wiped the tears from her eyes. "What?"

"You heard. He said, 'Tell Angie I'm on my way over.' I said, 'Okay.'" Rivera got up from the couch and shook her head so that her hair flew around her face in a short curtain of inky black satin with a beveled edge.

"Why," Angie said slowly, "would you do such a thing?"

Rivera rounded her eyes and blinked provocatively. "Because, chicklet, it's what's best."

The phone began to ring again. Angie leaned over and picked it up, her eyes fixed on Rivera.

"Hello."

"Angie?"

"Caroline." She tilted the phone for Rivera, who came over to listen.

"I just got back from the lake a little bit ago. I made pasta primavera and I've got way too much. Would y'all like to come share it with me?"

Angie was thinking about how best to inoculate herself against the trouble ahead, whether she should say, *John is on his way over here and I'll send him on to you for supper*, or *Did you know John was back, I saw him on the train talking to your sisters*, or *Why don't you bring that pasta over here?* Any of those statements might have put a stop to the gathering storm, but before she could open her mouth, Rivera took the phone out of her hand.

"Caroline. I haven't eaten. I'll be there in ten." Then she hung up, and in a single, graceful motion she turned and hugged Angie.

"You did too eat. You've been cooking all day."

"When have I ever turned down a free meal?" Rivera picked up the car keys from the table. "Besides, I'll be in the way here. Talk to John. Get it done, get it over with, once and for all. One way or the other."

Angie drew back, alarmed. "What in the hell does *that* mean?"

"Don't play dumb, Angie."

The screen door slammed behind Rivera, and Angie went to see if there was any more wine.

The rain had started to come down hard again when John Grant parked Kai's Mini in front of Ivy House. It was a warm rain and the air was sweet with it, and he had no idea, suddenly, why he had come here or what he wanted to accomplish. A half hour ago it had seemed the logical thing to do: he would apologize for being rude, settle whatever question Angie had about Miss Zula, and then calmly, rationally, he would make it clear to her that the past was past, and he was content to leave it that way. Surely once he opened his mouth the right words would materialize.

Then Angie was standing in the open door under the eaves, her arms wrapped around herself. She leaned against the door frame, her shape outlined by the light behind her.

John drew in a deep breath, unfolded himself from a car that seemed, from the inside at least, no bigger than a bread box, and sprinted across the street and the lawn, up the walkway, the paving stones slick underfoot. He stopped on the lowest porch step and forced himself to move forward slowly, deliberately.

She was looking at him with an expression he could hardly read: severe, unblinking, but curious, too. Certainly not angry or unhappy. At that moment it struck him, quite unexpectedly, that Angie was rarely unhappy; she could be angry better than anybody he knew, but nobody could accuse her of being morose, or even moody.

She said, "Come in out of the rain, John."

He went up the steps and onto the porch, where he stood dripping onto the floor. The house smelled of coffee and a meal cooked not long ago, meat and beans and spices. His stomach rumbled loudly enough for them both to hear it.

"Sorry."

Her arms were still crossed. She turned and went into the well-lit kitchen, pausing on the door swell. "Rivera's been cooking. *Chuletas*, and *arroz con habichuelas*." Then she plucked a folded towel from a laundry basket and tossed it to him.

Tony might be in Savannah, but Rivera was here, which meant they weren't alone in the house, and that was a good thing. A very good thing. Any moment Rivera might come down the stairs and sit down across from him. They would argue about movies or books or Ogilvie, and that would help him focus. Because he had come here to talk about business, after all. John fixed his mind on that idea and then he sat down to eat.

The table was cluttered with books and piles of paper and folders, some of them spilling photographs or newspaper clippings. Angie's mess, because Angie worked best like this, scattering everything around her and then standing back to see what patterns jumped out. It had irritated him and intrigued him too; sometimes, watching her work, John had the odd idea that he had been born without some particular kind of seeing that Angie— that many people—took for granted.

She moved Rivera's dirty bowl out of the way and put a clean one in front of him. For a few minutes they said nothing more to each other than strangers sitting at a restaurant counter: *please* and *would you like* and *thanks*. Then John was overwhelmed for a while by Rivera's cuisine of choice, which demanded his absolute attention. He drank the beer Angie put in front of him and accepted another thankfully.

Out of the corner of a tearing eye John watched Angie, who was playing with her food, drawing on her place with the tip of her knife. She looked less tired than she had that Saturday morning she had come to the house for breakfast, almost exactly a week ago.

First son of the local gentry sets up an ideal life for himself and discovers perfection is overrated. Or maybe you haven't got to that last part yet?

A week in the New York City archives up to his eyebrows in the most demanding, arcane, interesting material he could find, and still John had never been able to get rid of Angie's voice and the things she said to him over his own breakfast table. Now, when they were alone, she seemed content with small talk, because she said, "Where are Rob and Kai this weekend?"

"They found a house. It's empty and they talked the real estate agent into letting them camp out there tonight."

"So they'll be moving."

He nodded. "Pretty quick, looks like."

"Just in time."

She was looking at him. He raised his head slowly and met her gaze. "Caroline asked you to videotape the wedding."

"Harriet did. She said you had been dead-set against the idea but finally gave in. I expect that was the fallout from my indiscreet morning visit."

That was pretty close to the truth, though John neither wanted to admit it or to fill her in on the details. There was no better way to convince the Rose girls that he had no interest in Angie than to invite her to his wedding, and at the same time to give in on the video question. It had been a tactical decision on his part and it had worked well enough to put a crimp in Patty-Cake's plans to launch a major Angie-based offensive. The look of satisfaction on Patty-Cake's face was a relief and an irritation at the same time, even a week later.

Angie said, "Caroline and I don't talk about you, if you're worried we sit around comparing notes."

He studied the bowl of his spoon and the hard crescent of reflected light in its rim. There was nothing he could say that would make this situation right, no explanation, no rationalization that would fix things, and maybe it was good that he had come here tonight, if only because he might not have faced that fact if he hadn't. On the other hand, he was having trouble reading Angie's expression—nothing new there, he had made a career, it seemed, out of misreading her—and he was suddenly too weary to try. He said, "I thought you wanted to talk about Miss Zula."

Angie's eyes fluttered closed, and then opened. "I did. I do. But not now. It's been a really long day."

John felt a shiver of irritation slide up his spine. "We keep dancing around the things we need to talk about. Why is that?"

She leaned back and folded her arms, narrowed her eyes at him. "Okay," she said, "if you insist, I'll lay it out. You're getting married in a week. To Caroline Rose, who is a far better match for you than I ever was or could be. I wish you both every happiness, and a perfect life."

Now when she looked at him, full on, unapologetic, wanting something—but what?—there was a tic at the corner of her mouth. It took everything in John not to reach out and still it with his finger.

He said, "Maybe perfection is overrated after all."

She stood up so suddenly that the chair tipped over and crashed to the floor, and there she was, in a temper. He was asking himself what he meant by pushing her so far, what he meant to accomplish, what he really wanted, when the doorbell rang in a long shrill.

Angie threw up her hands. She said, "Of course." And: "Maybe you should just go."

"I'm not doing anything wrong," John said. *Not yet,* he thought. "I see no need to hide as though I were."

"Hello?" A man's voice bellowed from the front of the house, loud enough to rouse the neighborhood. "Hello? I know you're in there, Russo. Got-dammit. Come on out here and face me like a man."

"Christ," John said. "That's Tab. Maybe we should both take off."

"Tab Darling? Harriet's Tab?" Angie's eyes were bright with curiosity or maybe it was simply relief that the conversation neither of them wanted had come to such an abrupt end. John might feel the same way, if it weren't Tab Darling pounding on the door. The glass was rattling in the windowpanes with the force of it.

"That's him," he said. "He's been drinking. Let me handle him, okay?"

Angie's was curious about Harriet's infamous husband (*it would be best if he would just* die) and ready for just about anything. She waited for John to open the door.

Tab stood there with one arm resting on the door frame, the other fist raised to pound. He was a good-looking guy, or had been before his muscles had gone to beer, of which he reeked. On top of that, he was dripping wet but didn't seem to realize it.

"Tab," John said, "what is it?"

Tab blinked at him in the bleary, irritable way of the very drunk. "Is Harriet here? I know she is, she must be. Where's my wife?"

"She isn't here," Angie said.

Tab pushed past John and came to a stop in front of Angie. The fumes that came off him were enough to make her light-headed. He scowled at her.

"I suppose that wop you work with ain't here, either."

"You suppose right," Angie said.

Tab's whole face screwed up in frustration. "Girl, don't you know better than to come between a dog and a fire hydrant?"

Angie said, "Which one are you?" and John winced.

Tab was too drunk to follow the question, but not drunk enough to give up. He said, "The whole got-damned town is being overrun by got-damned wops."

His head wobbled a little as he leaned in close enough for Angie to count the oddly boyish freckles on his nose.

"Patty-Cake's got a hair up her ass with your name on it." He burped softly. "Says you're trying to take John here away from Caroline. Is that true?"

"No," Angie said. "I've got no hold on him." She made sure not to look in John's direction.

Tab sniffed loudly. "The hell you say. But there he stands, big as life and dumb as a sack full of hammers. What have you two been up to?"

"Work," John said. "Now, what can we do for you?"

He reared back to look at Angie down the slope of his nose. "I'm here to kill that got-damned pop-eyed skinny-assed woppish sumbitch that's been sniffing after my wife."

"That's something you'll have to take up with Tony directly," Angie said calmly. "But he's in Savannah just now. You could make an appointment to kill him next week, if you want. I can give him a message."

She had a moment to wonder if she had misjudged Tab Darling's degree of drunkenness, but his expression went from ornery to confused, and from there to sorrowful. "Savannah?" he said. "With Harriet?"

"Not to my knowledge," Angie said, and managed to look him directly in the eye. "Harriet came back on the train from Savannah. I know, I was sitting across from her."

"That's what Pearl said, too, but I thought she was just covering for her sister." Tab looked directly stunned at this news. "But then where is she?"

"If I knew," Angie said, "I would tell you."

John put a hand on Tab's shoulder. "Let's get you home. She's probably there waiting."

Tab gave John a hard look. "You're so got-damned superior. You Grants, better than everybody else. But not for long. You're almost one of us. One of the Rose boys." His grin was not pleasant. "One of the Rose girls' boys." Behind a cupped hand he stage-whispered in Angie's direction. "Poor bastard. Don't know what's coming at him."

Tab patted his head as if to settle a nonexistent hat, then walked out the door and fumbled his way down the steps. There was a huge old convertible at the curb and he lurched toward it with keys held out from his body in a perfectly straight arm, like a kid determined to pin the tail on the donkey.

Angie said, "You can't let him drive."

John closed his eyes and then opened them again. "Of course not." He raised his voice. "Hey, Tab, can I get a lift?"

From the bottom of the stairs he looked up at Angie. "Somebody will come by for Kai's car tomorrow." He tossed her the keys and then he bolted down the walkway toward Tab, who had already fallen into the driver's seat, sideways.

Five minutes later John waved to her as he steered the convertible away from the curb, though she was hidden behind the curtains in the parlor. He waved to her, though he couldn't see her at all, or know if she was even there.

Flat on her back on the old striped couch on the porch, Angie focused on the moth that was bumping its way around the lampshade. Her head felt too heavy, and her stomach too full, and that was the price to pay for chasing wine with beer.

"Ogilvie is not good for my health." She said it out loud to nobody at all. Tony was in Savannah, most probably in a bar scanning the women for a Harriet Darling look-alike, or maybe Harriet had snuck back there somehow and they were holed up in a motel. Rivera was at Old Roses with Caroline, and no doubt John would end up there after he dropped off Tab. Which was the way it should be.

Then Rivera would come back here and sit on the floor with her back against the couch and listen to what Angie had to say, no matter how absolutely ridiculous it might be. Because as many times as Angie turned things around in her head, the sentences that presented themselves were going to be hard to spit out.

I almost kissed John Grant was no better than *I wanted to kiss John Grant,* but certainly not as bad as *I still want to kiss John Grant* or, God forbid, *All I can think about is kissing John Grant.* All those things were true, and here was another one she would have to get out in the open if she was ever to sleep another hour: *John Grant wants to kiss me as much as I wanted to kiss him, but he's too dumb to figure that out. Dumb as a sack full of hammers.*

And the real kicker: *He's getting married in a week.*

The wonderful thing about Rivera was that nothing was ever complicated. An overdue gas bill, war in the Middle East, an affair gone sour, she could resolve any problem in three sentences or less. She would say, *Figure out what you want, calculate the costs, make your plans.* And: *Start by getting get your pitiful self off the couch.*

But Rivera wasn't back yet to shame Angie into saving her own life. Instead there was a moth bumping against the lampshade and rain on the roof and a smell of wet grass. It had been a very long day; Angie fell asleep.

John meant, once he had dropped Tab off, to drive over to Caroline's and instead found himself parked in front of his own house in Tab's convertible, which smelled of cigars and hot sauce and boys' sweaty gym clothes. It was surprisingly comfortable, and he might have gone to sleep just where he was, glad of the quiet and the dark and the rain.

He made himself reach for his cell phone. It felt warm in his hand as he listened to the ringing on the other end. He was thinking of hanging up when Caroline answered, a little out of breath.

"I was wondering about you," she said.

He said, "Caller ID takes all the excitement out of answering the phone. Leaves nothing to the imagination." And neither did the Rose girls, it seemed; Caroline had already heard from Pearl and knew all about his car trouble and the trip home from Savannah on the train. Her tone was light and friendly and solicitous as always, with an edge of something slightly frazzled. Of course, the story he had to tell about Tab Darling roving through Ogilvie fueled by beer fumes was the kind of news to make anybody nervous.

"I've got some pasta left," Caroline was saying. "And some beer, if you want to come over."

"Beer." John couldn't remember the last time Caroline had drunk a beer in his presence, much less brought any home to Old Roses.

"Rivera brought it. She came over to keep me company."

"Rivera?" He sounded like a parrot, and was powerless to stop himself.

"She brought some DVDs, too, of a sci-fi cult classic called *Farscape*. Strong women kicking butt and the men who love them."

"Much like Ogilvie," John said, and she laughed at that, a distinctly non-Caroline laugh. The idea of Rivera at Old Roses teaching Caroline how to appreciate beer and high-end sci-fi must mean something, but the one thought that presented itself to John was the fact that Angie had not exactly lied, but had certainly misled him. The whole time he sat in the kitchen with her he had assumed that Rivera was somewhere close by, and she had let him.

"Unless you wanted to come over?" Caroline finished, and John woke up enough to realize she had been waiting for him approve of her plans. No doubt Rivera was listening to that half of the conversation and shaking her head in disapproval, and with some reason.

Just that suddenly the question that had been nagging at him for a long time came into focus: Where did the intelligent, self-aware, confident Caroline, the one who chaired international meetings and wrote sharp critical reviews, disappear to when she left her office for home? Which of these two Carolines was he about to marry? And, most important—to him at this moment anyway: Why had he been avoiding this question for so long?

Right then the one thing John knew for sure was that he couldn't cope with Caroline and Rivera, not just now. Not this evening.

"I'm beat," John said. "I'm going to get some sleep."

There was a pause. Embarrassment? Relief? He couldn't tell. Then she said, "You do sound tired. Sleep is what you need."

They could agree on that much, at least, and so John left Tab Darling's convertible where it stood and went to climb into bed, alone, where he found, to his considerable irritation, that the thing he needed most was simply beyond him.

· ELEVEN ·

By rights I might have been Miss Maddie's brother-in-law, because my eldest brother Moses intended to marry her. He told Daddy so just before he
went off to Korea, but he didn't come back. Ever since the two sisters have
kept house together. If you can get Miss Maddie to invite you to Sunday
dinner, I'd be pleased to come along too. I'll bet I can get her to tell some
stories she keeps for special, and I've got a few of my own to share. Some of
them are even true.

Your name: Alfred White. I took early retirement from the railroad on account
of my bad knees, so most days you'll find me on the Liar's Bench outside the
barbershop.

At three o'clock on Saturday afternoon, just when Angie was
starting to believe that she might actually survive her hangover, the doorbell rang. Rivera, who had fallen asleep on the couch with a
book on her lap, didn't even flinch at the sound. Angie might have ignored
it, too, but then an image came to mind of a still-drunk Tab Darling come
back to find Tony, this time with a shotgun.

She unfolded her legs with some difficulty and made it to the door, where
she found Rob and Kai Grant. Until that moment she had forgotten completely about Kai's car, but the keys were still on the windowsill where she
had put them.

"Come for your Mini?"

"We have an invitation for you," said Kai, lifting herself up on her toes in
her excitement. "We are having an opened house. Will you come?"

"We just bought a house," Rob interjected, grinning.

"Time for a celebration," Kai agreed.

Angie said, "Now?" And: "Oh, I don't—"

"Come on," said Rob. "It'll be fun." He took the keys that Angie offered, tossed them in the air, and caught them again.

The two of them reminded Angie of kids on their way to a prom, which was both a little unfair and oddly right. More than that, she had the idea that they would come across in exactly the same way when they had been married fifty years.

"Right now?"

"No time like the present," said Rob. "We're paying rent until we can close, so the place is ours. You got something better to do on a Saturday night than come to a party with old friends?"

Angie heard Rivera's feet hit the floor.

"Party?"

"Oh, come along, too," Kai called. "Please come to our opened house, it will be good fun."

"I never say no to a party," said Rivera.

"But I—" Angie started, and felt Rivera's hand on her shoulder.

"—and neither will Angie. Can we ride with you?"

Rob took off in one direction in the Mini and the three women got into his old Volvo, Rivera in the front and Angie spread out on the backseat.

"We'll stop at the liquor store," Kai announced, then she hit the gas and they were off, roaring down the street. Angie didn't know if it was the idea of more alcohol or the way Kai was driving, but she was just about to lose the little bit she had eaten when they pulled, screeching, into the parking lot of the liquor store, which was called Dewey's Package for reasons Angie hadn't been able to pinpoint.

Kai was kind enough to park in the shade, and the breeze was cool. The smart thing to do, Angie decided, was to spend a few minutes lying right where she was. She propped her head on a book called *Complex Algebraic Surfaces*, put an arm over her eyes, and tried to remember how to breathe while she contemplated the evils of alcohol.

"Pardon me, miss?" The voice was deepest Georgia, baritone and hesitant. She moved her arm and opened one eye, squinting into the bright.

From this angle the guy looked to be seven feet tall and built like a refrigerator. Blond hair, green eyes, deeply tanned; Angie decided he could have been the model for every prince Disney had ever drawn, right down to his smile, which made him look like a sweet if somewhat dim ten-year-old. And he was a cop, by his uniform.

Either he was after Kai for her driving, or Angie was violating some local law, sleeping in the backseat of a car. In any case she could hardly work up any real worry, because the cop was smiling at her in a way cops in New Jersey never smiled unless you were related to them.

"Yes?" She couldn't quite make herself sit up, but she did manage what she hoped would be taken for a smile.

"Are you Angeline Mangiamele?"

She sat up after all while he kept talking. "I thought you must be, I've heard you described so often. I'm Winfield Walker? Win to my friends. I called and left a message with your coworker—"

"Rivera," Angie finished for him. She reminded herself not to stare at the man they had been calling Reverend Win behind his back.

"I just wanted to introduce myself," he said. He stuck his hand through the open window, and Angie shook it. Firm, warm, but not sweaty, big. And Patty-Cake's nephew.

"I think I had you confused with somebody else. I thought you were a preacher."

He ducked his head. "You're thinking of my cousin Walker. I might go for a deacon one day, but I don't think I'll ever be as hard-shell as he is."

Angie thought, *Is that good or bad?* and *What a waste*, which made her a little ashamed of herself, which didn't sit well on an already uneasy stomach.

"Wait," she said. "Let me—" She reached for the door just as he opened it. She managed to get out without falling on her face.

"You're looking a little green around the gills," said Win Walker. "Can I get you some water?"

He had other things to offer, too: aspirin, his grandfather Winfield's recipe for hangover, and a ride home.

"You should be in a dark room," he said. "An air-conditioned, very dark room."

"For a Baptist you know a lot about hangovers," Angie said.

He ducked his head again, which may have been calculated to make him seem boyish and sincere, in which case it was a complete success. "I sowed my oats, and just about every other grain known to mankind, while I was at it." Then he studied his shoes before he looked at her again. The beginnings of a blush were creeping over perfect cheekbones.

"Look," he said, "you must know my aunt Patty-Cake has been after me to call on you."

"Yes," Angie said. "That's been brought to my attention."

"I'm sure you're a good person and all—"

"I'm agnostic," Angie said. "And you're not."

He had a great smile and perfect teeth. "I'm not one to be scared off so easy," he said. "But truth be told, I'd just as soon not get wound up in whatever Patty-Cake is scheming."

"Me either," Angie said. "But I'm finding her hard to avoid. She's been sending my mail back as undeliverable."

"Well, damn." He looked off into the distance, his jaw muscles working. "Leave it to Aunt Patty to mess with the mail." He lowered his voice to a conspiratorial whisper. "We could call in the feds. Or would a stern talking-to satisfy you?"

"Please, no," Angie said. "I'll handle the mail thing on my own. You just tell your aunt that we gave it a try and didn't suit, and that will be the end of it." And: "It's not very nice of you to look so relieved. You could at least pretend to be disappointed."

"Oh, it's too early to be disappointed," said Win Walker. "I'm still planning on asking you out. Just so you understand it's got nothing to do with Patty-Cake."

His attention shifted, and Angie turned to see that Kai and Rivera were walking toward them pushing a cart filled to overflowing with cartons and bottles.

Kai called, "Win! I am so glad to see you. Will you come to our opened house?"

It was a very nice house, simple in design, only a few years old, and blessedly air-conditioned, which suited Angie very well on this first day of July. For the moment it was furnished with a scattering of upended crates and a dozen mismatched lawn chairs, one of which Angie claimed and dragged to a corner, out of the stream of people pouring through the door. Her headache had begun to recede but would be back howling if she pushed things.

"Hair of the dog," Rivera said, stopping by to press a plastic cup into her hand. Angie put it down where nobody would knock it over and thought of getting up to get water.

Rivera was weaving through the crowd, talking to everybody. Parties were Rivera's natural habitat, and this one looked promising. People came in bearing platters of chicken and cold cuts, bowls of salad, filled coolers, watermelons, Jell-O molds. Father Bruce showed up, peeking around a huge twenty-pack of toilet paper topped with a red bow. Everyone was talking to everyone, and loudly. Kai and Rob, both of them glowing with excitement and pleasure, moved back and forth from door to kitchen to stairs, eager to open closet doors and describe plans for the garden, the kitchen, the third bedroom they would turn into a study. All of this meant that Angie would be able to slip away within the hour, and maybe even before John showed up. She was gearing up for a long walk across town when Win Walker found her and hunkered down beside her creaky lawn chair.

""You've got to be dehydrated," he said.

"True," Angie said. "But I'm not courageous enough to go looking for the kitchen."

"No need." He handed her a cup of ice water. "Anything else I can do for you? Introduce you around?"

"That would take all night. Is there anybody not here?"

Win glanced around the room. "Kai and Rob are well liked. I think everybody in Ogilvie came to their wedding." He looked at her. "Why do you look surprised?"

She shrugged. "I'm not surprised. Just trying to figure things out. The whole South is a little strange to me, still. Probably would always feel that way if I stayed here the rest of my life."

It was an innocent enough thing to say, but Angie felt herself blushing. Maybe because Win Walker was looking at her so intently.

"You know when I said before I didn't want to get caught up in my aunt Patty-Cake's scheming?"

She nodded.

He rubbed a thumb along his jaw. "That wasn't the whole truth. I'm a little uncomfortable about people coming down here from way up north. I don't see how you can make a film about Ogilvie, not with your background."

At least he was honest, which Angie found refreshing. She was sure other people must be thinking the same thing, but mostly they kept their worries hidden behind a heavy curtain of good manners and hospitality.

"You might like it here, if you gave us a chance."

She looked at him in surprise. "I didn't say that I *don't* like it here. I like a lot of things about Ogilvie."

"Such as?"

Angie rested her head on her hand and thought. "I like the way you all sit on your front porches and talk in the evening. I like the Liars' Bench outside the barbershop, and I really like the men who sit there, the stories they tell. On Sunday mornings I like to watch tiny little old women with hats full of flowers—like parade floats, some of them—parallel parking huge old Cadillacs and Eldorados in front of the Assembly of God church. Like no-holds-barred bumper cars on the city street. I like spoon bread and grits and sweet tea. I like fried okra, but not boiled. I like pretty much everybody I've met. But I'll admit to you that I don't like everything."

He inclined his head, and Angie took a deep breath.

"I don't get this compulsion to put Coca-Cola into everything. Coca-Cola salad, what is that all about?"

"I can see you're not interested in a real discussion," said Win Walker, "but I hope you'll be fair, anyway, and not try to sell us to the world as another southern town full of crackers and rednecks."

He was a little angry, which made Angie tired and sorry she had ever got into the conversation. She also disliked being painted into a corner about a piece of work that was so early in its evolution. But it wouldn't do any good—and it might do considerable harm—to leave Win Walker with the wrong ideas just because she was hungover and wasn't feeling especially sociable.

She said, "We're not out to do a hatchet job, if that's what you're worried about, but we're not here to make a tourist commercial, either. That's not what documentary film is about."

For a long time they watched people walking by, though Angie could almost hear Win Walker thinking. Her irritation got the better of her, finally, and she turned to him.

"Look," she said. "I've been told that men down here don't take well to criticism, but maybe you're jumping the gun here a little, have you thought of that? A documentary is one way of telling a story, that's all. We'll work hard to get a clear picture and then we'll tell it the way we see it. Good and bad. Bad and good."

There was a flicker of interest in his eyes. "So you'll trot out the usual suspects, I guess. Racism, sexism, xenophobia, homophobia. You'll find all those things here, no denying it. But you've got them where you come from, too. Maybe people here are just more honest about their prejudices. Which makes it easier to chip away at them."

Angie said, "So how many gay people does your cousin Walker have in his congregation?" And then wished she hadn't.

He met her gaze straight on. "I don't know. He's not in the habit of discussing his parishioners' private lives."

"How honorable. And convenient."

There was a burst of laughter on the other side of the room, the kind that meant someone was telling jokes, and telling them well. Angie caught sight of Father Bruce, who had one arm around Rivera's shoulder. She was laughing so hard that tears ran down her cheeks.

The last time Angie had seen Father Bruce was at Miss Junie's birthday party. Behind his lopsided glasses his eyes were huge, sparkling, full of laughter. She wondered just then if Father Bruce, who had grown up in this town, knew about Miss Zula and Miss Anabel. If he had any idea about Rivera, and if he would care.

"Maybe we should start again," Win Walker said.

Angie suddenly regretted pushing him. She was about to tell him so when the door opened and Caroline Rose came in. She was carrying a pie plate, and John was just behind her. Rob was right there to greet them, kissing Caroline's cheek and then thumping John on the back, and then Father Bruce had come up to sniff at the pie. His put back his head and howled with glee.

From the other end of the room an ancient stereo system hissed and then began playing "Let's Give Them Something to Talk About."

"Y'all make room for dancing now," somebody shouted. "Get out the way, Marcy has got her dancing shoes on."

Angie said, "I think what I need is some fresh air. Want to go for a walk?"

Of all the odd things that had happened in the last day, John Grant thought, the oddest had to be the fact that it was Caroline who had insisted that they come to this party while he made excuses to stay home. He had given in, but standing just inside the front door of his brother's new house, his strongest, almost irresistible urge was to back out and head for home.

Caroline handed the sweet-potato pie over to Kai and took his hand. "Let's dance."

"Let's dance?" John let himself be pulled into the middle of the room. "What is up with you?"

It was a question he had posed at least three times in the last few hours, and each time she had laughed it off, or found a way to change the subject. Now her cheeks were flushed with color and there was a strangely stubborn set to her jaw. Caroline wanted to dance, and for once she was asserting herself. Which was a good thing, of course.

Except something else was going on, and he had the idea it had to do with Angie. Maybe Tab had told Caroline about finding him at Angie's place, which was something he could explain easily enough. Nothing had happened, after all. As soon as the right words presented themselves, he would tell to Caroline all about it.

I went over to Angie's to settle things once and for all, he could say. I went over there to tell her—to convince myself—that what's past is past. Those were exactly the words I was going to use, but somehow they never made it out of my mouth. I went over there with the best of intentions—

And that would be a lie, all of it would be a lie, so he had spent the whole afternoon with Caroline running errands, and hour by hour, it seemed more impossible to raise the subject. Instead they had made final decisions about floral arrangements and boutonnieres, gifts for the bridesmaids, and the menu for the wedding luncheon.

Thomasina Chance was catering the luncheon, and so John found himself at the back of the restaurant at a table crowded with covered plates while Thomasina, her chef, and Caroline debated mahimahi with citrus vinaigrette versus roast pork tenderloin with a port wine demi-glace and St. Agur cheese. For an hour John tasted what was put in front of him: persimmon and pomegranate salad, apple wood-smoked duck breast, fennel and Stilton soup. Thomasina was a transplant from New Orleans, about fifty, well padded, with a big smile and large laugh, but she was dead serious about food. When somebody thought to ask John his opinion he gave it, but mostly he was happy to leave the decisions to Caroline. He would have felt guilty about this, if she didn't seem to enjoy the whole process so much.

After they left Thomasina's, the heat and long afternoon caught up with Caroline in short order. She had said next to nothing to John in the car, and now she was hardly even looking at him, though she had insisted on dancing.

He said, "You know, you could just tell me what you're mad about. We could just talk about that, get it out of the way."

She tensed in his arms, but didn't lift her chin from his shoulder. "Look," she said. "Will Sloan is here. I wonder why he's not at the game."

It took a minute for John to remember the weekly baseball game at the park, which explained why none of the other Rose girls were anywhere to be seen.

"We can go over there," John said. "It's not five minutes from here."

Caroline said, "I think I'm entitled to skip a game once in a while. It's not like my brothers-in-law will miss me." And before John could think what to say to this unusual bit of rebellion, she said, "Look, Father Bruce is here too, he's not at the game, either."

Father Bruce was in the middle of the dance floor, with Rivera Rosenblum. Both of them were looking this way. The tip of his nose was cherry red, and as he danced, the Dixie cup in his hand sloshed.

"You two!" called Father Bruce. "Ask not for whom the wedding bell tolls!" With that, he put back his head and laughed uproariously.

John gave him a halfhearted salute and danced Caroline in the opposite direction. When they were in a less crowded corner of the room, he pulled back and made her look at him.

"Is it about me not coming over last night? Because—"

"No," Caroline said, shaking her head. "No, it's not that. Really it's not. It's nothing you did—"

"I was over at Angie's yesterday, just for a little while. I thought maybe Tab said something."

"—I've just got wedding jitters."

She was meeting his eye, but also trembling a little, and color flooded her throat. It made her look very young and innocent, and John felt himself flushing, too, with regret and guilt and weariness.

He didn't want to be here, half watching the door for Angie, who must surely be around if Rivera was here. He wanted to be someplace quiet, someplace safe. He thought of Old Roses, deserted just now with Miss Junie away. He thought of a puddle of light by an armchair surrounded by books, the kitchen table as big as a bed. He thought of being there with Caroline, away from the noise and the curious expressions, away from Rivera Rosenblum and the idea of Angie Mangiamele, away from the questions that were piling up into a tower that threatened to collapse around his ears.

He could sit in the kitchen at Old Roses with Caroline and they would talk, about the work he had done this week, about the article she was writing on the diaries of a medieval French nun, her mother's health, whether or not his mother would actually show up at the wedding, and if she would bring her newest husband, and how that might play out. Eventually they would end up in Caroline's room, on the pristine white bed. She would welcome him home in her quiet way, appreciative, amenable, softly murmuring.

He said, "Let's get out of here, why don't we. We haven't had any time alone together since before I went to New York. We could pick up some dinner on the way and spend a quiet evening at Old Roses. What do you say?"

Caroline's gaze flitted away, across the room, and then back to him. "Right now?"

"Why not?" John said, pulling her closer. "It would do us both some good." He put his mouth closer to the pink shell of her ear. "I've missed you." And it was true: he had missed her, this cool, intelligent, quiet woman who had been his friend first, before it had occurred to him that she was lonely, and he was lonely, and that there was no reason for them to be apart. That they would make a good couple, people of like minds and interests.

"But Kai and Rob," she said, a catch in her voice. "They'd be hurt."

"Kai and Rob have snuck off often enough to understand," John said. But the impulse to get away, to be alone with Caroline, was fading quickly, and irritation was taking its place.

She said, "We should stay for at least an hour, John. Let's go see the kitchen and get something to drink, why don't we."

He stopped Caroline with a hand on her wrist and the question that came out of his mouth surprised him. "Wait. Caroline, are you having second thoughts?"

Her expression was utterly calm. "Second thoughts?"

"Second thoughts about getting married."

The corner of Caroline's mouth quirked. She said, "Of course I am. Everybody has second thoughts at this point. I'm sure you do, too."

And she pulled away and started toward the kitchen.

The garden at the back of Kai and Rob's new house was fenced, and beyond the fence was a park. Angie was drawn to the sound of a ball game in progress, the crisp crack of bat on ball and the shouts that followed. Win Walker opened the gate with a flourish, and they started to walk in that direction.

"Are you one of those New Yorkers who live and die by the fate of the Yankees?" His tone was easy in the way of someone who was versed in making conversation with just about anyone. It was something Angie was good at, too, but in Win Walker she found it irritating for too many reasons to think about.

"I'm from New Jersey," Angie said.

"New Jersey, New York," said Win Walker.

Angie stopped and gave him a severe look. "Georgia, Alabama."

He held up his palms. "Point taken. So you don't like the Yankees?"

"I'm not much interested in the major league teams." She stopped short. "Is this just small talk, or are you interested in baseball?"

To that he had nothing to say, which was okay; Angie wasn't in the mood for the kind of conversation that went along with getting to know a new person. In fact, she admitted to herself, she wasn't in the mood for any conversation at all, and she wished Win Walker would take his flawless self and go back to the party. Then she could sit in peace and watch what looked to be a real game played by guys in their thirties and forties, men who had never quite given up on the idea that one day a Braves scout might show up to give them a chance at glory. When it was over she would walk home, by herself, in the twilight. If she was really lucky, she would cross paths with an ice cream truck. A sudden rush of homesickness made her draw in a breath.

They were halfway across the park when Win Walker asked her if she was mad.

"Listen, just because a woman isn't talking doesn't mean she's mad."

He nodded thoughtfully. "Was it John Grant showing up that made you want to take a walk, so sudden?"

She stiffened, but kept her voice light. "And would that be any of your business, if it were true?"

He shrugged. "Maybe not."

"Absolutely not," Angie said, and climbed up into the bleachers with Win following her. A man jogged by with a six-pack under each arm and called out. "Win! We've got 'em by the short hairs, boy."

The rest of the crowd was clustered on the far side of the bleachers. Angie saw that most of the Rose clan was here, probably because all the brothers-in-law were out on the field. Harriet was fussing with a picnic basket, batting her youngest son's hands away and laughing. Angie hoped none of them would look in this direction. All she wanted just now was to watch the game, which was fast moving and well played.

She was just starting to feel better when Win leaned close so that their upper arms touched and said, "Why don't you tell me about what's bothering you?"

She snorted out a laugh. "I thought confession was a Catholic thing."

"I'm a cop, remember?"

She looked pointedly at his uniform. "When I break a law, I'll be sure to look you up. Pay attention to the game, Tab Darling is about to steal second."

Win was studying her instead. He said, "Have you met Tab?"

Angie spared him a glance. His expression was interested but not judgmental, though she had an idea the question wasn't an idle one. She said, "He's been over to Ivy House. I know most of these guys." She shielded her eyes with the flat of her hand. "All except ZZ Top there playing shortstop."

"That's Wyeth Horton," said Win. "He teaches English at the public high school. Rumor has it he has never shaved in his life. So what do you think of Tab?"

Angie turned to face him. "I think Tab drinks too much when he's unhappy, and I think he's unhappy most of the time. Is the exam almost over now?"

Win leaned back to prop his elbows on the bleacher behind them. "You might actually want to talk to Tab sometime. He played Triple-A ball for a year, but his father wanted him to take over his practice, and that's all she wrote. Off he went to college and dental school."

That was a surprise, though Angie tried not to show it. "Good to know, for the next time I need bridgework."

Win shot her a sidelong glance. "Admit it, you had Tab down as a car salesman or an insurance agent or somebody who runs a still. Maybe," he said softly, "you don't know us as well as you think you do."

"Maybe I don't," Angie said. "But I'm starting to. Tell me, was it Patty-Cake who sent you on yet another mission to save Harriet from the invading Italian barbarians, or is there a Save Tab Darling Club you're president of? And wait, answer this one first. What makes you think I have any influence at all over Tony Russo, or that if I did, I would use it to interfere in his private life?"

There was a small silence. "Tab's a good guy at heart."

Angie threw up her hands. "Tab Darling is a good guy at heart. I wish him well, but there's nothing I can do—and I'd guess there's nothing you can do either—about whatever problems he's got with his wife. Why are you talking to me about this? Why not go down there and talk to Harriet?"

"Harriet talks to her priest," said Win Walker.

And everybody else, Angie might have added, but she held her tongue. For a while they were distracted by a shouting match on the field, umpire and pitcher nose to nose. Angie almost wished one of them would snap and throw a punch; it would have made her feel better.

"Is this general small-town nosiness, or family feeling, or you in your professional capacity?" Angie flared up, though she meant not to.

He shrugged. "A little bit of all three. I apologize." But he didn't look happy, or even very apologetic.

"And since we're on the subject," Angie said in a rush, "let me say this once and for all. Whatever is going on with Harriet, she's got a right to be happy, too, and if that means she has to leave Tab and find her own way, then that's what she should do. In my opinion. Which I will keep to myself, unless she asks me directly. And I'll say this, too. It's none of your business, either, not even if you were Tab's brother—"

She broke off. Win Walker was looking at her with an expression that was part grudging admiration and part embarrassment. Angie drew in an unsteady breath.

"Tab is your brother?"

"My half brother."

"Okay," Angie said, calmly. She counted to five and then, for good measure, to ten. "Tell me this. Is everybody in this town related to everybody else?"

"Pretty much."

Angie nodded. "Yes, okay. So Tab's your half brother. But I still stand by everything I said."

"Good," said Win Walker. "Because you're right, and I was wrong. I should never have brought up the subject."

"Okay," Angie said slowly. "Good."

"But I've got one more question," he said. "Just one more, and it's got nothing to do with Harriet or Tab."

Angie put her forehead down on her knees. "Let me guess, you want to know if I'm trying to break up John and Caroline."

"No," said Win Walker. "But I would like to know why you and John broke up."

Without raising her head she said, "Is this Patty-Cake's question, or yours?"

He shrugged, and against her better judgment Angie took note of the way his shoulders filled out his uniform. "I guess I deserve that. It's me asking."

Angie forced herself to breathe slowly and deeply. "I'll answer that if you'll tell me why you aren't married. You're what, thirty-five?"

"Forty-two."

She leaned back to look at him harder. "You're well preserved, and not hard to look at, either."

He grinned. "Thanks."

"And you've got a good job. So why aren't you married?"

"I was married," said Win Walker calmly. "I was married twice, as a matter of fact. The first time I was eighteen and way too young. The second time I was thirty-four. She died in a car accident just short of our fourth anniversary. I'm hoping the third time will be the charm."

Angie wasn't often at a loss for words, but this matter-of-fact recitation left her grasping for the right thing to say. "Okay, so I admit it: I had you pegged wrong."

"Thank you. Now it's your turn."

She took a moment to look out over the park while she thought of one sentence and then another, and finally decided, this once, to tell the simplest truth. To say it out loud.

"We broke up because John didn't love me. It's that simple."

After a long moment Win Walker said, "I never took John for an idiot."

"Thanks," Angie said, and meant it. "But he's not at fault. Things just . . . burned too bright and too fast, I guess you'd have to say." And: "Shit. Harriet wants me to come down there."

Harriet Darling was waving her arms over her head like a swimmer in trouble. "Angie! What are you doing way up there? Come on down and sit with us, girl."

"Be right there," Angie called back. She managed a stiff smile. Under her breath she said, "Have a nice life, Win Walker, and give my best to your aunt Patty-Cake."

For a short while, Angie had the idea that her evening—that her whole day—might just be saved by the miracle of baseball. The Rose clan, it turned out, were real baseball people, and she fit right in among them, or did, once the Rose grandsons in attendance—she was disappointed to see that Markus wasn't among them—had satisfied themselves that she knew enough statistical trivia and game history to be included in their number.

There were some great plays and colorful arguments and shouting matches at the mound, there was enough food to feed the entire crowd. The Rose sisters thrust plates at her, and Angie found that her appetite had come back, after all.

"Stick around," said Connie. "We'll feed you till you burst. It's a family failing, we just like food too much."

Pearl handed her a small open bag of Fritos.

"I don't think—" Angie began, but Pearl cut her off. "This is a southern specialty," she said. "You've got to try it. Never had Frito pie before?"

"Um, no," Angie said.

"Hold that bag open wide as you can."

Pearl pulled a ladle out of a casserole dish and dumped a serving of chili directly into the Frito bag. Then she held out small containers of chopped onions and grated cheese and shook them in Angie's face until she took a handful of each and dropped them on top of the chili.

"Is this a Georgia specialty?" Angie asked as she took the spoon Pearl held out to her.

"Hell no," said Connie, snorting a laugh. "That's Pete's favorite. He's an east Texas boy, born and raised."

It turned out that three of the four married Rose girls had not married local men: Pete McCarthy was from Texas, Len Holmes from South Carolina, George Shaw from Atlanta. Only Tab was from Ogilvie.

"Lots of folks come here for college and then stay, or come back to stay," said Connie. "Our husbands are prime examples."

Angie ate and complimented and talked about the game and the pigheaded umpire and the weather and the plans for the Fourth of July Jubilee. The game wound up and then down and out, and Angie was just realizing that she was feeling good, really good, for the first time in days, when she looked up to see Tony walking toward them from the direction of Kai and Rob's place just beyond the trees.

For a moment she just sat there among the Roses, who were still eating while they talked about the game and how the sun really was in Len's eyes or he would never have missed such an easy pop-up, and thank goodness Tab was right there to pull it out of the fire. The game was over, the day stood on its cusp, and the air was sweet and cooler than it had been in a week, suffused with the gold light of a high summer gloaming.

And Tony Russo was walking toward them, long and lean, scruffy with beard, dark circles under his eyes, a cigarette clamped in the corner of his mouth, and a halo of smoke hovering around his head.

Pearl saw him next, and after her Connie and then Eunice and finally Harriet. The men were standing with their backs to the field and were too wound up in their argument about the last play to notice much at all. Angie was just thinking that maybe she could avert disaster by sprinting off and turning Tony back the way he had come when Connie's youngest shot straight up into the air. At that moment Angie remembered him on the porch at Old Roses, his mouth pursed as he pulled back an arrow that sent

John Grant to the emergency room. He was called Scooter, and he had a voice like a siren.

"Look, Mama," he screeched. "It's the cameraman."

Tab Darling's smile faded as he turned his head, his whole body following. He hesitated for a split second, and then broke into a jog.

"Russo!" he bellowed.

Tony stopped where he was, looking confused and wary and like a third-grader who has just seen the school bully start toward him on the playground.

Harriet shouted, "Tab, you idiot!" and ran off after her husband at the same moment Tony bolted. For a fraction of a second the rest of the clan looked at one another in horror—and, Angie was sure of it, a deep and primal satisfaction—and then they tore off in pursuit.

For her own part, Angie sat right where she was. Out of shock and dismay and a certain sense of fate. Tony went through life dragging mayhem behind him; it was a fact, and now that the worst had happened—was happening—a calm came over her. She sat there with a half-eaten Frito pie in one hand and a spoon suspended in the other and watched two dozen men, women, and children streaming over the field. There was a dog, too, a goofy beagle mix with floppy ears, though Angie had no idea where he had come from. *Somebody tell the director to lose the dog,* she thought, *it's just too much.* And then she hiccupped a laugh.

Tony was cutting a wide circle that would—she saw this now—bring him right back to the bleachers, a bold move indeed if he thought she was any kind of protection when it came to Tab Darling. Then she realized that Win Walker was standing just behind her with a half dozen other men.

"Aren't you going to do anything?" she asked.

"It'll take care of itself," said Win. "It's just Tab working off a little frustration."

"Tab won't hurt him none," offered someone Angie recognized as a teller at the bank.

"Or not so much as you'd notice," somebody else said.

Tony came to a shuddering stop right in front of them. He was heaving hard for breath, but his eyes gleamed with his own familiar brand of crazy excitement.

She began, "Don't—"

But he wasn't even looking at her anymore. Tab caught up and plowed directly into Tony as if he were first base and the call was bound to be a close one. They went down into the dirt, whirling arms and legs putting up a cloud of dust.

Harriet shouted, "Tab, you idiot! This isn't about him, it's about you!" And then she threw herself onto her husband's back.

"Oh, Lordie," called out the third baseman. "Everybody into the pool."

Angie whirled on Win Walker. "What were you saying about nobody getting hurt?"

He shot her an irritated look and ran down the bleachers to wade into the fray, which was expanding—it seemed to Angie—exponentially. Tony, she saw with huge relief, was crawling away, and nobody seemed to notice.

"I guess old Tab is madder than we thought," said Wyeth Horton, the English teacher with the two-foot-long beard. "But you got to admit, the Roses sure do know how to throw a party."

City Hospital was a squat, homely building directly across from the park.

"Other ball teams go for a beer," Angie told Wyeth Horton. "But you all form a parade and walk over to the emergency room."

"Ogilvie," said Wyeth, stroking the beard that flowed over his chest, "is a place at odds with itself. The true native takes great pride in the old traditions, but at the same time he dislikes to be perceived as predictable. The Rose clan are quintessential Ogilvites, and I have no doubt that sooner or later one of them—my bet would be Tab Darling—will be overcome by that conflict and combust spontaneously."

Angie couldn't help herself, she burst into laughter. Wyeth nodded in acknowledgment but didn't smile. He said, "I've been waiting for you to come see me. I moved here from New Orleans to study at the university and stayed on to teach school these last twenty years. I do believe you might find my observations useful to your work. Shall we say—"

"Don't you let Wyeth lure you into his lion's den," said Eunice, appearing from around a corner. "He talks real pretty but really what he's doing is scheming on how to separate you from your panties."

"Eunice," Wyeth said smoothly, "you credit me with far too much ambition. I wouldn't aim so high as panties, at least not to start with."

The emergency room was very small and very clean, every seat occupied by the crowd from the park: the Roses but other people, too—players and their families, and one or two people who had just tagged along out of curiosity. The atmosphere was not exactly jovial, but nor was it tense.

"Any word yet?" Angie craned her head to see what the nurse at the reception desk was doing.

"Oh, the usual," said Pearl. "I swear we can't get through a summer without a half dozen emergency-room visits. Last year the staff had a pool going on how many times one of us would show up. I think the grand total was sixteen. I spend so much time in this place they should put me on the payroll."

"You all look healthy enough," Angie volunteered.

Pearl flapped a hand. "We are, healthy as pigs. But prone to accidents, and flights of temper." She sent Angie a sidelong glance, drew in a breath, and held it for a moment. "I wanted to apologize to you. We really are reasonable folks. It's just—" She paused. "We're all worried about Tab, but that's no excuse for his behavior or the way things got out of hand. I hope Tony in't the kind to hold a grudge."

Just then Eunice came down the hall from the examination rooms. She called out, "Tab sprained his ankle plowing into Tony, Drew has got a busted nose, and my Guy needed three stitches on his scalp. I hate to think what commotion y'all would get up to if you didn't like each other."

"Tab almost through back there?" Harriet was leaning against the wall with one arm wrapped around each of her two younger boys.

Eunice produced a forced smile. "I think Dr. Landry will be out to talk to you pretty quick. Angie?" She scanned the crowd and then smiled. "Len is just about done with Tony. He said to tell you to come on back."

Tony looked so pleased to see her that Angie was a little guilty about the scolding she had given him on the way over from the park. There was a bandage on his forehead now, but otherwise she couldn't see any real damage.

He said, "Angie. Tell this guy to let me go home. It's hardly even a concussion."

The exam room was smelled of disinfectant and rubbing alcohol and sweat. That was mostly from the doctor himself, as Len Holmes hadn't taken the time to do much beyond wash his hands and face and pull a white coat right over his baseball clothes. On the other side of the exam table was a nurse wearing scrubs the color of canned peaches and hair dyed to match, and beside her was Win Walker.

Angie stayed with her back pressed against the door.

"Tony, I'm not taking you home until the doctor says so, so forget it."

"Angie—" Win began, and she whirled around to face him.

"What? What do you want?"

"Win is here in his official capacity," said Len Holmes. The nurse was looking back and forth between Win and Angie with an eager expression.

Win nodded. "I'm just waiting to take Mr. Russo's statement. He may decide to press charges."

"Tony will not press charges," Angie said firmly. "Isn't that right, Tony? You're not going to press charges over a little misunderstanding."

Tony was scowling at the nurse, who had snatched the package of cigarettes out of his hand as soon as he fished it out of his pocket. He turned his scowl in Angie's direction.

"I won't press charges," he said.

"You're sure?" Win asked. "You've got every right—"

"No charges," Tony said. "I just want to go home."

Len Holmes said, "I'm going to hold you for a couple hours to be sure you're stable. Or as stable as you ever get."

"You see?" Tony said to Angie. "You see? They've all got the wrong idea about me."

"Of course they do," Angie said. "And later you can clear it all up. Once your head is on straight again."

When Angie made her way back to the waiting room she found it was almost empty. Harriet sat alone in the row of chairs nearest the desk.

"I sent them all home," she said. "Time to feed the boys anyway, and they were driving me crazy."

"You don't mind sitting here alone?"

"I called Caroline to come sit with me, but she wasn't answering, so I left some messages. I'm sure she'll show up. See, here's John's car now."

"Great," Angie said, not even trying to smile.

Harriet cocked her head and sent Angie a sidelong glance. "I can't figure you out, Angie."

"No surprise there," Angie said. "I'm not much good at that myself." The door swung open and she forced her expression back to neutral as John Grant came in and walked directly across the room toward them.

"John, darlin'," said Harriet, holding out her right hand. "Come and set with us. Where's Caroline?"

"I'm not sure, exactly. We were at a party over on Slow Down Lane—"

"Oh, did Rob and Kai buy the Reynoldses' place? Isn't that the sweetest little house? They'll be happy there, wait and see."

"They seem pleased with it." John had not yet met Angie's eye, which was beginning to irritate her. "Caroline had just gone off to the store with Kai and Rivera when I got your message. I'm sure she'll be here shortly."

Then he did look at Angie, though the expression he showed her was baffling. Regret, and distress, and a kind of unhappy resolve. He had looked like this the afternoon he introduced her to his grandfather Grant.

"I'm sure she will," Harriet echoed, but her tone had gone very flat. A doctor was coming toward them, a woman in her forties, small and neat and solemn.

"Dr. Landry," said Harriet, a smile faltering on her face, "you look like your dog just died. Is Tab back there giving you a hard time?"

They were all standing now, the three of them in a quarter circle around the doctor, whose attention was focused on Harriet. She said, "Tab's ankle is what brought him in, but I'm afraid it's more than that just now. He had a minor cardiac event while I was examining him, Harriet. He's not in danger of his life—"

"A heart attack?" Harriet said, flatly. "You're saying Tab's had a heart attack?"

"A minor heart attack," said the doctor. "Doesn't look like there's any serious damage to the heart muscle, but we have to run some tests—"

Harriet pressed her fist against her mouth and shook her head, held up a hand to stop the flow of words.

"Now listen, Harriet," said the doctor, "we've got a cardiologist coming in to have a look at him. Right now he's asking for you. I'll take you back to him."

Harriet had gone very still and pale, though her eyes were abnormally bright. She nodded and then turned to John.

"Don't call anybody, just yet. I couldn't cope with the boys just now and I want to tell them first, in my own way. Whatever there is to know, they should hear it first, and from me."

"Anything you need," John said. "Anything at all."

She produced a very wide, very forced smile. "It's a minor cardiac event, you heard the doctor. No need to get your knickers in a twist, John."

Harriet walked away with the doctor, but she stopped suddenly and turned back.

"It turns out I don't want him to die, after all. But I can't live with him, either. I told him so yesterday, which is why all this happened. Angie, you be sure to let Tony know. This is all my fault, it's got nothing to do with him."

"I'll tell him," Angie said.

Harriet nodded, and walked away down the corridor.

John asked, "Tony's okay?"

Angie nodded. "Really, it wasn't anything. Just some halfhearted punches thrown and a lot of people rolling around on the ground. Tony hit his head when he tried to crawl under the bleachers."

She sensed that John might have laughed at this image, if it weren't for what was going on in the examination room at the end of the corridor. Thinking of Tony sneaking off from the Rose mob on all fours did make Angie laugh; she couldn't help it, except the sound came out as something else, halfway between a hiccup and a sob. John reached out for her hand and then stopped.

"Things could be worse," Angie said quietly.

"Things are about as bad as they can get."

Angie's blood was thrumming loudly in her ears. She felt light-headed and weighed down all at once; she had the idea that her feet wouldn't obey her if she tried to walk away. If she tried to run away. So they sat side by side for a long time in the empty emergency room, in a silence that seemed to have a physical presence, words buzzing around their heads.

Angie leaned forward and folded her arms across her knees. She studied her feet, the fraying lace on one scuffed white sneaker, the smudge of clay on the other. John had stretched out his legs and so she studied his feet, too, sun-browned and long and strong and sinuous in immaculate Mephisto sandals.

She had been in Ogilvie for weeks, and in that time he had only touched her once, when she had collided with Patty-Cake Walker in his front hall.

His hand settled on her back, the touch light, the heat of his skin coming through the fabric of her shirt in a jolt that ran along her spine. Her throat swelled until it was almost painful, but when she turned her head she saw that he wasn't looking at her. John had put his head against the wall. She watched him swallow, the muscles convulsing along the arch of his neck, his Adam's apple riding the wave. His hand rested on her back, warm and firm and still.

A slow, bright anger started up someplace deep in her belly, and along with it the dull throb of desire. Angie thought of getting up and moving; she thought of putting her head on his chest and closing her eyes.

John's hand traveled up her back to the nape of her neck, slowly, tentatively, and then settled there. She could feel the curve of skin between thumb and first finger along her hairline, and then his fingers threaded into the curls, damp with sweat.

"John."

"Shhh. I've got something to say."

The fingers kept working, pulling gently, tugging. Angie closed her eyes and tried to close her mind to what he was doing.

"I'm sorry," he said. His tone was even and steady and considered, and with some part of her mind Angie wondered if he had practiced this speech.

"It was my fault, that summer. I pushed, and I didn't see what that was doing to you."

Angie steadied her breathing, counted to ten, counted again. The exact thing she had wanted to hear from him for these five years, word for word, and now it was said. She was gratified and relieved and unhappy, because it wasn't enough. She opened her mouth to say—what? And found he wasn't finished.

"I've been thinking about all this a lot these last couple days. There are a few things I know for sure. The first is, I don't want to be like them."

She said, "Like who?"

"I don't want to end up like Harriet and Tab. The second thing I know for sure is, I'm already halfway there unless I do something about it. And lastly, I know that I have a ways to go before I figure out why I did what I did. I've screwed things up."

Angie made a noise in her throat, though she herself couldn't be sure what it meant: *Stop, I can't bear it*, or *Go on, get it over with*. John came forward, leaned over so that their shoulders touched and their heads were side by side, like kids whispering secrets in the back of the classroom. His hand was still on the nape of her neck and his fingers moved in her hair.

"I ran into Win Walker out in the parking lot," he said.

In her surprise Angie turned her head, and found he was so close that her hair brushed his face. He smelled of the sun on skin, of perspiration and wine, of soap, and of whatever it was that made John himself. It brought a flood of memories with it, associations that came to her in half images and bright colors and tastes and ripples that skittered over her skin like ants, made her want to jump up and run away.

"What about Win Walker?" Her voice was small and creaky and unwilling, but she forced the words out.

"Did you tell Win Walker we broke up that summer because I didn't love you?"

"Damn it," Angie said, pulling away sharply. "Can't a person have a private conversation in this town?"

"Sometimes," John said calmly. "This conversation, for example, is completely private."

Angie spun around and saw that the nurse had left the desk, that all the chairs in the waiting room were empty, and outside the windows the lights had gone on in the parking lot, and that was empty, too.

She inhaled noisily. With her eyes closed she said, "This is a dangerous game you're playing."

"Angie," he said, his voice a little harder now. "I'll ask you again. Did you tell Win Walker—"

She cut him off with a short sound and then forced herself to look him in the eye. "I said that, yes."

He went very still. "I understand the need to explain things away, but, Angie, that's too much. There were things we couldn't get past—"

"Like what?"

He sat back. "You couldn't get comfortable, I couldn't figure out how to fix that. Maybe you didn't want me to. But you can't say that I didn't love you."

Those words in John Grant's voice, at a low whisper. Her whole body shook with it and her mouth was so dry, so very dry, that when she tried to speak, her voice whispered and cracked. But she swallowed and swallowed again until she could make herself understood.

"Not enough," she said. "Or you wouldn't have let me walk away."

He had turned his face toward the wall. She could see him struggling, with disappointment, with anger, with resolution; she had no idea what he was thinking. Then he swung back toward her and Angie saw that under his tan he was pale.

"Okay," he said. "I don't think it's so simple, but I'll let it go."

"You'll let it go?"

"I'll concede the point, for now."

"And?" she said, suddenly very tired and unsettled.

"And, I've got some things to straighten out before we can take this conversation any further. Before I can make you any promises."

Angie got up so fast that the chair rocked in place. She felt herself first flushing and then all the color draining out of her face, and all along her arms nerves were jumping. "What makes you think I want promises from you, you arrogant prick?"

He stood, too, caught her wrist and pressed his fingers to her wrist. Then he gave her a grim smile.

She pulled away from him. "Oh, please."

"You want me."

"Maybe I do," Angie said, anger pushing up and out. "But that's nothing an hour in bed wouldn't satisfy."

"No," he said, his expression utterly calm. "That wouldn't be enough, and you know it. This isn't about sex."

"So what is it about?" Angie said. "Just so we're clear, you tell me exactly what this is about."

His expression went still, and she recognized something in the way he tilted his head: John struggling for footing in a conversation that was spinning out of control, looking for logic in turmoil, for reason in the chaos of what he was feeling. Now he would take a deep breath and collect himself, and then he would apologize to her for this outburst, this completely unreasonable and uncharacteristic outburst, and he would walk away to find Caroline.

He opened his eyes and looked at her, but the embarrassment she was expecting to see wasn't there. He looked resolute and calm, a man who has made a decision.

John said, "I'm afraid, too, Angie. I'm scared out of my head. But I'm not going to let this get away from me, not again. Because this is our last chance, and I won't screw it up again."

The anger in her belly flowed away from her, as hot as blood, and was gone, just that simply. A muscle in her cheek was fluttering. She blinked at him and then she nodded, because she could not have spoken at that moment, not a word.

He managed a small smile. "Good. So I have some things to take care of, and then you and I will talk this through."

"Caroline."

He flinched. "I have to talk to Caroline. Yes."

Angie made fists of her hands and locked them by her sides, to keep herself from touching him. "John, listen to me. I can't promise you anything, not on the basis of this conversation. Remember that before you . . . before you do things that can't be undone."

"Too late," he said, and caught her face between his hands to kiss her.

She pulled back, a hand over her mouth.

"What?" he said. "What?"

"I've got chili breath."

He said, "I like chili."

She struggled a little at first, unsure suddenly of what she had wanted so badly just a few minutes ago. What she had wanted for the days and weeks since she had looked up to see him walking around the corner at Old Roses. Then the taste of him filled her mouth and her senses and he made a sound in his throat, a welcoming sound, a *Come to me* sound, and she gave up thinking completely.

Angie put her hands over John's where they cradled her face and ran them up his arms and twined them around his neck and kissed him back, openmouthed and deep and true. He held her so tightly that for a moment she couldn't breathe, and then he held her away from him to look into her face and she still couldn't breathe, didn't know if she would ever remember how to breathe. He pushed her hair out of her face, and then he smiled.

He said, "It won't be easy, the next few days. But I'll come to you when I've sorted things through. Maybe tomorrow I'll drive Caroline up to the lake; Miss Junie will need to know about Tab. That would be a good opportunity"—he swallowed hard—"that would be the right opportunity to talk to her."

"I'm not holding you to anything," Angie said. "I have no expectations. You could walk out of here and change your mind."

"Not going to happen," John said. "You may not be around when I get back, but I am coming back. And this time I won't let you run off until we know for sure, one way or the other."

Angie closed her eyes, and when she opened them Tony was standing a few feet away. It wasn't often that she saw Tony without a smirk on his face, and just now that sight was unsettling.

"Hey, John."

John ran a hand through his hair, cupped the crown of his head. "Tony. You in one piece?"

"I signed myself out. Angeline," he said. "Let's blow this Popsicle stand, what do you say? Cab's on its way." He held up his cell phone.

"I'll be in touch," John said. He touched her hand, ran a finger down her palm so that her muscles jumped. "Just as soon as I have news."

· TWELVE ·

There are many interesting folks here in Ogilvie, war heroes and politicians and men noted for their erudition and knowledge of our long and distinguished history. I hope you will not depend exclusively on sensational rumors and tall tales you must be hearing from the Liars (the name they claim with misplaced pride) who've got nothing better to do than sit outside the barbershop all day while their betters are working.

Your name: A concerned citizen.

Though she meant to sleep for most of Sunday, Angie found she was doomed to wakefulness, simply because her last conversation with John in the bright lights of the emergency room kept replaying itself in her mind, and as far as she could tell, there was no way to stop it. It was clear that she would have to find another way to distract herself through the rest of the weekend and, if she could not put John Grant out of her mind, at least minimize his presence.

Work, Angie told herself, was answer. She wrote long lists of things to do; she searched out her pens and color-coded and cross-referenced each item. First on her agenda was to organize all the materials that had been piling up on the kitchen table. On a raft made of paper she could float for a few days at least.

"This is serious," said Rivera when she came downstairs at three in the afternoon. "You bought a label maker."

Angie was sitting cross-legged on the floor, surrounded by neat piles. She said, "Don't step on anything."

Rivera tiptoed her way across the kitchen to the coffeemaker, boosted herself up on the counter, and sat there looking over what Angie had wrought. She wished, now, that she had picked another place for this project.

"Where'd you go for your office-supply fix?"

"Don't yell," Angie said. "Wal-Mart. I was desperate."

"I guess you were, to go thirty miles for paper and pencils and—oooh, nice paper clips."

"You'll be glad when I'm done; you won't have to go scrounging when you need something."

Rivera was fiddling with the filter. "I'm not complaining. An office-supply fix is better than getting drunk, any day." She began to scoop coffee, yawning while she counted under her breath.

Angie continued to work, but mostly she was anticipating Rivera's next question, which would be aimed at the very heart of the things she least wanted to talk about. She would ask about last night, and Angie's choices would be limited. She could refuse to talk about it, which was a kind of admission of its own that something big was going on, or she could spill the beans. She never had been able to lie to Rivera successfully.

Rivera turned the machine on, and when it began to hiss she slid off the counter. Her bare feet hit the linoleum with a thump. Then she sat down and reached for a pile of paper and began to look through it. "Hand me a couple file folders," Rivera said. "And the label maker, too, while you're at it."

They worked together for a few hours, stopping to make coffee or grab something out of the refrigerator. Angie was surprised, and then relieved, and then pleased. It was a comfort to sit like this with Rivera. They talked very little, and when they did, it was work or Tony, who was still in bed nursing his concussion.

"Who is this again?" Rivera asked, holding out a dog-eared black-and-white photo.

"Mr. Reston from Reston's Appliances."

"And he's important to us how?"

Angie picked up a pile of paper and looked through it. "I went to see him because of his entry in the memory book. 'If you are going to go digging up old stories best left buried, I hope you'll listen to both sides. If that's not too much to ask.'"

"Sounds promising," Rivera said, perking up.

Angie said, "His father was the one who kept turning Miss Zula and Miss

Maddie away when they first tried to register to vote. He told me the story himself. Worried about how his father will look."

"He's willing to go on the record?"

"Oh, yeah," Angie said.

Rivera disappeared again to check on Tony, and came back with the news that he was awake and cranky.

"On the mend," she said. She went back to sorting through photos: a river baptism, a picnic, a pile of watermelons with a baby perched on top, Miss Zula with a small white dog, Miss Maddie with an elegant woman wearing a long mink coat. John Grant on the cusp of puberty, his face bland with boredom on a Sunday-afternoon visit, Rob next to him, his eyes crossed and his tongue hanging from the corner of his mouth. A woman standing behind them, dark haired and light eyed, her hand on John's head.

"John's mother?"

"Yup. That would be Miss Lucy." And: "I'm taking this box out to the van."

She had been trying very hard to keep John out of her thoughts, mostly because Rivera could read sexual desire and frustration as easily as she could a fortune cookie. But then Rivera seemed fairly distracted herself. She was thinking about this, about how tired and strained Rivera looked, whether that came from last night's party or if something else was wrong, and how likely that seemed, given her long silence, when the phone rang. They both jumped, and then Rivera reached over to hit the speaker button.

"This is Win Walker. Is that Angie or Rivera?"

"Both of us," Rivera said. "You're on the speaker."

"Hey," Angie said, trying to sound friendly.

"Harriet asked me to call you to let you know that Tab is still in the hospital, and he'll be here for a few days at least. They're talking about bypass surgery. But the Rose girls want to make sure everybody knows that the wedding is still on for Saturday, as long as Tab is on the mend."

Angie dropped her head. There was a swipe of dried mustard on the cuff of her jeans. How that had got there, she had no idea. She studied it with great interest while Win Walker went on with his report. She fought the urge to ask him whether he didn't have other, more important phone calls to make, because she certainly had better things to do with her time.

"Okay," Rivera said finally. "Thanks for letting us know. Is the whole clan down there?"

"Pretty much," Win said. "Miss Maddie and Father Bruce are sitting with Harriet and the boys. Caroline and John went up to the lake to tell Miss Junie in person—"

Angie let out a small sound, one that Rivera caught. She shot her a questioning look, which Angie pretended not to see.

"—and Miss Zula has gone with them. You never know how Miss Junie will take the news."

Angie made another small sound; she couldn't help herself.

"Well, thanks again," Rivera said, still looking at Angie very hard. "Hold on a minute, Miss Maddie wants to talk to you."

There was a scuffling and then Miss Maddie's high, wavering voice came over the speaker.

"Rivera? I wanted to remind you about our appointment, sugar. We need to get started with the picnic baskets. I hope you're still planning on coming over to help? I'm going to drag Harriet out of the hospital. She needs a little time away."

"Of course," Rivera said, pulling a face at Angie.

"We'll be there," Angie said. She leaned over and turned off the speaker.

For a long moment the only sound in the kitchen was the flutter of papers as the fan moved in its arc through the room.

"Did you know about Caroline and John going up to the lake?"

Angie busied herself with paper. "And if I did?"

"Angeline," said Rivera, lowering her chin in a gesture that meant she was ready to go to war.

"Okay." Angie let out a strangled laugh as she collapsed back to the floor. She looked around herself at the piles of file folders with their neat labels, photos clipped together by subject and year, a legal pad bristling with sticky notes, her index in a half dozen different colors, the logbook riffling in the breeze. She closed her eyes and counted to ten.

She had imagined John and Caroline deep in conversation as the countryside flashed by, but now she had to give that up. Instead she saw Miss Zula sitting straight backed beside John, the head of her cane between her gloved hands and Louie at her feet. Caroline would be in the backseat, and what could the three of them possibly talk about? English department business? Grant deadlines? Tab Darling's medical condition? The fact that Harriet had left him?

She opened her eyes and saw that Rivera was still looking at her. She said, "You can't make me disappear by closing your eyes, so you might as well tell me what's going on."

"Everything," Angie said. "Nothing." Then she took another deep breath, and told Rivera what there was to tell.

When she was finished, the story seemed outrageous, simplistic, laughable, but Rivera looked neither upset nor surprised. For a moment she rocked herself, her chin pressed to her chest, and then she looked up.

She said, "I suppose it was inevitable."

Angie blinked. She had been expecting hard questions about John, and what Angie wanted from John, and why she thought she might be able to get those things. She was only half prepared to answer such questions, and that made her nervous, because if she couldn't make Rivera understand, she was lost.

The truth was quite simple, if she could only make the words come out of her mouth: she wanted John, she had always wanted him, and he wanted her, too. The connection had stretched over five years and many miles, but it hadn't snapped. It was still strong enough to draw them together, against everyone's wishes and expectations and maybe even against their own best interests. But there was no going back now, no way to pretend the conversation in the emergency room hadn't happened.

She was hoping that she would be able to say even part of this to Rivera, enough to make her understand that she knew what she was doing, but now Rivera had something to say.

"John isn't right for Caroline."

That was enough to jolt Angie out of her preoccupation with herself. She looked hard at Rivera and saw an expression there that, she realized now, must be a great deal like the look on her own face. Desperately hopeful, lovesick, pessimistic that anything so crucially important could possibly go right. The signs had been there, but Angie, caught up in her own mess, hadn't taken them in. Rivera was in love with Caroline Rose. Suddenly Angie found herself in the middle of a minefield.

"So," she said slowly, "what are you trying to tell me?"

"There's nothing to say," Rivera said, very clearly. "Not a thing."

A hundred questions flooded Angie's mind, but none of them could be asked outright; she could no more force a confidence from Rivera than she could stab her. And still she couldn't let things go as they stood.

She said, "What does Caroline want, do you know?"

Rivera made a face. "I'm not sure *she* knows what she wants. The only thing she seems clear on is her prime directive. Which is, not to disappoint her mother or sisters."

Angie's mouth closed with an audible click. "She'll go ahead with the wedding no matter—"

"Listen," Rivera interrupted her, "I am not going to discuss this, okay? I can't. Even for you." She looked at her watch and pulled herself, groaning, up off the floor. "Mangiamele, up and at 'em. Miss Maddie and the picnic baskets await."

Angie looked around the mess on the kitchen floor and felt suddenly deflated. She said out loud what she had been thinking for so many weeks. "I knew we shouldn't have taken this job."

Rivera said, "I'm starting to think you were right."

Miss Maddie's neat kitchen was Angie's favorite room in all of Ogilvie. It had white-painted cabinets that reached up to the ceiling and closed with small silver thumb latches, an ancient speckled linoleum floor, a sink deep enough for a three-year-old child to take a bath in, a cookie jar made to look like a gingerbread house, and a green Bakelite radio. The stove was squat and black and came to life with a hiss and a hint of gas.

Just now the kitchen was in chaos. Marilee and Anthea Bragg were busy chopping a great pile of onions, peppers, and cabbage while Harriet stood at the sink squeezing water out of cooked tomatoes. All three of them were wearing aprons with their names embroidered across the chest in swirling blue letters.

Food was everywhere: covered bowls and plates on the counter, pots on every burner, the oven glowing. Wicker picnic baskets with leather straps were stacked in a corner. An official-looking numbered ticket was tied to each with a piece of string.

Marilee pointed with an elbow. "Auntie's put out aprons for y'all, right there on the door hook? She'll be right in, she just went out to the garden to get some parsley."

"What are we feeding, the Second Fleet?" Angie slipped her arms into a huge red apron scattered with fat rosebuds. "How many days ahead of time do you start cooking for the Jubilee?"

Anthea laughed. "Two is cutting it close. You haven't seen the whole Bragg family together at once. And then there's the basket auction."

"Okay," said Rivera. "I need more information."

Harriet said, "We do it every year, to raise money for next year's Jubilee? You eat supper with your high bidder. It's an honor, you know. Auntie had to pull some strings for you to be Basket Girls. Most years they give out twenty tickets by lottery, and five more go to the baskets that brought in the most money the previous year. This time that's Miss Maddie, Caroline Rose, me and my sister, and Nan Ogilvie."

"And how did we score tickets again?" Rivera asked.

"The committee voted you honorary Basket Girls. The last time they did that was for Anita Bryant, the summer she was here visiting with Ben-Linda Stillwater and them."

Angie said, "I had no idea."

"You'll pardon me for saying so," Rivera said with a barely straight face, "but this is way Mayberry." She lifted the napkin over one of the bowls to sniff at it. "What is this stuff?"

"Granny Louisa's piccalilli," said Anthea. "And there weren't any black people with names in Mayberry, did you ever notice that?"

"They did send somebody from Atlanta one year to write us up for the paper," said Harriet. "We amuse them."

"Well, let them laugh. I don't care. I love the Jubilee." Anthea wrinkled her nose and then rubbed it with her wrist. "I plan on finding a husband this year. Or at least a really good time."

"You're all talk," said her sister. "But you do make me laugh."

Rivera wanted to know how often people hooked up at the Jubilee, and if that was the real purpose of the whole undertaking.

"Our folks got together at the Jubilee, back in the days before it was integrated and we had our own party on the other side of town," said Marilee. "But I met my George in Atlanta, when I was a resident."

Harriet said, "The first time I ever really talked to Tab was over my picnic basket at the Jubilee supper. That was the year I decided fried chicken was too country and I made mackerel cakes with dill sauce, but a disaster? Sick as dogs, the both of us. I thought he'd never forgive me, but as soon as he could pick himself off the bathroom floor he came by Old Roses with a bunch of flowers and a bottle of Pepto-Bismol. I fell pregnant with Tab Junior that same night."

"You're not the only one who tells a story that ends like that," said Marilee. "Nine months from now labor and delivery will be hopping, let me tell you. We got a lot of April babies in Ogilvie, always have had." She nudged her sister with an elbow. "Sometime I'll get up the nerve to ask Mama if it's just coincidence I was born in April."

That made Harriet laugh. "Don't be mean to your mama, Marilee. She didn't do so bad for herself, marrying Calvin Bragg. I should never've married Tab, pregnant or not, no matter what Mama and Father Bruce had to say." She shook herself slightly and gave them both a brilliant smile.

Anthea was watching her closely. She said, "You come and see me when you're ready, Harriet, and I'll draw up the papers for you."

At that Harriet looked at first confused, and then surprised.

"I'm not going to divorce him," she said. "I couldn't do that. Mama would just about die, and Father Bruce—" She shook her head. "But I am going to get a place of my own. We can live apart and still be married."

Angie said, "Anthea, you know the difference between a Catholic mother and a Rottweiler? Eventually the Rottweiler lets go."

Harriet hiccupped a soft laugh, and then she put her hands over her mouth and let go, her shoulders shaking. Rivera made a face at Angie, but she was grinning, too.

Miss Maddie stood at the end of the table, fists on hips and her head cocked at a thoughtful angle. Her apron fluttered a little in the breeze from the fan, and Angie wondered why it was that she had ended up yet again in one of the few unair-conditioned houses in Ogilvie on an afternoon as hot as this one.

"You girls are going to have the best picnic baskets," she said in an approving tone. "Wait and see if one of you don't walk away with the blue ribbon."

"Auntie," said Anthea. "The year you get knocked off the Basket Girls throne, hell has long since froze over and been sold for Popsicles."

"And when that day comes, it will surely be Caroline who takes your place," said Marilee.

There was a long discussion about Caroline's sweet-potato pie, followed by a debate on the proper packing of a picnic basket. By late afternoon Miss Maddie wasn't trying to hide her worry about her sister anymore. "I can't understand what is keeping them. Caroline has always been here when we start to put the baskets together, always."

Marilee said, "Most likely Miss Junie wanted them to stay for dinner, Auntie." But right then they heard Louie galloping down the hall toward them. Harriet said, "There, you see?"

Miss Zula stood in the kitchen doorway, smiling at her sister. "No need to get all flustered, Maddie, here I am. Louie, you are making a mess of that water bowl. Remember your manners."

She looked weary and more drawn than Angie had ever seen her, but Angie knew that her own expression had to be less than composed. She had the almost irresistible urge to jump up and ask about Caroline, who was nowhere in sight. She wondered if that was good news, or bad, and most of all she wondered how she could ask even the most innocent of the questions she wanted to ask. Rivera looked as jumpy as Angie felt.

Miss Zula didn't seem to take note. She let her sister fuss about her while she greeted each of them, spending the longest time with Harriet and holding both her hands in her own.

"Junie is just right as rain," she told Harriet. "Your mama is not the kind to fall into the faint at the first sign of trouble, and didn't I say so? Your Uncle Bruce is going this evening to fetch her down for the Jubilee, and I expect she'll spend most of the day at Tab's bedside."

"That's good news," said Harriet. "Because I'm going to be busy running the children's games. What did keep you so long? We expected you hours ago."

Miss Zula cast a glance at Angie, and smiled. A small, quiet smile but a smile, nonetheless, and what did that mean? Was it sympathy, or support, or nothing but good manners?

"Didn't you bring Caroline back with you, Auntie?" Anthea asked, and Angie thought, *Thank you.*

"Caroline is why we took so long," Miss Zula said. She took a sip from the wineglass her sister had pressed into her hand. Then she sat down and patted her lap. Louie jumped up and settled there with a contented sigh.

"Harriet, your sister decided to go to her bridal retreat, after all," she said. "So we dropped her off there on the way home."

"She *what?*" Harriet squeaked.

Rivera shot Angie a look. "A retreat? Like to a convent?"

"The Benedictine order has a retreat house about eighty miles from here," Miss Zula said. "She'll be back in a few days."

"Days?" Harriet looked like she was about to choke to death on the word.

Miss Maddie said, "It's a tradition, isn't that so, Harriet? All y'all went on bridal retreats before your weddings."

"Well, yes, but not five days before, not with so much to do. And she'll miss the Jubilee, and what about the bridal shower? What would make her do such a thing?"

"I don't know, dear," said Miss Zula, completely absorbed in the massaging of Louie's ears. "You'll have to ask her yourself."

"I would," said Harriet. "If they had a telephone. You'd think those nuns would have an emergency line at least. I'll have to cancel the shower. What am I supposed to tell people?"

"I expect Caroline trusts you to handle all that." Miss Zula gave her a serene smile. "You've done this four times before, after all. Exactly the same wedding, for all of you."

"But this is her wedding, not mine," Harriet wailed. And then an expression of complete dismay came over her face. "What about her picnic basket and her auction ticket?"

"Don't you worry about that," said Miss Maddie. "Neely Ogilvie is next on the list, and if I know her, she's got a basket together just on the hope one of us would drop dead."

Kai said, "A time of quiet reflection before a wedding seems to me a very good idea."

She was pulling books down from shelves and sorting them into piles. John thought again, as he often did, that Kai's approach to the world was as elemental and clear as water. He wondered about living in Japan, what that would be like; he thought of a quiet room on a mountaintop somewhere. Isolation seemed like a good idea just now, but then that would mean leaving Angie behind, again. He glanced at the phone, and then forced himself to concentrate on what his brother was saying.

"So what do they do all day long on a bridal retreat? I take it the nuns don't put on a lingerie show."

Kai said, "Nuns don't wear underclothing?"

"I have no idea," Rob said, straight-faced. "In fact, I don't particularly want to know."

"There is a bridal luncheon for Caroline on Thursday," Kai said. "Do you think it will be canceled?"

"And the bachelor party," said Rob. "What about that?"

"Hell if I know," John said.

He felt vaguely nauseated and completely hollow, in spite of the fact that he had eaten the entire dinner Kai put before him. He spent more than five hours behind the wheel today, which was part of it, but mostly his mental state had to do with Caroline, and the fact that he had never had so much as five minutes alone with her all day. Not even when she had announced her intention of going off to the retreat for the rest of the week. Junie Rose had been delighted, Miss Zula had seen it as a reasonable thing to do, and thus it had been settled.

There had been a moment, a mere fraction of a second, when Caroline had looked at him and he could have objected. For any number of reasons he could have objected, the first and most important being the fact that they were getting married on Saturday. He could have asked to talk to her in private for a few minutes—he should have done just that—but instead he had met her gaze and then let his own slip away, across the parlor of Miss Junie's summer cottage to fix on the view out the window and a single sailboat on the lake.

Two hours later she had climbed out of the car in front of the convent with a small suitcase—John had time enough to wonder when she had packed it before she had come around to his side of the car and kissed him, a brief touch of her mouth.

"Thank you," she said to him. "Thank you for understanding. This is what I need just now."

But he didn't understand, and how could he? The last real conversation he had had with her was at Rob's open house, which was less than twenty-four hours earlier and seemed at least a year. Because, of course, that party had been before the disaster on the baseball field and the mass exodus to the emergency room. It had been before he kissed Angie. Just now the world and all time could be qualified by the direction in which it flowed: up to the moment when he kissed Angie and she kissed him back, and then away from that moment.

As he turned the car toward Ogilvie and home, he realized that he remembered very little of that conversation in the crowded living room when Caroline had wanted to dance. He searched his mind and came up with no more than fragments: *bridal jitters* and *everybody has doubts*.

He had wanted to confess his own doubts to her; it had been his sincere intention to tell her everything. Caroline Rose, utterly meticulous and uncompromising in her scholarship, would ask hard questions and he would answer them honestly, and when that conversation was over, he would no longer be engaged. That would be the worst of it, though he knew the week would bring many difficult conversations: with each of the Rose sisters, with Miss Junie and Father Bruce and every male in Ogilvie who was in any way related to Caroline. But together they would come to an agreement on how to handle that, he and Caroline. They could work together still.

"John Grant," said Miss Zula. She was sitting beside him in the car and he had been so lost in his thoughts that he had forgotten her completely.

"Yes, Miss Zula?"

"You know I love Miss Junie like a sister, and her girls are like daughters to me. Caroline most especially."

He cast her a quick glance and saw that she was sitting as she always did, straight of back, hands folded. He had never seen her in anything but neat dresses, most of them in somber colors; he had known her all his life, and he had the idea that he didn't really know her at all. Now Miss Zula was looking straight out the window, and didn't turn her head toward him.

"Yes, ma'am, I know you do."

"You did a good thing today, letting her go without making a fuss. You did the right thing."

There were many questions that came to mind, but John couldn't think of where to start without revealing too much of his own mind-set, something he could not do out of fairness to Caroline. Something he would not be able to do until Friday, when she came home. The day before the wedding. Until that time he would have to pretend that everything was just fine, which would be one of the harder things he had ever done.

It occurred to him just then that maybe Miss Zula was trying to tell him something else.

He said, "You make it sound like she's not coming back."

At that she did turn to look at him. "She's coming back," said Miss Zula. "Sad to say, but she will most certainly come back as she promised."

The rest of the way home John had tried to think of ways to ask Miss Zula to explain that *sad to say*. He was good with words, and always had been. Students and colleagues both gave him high marks for his lectures, for the way he led seminars, for his ability to make the complex clear, to argue his point. He had made a career out of the careful weighing and arrangement of words until they sang on the page. Words were tools that could be used to uncover the truth, but this time they would not work for him.

Because, he must admit to himself, he was afraid of what Miss Zula might say if he could think of a way to ask her.

Now John half listened to Rob and Kai as they moved boxes. They were talking about curtains and telephone calls that needed to be made, address-change cards and utilities. They needed an answering machine and long-distance service, which made John think of his own telephone, because, he realized, it had been ringing for a while.

"John," said Kai, passing him with her arms full of books. "Aren't you going to answer that?"

By the time had had crossed the room, the machine had picked up.

"John? This is Eunice. What is this silliness about Caroline going on retreat five days before her wedding? Mama's no help, she says it'll do Caroline good. Except Mama's up there at the lake and we're down here with a list a mile long of things to get done before Saturday."

The machine clicked off. John looked at Kai, who blinked at him with the same look she got when she was working out the next ten or twenty chess moves: intrigued.

He got up and started filling an empty moving box with books from the pile on the floor.

For the next hour he and Kai packed books and carried the boxes out to the porch, listening to one message being recorded after another. John would have turned the machine off, but he had the idea that if he did people would start showing up at his door.

"Dr. Grant? John? This is Patty-Cake, in case you don't recognize my voice. I'm worried about you, John, and I'm worried about Caroline. Is everything all right? I can't get ahold of Junie, and there are rumors going 'round. Folks are saying Caroline's run off and the wedding's canceled, and I'm calling you direct, out of respect, you understand, because you should know what people are saying. I'm not one to spread rumors, but my daddy always said speak the truth and shame the devil, and so I'm speaking some truth here. The question is, who exactly is the devil in this situation? A few weeks ago everything was fine, and then . . . I just don't know what to think, Tab in the hospital and Caroline run away to those nuns. I do wish you'd pick up."

John stood there for a long moment after the machine had clicked off, sweat running down his face and body, feeling a little faint for the second time this summer, though this time a trip to the emergency room and a few stitches wouldn't fix the problem. Kai was watching him, her small heart-shaped face tilted to one side.

She said, "I wonder that Caroline didn't tell her family about her plans."

"She made up her mind all of a sudden," John said.

Kai nodded thoughtfully. She said, "Patty-Cake is thinking of Angie and her friends, that they have something to do with . . . whatever is going on between you and Caroline."

"I got that, yes." John managed a smile.

"It would be best if Angie stayed out of her way, I think," Kai said.

"Probably."

The phone began to ring again.

"Dr. Grant? Professor Grant? This is Jean Marie Stillwater? I'm Caroline's second cousin once removed on her daddy's side? I do the bookkeeping for Abby Shaw, the florist? I'm calling because the balance is due on the bill for the flowers, the corsages, and arrangements for the church and all that? And I can't get hold of Caroline. Her sister Eunice said I should call you direct? I surely would appreciate it if you'd come by the shop tomorrow and take care of business. Bye now."

In the silence John could hear Rob singing to himself while he lugged boxes to the car, lots of volume and enthusiasm, but what song it might have been was known only to him.

"Mama always said Rob couldn't carry a tune in a bucket," John said. It wasn't often he thought of his mother, but she seemed very close at the moment. Lucy Ogilvie Grant Bradshaw Butler Chatham Black would know how to handle this situation. She would look Patty-Cake Walker in the eye and say just the right thing, words as pretty as oleander and twice as deadly. If John were to ask her for advice, she would cluck sympathetically and offer anecdotes from her many ventures into matrimony. Who else of his acquaintance had as much experience with weddings, and the multitude of ways that the whole thing could go wrong?

"You must be very distressed if you are thinking of asking your mother for advice." Kai was watching him, her arms filled with books.

John was getting used to the way Kai sometimes picked up his thoughts, but this made him jump. He said, "The one person I need to talk to is the one I can't call. No phones at the retreat."

He wanted to talk to Angie, too, but he couldn't say that aloud, not even to Kai. And he had made a promise to himself: he would stay away from Angie until he had something concrete to say.

She shook her head at him as if he were a lazy student. Then she put down the books and went into the kitchen. She came out again with a pad of paper and a pen, which she thrust into his hands.

"Write," she said. "They have no phones, but surely she can read a letter. If you have things you must say, then say them. Get it into the mail tomorrow morning and she will have it on Wednesday."

"Tomorrow is a holiday," John said.

"Then she will have it on Thursday, unless you want to drive up there and leave it for her. Is it that important?"

"Yeah," John said. "It is."

"Then write," Kai said. "And Rob and I will drive with you, to keep you company."

When Angie and Rivera got back to Ivy House the phone was ringing. They bumped into each other in their race to get to it when Tony's arm snaked out from the couch and snagged the receiver.

He sat up and waggled his eyebrows at them.

"He's feeling better," Rivera said.

"Good," Angie said. "Then I can kill him with an easy conscience."

On the phone Tony said, "Your lovely daughter is right here, planning my murder. Here you go." He held out the receiver and gave Angie a beatific smile. "Your father."

"Angie!"

"Dad."

"Tell me, they got a different calendar down there in Georgia? A different number of days, or maybe in a different order? I only ask because my calendar here, the one cousin Benny sent me from Florida, that calendar says today is Monday, July third. Which means—up here in Jersey, anyway—that yesterday was Sunday. And I got this idea, call it crazy, but I got the idea that yesterday was Sunday where you are, too, because this beauty-ful Florida calendar says so, and Florida is south of where you find yourself at this point in time. And the last I checked, time zones run east to west, not north to south. Am I right?"

Angie grimaced at Tony, who shrugged dramatically. "Sorry, Dad. Things got busy yesterday."

"Angie, this is your mother on the other line. You've got my permission to ignore your father. He misses you, but that's no excuse for bad manners, Tommy. Now, tell me, how is work going? How's Rivera?"

"Good, we're all good, everything's good." Angie shot a look across the room to Rivera, who was scowling at the screen of her cell phone. She might have said, *Rivera seems to be in love with a woman who just ran off to a nunnery.* Her mother took an academic interest in Rivera's love life and would certainly be intrigued by this newest chapter, but now was not the time for a lesson in modern-day lesbian mating rituals.

"Tony got himself in trouble yet?" Angie's father yelled.

"Oh, yeah," Angie said. "I'll let him tell you about it." And she handed the phone back to Tony, who performed, as he always did when pressed. While he related the story of the rumble in the park, Angie went into the kitchen and got herself a glass of water. Rivera followed her in, and they stood there together in the dim cool listening to Tony, who paced up and down with the phone under one arm, the unlit cigarette in the corner of his mouth jerking as he talked.

"We've got a busy day ahead of us tomorrow. We should get some sleep." Rivera said this flatly.

From the other room Tony called, "Your father wants to know what you two put in your picnic baskets."

"Lasagna in mine, cannelloni in Rivera's," Angie called back.

Rivera snorted a laugh.

"Oh, like I can tell Tommy Apples what southerners eat. He'd be on the next plane."

"Your mother says it sounds like a slave auction," Tony shouted.

"Tell her enough with the old *Roots* tapes, they've made some good movies in the last twenty years."

Rivera produced a giggle like a burp and then they were both laughing in near hysterics, covering their mouths and bent over double. Finally Angie caught her breath. She said, "Did you have any idea Caroline was going to do this?"

"Run off?" Rivera flung herself down on the couch, looked up at the ceiling, and frowned. "I knew she was feeling trapped, but this? No. Do you think the Mother Superior looks like Rosalind Russell in *The Trouble with Angels*? Caroline reminded me of Hayley Mills the minute I saw her. I had such a crush on her in that movie."

Angie leaned forward and pressed her forehead against Rivera's shoulder. "What a mess we've got ourselves into."

Rivera said, "It's a record, even for us."

In the other room Tony was talking to Tommy Apples about the odd habits of southerners, and they listened to him for a while. Finally Angie said, "There are questions I'd like to ask you."

"No," said Rivera. "Please don't, because I've got nothing useful to tell you."

Less than a half hour after Kai handed him paper and pen, John folded three closely written sheets into an envelope and sealed it quickly before the urge to edit got the better of him. This morning he would have told anyone who asked that he was so used to composing on the computer he couldn't write longhand anymore, and yet this particular letter had poured itself across the page without hesitation or pause.

Rob and Kai were waiting for him on the porch, Rob tossing the car keys from hand to hand.

"You don't have to do this," John said. "But I'm glad you offered."

"Can't have you driving into a ditch," Rob said. "Not just when things are getting exciting around here."

"I owe you."

"Yes," Rob said, clapping him on the back. "You do."

For the next hour and a half John drifted in and out of a twilight sleep, vaguely aware of the darkening sky, of Kai's profile when she turned her head to talk, of the weight of the letter in his shirt pocket. He thought of Caroline reading it, her head bent over the paper, and he was overcome by sadness and affection and fear. He didn't want to hurt her and he couldn't marry her; he couldn't even remember how he had imagined he could make her happy.

He had loved her—he loved her still—for her intelligence and quick mind and shy smile, for her quiet thoughtfulness and her empathy, her kindness, but he had no idea what touched her most deeply. She never lost her temper, though there were times he had been angry for her, at her sisters, for the way they passed her back and forth like a doll; at her mother, for letting that happen. He had asked her, more than once, how she managed and she had given him her enigmatic smile.

Anything for a quiet life. It was her mantra, and a joke in the family. Eunice had given her an elaborate purple velvet-and-silk pillow with those words embroidered on it. Caroline kept it on her bed, the one spot of color in her cool white bedroom.

No matter how Caroline felt about this letter, about him, about the trouble he was bringing down on her head, she would never allow it to come to the surface, just as she kept everything else just out of touch. The evening he asked her to marry him she had smiled so sweetly and turned her face to his shoulder and trembled. Because she was happy, he had thought then, because—he remembered resorting to cliché without hesitation—*still waters run deep.*

Once he set himself the task of examining the things he had so studiously ignored for the past year, John found he couldn't stop. Caroline's solemn nature, her shyness, her inability to stand up to her family when it came to something as basic as her own wedding, all these things he pulled forth from his memory like rabbits out of a hat, and taken together they spelled out an indictment, not of her but of himself. He had treated her no better than her sisters; he had used her as a mirror, and she had done that job well, reflecting back to him what he wanted to see. Now John promised himself that sometime, somehow, he would confess this failing to her and ask her forgiveness.

Rob said, "We're just about there. You're sure you want to do this?"

His first impulse was to brush the question off, but John caught his brother's glance in the rearview mirror, wary, concerned.

Step by step he reviewed what must come. He would hand this letter over to whichever nun came to the door. Caroline would read it, tonight or tomorrow morning, and with that, their engagement would be ended. Sometime in the next few days Caroline would make the announcement that the wedding was off, because he had left it up to her to decide how best to do that. She might come home to Ogilvie, or find a phone and call one of her sisters or, more likely, her mother. At that point, the wedding guests would be contacted and the rumor mill would go into overdrive. When he showed his face in town, he would be accosted on the street by third and fourth cousins, Caroline's and his own, who believed it their right to hear the whole story of what went wrong, and who was at fault. No matter what story Caroline told, no matter how kind she was to him in the telling of it, blame would be parceled out, the largest portion would fall to him. Because he deserved it, first of all, for getting into this situation.

He would deal with all that and more, because it was necessary, and because it was the price he had to pay to claim Angie. Or to try to claim her; there was always the possibility that she didn't want him.

Except that she had kissed him back, and meant it.

He said, "Yes, I'm sure." And he was overwhelmed, just that simply, with relief.

Kai turned to look at him. "What happened to change your mind?"

He could have told her the whole story. Most probably he would tell her, one day, but as the redbrick wall of the retreat house came into view, a simpler answer came to mind.

"Something a man on a plane said to me," John said. "And Angie. Angie happened."

THIRTEEN

If you can get Miss Zula to open up and tell you about how she bases her characters on people here in Ogilvie, you can be sure we would all love to hear about that. To tell you the truth, I think most folks in this town only read her work because they are looking for themselves. For example, I am sure she based Daddy Sam in her second novel on Emmet Preston, but I have never got up the nerve to ask her.

Your name: Please don't be offended if I don't sign my name. This is a small town.

I took organ lessons from Miss Zula's daddy from the time I was five years old until the day Brother Bragg died. I was ten years old when our Lord sent down His band of angels to pick up Martin Bragg to be the leader of His choir in Heaven. There must have been two hundred people at his funeral, come from as far as Atlanta and Tallahassee. Sister Bragg looked like a marble statue sitting there in the front pew, but the three children wept so. Brother Bragg was much loved by all the congregation, for his kindness and generosity and for his music. I know that he will spend eternity playing and singing His holy praise. I look forward to shaking his hand on the other side, someday soon.

Your name: Alvin Lee Downs. My mama played the organ at Mount Olive AME after Brother Bragg passed on, and I took her place when Mama was called to Heaven thirty-seven years ago this March.

On the long drive back from the retreat house John slept like a man suddenly and unexpectedly relieved of a burden, deeply and without dreams. When they pulled up in front of the Lee Street house, he woke disoriented but not unhappy. He couldn't even claim to feel guilty, though he figured he should; he was about to cause considerable pain and discomfort to people he cared about. Had probably already caused such pain. His general lightheartedness, he told himself, had less to do with Angie than it did with the fact that marrying Caroline would have been a mistake.

He wanted to go over to Ivy House on the spot and tell Angie so, but she wouldn't thank him for that; not tonight, not ever. The things they had to work out between them were tough enough without bringing Caroline into the picture, and his position would be far stronger if he waited until he could tell her with complete certainty that the wedding was off. Which he couldn't do until he heard from Caroline.

Rob and Kai went right back to packing, but he went straight to bed and had the best night's sleep he could remember in weeks. He woke up thinking about work, and eager to get to it. At the English department he could barricade himself in his office, where things were neat and organized and problems were easily mastered. Rob would keep the Rose girls and Patty-Cake at bay. It was a workable plan, except, as it turned out, he was wrong to assume Caroline would be quick to get in touch.

By midmorning it was clear that she was the only person in the world who wasn't eager to talk to him. The phone in Rob's office rang and rang and rang, vague and far away and as hard to ignore as a buzzing mosquito. The only phone call Rob was supposed to put through was the one from Caroline, or Angie. John's phone sat squat and silent and mocking.

At three Rob came in to stretch out on the couch and recap the highlights, which were as bad as John had feared.

"Blood in the water, scandal in the air, it's all the same to the good folks of Ogilvie," Rob finished.

"What a mess," John said. "Christ, I wish she'd call, but I can't blame her for making me sweat."

Rob had no solutions to offer, but he did the next best thing: he took John home with him and they sat in a mess of moving boxes to eat carryout barbeque and drink beer until the sun went down.

Kai said, "You need a distraction. I suggest poker."

John snorted a laugh. "I'll just hand you my wallet, why don't I. Get it over with."

"We could call Angie and Rivera and Tony to come join us," Kai went on blithely.

"Fresh meat," said Rob. "My wife, the hunter."

"It would be a way for you to see Angie," Kai said to John. "It's what you need, to see Angie."

John stood up and stretched. He had a very slight beer buzz, just enough to make him relax to the point where he could see the truth of things.

"You're right," he said. "I do need to see Angie. I'm going to walk over there."

They didn't try to talk him out of it, maybe because they wanted to be alone; maybe because they really understood. John set out on the two-mile walk at a good pace. It had always been the best way to clear his head, walking through the town he loved so much. The night was full of echoing sounds, insects and water and wind. Most of the houses he passed were darkened, quiet, watchful. Here and there curtains fluttered at an open window. A radio news report rough with static came to him from a screened porch.

He crossed into campus and heard the sound of voices in a good-natured argument, and at that moment he remembered for the first time in hours that tomorrow was the Fourth of July Jubilee, which started off with a 5K run. A run he and Caroline were supposed to take part in, together.

He thought of taking another route, but the workers had seen him already. Half the Ogilvie Police Department was still here, putting the finishing touches on the security and first-aid pavilion. Spotlights made it look like a stage populated by a troupe of very tired actors.

"John!" called Louanne Porter.

"If it isn't the chief of police," John said. "Louanne. Bob, Mary Beth, Lee, Howard, Win." It was bad enough running into a crowd of old friends at this moment, but he really didn't need Win Walker telling people he had been wandering around after dark, not with Caroline gone off on a retreat and the rumors already getting started. He put Patty-Cake Walker's voice out of his head and steadied his resolve.

"What are you up to?" Louanne asked him.

"Just getting some fresh air. You got the whole police department out here?"

"No rest for the wicked," Louanne said. "John, you been back in town a couple weeks at least and I don't recall seeing you down at the Hound Dog even once. Caroline got a tight hold on you, does she?"

"No tighter than you've got on Jimmy," said Mary Beth dryly, and Louanne let out a squawk of laughter and swung out, halfheartedly, to smack at the woman who was both her sister-in-law and her community-relations officer.

"You'll see him there on Thursday," said Win Walker. He had been sitting on the ground and he stood up, pulling his cap off his head to scratch at his scalp. "The Rose girls' men have got one hell of a bachelor party planned, is what I hear."

John felt the smile freeze on his face, and hoped nobody took any note of the fact that he was standing there like a rabbit looking at a truck barreling toward it.

"Oh, Lord," said Louanne. "I'll have to put a few extra men on duty that night."

"Alert the emergency room."

"Call up the National Guard."

"Y'all go ahead and have your fun," John said, starting to back away, slowly. "We'll see who has the biggest hangover the next day."

Win walked toward him, looking concerned and as if he had questions he wanted to ask. "John, where you headed? You need a ride?"

John held up both palms. "Just talking a walk. See y'all tomorrow."

He should have headed home right then. He stood for a moment in the dark trying to do just that, but then he thought of Angie, and a sense of purpose came over him. Every nerve in his body jangled, his fingers buzzing with adrenaline, and he had to laugh at himself. He was being drawn across town like a sixteen-year-old boy with an itch.

It's not about sex, he told himself. And then: *It's not just about sex.*

Because he couldn't deny that he was going to talk to Angie, but he wanted her, too. He had been wanting her for weeks, and there was no more sense in pretending he didn't. At least he wouldn't need to make excuses to her; she would be more comfortable with what drove him through town in the middle of the night than he was himself.

Angie's approach to sex had taken some getting used to that summer; her ability to ask for what she wanted, her preference for plain words. She cringed at *making love* and told him in all seriousness that she preferred the Anglo-Saxon alternative. *Fucking* was a strong, healthy word that didn't pretend to be anything but what it was.

This conversation had happened in bed, the first night they spent together. They were lying exhausted in a pool of heat and sweat under the overtaxed air conditioner in the window of her bedroom on Eighth Street.

He said, "Tell me again, what's wrong with 'making love'?"

Lying on her stomach, her hair floating across her back, she had turned her head to look at him. "It's coy. It's insipid. It's euphemistic, and it complicates something that doesn't need to be complicated. Do you like the term, really?"

He had to admit he didn't. "What about 'having sex,' then?"

She wrinkled her nose. "Grammatically suspect, and definitely not the thing to say when you're inside somebody. At least not when you're inside of me."

It had taken all his self-control to hold on to the conversation, but he managed. "Hasn't 'fucking' been co-opted," he asked her, "by just about anybody who ever stubbed a toe or got cut off in traffic?"

"Not by me," she said. "It's far too powerful a word to waste on casual cursing." She ran a finger up his thigh. "Have I hit a sore spot? Stumbled on a slumbering inner prude?"

He caught her wandering hand and leaned forward to kiss her mouth, her impossible mouth, her swollen mouth. She liked to kiss as much as she liked fucking.

"Maybe so," he said. "You know any exorcism rites?"

In the first weeks they had had many conversations about words, the ones she liked and didn't like, the different associations he had for "tit" and "boob," "cock" and "dick." Mostly these talks led them to bed, or to an abruptly cleared table or to a chair—she had a particular affection for fucking face-to-face sitting up—or on one memorable occasion, to the stairs outside his apartment door. She was the most sexually curious person he had ever run into, exhausting, intriguing. Other women had discovery fantasies, rape fantasies, multiple-partner fantasies, but Angie liked the sound of his voice and plain talk.

At first he considered himself fortunate to have found a woman he liked in bed and out of it who wasn't in a hurry to talk love, commitment, what was going to happen next week, next year, forever and ever. Angie knew he was leaving Manhattan at the end of August, but if she ever thought about the fact that the office she was setting up in Hoboken with Rivera was within easy driving distance of Princeton, she never raised the topic, and really, what more could a man ask for? A smart, funny, sexually curious, challenging, attractive woman who was capable of living in the moment. She was eight years younger than he was and ten years younger than the last woman he had dated for any period of time, but in some things—in most things—she seemed older.

It was midsummer before he realized that the very words he would have withheld had she been looking for them were pushing themselves more and more often into the front of his mind. That tingling of nerves in the solar plexus, the flush of blood when he came around a corner and saw Angie— such extreme reactions were outside of his experience, and unsettling.

John called his brother to confess. He said, *I'm in love with a woman who doesn't want to talk about love.*

Reverse psychology, Rob had said. *I can't believe you fell for that one.*

The only response to that was a weak laugh; he couldn't even work up any hurt pride, much less anger. He was too busy, suddenly, wondering where he fit into Angie's view of the world. For once John was the one with the questions, and he could appreciate the irony, if not the discomfort.

The very evening he first talked to his brother about Angie, she showed up at his door with take-out Korean food. He tossed the bag onto the table and drew her into the bedroom and onto the bed. If he was going to be out-maneuvered he might as well enjoy it. Surrender with grace and dignity; hand over the keys to the castle. So he said the words: *I'm falling in love with you.* It was surprisingly easy, even liberating, but her response was nowhere near anything he had imagined.

He remembered her turning and stretching beneath him, the weight of her, the heat, the way she caught her breath and let it go. The smile at the corner of her mouth, banished before it could blossom. She flexed around him, and he gasped, too.

Good, she had said solemnly. *Good.*

Thinking it over later, he had laughed out loud, in relief and acceptance. The next day on the phone Rob said, *You've met your match.*

As he walked across campus in the humid dark, all these memories came rushing back, bright and clear and detailed. As if the five years they had spent apart had never happened; as if that weekend on Long Island had been nothing but a very vivid, very unpleasant dream. He remembered his grandfather at the head of the table staring at Angie, bristling with displeasure. Heart failure had turned his lips and fingernails as blue as her hair.

Now was not the time to allow Matthew Grant out of his grave. John didn't want to have to deal with that rasping, wavering voice, so he thought of Angie, not as she had been that disastrous Long Island weekend, but as she was Saturday night in the fluorescent glare of the emergency room lights, the smile she had given him, sweet and sorrowful and hopeful all at once.

He looked up to find himself in front of Ivy House. There was a light on in the parlor, which might mean she was sleepless and worried or maybe she was in there watching sci-fi with Rivera, the two of them stretched out on the floor discussing camera angles and lighting and dialogue.

But it was Tony Russo who answered his quiet knock; Tony with his trademark cynical smile, his eyes a little glassy. There was rockabilly coming over the speakers and the smell of grass in the air.

"Hey," Tony said. "Here for Angie?"

That woke John out of his trance. Tony and everyone else in Ogilvie outside his own immediate family thought of him as a man about to get married—a man as good as married, to a woman who happened to be out of town. And here he was looking for Angie.

"I'll go get her up," Tony said, not waiting for an answer. "Unless you want to go up yourself: it's at the top of the stairs." One brow lifted, curious but not too; willing to live and let live.

"I'll wait here."

She woke because someone was sitting on her bed. In the near total dark of the bedroom she sat up, her heart beating so loud in her own ears that she felt dizzy.

"What?" she said. "Who?" But she knew already. That particular combination of tobacco and pot, coffee and licorice could only be Tony.

"I hope you didn't wake me up to do a taste test." Tony had been experimenting with mint julep recipes, and often required the opinions of his housemates. "What time is it?"

"Just past midnight. John's downstairs."

She couldn't make out his expression in the dark, and his tone was unremarkable.

"I said, John's downstairs."

"I heard you. Give me a second." Her pulse was racing and her throat felt swollen and rough. The room was cool but a fine sweat broke out all over her body.

Tony said, "Are you sure about this?"

"I'm not sure about anything," Angie said, throwing back the sheet. "Except that I have to go down there."

"Well, this is ironic," Tony said. "After all the trouble I've caused on shoots because I couldn't keep my pants zipped, I'm about to tell you to remember why we're here."

"'Ironic' is one word," Angie said, pulling on a pair of sweat pants. "'Bullshit' is another. I know why we're here, Tony. I've never lost sight of that and I never will."

"Yeah, but. If you break up the wedding of the season, how's that going to play down at the Piggly Wiggly?"

She could stand here in the dark and argue with Tony, Angie realized, or she could go down and find out from John if there was anything to be fighting about in the first place. In the two days since that kiss in the emergency room she had pretty much convinced herself that it was all her imagination; John was avoiding her because he was embarrassed and didn't know how to tell her he had been drunk and couldn't be held accountable for outrageous promises. Now she had to go downstairs and let him tell her that. Or she could refuse, simply send a message down: get lost.

A third possibility occurred to her, fantastic but oddly appealing: she could jump into the van and drive down the road to Orlando and see what minimum-wage jobs were hers for the asking at Disney World.

"You already blew the Piggly Wiggly when you dumped DeeDee," Angie said, and left him there sitting in the dark on her bed.

John spent the few minutes it took Angie to come downstairs speaking firmly to himself, going over the best way to handle things. Then she came in, smelling of sleep, her shape rounded in the old blue T-shirt he had tried so hard to put out of his mind. The battle for reason, for self-denial and patience, was lost at that moment.

Angie stood breathing deeply, her hands twitching at her sides. She noticed how sweet the air was here; it always took her by surprise, jasmine and honeysuckle, like sugar on the tongue. The branches of the old oak that overhung the porch brushed over its roof with the breeze. She heard the low hum of the kitchen light, crickets and tree frogs and the beat of her own heart.

She heard those things, but she saw John. She went up to him and touched him, lightly, on the shoulder.

He turned toward her gracefully, quickly, and put an arm around her waist to pull her up against him, half lifting her off her feet.

"Hey," she said, putting the flats of her hands on his back. "Hey. I wasn't expecting to see you."

He rubbed his cheek against her hair and drew in a deep breath. "I couldn't stay away. I meant to, but I couldn't."

She stepped back and caught his hand. "Come sit down." With a small tug she pulled him toward the couch and the oblong of yellowish light put out by the single lamp at its far end. She tried to read his expression and saw nothing good there. Angie's throat constricted but she forced the words up and out.

"John," she said. She dropped his hand and curled herself in the corner of the couch, feet tucked up, arms tight around her knees. "Just tell me, okay? Don't drag it out, that won't make it any easier."

Something clicked in his face, some understanding and following quickly, surprise. He sat down, his body twisted toward her.

He said, "I never had a chance to talk to Caroline when we drove to the lake, not once. I meant to tell her. Maybe she knew that, somehow. Maybe she guessed. But I couldn't leave it, so I wrote a letter, and Rob drove me up there to deliver it last night. She must have it by now, but I haven't heard from her yet."

"A letter," Angie echoed. "You took a letter up to the retreat house?"

He nodded, started to say something, stopped.

They were silent for a long moment. Angie tried to imagine such a letter, the things he might have said; whether or not he had used her name. She hoped he had left her out of it, and knew that it was a cowardly thing to wish.

"Go on," she said. "Tell me the rest of it."

"I thought she'd call today, but I haven't heard from her yet. I can't even begin to guess why."

"I can," Angie said. "But then I've had some experience."

There was a small, hard silence. John said, "I wondered if you'd ever bring up the subject of that letter."

"It was a good letter," Angie said. "It was all generosity and kindness, and you have nothing to apologize for."

He touched her hand where it lay on the couch, lightly. "When I wrote it I thought you might answer it."

"I wasn't ready," Angie said. "I wasn't ready for the things you were offering me but I didn't want you to give up, either. I was afraid. I still am."

She met his gaze steadily, and saw that she hadn't surprised him or made him mad, which gave her the courage to let the subject go for the moment.

"So you're waiting to hear from Caroline."

"That's about it. It's going to be rough over the next few days."

Angie might have said, *It's rough now,* even knowing how terrible it would sound, how unfair.

He was saying, "So I'm thinking it would be best for us to wait until things have settled down a bit."

"Yes," she said slowly, "that makes sense." And: "How long do you think that will be?" Angie rarely blushed, but she felt herself coloring now. She put her forehead on her upraised knees to hide her face.

"Hey."

She made herself look up.

"Another ten minutes is too long, as far as I'm concerned."

Angie swallowed. She closed her eyes and nodded and kept them closed, because her self-control was shaky at best, and he was so close.

"The thing is, I have to go along as if nothing's changed until she tells her family otherwise. That may be tomorrow, or the day after, or maybe even Thursday. I can't think she'd leave it that long, but she might. Then you and I will have to have a serious conversation."

Angie felt a pulse throbbing in her temple, and made the tactical decision to overhear this last statement. She said, "We've got a lot of work over the next couple days, so it won't be too hard to stay out of your way." She managed a small smile, one that must look as insincere as it felt. "Probably wasn't the best idea for you to come here just now. For all we know Professor Hillard next store is watching us. She has insomnia."

She meant to strike a playful tone, but instead her voice wavered.

John turned his face away from her as if she had said something painful, his gaze fixed on a point in the dark yard. Then he made a small sound, a half sigh of surrender, and without warning he leaned past her to turn off the lamp with a sound like the snap of a wishbone.

"There," he said, his voice low and steady. "That takes care of Peggy Hillard. Now let's take care of you."

He put his hands on her to draw her toward him. John felt her first startle and then soften in acquiescence, in welcome, in pleasure. She curled against him and he put his hands in her hair, tilted her head up.

"I shouldn't have come. Maybe if you weren't wearing this particular T-shirt I could leave. But you are, and I can't."

She met his kiss with a hint of nervousness that gave way immediately, her mouth soft and warm and familiar, the kiss spiraling down and down, drawing them together at breast and belly and hip. There was an instantaneous heavy stirring in his groin. He ran his hands up her back under the T-shirt, his thumb skidding along the indentation of her spine and drawing a shudder from her.

John smiled against her mouth and she took his face between her hands and drew him down over her, smiling, too, both of them on the verge of laughter that they should find themselves like this after so long. Finally. She nipped his ear and he yelped and she ran her tongue down the bristling line of his jaw. And then she did laugh, a low laugh full of anticipation.

"This is right," she said, a little breathlessly. A statement of fact.

"Oh, yeah." He smoothed her hair away from her face. "I should never have let you go. I never did let you go, not really."

He kissed her breathless while he rocked into her on the broad old sofa, pressing himself against her, relearning her touch and feel, the curves and hollows and the taste of her. She flexed, and then gave in and up and let go, went fluid beneath him. Her T-shirt came off first, leaving her in nothing but the shorts that she wouldn't let him draw down her legs, not yet, not yet. Not until she had pulled his shirt over his head and set to work on his pants, peeling them down over his hips and stopping to kiss his belly, her mouth open and wet. She looked up at him, her face an oval in the dark, her eyes gleaming, and reached into his pants pocket, pulled out his wallet and flipped it open, fished with two fingers and then held up the condom like a magic coin.

"You are such a boy scout. Always prepared."

"Ever hopeful," he said, and pulled her up along the length of him until her breasts were pressed against his chest. Then he flipped her neatly onto her back and paused, touching his forehead to hers.

He said, "There are so many things we haven't talked about yet."

She groaned, reaching for him, but he held her down with no trouble at all, both of her wrists in his one hand.

"I've got things to say to you," he whispered. "I don't think you'll mind hearing them."

John wanted to talk, and really, Angie tried to tell herself, wasn't that what they needed to do? This was serious business, after all, he was walking away from another woman, another kind of life, and why? To what end? What did he want from her, really, and what could she expect from him?

Important questions, crucial questions, for tomorrow or the day after, for anytime but now. As much as she loved John's voice, right now she loved his mouth more. She arched up to kiss him, rich and deep and full, a kiss that flowered in the belly and sent little shocks back up her spine, flowing out and out. He made a humming sound. How had she forgotten that sound of his, that click in the back of his throat? Angie rubbed herself against him, spread herself open beneath him, beckoned. *Now now now.*

But John would have none of it; he held himself over her with his knees between her thighs, his shoulders wide as a raft, his arms and legs like oars, his chest pressed against her breasts. He held her effortlessly away from him, only his cock reaching toward her, Angie thought, biting back a burp of laughter, as if it meant to handle this on its own, with or without the rest of him.

He was whispering in her ear. *Wait,* and *Christ, Angie, please.*

She cupped his face in her hands and pressed small nipping kisses on his mouth. "What?" As if she didn't know. As if she couldn't see it, the things he was wanting to say and hear. They had been here before, the two of them, on the verge of words.

"Tell me."

She said, "Of course I love you. I always have, you idiot. You dope. From day one. Didn't you know?"

His closed his eyes, nodded. Sweat glistened on his face and throat and shoulders, his beautiful shoulders. "Good," he said, and claimed her, finally, absolutely. "Good."

· FOURTEEN ·

You must understand how much things have changed in Ogilvie if you truly want to tell Miss Zula's story. For example, when she was coming up in the forties and fifties, political, social, and racial distinctions were sacrosanct. At the First Baptist Church (and the First Baptist congregation was far more powerful and bigger than the Episcopalians) Pastor Tate was a great adherent of Leviticus ("Both thy bondmen and thy bondmaids shall be of the heathen that are round about you. . . . And ye shall take them as an inheritance for your children after you, to inherit them for a possession; they shall be your bondmen for ever."). For Pastor Tate and his parishioners, the idea of equal rights for blacks was truly nonsensical and offensive, and one more thing: he would be outraged if he knew about the way the Catholic congregation has grown and prospered in Ogilvie. I know this, because he was my grandfather and he turned his back on my father because he came back from WWII with an Italian Catholic wife.

Your name: Dab Tate. I'm a partner in the same physicians' group as Marilee Bragg.

A program," Tony said, running a thumb along his jaw. "There is a full-color, printed program for Ogilvie's Fourth of July Jubilee." He was holding it at arm's distance, squinting to read down columns printed in blue and red on white. "Fifty people have been working on this for six months," he informed Angie and Rivera, the unlit cigarette in the corner of his mouth jiggling. "Starts at eight with a five-K run/walk that snakes all over town and campus, ends up—oh, this is good—at the Kiwanis Pancake Breakfast. They've got a tent in the park. I could use some pancakes, should we start there?" Without waiting for an answer he flipped the page and kept reading. "Sack races, tug-of-war, water-balloon toss, logrolling on the river, a band concert, a gospel choir, an orator's corner, a softball game, oh, a chili cook-off and"—he glanced at his watch—"there's a pig roast. The barbecue pits have been going for two hours already."

"We get the idea," Rivera said. She handed Angie a camera lens.

"But wait, I haven't got to the best part," Tony said. "A parade before the auction. And you're in it."

Angie looked up from the open camera bags. "Come again?"

"Everybody with a basket for the supper auction walks in the parade. To show off the goods first, I guess, before the bidding starts." He grinned at them. "I'm almost sorry I don't have a basket myself."

"Work first," Angie said. She meant to sound firm, but found that she had lost that knack. Which went along quite nicely with the fact that the bones in her legs, once very reliable, were now partially jelly; John's doing. With a jerk of the head she went back to counting film canisters and battery packs.

Both Rivera and Tony would be taping, Rivera staying close by Miss Zula and Miss Maddie, Tony roaming. They had started the day with the usual argument about who got which digital video camera. Angie herself was loaded down with two still cameras, one digital, one 35mm, a small voice recorder, multiple notebooks, a phone, a beeper, and a walkie-talkie that would put her in touch with Rivera or Tony if she needed them.

The idea of a day running around in the July heat should have had her dragging with exhaustion, but in spite of the fact that she had had very little sleep—or maybe because of that—she flushed with adrenaline, fired up, ready to go. Work could do that for her when it was going well; good sex had the same effect. No wonder she was flying.

Rivera poked her in the ribs. "Wake up, Mary Poppins, we've got company."

Markus Holmes was standing at the screen door, looking eager and embarrassed all at once.

Tony said, "I told Markus we could pay him for helping out with the gear, and if that works out, we've got the assistant position still open, right?"

"Sure," Angie said. "Good idea."

Tony put his palm on the crown of her head and wobbled it. Then he leaned in and whispered, "It's okay to be happy, you know."

Angie was suddenly very aware of how fortunate she was in her friends. If she asked for opinions she'd get them, unvarnished, but right now they were both studiously looking the other way, which was exactly what she needed. Sooner or later she'd want their thoughts on this situation she'd gotten herself into, but not now. Not today. Today they had to concentrate on work.

Just a few days ago Memorial Park had seemed huge, but at nine o'clock in the morning it was obvious that just about every inch of it would be put to use for this Jubilee. Tents had sprung up like mushrooms, all of them with official-looking banners in bright colors.

"Whole families just about move in for the duration," Markus told them. "They won't break camp until the fireworks are done, close to midnight."

In New Jersey, a day at the park or down the shore meant a blanket, sunscreen, some sandwiches, beer and soda, and money for ice cream. Angie found the scene in front of her hardly credible, a carnival sprung out of the mist, *State Fair* meets *Brigadoon*. She was actually relieved to see a half dozen small enclaves of teenagers who were making it their business to stand out. Markus talked to many of them in passing, including one group of Goths who must certainly die of heat prostration before the day was out.

Angie caught sight of a kid at least six and a half feet tall with Day-Glo yellow hair; Alice Cooper eye makeup; studs in his nose, lip, ears, and eyebrows; and a black T-shirt with stark white lettering: I'm the Shit That Happens.

Markus took his job seriously, pointing out details that were often funny, whether he meant them to be or not. "The Parkhams have had that spot for fifty years or more," he said. "Same with the Ogilvies, over there, and the Roses and the Walkers. Over there by the band shell, that's Deacon Beasley and his whole clan. The Assembly of God families all set up closer to the river and Four Square Gospel way over there. The Four Square ladies and the Assembly of God ladies don't see eye to eye. There was a falling-out over tomato chutney back in the seventies, and they haven't got along since."

A man in an Uncle Sam costume walked by on stilts, his cotton beard fluttering in the breeze. A line of children ran along behind him like the tail on a kite. There were strolling vendors selling balloons and lemonade and miniature flags.

"Wait," Tony said. "Is that a couch?"

Markus grinned. "Folks are going to be here all day, they want it comfortable." That seemed an understatement to Angie, looking over a sea of sun umbrellas. One family had set up what looked like the pavilion of an Arabian prince under a striped awning.

"The Lawsons," said Markus. "That's Weezie Lawson there, I expect you've met her."

"Vice president of the Junior League," Rivera said.

"At the very least," said Markus. "What the Ogilvies don't own, the Lawsons do. You saw Weezie's oldest boy, Chris, back there." He jerked his chin back in the direction of the teenagers.

Tony laughed. "'I'm the Shit That Happens' is a Lawson. I like it."

Markus led them toward an open area under a canopy of live oaks. Louie came shooting out from under a table, his whole rear end wagging frantically, to launch himself at Markus. The boy caught him neatly and tucked the dog under his arm like a rolled newspaper.

"We set up for you right next to the Braggs. I hope that's okay."

"Perfect," Angie said, and put her bag on a picnic table topped with a huge sun umbrella and spread with a bright yellow-and-pink tablecloth. There was a pitcher of lemonade and one of sweet tea, a number of covered dishes, and a tub of ice. There were also four reclining lawn chairs with pillows, a paper fan sitting on each of them. "You didn't have to do all this," Angie said.

"But we're glad you did," Rivera added, scooping ice into her hand and holding the cubes to her neck. "We need a home base. We're not paying him enough, Angie."

"You're not paying me anything at all," Markus said.

"See?" said Rivera.

Markus looked uncomfortable at the mention of money. "It was all Miss Zula and Miss Maddie who arranged all this," he said. "You know Miss Maddie has been on the Jubilee committee for forty years? Folks will tell you it was the preachers from all the different churches who were behind the push to integrate the Jubilee—this was back in the sixties—but it was Miss Maddie pushing the preachers."

Tony looked up from his viewfinder. "Where are the Braggs, anyway?"

"Over at the Kiwanis tent," said Markus. "I'm supposed to take you over there."

"Right," said Tony. "Lead on to the pancakes."

By ten o'clock Angie needed a break, so she headed back to their base under the oaks, where she found Miss Zula and Miss Maddie sitting comfortably in the shade, surrounded by some fifty of their closest relatives. Angie had never seen the three nephews in anything but suits, but today they were wearing Hawaiian shirts and Bermuda shorts and baseball caps. There was a sleeping toddler sprawled across Dr. Bragg's lap—which one of the dozens of younger Braggs, Angie could not say—and a hound of some kind sitting at his feet, panting madly. She shot a half dozen frames before the doctor realized she was there, and then went to the table where Rivera was pouring her a tumbler of sweet tea.

Rivera squinted up at Angie and inclined her head toward the old women, who were admiring a baby with a great ruffle of chins and dimpled knees.

"It's like a court session," Rivera told Angie. "Everybody comes to pay their respects. Half the board of regents has been by already, and every preacher from every church."

Angie took a long swallow, closed her eyes in appreciation, and took another. Her tank top was already soaked through with perspiration; her hair, bundled up under her sun visor, was just as wet at the scalp.

"You getting anything?"

Angie said, "Lots of good sound bites, seven interviews set up for next week, twice that many invitations to supper, and a couple dozen questions about the contents of my picnic basket."

There were other numbers she could have recited for Rivera, but kept to herself. She had seen John five times, four times from a good distance away; once when Connie and Pearl had called her over to give her a glass of lemonade so cold it made her teeth ache. In that one meeting he had met her gaze three times. She had managed to keep her voice even and steady, and hoped that the flush that crawled up over her neck would be attributed to the heat, by the Rose girls, at least.

All morning she had been stalking him with her camera, though she did her best not to make it obvious. She caught him as he came over the finish line, at the pancake breakfast, in conversation with children and his brother and a dozen other people, leaning down to hand Miss Junie a plate, throwing a ball, laughing. At one point she went to the top of the slide in the playground with her camera, taking an occasional shot of the ring of disgruntled kids' faces below her, but mostly looking for John.

She was acting like a horny sixteen-year-old, but couldn't stop herself from shooting a few pictures of him stretched out on a lawn chair in a row set up, it seemed, specifically for the Rose sons-in-law, minus Tab, who had had bypass surgery two days earlier.

"Where to now?" Rivera asked.

"Some church ladies are judging jams and preserves in the food tent, and then there's the tug-o'-war." Angie took an ice cube and rubbed it on her throat. "Apparently the Lawsons and the Ogilvies will be going head to head. Any sign of Tony?"

Rivera shrugged. "I'd check down by the river. He's staying away from Harriet, at least." Her gaze flicked to Angie's right. "Heads up," she said. "Patty-Cake."

Angie took a deep breath and pasted on a smile before she turned. Patty-Cake was leaning over Miss Maddie, teeth flashing, eyes rounded.

"Cue the *Jaws* music," Rivera said, and started filming.

"Miss Zula," Patty-Cake was saying, "maybe you can tell me what our Caroline was thinking, running off right before her wedding." She crossed her hands on her chest. "Makes no sense to me, no matter what angle I look at it."

"Is that so?" Under the broad brim of a straw hat Miss Zula's eyes seemed especially dark and very large. "Best you leave such complicated problems to the folks who aren't so easily confused." There was nothing even remotely friendly about her smile, something that seemed, finally, to register with Patty-Cake. She bit her lip and looked to Miss Maddie for help, but got only a vaguely polite, distant look from that normally friendly face.

"Um," Patty-Cake said. "Well, all righty, then." She half turned, caught sight of Angie, and her expression shifted again, from embarrassment to annoyance.

"Busy today, I see." Her mouth twitched convulsively.

"Yeah," Angie said. "It's a good opportunity."

With a sticky-sweet smile Patty-Cake said, "You take care now, things can get a little rough around here once the games start."

"Is that so?" Angie could feel Rivera hovering nearby, and hear the low hum of the camera. She counted to three and found that she couldn't keep quiet. "And here I thought you were already playing."

Before she turned away she caught Miss Maddie's expression, bright and amused and not at all displeased, and Miss Zula's more thoughtful one.

Angie saw Harriet Darling for the first time that morning in the food tent. There was a red ribbon attached to the placard on the table that introduced Mrs. Harriet Rose Darling's brandy peaches.

"Those judges," she told Angie, "have got no imagination."

It was hot in the tent and not especially interesting, but Harriet looked so downtrodden that Angie couldn't bring herself to rush out. She asked about Tab.

"Surgery went just fine," Harriet told her. "He's cranky as that wet hen folks are always talking about, making trouble for the nurses, generally being himself. Mama's over there now, playing five-card stud with him. Which is a good thing, because all these rumors flying around would give her a heart attack of her own."

She gave Angie a hard look. "You heard the nonsense people are talking?"

"Patty-Cake filled me in," Angie said, looking longingly toward the exit.

Harriet snorted. "I'll bet she did. She's the worst offender. Blood or no blood, I'm going to have to clear the air with Patty-Cake." She frowned elaborately. "If people ask you, just say Caroline will be home tomorrow or the day after, and the wedding will come off perfect."

The smart thing to do was to agree and walk away, but Angie wasn't feeling particularly smart, and so she said what was on her mind.

"I'm surprised you're so eager to see your little sister married," Angie said. "Seeing how your own situation has gone bad."

Harriet's mouth fell open in surprise and then snapped shut. "Well, I don't think you can compare the two, not at all." She lowered her voice and leaned toward Angie to whisper. Her breath was ripe with brandy and mint.

"I never should have married Tab, but I was desperate. It was that, or break Mama's heart."

Angie took a deep breath and then the words came out, because they must. "But, Harriet, how do you know Caroline isn't feeling exactly the same way?"

Harriet blew out a surprised breath that made her hair flutter around her face. "What would make you say such a thing?"

Angie shrugged. "She's not here, is she?" And very calmly she hoisted her pack over one shoulder and walked away. There was sweat running down her neck and back that had nothing to do with the heat, and she shivered.

Once Angie had allowed herself to get involved in a discussion about Caroline the topic followed her around for the rest of the day.

"Now, everybody knows the Roses are the finest, most upstanding folks you'll find anywhere," Miss Annie told Angie. The librarian pressed a plump hand over her heart. "But you Catholics got your own ways of going about things. Not that there's anything *wrong* with that, understand. But could you please explain to me what this retreat business really means?"

At lunch Angie found that she wasn't the only one getting questions. The high school football coach had cornered Rivera, wanting to know if Caroline's being sent off to a retreat was some kind of penalty phase.

Miss Maddie said, "What did you tell him, Rivera?"

"That I was raised by a Jew and a Quaker," Rivera said. "And I sent him to ask Father Bruce. Actually, I'm curious what kind of answer he'll get."

"They could ask one of us directly," Markus said. He had barbecue sauce on his chin and he was flushed with heat and irritation. "But that would take all the fun out of the gossip."

Miss Zula said, "Son, if you can't learn to ignore the talk, you'll have to move away from here as soon as you're old enough. It's the price of admission."

Markus tossed a bit of gristle to Louie, who caught it with a neat jerk of his head. "It's a high price."

"It is," Miss Zula said. "You'll have to figure out for yourself if it's too high, because there's no changing the way things work in a town like this."

Tony caught Angie's eye in a look she knew very well. Hours of film shot, and still they missed such crucial moments. In Miss Zula's case, they seemed to miss more than usual, because—Angie had figured this out quite quickly—she rarely talked when they were actually filming, unless she was asked a direct question. The one exception had been the afternoon they spent in Savannah.

She said, "Miss Zula, I thought maybe Miss Anabel would come down for the Jubilee?"

Miss Zula looked at her, her gaze even and sharp and calculating. Whatever she was looking for she didn't find, because something softened in her face. She said, "Anabel doesn't ever come to Ogilvie, for the same reason that Markus might someday find he has to move away."

Angie was finishing up her tenth roll of film when the heat and lack of sleep caught up with her. The Stillwaters were just about to pull the Prestons over the line in front of a hugely appreciative crowd when the world began to sway in such an alarming way that she sat down, abruptly, just where she was. The forest of legs around her began to revolve like a carousel.

She was concentrating very hard on a pair of coffee-colored knobby knees below polka-dot shorts when a familiar face appeared beside her looking concerned.

"Come on," said Rob, grasping her by the elbow to help her up. "Let's get you out of this crowd, Angeline. Give me that camera bag before you drop it."

"But I've got work to do," Angie said.

"Later." Rob grinned down at her. "Right now you need some shade and a lot of water."

She would have protested if her head hadn't been spinning; as it was, Angie let herself be propelled toward an open space, where Kai was standing with her arm raised, like a woman hailing a cab on Fifth Avenue. A golf cart came to a lurching stop right in front of her. There was a red cross painted on the side and a very thin man in medical whites at the wheel. His arms and face were burned a deep reddish brown and covered with a mat of curly blond hair, and above a shaggy beard bleached white by the sun his eyes looked almost colorless.

"Too hot for a Yankee," he said, sizing up Angie quickly. "Help her in, Rob, and I'll take her to the first-aid tent."

Angie said, "I'm Italian. I can stand the heat."

"We'll take her to our place if you can swing by there," Rob said, ignoring her. Kai was climbing into the rear seat and gesturing for Angie to follow her, and the world started to wobble again. She climbed in, and the cart took off with a jerk.

"Italians are a Mediterranean people," Angie announced. "And I'm southern Italian on both sides. A hundred percent." Her stomach lurched up into her throat and she burped.

"Yankees," said the paramedic to Rob.

"Neapolitan on my father's side," Angie said. "Calabrese on my mother's."

Kai handed Angie a bottle of water. "Small sips," she said. "Slowly."

Angie gave in, mostly because her muscles didn't seem willing to obey her beyond the energy it took to accept the water bottle. She sipped as the cart zipped through the park and wound around crowds. In the distance she saw Tony filming what looked like Miss Zula playing a game of horseshoes with a dozen other elderly women.

"I should . . ." she began, and Kai interrupted her. "We'll come back and tell them."

"Okay, then," said Angie meekly, and folded her hands in her lap. She wondered briefly what the paramedic would say if she should vomit all over his neatly kept golf cart, and then realized, looking at the back of his head as he talked to Rob, that the round bald spot at the crown of his head framed a bright red tattoo, two scrolling words: Jesus Saves.

The golf cart came to a stop at the path that led to Rob and Kai's garden gate. Angie got up to step out, bent over at the waist, and let her lunch go in a rush.

"Oh, yeah," said Rob lightly. "Nothing wrong with you."

"The heat doesn't bother me," Angie said. "I'm Italian." And she leaned over again to spatter the rest of the seat.

"Yankees," said Jesus Saves. "Y'all need to stay out of politics and the sun, too."

Angie woke up in a wide bed in an otherwise empty room, unsure of much at all except that she was thirsty. She vaguely remembered Kai helping her strip down and get into the shower. She had put her underwear back on at some point. Angie stared at the ceiling fan for a while, hypnotized by the gentle whoop, whoop, whoop, letting questions drift through her mind without trying to sort out answers. She had no idea how long she had been here, what time it might be, how much of the Jubilee she had missed, whether Rivera and Tony were looking for her or coping fine without her, or—and this question seemed the most important of all—why she should ever want to move from such a cool, comfortable, quiet spot.

Finally she raised her head and saw that there was a note on the sheet near her left hand, the writing painfully neat: *Your clothes are hanging in the bathroom. I've left fresh towels if you want to take another shower. Your camera bag and telephone are beside you on the table. We have gone back to the Jubilee. If you wake before we come back, drink water. Kai.*

There was a carafe of water with shards of ice and lemon slices floating in it and a glass. The water was delicious. It ran in rivulets over Angie's chin and throat and she shivered with pleasure, almost missing the fact that somebody was coming up the stairs. She pulled the sheet up to her chin as the bedroom door opened.

John stood there, looking sheepish.

All Angie's nerves began to fire at once. "Harvey. How nice of you to drop by." She was grinning like an idiot, but she couldn't help it. And she didn't need to, either, because he was grinning, too.

He leaned against the door frame and crossed his arms. "I don't suppose you're ever going to give up on this Harvey thing, are you."

"Probably not."

"Even though we are agreed that Harvey Carson was in no way based on me."

"Who knows why one nickname sticks and another doesn't?" Angie grinned at him. "A more important question: Who knows you're here?"

"Rob told me what happened. I came by to check on you, see if you need anything."

Angie slung her arms around her upraised knees and considered. "I just didn't get enough sleep last night."

He made a sound deep in his throat. "I hope that's not a complaint."

"It's a compliment, and you know it."

He reached behind himself to close the door. "Rob said you fainted."

"Actually, the truth is much less romantic. I threw up. But I distinctly remember brushing my teeth, if that's what's keeping you all the way over there."

He came over to sit on the edge of the bed. "Heatstroke?"

Angie threw back the sheet with a flick of her wrist. "Yes, please."

He caught her head in one hand and pulled her to him. It was a light, curious kiss that involved mouths alone, and it wasn't nearly enough. Amazing what a nap could do for a person's energy.

"Hey," she said. "I missed you."

"I've been grinning like an idiot all day." He kissed the corner of her mouth, her jaw, the soft spot behind her ear. "When Rob told me you were here—" He stopped and kissed her again.

What she wanted to do was pull him into bed, but Angie forced herself to break the kiss. "You know, I have to get back to work."

He mumbled something against her neck.

"And you have to be more careful, John. I wouldn't be surprised if Patty-Cake put a tail on you."

"It's your tail I'm concerned with just now," John said, a finger running over her shoulder to catch the bra strap and slide it down. In spite of the cool air he was flushed, his blue eyes glassy and heavy-lidded, the muscles in his jaw clenching like a roll of nickels.

"Wait," Angie said. "Wait."

"We've wasted enough time," John said. "No more waiting."

And he was right. For years Angie had put the memory of him like this away from her, and now here he was again, John Grant, wanting her as much as she wanted him, and what idiots they had been. She wondered at the strangeness and rightness of it, and then she put her hands on his cheeks and smiled against his mouth.

"We'll have to be quick."

He took her down, rough and sweet. "Not a chance in hell."

Some time later Angie said, "Do you think anybody saw you heading over this way?"

They were pressed together still, John's face against her neck, arms and legs intertwined, comfortably messy, warm, nerves still jumping. If she looked in the mirror Angie knew she would see that her skin was mottled from her chest to her hairline, something that would take a good hour to go away. Maybe she could blame it on heatstroke.

She'd have to avoid Rivera for a while, at least. And Tony, too.

"I'm too tired to worry about that just now," he was saying. "You wear me out." And then jumped when she pinched him. They wrestled for a moment and then she gave in, as she'd always meant to, when he got hold of her. She was trying not to think about time or work and was almost there when she heard someone downstairs.

John heard it too. He went very still and then all at once he moved, rolling off her and crossing the room in three long strides to turn the lock on the door. He looked so good standing there naked that Angie forgot to be worried for all of three seconds.

"Hello? Angie?" The voice on the other side of the door was not unfamiliar to her. "It's Win Walker."

"Win? What are you doing here?"

"The dispatch people sent me over here to check on you. I'm the paramedic on duty."

Angie gulped down a giggle while John began to pick up his clothes.

"That's nice of you. Tell them I'm fine, would you?"

"I'd be happy to. But first I have to check your blood pressure and pulse."

John began to tiptoe toward the bathroom while Angie fumbled for her underwear.

"Angie? You okay?"

"Just a minute, I'll be right with you." She wished she had paid more attention to her clothes this morning, but then maybe a hot-pink bra held up by two safety pins and a pair of lime green jockey shorts decorated with poodles would distract Win Walker. Maybe he wouldn't notice that the room smelled like sweaty sex.

She ran to the windows and opened them as far as they would go, and then she wrapped the top sheet around herself. Through all of this a sermon came droning from the other side of the door.

"Heatstroke is serious business, you know—"

"Is that so?"

"Folks die of heat prostration all the time. Down in these parts we lose a

Yankee every year or so because y'all can't remember to put on a hat when you go out in the summer sun."

Angie flipped the lock and walked backward to sit on the bed.

"Come in," she said, and put on her biggest, brightest smile.

He stood there frowning. "You're not dressed."

Angie glanced down at herself. "I'm more covered up in this than I would be in shorts and a T-shirt. I need to get back to work, can we get this over with?"

He pulled a blood-pressure cuff and stethoscope out of a bag. "Have you fainted again?"

"I didn't faint before," Angie said. "I threw up."

"You fainted," he corrected her. "That's what Walker wrote on his duty sheet. He had to carry you into the house."

"I don't remember that," Angie said, trying not to laugh. "I hope he was a gentleman."

Win's whole lower face twitched. "Stick your arm out here," he said. "And stop trying to distract me."

Angie had the sense that the best way to get rid of Win Walker was to cooperate, so she bowed her head in what she hoped looked like contrition and did as he asked. She put out her arm for the blood-pressure cuff, and got a look at his watch. It was just before five, and that meant she had been gone from the Jubilee for more than three hours. In an hour she had to be changed and ready for the parade.

Win was frowning at the dial on the blood-pressure cuff. "You been getting enough sleep?"

She tried not to tense, and failed. She thought of saying, *I got no sleep at all last night because I was otherwise occupied with John Grant. In fact, that salty smell you're trying to ignore is more of John, who is hiding in that very bathroom. And do tell your aunt Patty-Cake I said hey.*

"Normally, yeah."

"Your blood pressure usually on the low side?"

"So I'm told."

"Okay." He sat back on his heels. "You're free to get up and go as long as you stay hydrated and out of the sun. Now I need to wash my hands and I'll be on my way."

Shit.

Angie said, "Um, okay, but can I go first? I really have to. I'll just be a minute, I promise, if that's okay." And she lurched across the room with the sheet wrapped around her. At the door she turned to smile at him.

"Thank you," she said, reaching for the magic words that would take the suspicious look off his face. "It's . . . it's a feminine hygiene issue, you understand." Then she opened the door and stumbled in, slamming the door behind herself. She turned, breathing heavily.

John stood at the far end of the small room between the shower stall—clear glass, no curtain—and a window, his face red with suppressed laughter. This in spite of the fact that there was no place to hide, and Patty-Cake Walker's nephew was on the other side of the only door.

Angie turned on the water taps in the sink and then went over to him. "Either you're willing to come out to Win Walker right now and admit you're cheating on your fiancée, or you're going out that window," she whispered.

"I think Win's sweet on you," John said. "He wants your soul for Jesus but he'll keep the rest of you for himself."

"Don't be an idiot," Angie said, trying not to giggle.

John grabbed her and kissed her, hard. "I'll call you later." And then he opened the window, chinned himself up and through it feetfirst, and disappeared. Angie watched him shimmy down the drainpipe and run off through the shrubbery, long and lean, the muscles in his legs working, which could not be good for her pulse or blood pressure but was a joy in every other way.

Then she used the bathroom—because that had been no lie—washed her hands and face, retrieved her clothes from the hook on the back of the door, and dressed as quickly as she could. All the while she was lecturing herself on the importance of keeping a straight face, making the right impression, and disabusing Win Walker of his suspicions.

With all the dignity she could muster Angie opened the door and found him still waiting, his expression closed and cold as he passed her on his way to wash his hands. Angie was trying to make sense of that as she went over to the bedside table to get her things, where she stopped dead. Dizzy again, but this time it had nothing to do with the Georgia sun.

Wrapping the top sheet around herself had seemed such a good idea at the time, given the state of her underwear. Now she saw—as Win had surely seen—a perfectly round wet spot in the very middle of the bottom sheet. Just to make things absolutely clear, a wilted, glossily damp, bright orange condom glistened against the cobalt blue of the sheet. A study in color contrasts, and the wages of sin.

John found himself laughing all the way back to the Jubilee. In spite of the close call, in spite of the seriousness of the situation, he was giggling like a girl, something that would have to stop.

He covered his mouth with his hand and bit his tongue. With some effort he called up images of Miss Junie, Miss Zula, Patty-Cake Walker. Caroline. That worked.

The thing was, he told himself, he had needed a rest. Even Miss Junie had told him to go take a nap. So he had gone to his brother's spare bedroom. What could be more sensible that that? He sure felt a lot better than he had an hour ago, in spite of the fact that he had done a 5K run this morning after spending the night with Angie.

It was harder than he had imagined, having to field questions all day. People he barely knew stopped him, wanting to know where his pretty fiancée had got to, and how Caroline was holding up under the pressure, and wasn't it just a bear, getting ready for a big wedding, and did he know how lucky he was to be walking off with the fairest blossom that Old Roses had to offer? This last bit of overextended imagery came from Missy Stillwater, whose sister Midge—he remembered with a combination of embarrassment and glee—had spent some time in the backseat of his car the summer he turned seventeen. John was very aware that every single person who came to talk to him about Caroline was looking for him to trip up and contradict the story that the Rose sisters were telling.

And still the worst part of the day was that he had to ignore Angie, which felt wrong in every possible way.

So he had fixed that. When Rob had told him that Angie was taking a few hours off in a quiet, private bedroom not ten minutes away, it had seemed the only thing to do.

Now Miss Junie would be waiting for him to escort her to the parade, and there would be more questions, of that he could be sure. He didn't want to make Miss Junie wait, and still somehow he found it hard to walk any faster.

Like most of the matrons of her age and standing, Miss Junie had been watching the Jubilee parade from the corner of Main and the Parkway for the last thirty years. It was a good spot, just across from the university, made better by the fact that the Jubilee committee went so far as to build a raised platform. Every year Miss Junie picked one of her sons-in-law to accompany her there and get her settled. This year Miss Zula had decided to join her, so John, who had been given the honor, had both of them to contend with, chairs to adjust and readjust, and a sun umbrella to position.

At least it took his mind off the fact that Win Walker and Walker Winfield were leaning up against the ambulance parked down the street, arms crossed and heads bowed close together as they talked. He had got away from Rob's without being seen, but still it gave him a bad feeling to see the two cousins in deep conversation.

When they first heard the high school band approaching, the ladies dismissed him and John loped across the street to stand with Rob and Kai.

"How's Angie?" Rob shouted at him, and John had to be satisfied with giving his brother a dirty look. It did no good to lecture Rob, so he turned his attention to the floats, elaborate platforms heaped with bunting and flags and flowers in primary colors. Ogilvie was a socially active place and every club, league, and association had a float: the Junior League, the Garden Club, the Knights of Columbus and the Holy Name Society, the Veterans of Foreign Wars, the Rifle Club. Every one of Ogilvie's churches had some kind of float, some more than one. The First Baptist gospel choir went by in scarlet robes with golden tassels around their necks, followed by a whole battalion of Confederate reenactors in full uniform. John was just starting to feel more cheerful when the Basket Girls' float appeared.

Miss Maddie sat on an elevated chair in the middle, her gloved hands folded decorously on the basket in her lap. There was a great blue ribbon rosette on its handle, which meant that last year her basket had brought in the most money toward this year's Jubilee. The rest of the Basket Girls walked alongside the float, all of them dressed to the teeth. Rivera was in a red polka-dot dress with a tiny cinched waist that made her look like a very tall and exotic Donna Reed, and even Angie, John saw, had been talked into dressing up.

He knew with absolute certainly that the sundress she was wearing—butter yellow with a scattering of purple flowers—had been borrowed from somebody else and pressed on her by Miss Maddie. He couldn't think of another person in the world who could have talked her into that dress, which made him think of talking her out of it, which was not a good thing to be thinking about just now.

Not that he could look away from Angie in a dress. She pulled at the low-cut bodice, fiddled with the wide brim of the straw hat. For once her hair was neither pulled back in a ponytail or hidden under a scarf, and the breeze sent the curls dancing around her flushed face.

"Wow," said Rob.

"Very sexy," said Kai.

Together they turned to watch the Basket Girl float disappear down the street toward the park. At the next corner Patty-Cake Walker was watching John, her expression all fire and brimstone.

Ridley Smith was a nondescript forty-year-old mortician who was also Ogilvie's mayor. The only thing southern about him, outwardly at least, was his voice, which was deep and melodious.

"Bless Ridley's soul, he's as boring as vanilla pudding without the bananas," said Marilee Bragg when Rivera asked about the mayor. As Basket Girls, they were sitting together on the stage, the baskets lined up in front of them. They were waiting for the Shriners to stop fussing with cables and the microphone so that the auction could start. Angie thought again how odd it was that none of the three black women who were participating were uncomfortable with this, and made a note to herself to ask the Bragg girls about it when she had them alone.

Marilee's sister Anthea was saying, "It's true. It gives me gooseflesh just to listen to the man talk."

Miss Maddie giggled. She said, "Ridley's talents were being wasted at his daddy's funeral home. That MBA don't mean much to the dead, but he balanced the town's budget straightaway."

"Truth is," said Anthea Bragg, "folks were tired of the Ogilvies running everything all the time." She said this in a whisper, as Nan Ogilvie was sitting on her other side.

"He's a good auctioneer," said Miss Maddie. "He's got the patter."

"Uh-huh," said Anthea. "Got a tongue hung in the middle so it can flap at both ends."

"Lucky Mrs. Mayor," said Rivera, and Angie elbowed her.

Miss Maddie said, "Angeline, dear, stop fidgeting. You look lovely. Very ladylike. Wouldn't your mama be proud?"

"Her mama would fall over flat," said Rivera.

"I feel like ten pounds of potatoes in a five-pound bag," Angie said.

"Don't be silly," Miss Maddie said. "You've got a lovely figure."

"That dress looks better on you than it ever did on Anthea," said Marilee, and: "Ouch. Leave off, sister, you know it's true."

"The whole town must be here," said Rivera, rising up from her seat to look over the crowd. "Wasn't Shirley Jackson from the South? I keep thinking about 'The Lottery.'"

Nan Ogilvie turned to Rivera, her perfectly made-up face glowing beneath the brim of a hat the size of a small car. "It's an auction, dear, not a lottery."

"Nan, she's talking about a short story," said one of the Stillwaters. She gave Angie a quick apologetic smile.

"Oh," said Nan Ogilvie, spreading her skirt around herself more artfully. And: "I'm far too busy to bother with fiction."

Miss Maddie said, "Hush now, he's about to get started. Girls, sit up straight, and smile."

Here goes," said Rob. "I bet Wyeth Horton twenty bucks that Ridley could shave fifteen seconds off Miss Maddie's time."

"I hope you got odds," said Kai. "The volunteer firefighters have been raising money for months."

Ridley held up Miss Maddie's basket and started the bidding. The volunteer fire department went head to head with the college Faculty Club and the combined resources of the Mount Olive AME church. An individual had no chance at all, unless he was willing to put a second mortgage on his house.

"Sold!" Ridley Smith slammed the gavel down less than thirty seconds after the first bid had been shouted out. "To the deacons of the Mount Olive African Methodist Episcopal Church, two thousand forty-one dollars and fifty cents. Miss Maddie?"

There were hoots and whistles of appreciation as Miss Maddie walked off, head held high, on the arm of her nephew Martin.

"Granny Junie sent me to say you should go ahead and bid, if you care to."

John turned to find Markus Holmes standing behind him.

"She thought maybe you'd feel like you couldn't bid because Caroline isn't here. She said you should go ahead, if you want."

"I wasn't planning on bidding," John said.

"Because," Markus said, as if John hadn't replied at all, "you could go in with me and Tony." He pointed to Tony Russo, who was standing on a chair with a video camera pressed to his face. "We're going to bid on Rivera's basket. Unless you were going to bid on Angie's?"

John met his brother's eye over Markus's head. "Sure," he said. "I'll go in with you on Rivera's basket. Put me down for fifty dollars."

"It'll take more than that," Markus said. "How about a hundred? It's for a good cause."

"It's for fireworks and watermelons," said John. "But okay, count me in."

Unless I miss my guess," the mayor was saying in a voice that reverberated through the microphone, "I smell somebody's mama's secret recipe for macaroni and Vienna sausage casserole. Let's see what else we got." He held up the sheet of paper that listed the contents of each of the baskets.

"Well, now, look at this. I can't remember the last time I had Coca-Cola cake. I believe I'll have to start the bidding at fifty dollars."

"I hope Tony is getting this," Rivera said to Angie when Marylou Scott went off with Ogilvie's high school football team. The boys had come up with close to three hundred dollars among them so they could each claim a spoonful of casserole, a chicken wing, and a few crumbs of cake. Now only two baskets remained on the table, but it seemed to Angie that the crowd was significantly bigger than it had been.

"I feel like the kid who gets picked last for kickball," Angie said. There was a warm wind but she was wishing for a shawl or a sweater or a blanket she could hide under. She alternated between wondering where John was in the crowd and hoping he had stayed away. She needed to tell him about Win Walker and the condom debacle, but there would be no chance to do that for the next few hours.

"I'm glad they do the guest baskets last," Rivera said. "I wouldn't want to miss any of this."

Angie said, "Did you see Little Billy Munro?" She pointed with her chin. "The entire population of the Liars' Bench is over there giving you the eye, and they haven't bid on a basket yet. Look," she said, "you're up."

The mayor was holding up Rivera's basket in one hand while he peered at the list in the other. "Folks—"

"One hundred dollars!" The decidedly female voice came from the back of the crowd.

"Oh, shit," said Rivera, sliding down in her chair. "Weepy Meg."

Ridley Smith laughed, though he didn't look much amused. "I haven't even—"

"One hundred twenty!" Markus Holmes called, his voice cracking.

"One thirty." Meg's voice boomed like a soprano foghorn. Angie wanted to get a look at the woman she had only heard about, but there were enough people craning their necks. She settled for sending a furtive glance in John's direction. He was talking to Kai, his head bent down solicitously. A flush started deep in Angie's belly, but luckily nobody was paying any attention to her just now.

"The Liars bid one hundred fifty!" called Little Billy.

"Wow, Angie." Rivera gave a nervous giggle. "I've got the Liars and the lesbian competing for my company at dinner."

"Supper," Angie muttered. "It's called supper in the evening."

The mayor was trying to impose some order on the bidding, and not having any luck at all.

"One fifty-five!"

"One hundred sixty!"

"Is that you, Meg?" The mayor squinted into the late-day sun. "Are you bidding for the ladies' auxiliary?"

"I'm bidding for myself," Meg called back. "You got a problem with that, bubba?"

Angie turned to hiss in Rivera's ear. "Weepy Meg is the mayor's sister?"

Rivera bit her lip. "Who knew?"

"One hundred sixty-five dollars!" Little Billy had worked his way to the stage and he held up a fistful of bills. "Cash money."

"Two hundred fifty dollars," Meg yelled.

"What a time to come out of the closet," Angie said.

Rivera slid slower on her seat. "I don't know whether to be flattered or pissed off."

"I'd go with flattered," said Angie. "There's lots of people here got pissed off covered already." But when she really looked, she didn't see as many thunderous expressions as she might have expected. She did see I'm the Shit That Happens and his friends, all of them looking uncharacteristically interested in the proceedings. Somebody else was making trouble for once, which might be an irritation or a relief; it was hard to tell.

"Maybe I could lend Markus some money," Rivera said, just as the gavel thwacked on the podium.

"Sold," said Ridley Smith. "To my little sister Meg, for three hundred fifteen dollars."

"Eat in plain sight," called Angie as Rivera walked off.

The only safe thing John could think to do was to leave before the bidding started on Angie's basket, and that with as little fanfare as possible. If he was gone and Angie was in plain sight, Patty-Cake Walker's suspicions could be put to rest for tonight, which would be a good thing for all parties.

He kissed Miss Junie's cheek and made excuses that were at least partially true: he was near dead on his feet, and he did have a big day ahead. On Thursday five different reunions would get started, and in the first flush of enthusiasm for his new job he had said yes to every invitation. It had seemed like a good idea at the time, a way to keep busy on the two days before the wedding and while making clear to the administration that he was willing to do his share of the work. Now he found it hard to think about giving a dinner talk on new directions in academia, but he would have to do just that, in about forty-eight hours.

Which would hopefully take his mind off both Angie and Caroline.

He saw Louanne Porter getting into her squad car as he came to the edge of the park and waved her down to get a ride home, glad to let her distract him for ten minutes with stories about things that had kept her busy: kids smoking weed out in the open, Charmaine Walker just drunk enough to think it would be a good idea to jump in the river topless, the theft of a half dozen pies from the food tent, and a night in jail for Peter Robeson, whose wife had been taken to the emergency room with a broken jaw and a black eye.

"The Jubilee isn't much fun for you," John said.

"More fun than it was for Georgia Robeson," said Louanne. "But she never learns. Tomorrow she'll get him out of jail and refuse to press charges, and about Labor Day we'll go through the whole thing again. I'll never understand women who go looking for exactly the wrong man to marry." She seemed to remember that John was about to get married himself and threw him an apologetic smile. "Caroline being one of the exceptions, of course."

"Of course," John said.

He got out near campus to walk the last block in the twilight, thinking about Caroline and the choices she had made. She would be coming home tomorrow or the day after, and they would have to sort it all out between them. He might say, *I went about this all wrong,* and *I couldn't be the husband that you deserve to have.* Which was only part of the truth, but she deserved all of it. If she wanted a play-by-play confession, he'd give that to her, too, because he might be stupid at times, but he couldn't be a coward about this. That would be unfair to everybody.

He'd take the blame, pay the bills, make the phone calls. The long list of wedding plans in reverse: cancel the caterers, the church, the flowers, the honeymoon, send back the presents. He'd be the one to tell people to stay home, the wedding was off.

John stopped just where he was, overcome by a jolt of guilt so great that his stomach cramped with it.

On the other side of all that was Angie, or the hope of her. There was a long list of potentially troublesome practical questions that had to do with logistics and jobs and where they would be spending their time. To all that, Angie had added another item, one he hadn't let himself think about.

They had been pinned together on the old couch on the Ivy House porch, the night breeze gentle on his sweaty skin, when she had put her forehead against his. "You're going to be mad, at some point," she had said, "when you realize what you've thrown away for me."

It had taken him by surprise, but it shouldn't have. Angie had a way of cutting to the bone, and he was smart enough to recognize the truth, even if he didn't know what to do about it.

John let himself into the house, cool and dim with the shades drawn against the afternoon sun. There was a scattering of half-filled moving boxes and packing paper, a pile of math books on the coffee table, and a note on the table next to the phone.

I have deleted all the phone messages that were not of importance, Kai had written. *Here are the rest: 1. Your car will not be ready until next Monday. 2. President Bray's assistant called to ask if you will have dinner with him and some of the alums on Thursday after your talk. 3. Lucy will arrive here on Friday morning by car.*

His mother, on top of everything else. John collapsed on the couch and concentrated on thinking of nothing at all. Not Caroline or Angie or work, and certainly not of his mother or Saturday, when he was supposed to be getting married.

All the things he wanted to stop thinking about followed him, as he half knew they would, and ran amok in his dreams. John dreamed of his mother driving toward Ogilvie in a huge old Pontiac convertible, her eyes hidden behind dark glasses and her hair and long neck wrapped in a silk scarf. In the dream he was in the backseat, and they were talking to each other on cell phones that beeped and buzzed and faded in and out.

He woke to the sound of fireworks, a long hiss followed by a muffled boom. Outside the sky would be filled with cascades of hot color, but the house—this house he loved so much and would live in for the rest of his life—was a safe place, cool and dark. John sat up, pressed the heel of a palm into an eye, and took stock: he was thirsty, and he smelled of barbecue smoke and sweat and Angie.

He thought of calling her. She could come over here, if they were careful.

She could spend the night with him in his own bed, and he would wake up to find her hair a tangle across the pillow. John glanced at his watch and cal-culated when it would be safe to try her cell phone. Time to take a shower and change.

On his way through the front hall he saw the FedEx envelope. Either he had stepped over it as he came in the door, or it had been delivered while he was asleep on the couch. For a long moment John stood looking down at the colorful cardboard rectangle, then he turned on the hall light and picked it up.

His name and address had been written by Caroline. Her handwriting was unmistakable, sharp and black and slanting backward. The only return address was a FedEx office outside Savannah, nowhere near the last place he had seen her. John took a deep breath and opened it.

> *Dear John,*
>
> *I left the retreat house yesterday afternoon shortly after you dropped me off, because I have some crucial things to think about and I can only do that in a more neutral setting. Please don't worry. I'll be back on Friday and we'll sort things out then, I promise.*
>
> *Love,*
> *Caroline*

John read the letter twice without moving from that spot, and then he sat down on the hall stairs, where he stared at his own hands for a good while. Finally he let out a hoarse croaking laugh.

Yesterday in the late afternoon Caroline had sat at a motel desk some-where and written this letter. She had never got the letter he had brought to the retreat house. He looked at the words on the page.

We'll sort things out then.

At least, he told himself, he could be not be accused of being dense; any reasonable person must admit that there was no useful information here at all beyond the simple fact that Caroline had gone off. It was the kind of let-ter a sister might write, or a close friend. A woman about to get married—a woman who was happy about the fact that she was about to get married—would hardly write such a letter.

John realized now that Caroline had been increasingly distant over the last month, vaguely ill at ease, almost, at times, untouchable. At first he had seen all that as pre-wedding jitters, symptoms of the stress that came from dealing with her sisters; then he had been too distracted by Angie, and he hadn't paid close enough attention.

"Christ, I'm an idiot." He said these words out loud in the empty house. Worse still, he was a clueless idiot, one with no answers, and no way to get them. Caroline would come back on Friday, but what then? The worst-case scenario was that she would show up relaxed, refreshed, looking forward to the wedding.

What if Caroline doesn't want to let you go? Angie had asked that question the night in the emergency room, and what had he said?

Caroline is nothing if not practical. He had never anticipated something like this, and had no idea what to do next. He had three days to manage the Rose girls and Miss Junie, three days to pretend that he was about to get married. In good conscience he could say nothing about calling off the wedding until he had spoken to Caroline. If he still had the courage to do it at that point.

John got up to go take a shower. Outside, a triple burst of fireworks echoed across the sky, and all across Ogilvie dogs put back their heads and howled.

· Fifteen ·

To: Patricia C. Walker <pattycake@ogilvie.edu>
From: Angeline Mangiamele <apples@tiedtothetracks.com>
Re: follow up (2)

Just a note to inquire about the status of my memo dated one week ago. The most important matters:

1. The beta monitor in the editing suite is still waiting for repair or replacement. This is our most urgent need.

2. My mail is still not reaching me. Have you had any success with central mail services on sorting this out?

3. We understand that Rob Grant has okayed an additional two hundred photocopies a month be added to our allowance, but thus far our PIN code is not working. Could you please clarify this situation for us?

Thanks for your help.

A.

To: Angeline Mangiamele <apples@tiedtothetracks.com>
From: Patricia C. Walker <pattycake@ogilvie.edu>
Re: follow up (2)

1. The necessary requisition forms have been sent. In the summer Technology Assistance—like this department—is understaffed, but I will call and see what the estimated wait might be.

2. As I put a number of things in your inbox just yesterday I thought this problem was resolved.

3. Your PIN numbers have been updated. During your short stay with us, requests regarding the photocopier, its use and access issues, should be directed to me, in accordance with official departmental policy.

Patricia C. Walker
Senior Secretary and Office Manager
English Department

To: Patricia C. Walker <pattycake@ogilvie.edu>
From: Angeline Mangiamele <apples@tiedtothetracks.com>
Re: follow up (3)

Just a note to inquire about the status of my memo dated ten days ago. The most important matters:

1. Still no progress on the monitor.

2. The mail in my box includes two credit card offers addressed to (a) Andrew Malone, and (b) Anil Mustafa; a flier for a sale at the campus bookstore; and three internal memos, all from you. I have not received any outside mail addressed to me since I arrived.

3. PIN number still not working.

Thanks for your help.

A.

To: Angeline Mangiamele <apples@tiedtothetracks.com>
From: Patricia C. Walker <pattycake@ogilvie.edu>
Re: follow up (3)

1. Technology Assistance tells me the monitor is scheduled for pickup today or tomorrow.

2. Maybe you gave out the wrong address?

3. I see that I forgot to give you the new PIN number. Please check your inbox for it later today.

Patricia C. Walker
Senior Secretary and Office Manager
English Department

To: Patricia C. Walker <pattycake@ogilvie.edu>
Cc: John Grant, Department Chair <jgrant@ogilvie.edu>, Robert Grant, Executive Assistant <robgrant@ogilvie.edu>
From: Angeline Mangiamele <apples@tiedtothetracks.com>
Re: follow up (4)

Just a note to inquire about the status of my memo dated two weeks ago. The most important matters:

1. Our progress is seriously compromised by the lack of a working monitor. If Technology Assistance cannot repair or replace it today, I will submit an urgent request for a new monitor through Rob Grant immediately.

2. I have a phone call into the US post office to see if they can track down the problem from their end.

3. Please e-mail the PIN number ASAP.

Thanks for your help.

A.

To: Angeline Mangiamele <apples@tiedtothetracks.com>
Cc: John Grant, Department Chair <jgrant@ogilvie.edu>, Robert Grant, Executive Assistant <robgrant@ogilvie.edu>
From: Patricia C. Walker <pattycake@ogilvie.edu>
Re: follow up (4)

1. The new monitor has been ordered and should arrive tomorrow. Rob tells me he has e-mailed you the UPS tracking number directly.

2. As you will have heard from Mason Campbell at the post office, it seems they had a request on file for your mail to be held there for pickup. Their hours are 8–4 weekdays.

3. According to official university and departmental policy, e-mail may not be used to transmit any sensitive information including (but not limited to) computer passwords and PIN numbers. I have put a photocopy of the relevant pages of the technology guidelines manual in your inbox, and deducted those six pages from your monthly allowance.

Patricia C. Walker
Senior Secretary and Office Manager
English Department

To: Patricia C. Walker <pattycake@ogilvie.edu>
Cc: John Grant, Department Chair <jgrant@ogilvie.edu>, Robert Grant, Senior Administrative Assistant <robgrant@ogilvie.edu>
From: Angeline Mangiamele <apples@tiedtothetracks.com>
Re: follow up (5)

While the promised pages from the technology guidelines manual were in my box, the PIN number was not.

Until this matter can be resolved, Rob has given us his PIN number to use.

To: Angeline Mangiamele <apples@tiedtothetracks.com>
Cc: John Grant, Department Chair <jgrant@ogilvie.edu>, Robert Grant, Executive
Assistant <robgrant@ogilvie.edu>
From: Patricia C. Walker <pattycake@ogilvie.edu>
Re: follow up (4)

The English Department has an official policy on the use of the photocopier. This
policy was reviewed by the faculty on March 18, 1989, and approved by Professor
Calhoun, the presiding chair, the next day. Quoting from page four, paragraph four:
"No person shall lend out his or her PIN number to any other person, or take other
steps to share, barter, or distribute photocopy allowances."

   Rob Grant transferred into the English department from central administration
just a month ago, so I'm assuming he hasn't had time to review the relevant departmental guidelines. I have put photocopies of the relevant pages in his box and
yours. Those ten pages have been deducted from your monthly allowance. The PIN
number for Tied to the Tracks is in a sealed envelope in your box.

Tony laughed out loud over the e-mail printouts and memos Angie
handed him when he showed up past noon on Wednesday. "By God," he
said with sincere appreciation. "The woman has balls, you got to give her
that. Did she really give us six-six-six for a PIN?"

They were in the reception area of the editing suite, where Angie and
Rivera had spent the morning trying to impose some order on the miles of
video from the Jubilee.

Rivera was rummaging around in the bags of Mexican carryout that
Tony had deposited on the coffee table. It was meant to make up for the fact
that he had slept in while they had been busy, and it worked. Angie took the
bag of tacos Rivera was waving in front of her.

"Six-six-six," Tony snorted. "The minx. She knows not with whom
she toys."

Angie flicked a glance toward Markus, who was, after all, one of Patty-
Cake's numerous blood relatives. She said, "The monitor was sent express
overnight. It should be here tomorrow morning if not this afternoon."

"The sisterhood would be proud of Patty-Cake," Tony said, ignoring the
change in subject.

"Which is a good thing," Angie said more loudly. "Because it's going to
take us days and days to catch up with the screening."

"What sisterhood?" Markus asked.

"The High Holy Sisterhood of Administrative Assistants," Rivera said, sending Angie a *Give it up* shrug. "The source of all true power."

"And staplers," Tony added. "If there had been a dozen of the sisterhood around during the Civil War, we'd all be whistling 'Dixie.'"

"Don't call it that," Angie said. "Some people take offense."

"They do?" Tony said, and craned his head around to Markus. "Hey, are you offended if I say the words 'Civil War'?"

"Not me, but plenty are," Markus said. He had been organizing newspaper clippings, and there was a smudge of ink on his cheek, which made him look especially young. He said, "Try calling it the War Between the States, that's pretty neutral."

"Then by all means," Tony said with a royal wave of one hand. He was in an excellent mood, which probably meant he had not spent the night alone. Angie tried to remember when he had left the Jubilee and who had been with him, but the Liars had monopolized her attention from the second they won her picnic basket and company at supper. She had been so busy with them that she hadn't even seen John go, nor had she heard from him last night. For which, she was sure, there must be a very good explanation.

She stretched out on the couch, trying to find a comfortable position, and finally sat up to dig beneath the cushions. From the depths she retrieved a shoe, the cell phone Tony had lost days ago, a half-eaten packet of crackers, a DVD case, and a bright purple plaid bra, 38DD, which she threw at Tony's head, where it hung, one cup over each ear.

"Rakish," Rivera said. "A fashion gamble, but I think it's working."

Markus barked a laugh, and then dropped his head and hid his mouth behind one hand.

"Tony," Angie said, trying to sound stern, "the editing suite is not your personal clubhouse."

"Why not?" Tony pulled the bra off his head and sniffed it with his nose wrinkled. "Bathroom, shower, microwave, television, a couch to sleep on, and every bit of hardware and software the geekish heart beneath this oh-so-debonair exterior has ever lusted after. Best of all, my mother doesn't have the phone number here and there's no cell phone reception."

"Your mother." Markus stood up suddenly. "Tony, I forgot to tell you that your mother called and said she'd call back"—he glanced at the clock, which read five minutes after noon—"on her lunch break."

Tony was just getting to his feet when the phone rang.

"Too late," Angie said, and Rivera added: "Don't be a coward, Russo. Millie's on the phone."

Rivera had been saying for years that they could make a whole film around Millie Russo's phone calls to her only son. Tony refused to discuss the possibility, but he always put his mother on speakerphone. Angie had yet to figure out if his purpose was to spread the misery around, or entertain them.

"Tony," Millie said now from her kitchen in East Orange, "I'm calling to ask, you ever think about real estate?"

"Hi, Ma," Tony said. "How you doing?"

"You know, same as always. So, you ever give real estate a thought?"

"Real estate? What for?"

"Real estate. Why not."

"Ma, would you just spit it out?"

"Listen to Mr. Impatient. You don't got ten minutes for your mother?"

"Sorry, Ma. Go ahead."

Millie sniffed. "You remember Jerry Tedesca, the tubby boy with the overbite was in high school with you? His uncle Mario died. His heart, and him only seventy-nine."

"And Jerry was at the wake."

"That's what I'm telling you. You know what Jerry drives? A Mercedes, the biggest one they make. Still got that new-car smell, leather seats as soft as butter. He drove me and your aunt Dot home."

"And Jerry Tedesca is in real estate."

"That's what I'm telling you. Real estate. He made close to *a million dollars* last year."

"Real estate, Ma."

There was a moment's silence. "What, you can't sell a house?"

Angie let out a squeak, and Rivera poked her.

"Ma."

"I'm just saying. How hard can it be to get a real estate license? Your second cousin Eddie got one, and God knows he's got nothing much going for him in the brain department."

"Ma, I've got a job."

"You drive around all day in a nice car, looking at houses. You want, you can fill the trunk up with cameras, take pictures on your lunch hour."

"I'm fifty years old, Ma. I've got a job I like and I'm good at."

"It's never too late to improve yourself. You could go back to school. Move in here with me to save some money, go and study business. Angie, you tell him," Millie shouted so that the speakerphone vibrated. "A backup plan is a good thing."

"A backup plan is a good thing," Angie echoed obediently, and Tony shot her a dirty look.

"Why do I bother?" Millie asked with a sigh. "He never listens. You never listen, Tony."

"We'll talk to him about it, Mrs. Russo," Rivera volunteered.

"I know you will. Such good girls, and single. Tony—"

"Ma."

"I'm just saying."

By six o'clock Angie had finished setting up the new monitor and done all the prep work for the screening sessions they meant to start first thing Thursday morning.

She should be exhausted, but instead Angie found it impossible to dial down the rapid flow of her thoughts. She considered going back to Ivy House and starting dinner, or to the Piggly Wiggly to look at new entries in the memory book. Miss Annie had called to say the local histories she had requested were finally available, there was two weeks' worth of mail to catch up on and bills that were surely overdue.

All this was true, but there was another truth, a more important one: John was downstairs in his office, and she hadn't seen or heard from him all day long.

There had been no lack of other visitors. It seemed as if a dozen people had dropped by, including Rob, who had come up on his lunch hour to look through old photos, something she had asked many different people to do.

The photo box was meant to look like an odd assortment thrown together hastily, but in fact Angie and Rivera had spent some time deciding what would go into it. Most of the pictures were of Miss Zula and her family over the years, some which Angie knew a great deal about, some which were more mysterious. Most of the photos were candid and many were badly composed.

Angie left Rob with the box and a notepad for more than half an hour, because she had come to the conclusion that it was best to leave people to sort through things on their own, and to take what information they provided without questions or prompting.

From the box she had left him Rob pulled out a half dozen photos to study, and he had written a few sentences about each of them. One of the pictures he had put aside to talk to her about, and Angie felt the small, sharp thrill that came with the feeling that a crucial piece of a larger puzzle was about to be turned over.

This particular photo, badly framed, overexposed, was of Miss Zula as a young woman, standing on a porch. She was dressed in what must have been her very nicest clothes: a tailored suit with a flower pinned to her lapel, more flowers on the rim of a small hat, white gloves, and a dark wool coat with a fur collar hung over her shoulders. She was laughing into the camera and she looked unreservedly happy. To her right was her mother, dressed in dark colors. There was a resemblance between Zula and the older woman in the shape of the mouth and eyes, but while Miss Zula was smiling, her companion's expression was grim, almost disapproving.

"Miss Louisa," Rob said. "There aren't many pictures of her around that I'm aware of. My grandmother used to say she was as sour as June apples. Have you heard much about Miss Louisa?"

"I had an interesting conversation with Sister Ellen Mary at the rectory," Angie said. "But we haven't had much luck getting Miss Zula to talk about her. What's your take on her, clinical depression or borderline personality or just plain mean?"

"All three, probably," said Rob. "If you get a chance, ask my mother while she's here. Lucy has some Miss Louisa stories."

Angie shouldn't be surprised to hear that Lucy was coming; the wedding hadn't been canceled yet, after all. She said, "When do you expect your mother?"

"Friday morning."

There was a bit of an awkward silence in which they both must be think-ing the same thing. Rob must know about his brother's plans—about his change of plans—but he could no more bring up the subject than she could. Angie studied the photo in front of her, afraid that if she opened her mouth, words she could not take back would spill out. Then she remembered another photo, one she had shown to almost everyone who came into the office. She pulled it out of a drawer.

She said, "I've shown this to five people and every one of them has given me different names."

This was a black-and-white photo, too, but the contrasts were sharp and true. On the back someone had written 1947 in a slanted, wavering hand. There were three people in the picture: a tall black man wearing an over-coat and a fedora standing behind two women, one in her late twenties and white, the other an elderly black woman with thin white hair and the kind of large, even white teeth that Angie recognized from the glass on her grandfather's bedside table. Both women were dressed for church or some other formal occasion, and the photo had been taken on a porch.

Angie looked at this photo every day and she was always struck by it for some reasons she could name, and others that were still unclear. The man's posture had caught her attention first. He had put his hands on the shoul-ders of the women before him, his right hand on the younger woman's right shoulder, his left on the older woman's left, and he was leaning forward slightly with his upper body, as if he wanted to draw them both closer. The younger woman had begun to turn her head toward him. She had a beautiful profile, her jaw strong and clean and the line of her cheek a perfect curve, but what caught Angie's imagination was her hand, which she had lifted as if she meant to touch her own right shoulder, where the man's hand rested. The camera had caught that motion and turned her hand into something alive, trembling and full of life just over her heart. Angie followed the arc of the moving hand as she had every time she picked up this photo, but this time a flash of recognition came to her.

Rob had already reached back into the photo box to bring out the one he had found of Miss Zula and her mother. When he put it down on the desk, it was clear to see that the two photos had been taken on the same day on the same porch, maybe only moments apart. The flash had malfunctioned on one but not the other, so that Miss Zula and her mother were overexposed while the other people—and who were they?—were in focus.

"Look," Rob said, "you can see a little of Miss Zula's shoulder here."

His finger hovered over the edge of the first photo and traveled to the one next to it. "Like a bridge," Rob said, putting exactly the right image in Angie's mind. They stood for a moment trying to understand the story the two photos made when they were put together.

"That's got to be Abe Bragg," Rob said finally. "I've never seen of photo of him out of uniform before, and the hat put me off at first."

Of course, Angie thought. Another missed connection, but like Rob, she had seen very few photographs of Miss Zula's older brother. There was one of him in the parlor at Magnolia House, but in his Air Force dress uniform.

"I don't know who the two women are," said Rob. "Did you ask Miss Maddie? She might be the one who took the photos, as she isn't in them."

"I'll have to remember to show them to her next time I'm over there." Something she would do as soon as possible, but Angie didn't want to say so, for reasons too complicated to consider.

"Why not ask Miss Zula directly?"

Rob's law degree made itself evident at the most inconvenient moments, as with this completely reasonable question that Angie didn't want to answer. If she tried to mislead him with a partial truth by telling him that she didn't want to force a confidence, he would see through her. The whole truth was that she didn't want to take the chance that Miss Zula would appropriate the photo and ask her not to pursue it without further explanation. There were few subjects that Miss Zula seemed reluctant to discuss—at least thus far—but her brother was one of them.

"I will," Angie said. "At some point. But I have to tread carefully with Miss Zula."

Rob was looking at her closely. "Of course," he said finally, the lawyer still foremost in his expression. "I can see that."

The last visitor of the day had been the one Angie least wanted to see. Harriet Darling came rushing in, out of breath and sputtering apologies, because, she told Angie, her appointment with Tony had been for 3:30, and here it was a full hour later.

To Angie it made perfect sense that Tony himself was late. He was no more reliable than Harriet when it came to being punctual.

"I guess he forgot. He's out showing Markus the fine points of using a light meter."

Harriet's face broke into a smile that made her look so young that Angie wished she had a camera to record it.

"In't that just sweet?" Harriet said. "Taking Eunice's Markus under his wing like that."

"What did you need to talk to him about?" Angie asked.

"Why, the wedding, of course. Y'all are doing the videotaping, and I've got notes here"—she dug in her bag and pulled out a leather portfolio—"I'll just have to go over it all with you."

"You wouldn't rather come back tomorrow?"

"Heavens, no." Harriet sat down with a plop on the sofa and threw back her head. "Tomorrow I won't have time to breathe much less come back here. It's a good thing I took this week off." She dropped her chin to her chest and glared at Angie.

"You know I love her dearly, but I could kill Caroline. Leaving us with all this, and Tab in the hospital—no, no, don't make a face. He's doing fine."

Angie said silent thanks that Harriet was so easily diverted.

She was saying, "He's doing so much better, the nurses are going cross-eyed dealing with him. Tab is not a good patient, you had best believe me. Mother Teresa would end up slapping him silly, and I'm no Mother Teresa."

"He's got to be in some pain," Angie offered.

"Well, of course he is," Harriet said. "But I guarantee you whatever he's feeling has got nothing on childbirth, and I got through that three times without offending half the hospital." She closed her eyes for a moment. "You know he can't keep a dental hygienist? The longest one ever held on was three months, and she was deaf in one ear. I swear, once this wedding is over and he's out, I'm going into hiding myself."

"A retreat must sound like a good idea just about now."

Harriet snorted. "To hell with retreats, I'm thinking Mexico, or Bermuda maybe. Can we get down to it, sugar? I'm running late."

Angie cast a longing glance at the closed darkroom door and the red light burning above it. There would be no rescue from Rivera, and so she sat with Harriet Darling and took exhaustive notes about a wedding that was not supposed to happen. Because the groom had already backed out, but Harriet Darling didn't know that. Angie tried not to think of Harriet's reaction when she finally found out that all this rushing around had been for nothing.

"You all right?" Harriet asked. "You're looking a little pale. I hope the Liars didn't keep you up too late." She winked suggestively and laughed.

"They were very sweet," Angie said.

"Well, you were worth every penny. Didn't you look a treat? I swear, girl, I don't know why you dress the way you do. I've seen nuns with more fashion sense." And then she bit her lip. "I'm sorry, that was rude."

"It's okay," Angie said. "It's not the first time I've heard it. My mother is always after me about clothes."

"Tell you what," Harriet said. "After the wedding, once Tab is out of the hospital and on his feet, I'm going to start looking for an apartment. You help me with that, and I'll take you *shopping*." Her eyes gleamed at the thought. "We can spend the day in Savannah, get you a whole new wardrobe."

Angie was trying to find a way to let Harriet down easily when Rivera popped her head out of the darkroom.

"I'll be ready in fifteen," she said. And: "Hey, Harriet."

"I've got to go too," Harriet said, her expression suddenly much more subdued. She stood up and wiggled so that the crease in her linen slacks fell into place. "Rivera, I don't know if you realize it, but it's likely you're going to get some nasty comments, now that people know—" She tilted her head. "After what happened at the picnic auction. I hope you're ready for that."

There wasn't exactly disapproval in her tone, but something of a frustrated mother scolding a teenager daughter, one who had gone against all good advice and now had to face the consequences.

"I'll manage," Rivera said. She stood in the open door like a queen, straight of back, her head held high on her long neck.

"I suppose you will," Harriet said dryly. "But then again you'll be gone by next summer and Meg has to live here."

"She'll manage, too." Rivera said, in a particular quiet tone that set alarms ringing in Angie's head. "You'd be surprised how liberating it is to put lies behind you. But you know that, don't you? You're just about to leave your husband."

"That's not the same thing," Harriet said stiffly.

Angie said, "Rivera. Don't be a mope."

That earned her a flashing grin and one shoulder lifted in acknowledgment, and just that suddenly the crisis was past.

Harriet turned and took Angie's hand to squeeze it. "Thank you, sugar. You're so sweet to help out with the wedding. I guess it can't be easy, but you don't let on, and that's got to cost you something."

Angie felt herself flushing. "Don't mention it," she said, trying not to look at Rivera. "Please."

· SIXTEEN ·

Ogilvie Bugle

NEWS ABOUT TOWN

Will Sloan, director of WOTV, Ogilvie Public Access Television, asks us to remind our readers that there are some exciting programs coming up at OP-TV. Today and through the weekend *The Eye on Ogilvie* team will be roaming the campus during the reunions to find out what the alumni have been up to. On Saturday there will be a special broadcast of Patty-Cake Walker's popular *Girl Talk*, live from the wedding of the season. Rumor has it that Lucy Ogilvie Black will be coming home to Ogilvie to see her son John Grant married to Caroline Mae Rose, both English Department faculty members at the university. See it all on Channel 12, starting at 10:30.

Thursday morning John called his brother into his office and handed him the letter from Caroline. Rob leaned against the wall to read it, and though John watched him closely, he saw no change in Rob's relaxed posture or in his expression. Which might mean that John had been thinking about it too hard and long and blown it all out of proportion. A less appealing option occurred to him, but couldn't be rejected out of hand: Rob was hiding his real reactions behind his lawyer's face.

"Well, that explains some things." He folded the letter and put it back in its envelope.

"Really. Then maybe you can fill me in," John said. "Because I'm confused as all hell."

"What I mean is, it explains why you didn't show up for your bachelor party last night."

That hit John like a fist to the gut. He let his head drop to the desk, and groaned.

"Don't worry," Rob said. "I told them you had gone up to the retreat house to see Caroline, but that her sisters weren't supposed to know about it. The guys were so busy talking about how you'd sneak into a convent that they went along with the whole thing."

"I was at home," John said dully. "With the phone turned off."

"It wasn't a good day for you yesterday," Rob agreed. He looked at the letter for a long moment. "I thought you were going to take a chunk out of Patty-Cake a time or two. Not that she doesn't deserve it."

John pressed the bridge of his nose with thumb and forefinger and counted to three. "Okay, I did let that crap about the photocopier get to me," John said. "A mistake, huh?"

"Let's just say you gave her what she wanted." Rob crossed over to the couch and sat. "So what do you think is going on with Caroline?"

"You first," John said. "Please."

Rob thought for a minute, his head turned to one side. "A couple of possibilities come to mind. I would say she hadn't got your letter when she wrote this, so my first guess is that she has got some idea about Angie and is about to dump you."

"But—"

"Let me finish. That's the most obvious answer, but it doesn't sound like Caroline to me."

John, who had come to this same conclusion almost twenty-four hours ago, nodded. "Go on."

"The list of things serious enough for her to run off like this is pretty short. I'd guess her sisters are worried about her wanting to be a nun."

"Probably they are," John said. "But I can't see Caroline going into a convent."

"Too melodramatic by far, you're right. Have you considered that she might be in love with somebody else—"

"Nope," John said.

"Okay." Rob was looking at him closely. "You're sure?"

"As sure as I can be. You know Caroline, she's not adventurous. And I can't think of any man around her who might have . . . distracted her."

"Maybe it's somebody from her past," Rob said. "Maybe it snuck up on her."

John heard an unusual tone in his brother's voice. "Is there something you know you're not telling me?" he said. "Something about Caroline and somebody else? Are people talking?"

"Hold on there," Rob said. "Don't get carried away. No talk, no gossip, no rumors, no suspicions. Caroline isn't Mama, okay?"

John nodded, relieved. The idea of people snickering behind his back was enough to make his gorge rise. "So what do you think it all means?"

"I don't know," Rob said. "Beyond the fact that you're stuck until she comes back here and you can ask her. What was Angie's take?" And after a moment: "Please tell me you've talked to Angie about this."

"I wanted to figure it out for myself first." John heard the defensive note in his own voice and winced.

Very quietly Rob said, "You haven't talked to Angie since you got this letter on Tuesday evening?"

"Now, wait—"

"Since Tuesday," Rob repeated. "A good part of which you spent with Angie in my spare bedroom."

John closed his eyes. "Look. The whole town thinks I'm getting married the day after tomorrow, and I can't call the wedding off because the bride has run away. What exactly am I supposed to say to Angie?"

Rob got up and began to pace. "I want you to listen to me now, and carefully. My advice is, go find Angie and tell her what's going on. Leave not one detail—not one—out. Show her the letter, and run through every reaction you've had. Then throw yourself on the mercy of the court, and maybe, if you're lucky, you'll pull your ass out of the fire with nothing more than a few blisters. I hope you do, but you're going to have to work at it."

A pulse picked up in John's temple, not because he was angry, or at least he wasn't angry at his brother. His heart was racing because he knew the truth when he heard it. He swallowed. "I've got to be at this alumni thing in a half hour."

"Then you had best get a move on," Rob said.

At the door John hesitated. "I'm going to need all the help I can get these next two days."

Rob said, "You know where to find me."

It took every bit of persuasion she could muster, but Angie managed to get the whole crew into the editing suite by seven on Thursday morning.

The novelty of working in such a well-equipped and comfortable space put them all in a good mood. They could spread out logbooks, files, comput-ers, and their personal gear, along with an array of cups and carryout bags. Best of all, they had enough computing power and no restrictions on how much of it they used, or how long they spent here. That was such a luxury that it took Angie a full hour before she relaxed enough to stop constantly looking at her watch.

Big companies with large staffs allocated the logging to assistants, but Angie liked everything about this part of the process. Most of all, she loved the working together and the talk about the story while the digital counter at the bottom of the screen ticked along steadily. The entire time she scribbled, writing down minimal information about the scene and its loca-tion while Tony did the same on a laptop.

Markus wanted to know if Rivera was going to take notes, too, at which she flexed her fingers in the air like a surgeon wiggling into sterile gloves.

"Hell no," she said, settling down in front of the controls. "Somebody's got to drive."

They had been working together like this for so long that it was like dancing with a very well known and trusted partner. Rivera often froze the flow of the video in the split second before Angie or Tony could ask her to, either to catch up with note taking or to talk about a particular shot. Some-times it was no more than an expression on a face perfectly lit by the late-afternoon sun, but there were dozens of segments that made Angie catch her breath and remember, with complete clarity, what she loved about her work, and why she was here.

Which had nothing to do with John Grant, not in the first line.

"Angie?" Rivera was saying.

"Sorry. What?"

"Could you put my mark next to this bit of John and Miss Zula talking?

"Sure." Angie picked up her red pen to draw a star next to the entry that read 02:02:38:13, 02:04:04:13, JG talking 2 ZB re fall schedule. Z 2 Louie asleep & pan around office and got a blob of ink instead. She turned her head.

"Where's Markus?"

"He left a half hour ago to run errands for his mother," Tony said. "Jeez, Ang. You drag us in here at the crack of dawn and then you fall asleep yourself."

"I'm not sleeping," Angie said steadily. "I was concentrating. Hold up, I've got to go get another pen."

John came into the reception area just as Angie was closing the door to the supply closet. She stopped where she was and tried to smile, but didn't quite manage. Breathing was almost as hard.

He was dressed in a dark gray summer-weight suit with a deep red tie over a snowy white shirt, and Angie had a sudden memory of the dry cleaners he used in Manhattan. The woman behind the counter—small and round with a heavy Slavic accent—had talked to John as an indulgent but hard-to-please grandmother might have. Angie had come to the conclusion that he liked it, or he would have taken his business to one of the hundreds of other dry cleaners in the city.

She said, "What was that woman's name, the one who called you *booby?*"

John smiled so suddenly and so beautifully that Angie's breath hitched and caught and she thought, *Where the hell have you been?* But she bit her lip to keep from saying it.

"Mrs. Pulaski. I think about her, too, every time I put on a suit. The dry cleaner here is Miss Nellie, and she calls me John-John. I miss Mrs. Pulaski."

"You haven't been back here all that long," Angie said. "Cheer up, I'm sure you'll find some shop clerk willing to abuse you to your face."

"Probably not in Ogilvie," John said. "Mostly people wait until you're out of hearing to bad-mouth you."

That made Angie think of Win Walker. She realized that she had successfully put the condom episode out of her head—so successfully that she had yet to tell John about what had happened after he shimmied out the bathroom window. But then she had run into Patty-Cake at least four times since the afternoon of the fourth, and there was no indication that her nephew had been whispering in her ear. Angie had to assume that he kept quiet out of professionalism, which made her feel guilty all over again, this time for underestimating him. She was thinking about that when she realized John was saying something quite important.

"—and then Rob called me an idiot."

Which he was, most certainly. An infuriating, frustrating, gorgeous idiot she had missed beyond all reason for almost forty-eight hours, and what did that make her?

She said, "We agreed it was best to keep contact to a minimum."

"I should have called, at least."

True. Another thing not to be said aloud, not at this moment. Instead Angie said, "You look like you're on your way someplace."

"Reunions on campus, I have to go to a luncheon."

"That explains all the people wandering around."

"I have to give a talk this evening, too, and then there's a supper—"

"Isn't Miss Zula giving a talk, too? Because we're supposed to shoot it."

"Ah." John looked disconcerted at this news. "Well, I suppose I'll see you there."

"I suppose you will."

He cleared his throat again. He said, "There's a letter from Caroline." He said it lightly, but there was a tension in him that she could see in his shoulders and the tilt of his head.

Angie leaned against the closet door and crossed her arms on her chest. "She's told her family?"

"No. Not yet. It's complicated," John said. "I need to talk to you, but I have—"

"This alumni thing, you said."

"Are you around later this afternoon?"

The urge to hear what he had to say, good or bad, to get it over with once and for all, that urge was at war with the far less pleasant compulsion Angie was feeling. If suffering and regret were going to be on the itinerary, she would take him along for the ride. She said, "We're in the middle of a big logging session, and we'll be at it all day."

His face fell. "Okay, well. Maybe after this alumni supper thing? You could come over to the house, that might be safer."

Hours and hours and hours from now. Angie nodded.

"Good." He turned toward the door and then suddenly changed direction and came across the room in four long strides. He put one hand on the door over her head and leaned down and kissed her, short but sweet and thorough, a kiss that said the things she needed to know. She heard herself let out a shuddering sigh of relief.

"Don't worry," he whispered. "It's nothing about you. Nothing bad about us. I don't want you to worry. I'm trying, Angie, I'm really trying. I don't want to screw this up."

Angie nodded. "Good." This time she managed a smile. "Good."

As president of the university, Karl Bray lived in the small mansion on campus that Captain Joshua Ogilvie had built in 1820 when he first settled the town and gave it his name. Karl was an excellent administrator and a nice enough man, but he was also a native of Vermont, an art historian, and an unapologetic atheist, so it was no surprise to John that after fifteen years in town, Karl had never really become part of the community.

And still Karl should have known enough about how Ogilvie worked and the old quarrels not to seat Zula Bragg next to Button Preston Ogilvie. They both had to be included, that much was clear—Button's husband, Harmond, was the chair of the board of regents, and she herself was an alumna.

John sat across the table from the two elderly women who so studiously ignored each other. Miss Zula was as reticent as ever, answering politely whenever one of the guests addressed her but never allowing a conversation to go very long. The fact that the people around this table would each be contributing tens of thousands of dollars to the university impressed her not at all. Button, on the other hand, never stopped talking. She had gotten onto the subject of the town's history and genealogy, the worst possible place to go when she was sitting next to Zula Bragg.

"Your husband and son are the last direct descendants of the original Joshua Ogilvie, the man who built this house, is that right?" This from a middle-aged alumna who was president of a small bank in Atlanta.

"That's right," Button said. "Most of the Ogilvies in town are descended from *John* Ogilvie, Joshua's younger brother? Dr. Grant's mother is an Ogilvie of that line." She shot him a patronizing smile, which John pretended not to see.

Button went on for a while about the Ogilvie lineage, fabricating where it suited her and skipping over the less savory bits, such as the fact that Zula Bragg was herself directly descended from both Joshua and John Ogilvie, who had been visionary men when it came to everything but slavery and the persons of their female slaves. It was exactly this kind of talk that had gotten

Button Ogilvie written into *Sweet-Bitter*, the novel that had won Miss Zula the National Book Award.

Karl Bray said, "To be completely fair, Button, you have to remember that Captain Ogilvie had children outside his marriage. Those descendants are here in town, too." His gaze flickered toward Miss Zula and away again.

Button smiled stiffly. "That's a theory," she said. "One without any sound *proof.*"

The man to Karl's right cleared his throat. He was twice Karl's size, with a great slope of belly and jowls like the flaps on a rooster, and he had a deep, resonating voice that almost echoed off the high ceilings. "These days we can prove or refute such claims on the basis of DNA testing."

"But, Dr. Beasley," said Button, "why? Why go stirring up all that dusty old history? We need to look forward, and forget this obsession we have with hashing over the past."

"Such as genealogy," said John, but while her expression stiffened, she didn't rise to the bait.

"But his other descendants—" a younger man began, and then stopped when Button turned a glittering glance in his direction. Before she could launch into what John suspected was a set piece, her husband spoke up.

"This is a matter of some delicacy," he said in his high, breathy voice. "But really, if you don't allow emotion to cloud the issue, it is quite simple. Outsiders who don't understand the social nuances sometimes get the idea that we descendants of Joshua Ogilvie are racists, but the truth is, we're just snobs. Not that the two failings are *necessarily* mutually exclusive, but they are in this case."

There was a ripple of vaguely uneasy laughter around the table, and John reminded himself that he had come back here knowing full well that he would be dealing with people like this, who dealt out such casual arrogance like loose change. There were fewer of them around these days, it seemed to him, and of course there was also Zula Bragg, who had never flinched at defending herself.

Miss Zula said, "Mrs. Langley, have you been to the family cemetery on the grounds behind the mansion?"

"Why, no," said the bank president. "Now that you mention it, I never have."

"I'm not surprised," said Zula. "It's not generally open to the public. But I'm sure Dr. Bray could arrange for you to see it."

"My sister and I visit the cemetery a few times every year," Miss Zula went on. "We've got four great-grandparents and four great-great-grandparents buried there—all but two of them in the section reserved for slaves." Her tone was matter-of-fact, but there was a light in her eye that John knew better than to challenge. Apparently Button did, too, because she kept quiet.

"Is that so?" The doctor looked interested. "I'll bet your documentary people have been all over that piece of history."

Button made a tight little circle of her mouth and then said, "I'm afraid you're probably right."

Such an opening was more than John could ignore. He said, "Mrs. Ogilvie, you don't approve of the documentary?"

Button Ogilvie's papery-thin cheeks flushed, Miss Zula smiled at him openly, and John settled back. Not satisfied, exactly, but more comfortable now that he had cast a vote.

"I'm sure I don't care one way or the other," Button said loftily, though John knew she had lobbied behind the scenes to keep the regents from commissioning the documentary. "The film people seem nice enough, though a trifle bohemian. Sooner or later I'll have to let them interview me, but I wouldn't mind so much if they weren't so young and inexperienced."

"They came with the highest recommendations, my dear," said her husband. "And Miss Zula chose them, after all. She has every faith in them, and so does the board of regents."

Button's mouth went very small and round, a disapproving coin in the middle of her face. "Of course. I had forgotten." She turned a stiff smile toward Zula. "Why this particular film company, if I may ask?"

"I brought Tied to the Tracks to Miss Zula's attention." A guest at the other end of the table spoke up for the first time. Her name was Judith Parris, and while John had met her once or twice over the years, he knew her primarily by her reputation. She was a professor of film and women's studies, a powerhouse in academia known for her razor-sharp critical work. Among other things.

Judith Parris was somewhere close to forty, with a long face and patrician bone structure under a razored shock of prematurely white hair. She stood out among these frail, conservative older women like a Picasso among stolid still lifes, her long frame wrapped in a jewel-colored silk caftan over wide pants. There were loops of silver wire around her neck strung with great chunks of polished stone and amber and bits of what looked to John to be barbed wire.

Miss Zula said, "Dr. Parris took creative writing with me when she was studying here, and then she had Rivera Rosenblum—one of the film company people, the tall young woman with very dark hair?—in some of her undergraduate classes when she was on the faculty at Smith. She's kept track of Rivera, and I keep track of Jude, and so the wheel goes round. We are a very small world."

"Academics?" said the bank president.

"Feminists?" said Button Ogilvie.

"Academic women out of Ogilvie College," said Miss Zula with a small smile.

"With a weakness for gambling," added Jude Parris.

The two women exchanged glances, and John thought: *Oh.* There was something going on here beneath the surface, and curiosity flooded through him. To Jude he said, "So we have you to thank for *Tied to the Tracks?*"

"Essentially," she agreed. "And now that you've raised the subject, I didn't get a chance to talk to Rivera earlier, but I'm supposed to meet her and her friends a little later for drinks. If somebody can give me a ride to the Hound Dog?"

The Hound Dog, which Angie had successfully avoided for so long, turned out to be just what she expected. Bars were bars no matter where you went. Right now in Hoboken there were a dozen that could be mistaken for this one, with adjustments for décor and musical tastes. The Hound Dog was underlit, overcrowded, smelly, and loud, and while her first and only beer had tasted very good after a long day in the editing suite and then at the stuffy reunion reception, she really wanted to be somewhere else. She glanced at her watch again and told herself that John wouldn't be home just yet. And if he was, well, then. She had waited, and so could he.

"You can't have the keys to the van," Tony was explaining to her in a ponderous tone. "You've had too much to drink."

"No, *you've* had too much to drink," Angie said. "I'm sober."

"I knew it was one of us." He pulled out his shirt pocket and crossed his eyes trying to look into it. "No keys. Ask Rivera."

"She said you have them. Check your rear pockets."

There was a hand on Angie's shoulder, a firm touch that made her jump and her heart speed up. She turned her head.

"Hey, Wyeth," she squeaked. "How you doing?"

Above his beard, Wyeth Horton's cheeks were cherry red, from drink or dancing or both.

He said, "Come on and dance," and towed her through the crowd by the hand without bothering to hear her thoughts on the subject. There was no chance of making herself heard over the band, she thought, but she'd be able to get away once they reached the dance floor.

Except there never was that chance, and after a while she stopped trying to make excuses. For an English teacher of considerable and ponderous girth, Wyeth could really dance. So could the other men who claimed her one after the other. Angie knew how to dance, too, for the simple reason that all four grandparents had been avid ballroom dancers. Through her childhood and much of her high school years they had dragged her to every competition on the East Coast.

When the band finished its set and left the raised stage to take a break, Angie was breathless and laughing when she looked up to see John standing at the edge of the crowd. He was still dressed as she had seen him last at the alumni reception, but he had loosened his tie and had a long-necked beer bottle in one hand.

Tony came up and draped an arm over her shoulders. "Aren't you glad you didn't rush away?"

Angie shot him a warning look that didn't even register.

"Get this," he was saying. "John brought Jude Parris with him."

Angie had been ready to disavow any interest in John Grant, but this last piece of news took her by surprise. "Jude Parris? At the Hound Dog?" And then: "The reunion. I didn't even think about it: she's an alumna."

"Who's Jude Parris?" Wyeth asked, looking interested.

"Rivera's adviser from Smith," Angie answered absently. She caught sight of the table where Jude sat with Rivera and Meg and—she sighed— John. Wyeth was looking in the same direction.

He said, "Judith Parris? Author of *Man of Pain*?"

Angie thought, *Oh, shit.*

Wyeth said, "She's got a new book coming out, I forget the title."

Tony said, "*Studies in Sexual Indiscretion*," and Angie punched him, hard enough to make him yelp. He rubbed his arm and scowled at Angie, but he spoke to Wyeth. "Hey, Urban Cowboy. Stay away from Jude Parris. She eats her dead."

"John and Win look comfortable enough," said Wyeth, and Angie saw that, indeed, John Grant and Win Walker had been induced to join Rivera, Jude, and Weepy Meg.

"I'll come with you," said Wyeth. "Is she one of the Savannah Parris girls?"

A half an hour later Angie had pretty much given up on ever getting away to be alone with John. There were eight of them crowded into a round corner booth, and somehow or another she had ended up between John and Tony, directly across from Win Walker and Wyeth Horton. Wyeth's attention was mostly on Jude, but Win kept a close eye on Angie, and his expression was less than friendly. Of course, the last time they had talked to each other it had been in the presence of a loaded condom, which probably explained a lot.

The table was crowded with glasses and bottles and open cans of Vienna sausages, at Wyeth's insistence that they needed the full Hound Dog experience before they went back north and proclaimed themselves experts on the subject of drinking habits in the Deep South.

"You really did miss something fantastic," Jude was saying. Her thin cheeks were pale even in the heat of the overcrowded room, but her eyes flashed with pleasure, as they always did when she had a new audience. Jude was ignoring Wyeth to size up Win, and Win was not completely immune. Angie reminded herself that it wasn't her job to protect the gentle souls of the world from the more predatory ones, and Win Walker was a big boy.

"I can't remember the last time I saw Miss Zula take somebody apart with such obvious delight. I almost felt sorry for the woman," Jude finished.

"I wouldn't feel sorry for Button Ogilvie," said John. "She provokes Miss Zula because she likes the excitement."

Wyeth said, "Sometimes I think they should just have an old-fashioned duel and get it over with."

"Gunfight at the Ogilvie Corral," said Tony. "We could tape it."

"Oh, now, it's not that bad," said Win. "They just squabble a little."

Meg said, "If you ask me, it's all about unrequited love."

Rivera's head jerked up. She had been uncharacteristically quiet, sitting there between Jude and Meg. The problem was that Jude took some finessing at the best of times, and Meg was complicating matters considerably. She was leaning against Rivera's arm, radiating a combination of satisfaction and smugness that was bound to get on Rivera's nerves. Angie, who had watched Rivera negotiate her fair share of relationships over the years, could see that her interest and her patience were close to exhausted. Meg might have sensed that herself, because she was working very hard to impress.

"Are you saying Button Ogilvie is a lesbian?" Win asked, looking more amused than shocked.

"Not Button," Meg said in an aren't-you-silly voice. "Miss Zula."

"Meg," Rivera said in a weary tone. "Shut up."

"I second that," said John.

There was a small and very tense silence. "Why would you say that to me?" Meg said finally, blinking hard. "Aren't I entitled to an opinion?"

"You're not entitled to spread false rumors," said Win, his smile gone now. "Maybe you shouldn't have anything more to drink."

"Meg, darlin'," Wyeth said, smacking the table with both palms. "You and I haven't been out on the dance floor yet tonight."

She ignored him. Her expression was almost comical, a combination of hurt and irritation. "I think I know more about lesbians than you do, Win Walker. Shouldn't you be someplace conducting a Bible study or something?"

John said, "Drunk and rude, both. Win, let me buy you another beer."

"Well, I'm sorry," said Meg, though it was clear she was no such thing. "Rivera, aren't you going to back me up about Miss Zula, sugar?"

Rivera winced. "I don't want any part of this. This is so not kosher, Meg."

There were blotches of color on Meg's cheeks and her chin trembled in a way that some men might find disarming, but would get her nowhere with Rivera. She said, "I thought y'all were interested in the *truth*."

Jude said, "Who said you can't have an intellectual conversation in the Hound Dog?"

John smiled grimly. "Miss Zula is not a lesbian. Can we change the subject?"

Meg said to Rivera, "You were ready enough to help me come out of the closet."

"That sounds like a *no* to me," Wyeth said to John.

"That was your decision," Rivera said, and Angie, compelled to speak up, added: "You don't push somebody out of the closet."

"Not down here, especially," said Tony cheerfully. "Down here you lock the door."

John gave Tony an irritated look. "You can't push somebody out of the closet or lock them into it if they aren't in it to start with. This is stupid. Miss Zula is not a lesbian."

Meg said, "If you're so smart, John Grant, then what about Miss Anabel? Rivera, tell them about Miss Anabel."

Angie, feeling slightly dizzy, covered her face with her hands and took a deep breath.

"I've got nothing to tell," Rivera said. "I've never even met Miss Anabel. Angie interviewed her."

Jude had been watching the conversation escalate with an avid curiosity that did not bode well. Now she leaned across the table. "You didn't really interview Anabel Spate."

"She did," said Tony. "*We* did. Miss Zula took us with her on a visit."

"Anabel Spate is a legend around here," said Wyeth.

"She is indeed," said Jude. "Can I see the footage?"

"No," said Angie and Tony together.

"But we sure would like to hear your Miss Anabel stories," Tony said.

John said, "Meg, do you want to dance? Wyeth, Meg wants to dance."

Meg said, "I'm not the only one who thinks Miss Zula and Miss Anabel are more than just friends. Rivera said—"

Rivera turned to her. "Don't take what I said out of context, and do not quote me. Ever."

Angie said, "I'd like to dance." She said it loudly, but things were too far gone and not even John paid attention; he was too focused on Rivera, and he looked seriously aggrieved.

"I hope y'all have better things to do than sit around and take apart Miss Zula's private life."

That made Angie's stomach clench, and Tony laugh out loud. "That's what we're here for," he said. "That's what you're paying us to do." He belched again, and gave his chest a ponderous thump.

"Within reason," John said.

"Oh," said Tony. "The 'within reason' clause. Ang, is that before or after the part of the deal where they promised us artistic freedom?"

"Excellent question," Jude said. "How exactly would you define 'within reason,' John? Are you forbidding them to touch on issues of sexuality?"

"Folks in Ogilvie don't *talk* about sex," Wyeth said.

Angie didn't like the look on John's face; she didn't like the discussion or the way people's voices had gone so sharp; she wanted to be someplace else. She was about to say so when she felt John's hand on her knee, pressing hard, the universal *don't go* gesture. She felt Win Walker's gaze resting on her and shot him a mind-your-own-business scowl.

John said, "I trust Tied to the Tracks will respect whatever agreements they've made with Miss Zula."

"Evasive, but effective," Jude said. "But I'm still wondering why Meg is so sure that Miss Anabel and Miss Zula are lovers."

"I've heard people talking," Meg said defensively. "You said yourself Anabel Spate's a legend."

"A legend, as in civil rights," said Rivera. "Not as in gossip. Which you should avoid at all costs."

"Don't knock small-town gossip. There's usually some hard truth at the bottom of it," Wyeth said.

"But not in this case," said Win Walker.

Tony said to Meg, "Let me guess. You're saying that Miss Anabel left Ogilvie and moved to Savannah because people suspected she and Miss Zula were—"

"Yes," said Meg, trying to look injured and dignified at the same time.

"No," said John and Win together.

"Unlikely," said Jude, at which Rivera looked grimly satisfied and Meg crestfallen. To Jude she said, "I thought you were on our side."

"What side is that?" Jude said, laughing at her openly. "This isn't a club, you know. There's no secret handshake, no policy handbook or oath of loyalty. I for one don't think Miss Anabel is one of the girls: it just doesn't fit with what I know about her."

"But you are?" Win asked, looking confused and disappointed, which might have amused Angie if it weren't for the fact that she could sense how angry John was, sitting beside her, barely holding it in, thrumming with it.

"I like women," said Jude. "But I like men just as much. What about you?"

Win's expression was enough to make Angie cough a laugh. He blinked as if Jude had asked about the size of his sexual apparatus, and then he cleared his throat.

"I like women," he said. "Exclusively."

"Well, then," Jude said, "maybe you shouldn't be sitting so far away from me."

"Okay, time to go," Angie said. "This is definitely more than I need to know."

"Wait," Meg said. "First I want John to tell me why he's so sure Miss Zula and Miss Anabel *aren't* lovers."

John got up and leaned across the table toward Meg. "Listen to me now, Meggie. Nothing in this world would ever convince me to sit here in the Hound Dog, of all places, and talk to you or anybody else about Miss Zula's private life. She deserves better than that, and you know it."

Meg held her head high and backed down not one inch, which surprised Angie and alarmed her too.

"No, *you* listen," Meg said. "From what I understand, documentary film is about a story. And this sounds like a story to me, John Grant, one that in't going to go away. And while we're talking about stories that won't go away, think about this: you're supposed to be getting married to Caroline Rose on Saturday, but you've been making eyes at Angeline there all week, and Caroline is run off to a convent someplace. Don't think folks haven't noticed. In't that so, Win?"

Wyeth said, "Meg, sugar, you are determined to offend everybody at this table. I'm going to drag you off to the dance floor before you get yourself strangled."

Everyone watched Meg let herself be cajoled away to the dance floor. Or almost everyone, Angie thought. Win Walker kept his gaze firmly on her, his expression implacable.

· SEVENTEEN ·

Ogilvie, Georgia. Bearing Cross Church of God in Christ; Big Creek Baptist Church; Christ Church; Church of God of Prophecy; Church of God; Church of Jesus Christ of LDS; Elizabeth Chapel Church; First African Baptist Church; First Baptist Church; First United Methodist Church; Friendship Baptist Church; Blue Ball Free Will Baptist Church; Ogilvie Church of Christ; Mount Olive African Methodist Episcopal Church; Ogilvie Church of God; Ogilvie Methodist Church; Old Pine Grove Church; Our Lady of Divine Mercy Catholic Church; River Run Baptist Church; Seven Star Missionary Baptist Church; Turn Around Circle Gospel Fellowship; Unitarian Universal Fellowship.

"Looking for God in All the Right Places." Your Guide to Places of Worship in the South. www.southernvoicesraisedinprayer.org

Hey," Tony said to John about a half hour later, "you know Angie isn't coming back, right?"

They were alone at the table, the two of them hunched over beers. After Jude had dragged Rivera away and Win had disappeared into the crowd, Angie excused herself, too, and went to the bathroom.

"I was starting to wonder," John said.

"Yeah, well, the van keys are gone," Tony said, patting his pockets. He took a huge swallow of beer, narrowed one eye in John's direction.

John lifted up Angie's purse to show Tony. "Does this mean what I think it means?"

"Sure," he said. "She wants you to come after her."

"Huh." John looked at the small leather sack doubtfully. "I've never been good at reading the signs."

"This one is in blinking neon," Tony said. And: "Don't screw this up."

"That's what I've been telling myself all day."

"So you're going after her," Tony said. "Good. You can give me a ride home."

Tony had fallen asleep before John got the car out of the parking lot. He snored all the way to Ivy House, where the van stood at the curb and the house was completely dark. John was trying to figure out what that meant when Angie's cell phone began to ring and Tony woke up, snorting in confusion.

John dug the cell out of Angie's purse and handed it over to Tony, who scowled, but flipped it open. "What?"

He listened and then handed the phone to John while he got out of the car. While Tony lurched off toward the house, John counted to three, took a deep breath, and put the phone to his ear.

"Hey."

"You are slow sometimes, Harvey."

"But you love me anyway."

There was a small silence. "Should we talk about Meg?"

"Not first thing. Not even second thing." He heard her catch her breath, and his throat got dry, thinking about that.

"I thought you were mad at me, about the Miss Zula stuff."

"Third thing," he said. "Or maybe fourth."

"So are you going to sit there all night, or are you coming over here?"

John looked at the dark house. "Huh? Over where?"

"I'm sitting on your bed," she said. "You don't lock your doors."

"It's Ogilvie. I doubt you could find a locked door if you tried a hundred of them. So you parked here and walked over there, because of what Meg said?"

"Yup. Relieved?"

"A little, I guess." A *lot*. But he didn't want to admit that, not even to himself.

"So will you get over here?"

"I'll be as quick as I can."

"I hope not," Angie said, and hung up.

The phone rang again almost immediately.

"Angie—"

"John?" The voice was familiar, but it wasn't Angie. "John Grant? Is that you?"

"Hi, Mrs. Mangiamele. Yeah, it's me."

"What's with the Mrs. Mangiamele? We're strangers now all of a sudden? You call me Fran like you used to. So are you and Angie back together? 'Cause that would be good, John. For both of youse."

He found himself grinning into the phone. "It would be good," he said. "But give me a couple more days, okay?"

"So you're not getting married Saturday? Never mind, tell me this. Angie anywhere nearby?"

"Not at the moment."

"Good," said Fran Mangiamele. "'Cause there's something I always wanted to tell you back when you two were dating, but there was never a good time and then things went sour. Which was a shame."

"Fran—"

"When Angie was a little girl," Fran Mangiamele plowed ahead, "she had what they call anxiety issues. She had trouble talking to other kids when she started school, that kind of thing. Did you know about this?"

"No," John said, "she never told me." He thought of Angie as he knew her, approaching strangers to talk to them on the street. "Hard to believe."

"I know, looking at her now. But it's true, as a little girl she'd get all *agita* about the littlest things. You know how she handled it? Clothes. She couldn't control school or the kids, but she could decide what she was going to wear. The whole year she was in kindergarten, every night I'd wash the same jeans and T-shirt, and every morning she put them back on. Socks, too. She didn't care that the other kids had fancy clothes with Elmo and Miss Kitty and sparkles. None of that mattered to her, she just wanted to be comfortable in her clothes."

"Okay," John said, "but I don't get it. I have never complained to Angie about what she wears."

Fran made a *pffft* sound that meant he had misunderstood her point.

"Pay attention, you'll get my drift sooner or later. So once she got into grade school, things got a little better, but it took time. We'd go shopping and she'd pick out the plainest things, T-shirts, jeans, sweaters. I'd pick up a dress in a color that would look good on her and she'd turn her back on it.

So we'd take the clothes home and hang them up in her closet and they'd be there for months, sometimes as long as six months, before she'd put something new on."

There was a pause.

John said, "She did this—"

"She still does it, with everything. Shirts, shoes, jeans, later on dresses and skirts. Like, she can't put something on until she gets comfortable with it. But once she gets used to something—"

"She never gives up on it," John said, thinking of the Nirvana T-shirt hanging over her footboard.

"That's it," Fran Mangiamele said. "She's a cautious person, and you're a change. A big change. She likes the look of you hanging there, but she needs time to get comfortable. That's what went wrong last time, you rushing things."

"You're talking about somebody who cut her hair and dyed it blue on a whim, to shock me."

"Hair grows out," Fran said. "Nice and easy and gradual, it comes back, no matter what you do to it. You can count on it, but you can't rush it."

"Ah," said John, a little confused but also intrigued.

"So get to work, and call me back when you two have got things fixed up. Believe me, I'll be waiting by the phone."

John's house was beautifully furnished, comfortable, well laid out, preternaturally neat, and so unlike Angie that she could hardly imagine living here. If that ever became an issue, a prospect that suddenly seemed less likely, especially after she found the suit bag hanging on the back of the bedroom door with the words *Grant-Rose wedding* on the slip.

That's what you get for snooping, she told herself, and sat down on the bed. Then she picked up the phone and dialed her own cell number again.

"So how long does it take you to drive across town?" she asked when John answered.

"Missing me, are you?"

"I'm about to start looking through drawers, just so you know."

He gave a sharp laugh at that, more surprise than worry. "Your phone rang."

"Wait, don't tell me. Apples or Peaches."

"Peaches," John said. "You never told me how much your mother likes me."

Angie closed her eyes and lay back on the bed. "She's a sucker for a pretty face. So what did you two talk about?"

"She had a story to tell."

"The one about how when I was five I gave a kid down the block a bloody nose when he tried to kiss me?"

"No," John said. "I see some thematic similarities, but no blood was shed in this particular story."

"So tell me."

"It seems I'm a pair of pants hanging in your closet."

"Shit." Angie bit her lip. "Turn off the cell phone, would you? And get over here."

Much later Angie said, "Do you think it's twisted of me that I like it when you get mad? Because let me tell you Harvey, that was spectacular."

John was lying on his back, eyes closed. "God help me, I'm starting to like you calling me that. What do you think that means?"

"Wait," Angie said. "Are you going to tell me you've got a crush on Tony?"

He grabbed her and she shrieked and struggled and then gave in. "Okay, okay. Whoever Miss Zula was thinking about when she put Harvey Carson on the page, it wasn't you."

"Good." He let her go, which was a little bit of a disappointment, though the way he was looking at her was promising. "Now what's this about me being mad?"

"You forget to be polite," Angie said, running her fingers over his sweaty skin. "You stop thinking, and all the gloss comes off, and things get . . . interesting."

"So are you saying I was too rough? Because if I hurt you and you liked it, that would be sick."

"Christ no, you didn't hurt me. You've got that analytical gleam in your eye, and now I'm sorry I raised the question."

"So tell me," he said, still grinning, "are things less than stellar when I'm not angry?"

"You're fishing for compliments."

"I repeat, when I'm not angry—"

"You fuck like a god, regardless of your mood."

That made him laugh out loud. "Okay, I deserved that." He turned away to take care of the condom, which made Angie remember why Win Walker had been in such a sour mood at the Hound Dog.

She said, "We need to talk."

John groaned and swung his legs out of bed. "Yeah, we do. but I was hoping to get you into the shower first." He looked at her over his shoulder. "That would be the first stop on the tour of my adolescent fantasies."

"A girl in the shower?"

"A girl in that shower," he said. "Hot water and soap and a girl, all together."

"So how old were you when you got to try that out?"

He grinned at her. "Thirty-six."

Angie sat up. "You're kidding. That's a virgin shower?"

"As far as I'm concerned it is. My great-aunt Helen lived here for the last twenty years, you know. She was a sweet old lady but proper, and she had ears like a bat."

"When did she die?"

He cleared his throat, looked away. "Last summer."

For the last year John had lived in this house whenever he could get away from Princeton, and for most of that year he had been engaged to Caroline Rose. Had Caroline declined an invitation to join him in the shower because Rob and Kai were down the hall, or had he never asked?

"What was the plan, anyway?" she asked. "Was Caroline going to move in here, or . . ." Her voice trailed away when she realized she didn't really want to hear the answer. John was going to tell her anyway, she could see that.

"She was supposed to move in this week," John said. "Or at least I thought she was. Her sisters still think I'm going to move into Old Roses. I don't know what Caroline was actually thinking, which I suppose should have been my first hint."

He rubbed his knuckles over his jaw and the bristles of his new beard made a hushing sound.

"Is that what you needed to talk to me about?"

"In a way. Caroline wrote me a letter."

Angie pulled her knees up to her chin. "Okay. Go ahead."

She listened, her head tucked forward as he read what couldn't have been more than fifty words, and still Angie wished the lights were out; she wished they had had this conversation on the phone. She didn't know how she was supposed to react. Except that wasn't exactly true. *Mangiamele*, she told herself, *you are such a fake. You don't want to say what's on your mind because you have never known a man, no matter how open-minded, how liberal, how smart, to take such speculation with a shrug.* If a woman left for another man, that might be a relief or a tragedy, but the guy whose wife left him for another woman was the butt of the joke. In a town like Ogilvie, how would this play? Angie closed her eyes, trying to imagine it, and then, slightly nauseated, opened them again.

You don't know this for a certainty, she told herself yet again. *So shut up.*

"I have to admit," he was saying, "I'm at a loss. I don't know how to read this."

So John was clueless and Caroline was cowardly, and what a great combination that was.

"What do you think?"

He was standing at the window that looked out over the garden, his back to her, oblivious to his nakedness or the picture he made. He had the build of a rower, his arms and shoulders and neck broad and strong. She could count his vertebrae, trace the flexing muscles in his back, the sun-bleached hairs on his long legs. His hips were narrow, his buttocks perfectly round and pale as milk compared to the rest of him, the color of toast. *Turn around*, she wanted to say. *Come here. Touch me.* Angie closed her eyes and counted to three until the tide rising in her subsided.

"You know Caroline much better than I do," she said.

He sat down on the edge of the bed. "Bullshit."

That took her by surprise. "Huh?"

"Bullshit. I'm missing something obvious. I know I am, for the simple reason that I always do, as you have pointed out to me before."

Angie cleared her throat. She said, "Let me read the letter, then." Not that it would be of any help, but it would buy her some time. She took the letter from him and ran her eyes over Caroline's strong handwriting, but she was really weighing one statement after another and dismissing each in turn. When she was done, she put the letter down on the bedside table.

John had come back to bed and was stretched out beside her, his head propped on his arm.

"A few ideas come to me," she said. "But first let me ask you. Does it matter?"

"Does it *matter?*"

"She'll be here tomorrow—" Angie glanced at the sky outside the window. "She'll be back here *today*, and she'll . . . explain." And then, in response to his blank expression: "I just mean—"

"You think there's some simple answer to all this?"

"I think there's no sense in anticipating trouble. We've got enough of that as it is."

"Christ, I wish she had got that letter I wrote. The way things stand, I have no idea what to think. Rob took this as an indication that she wants out."

Angie shrugged. "Sure, you could read it that way."

"If that's the case," he said slowly, "then I've got to wonder why. Do you think she could be—" He stopped, and Angie could almost hear the words in her head: *in love with somebody else.*

"Angry—about you?"

She wanted to bury her face in the pillow, because the urge to scream or laugh or both at once was almost overwhelming. Luckily John's mind and his attention were elsewhere. And he was trying, and so she made an effort and calmed herself down so she could listen.

"I'm drawn to women who are hard to read, I always have been. But I'm learning, because I can tell that you're not saying what you're thinking, right at this minute. Are you?"

His voice had gone slightly blurry, as if he were drunk or near sleep. There was resignation in his expression, and that cut her to the quick.

Angie pressed herself against him. She put an arm across his chest and her face against his neck and she kissed him, softly, on the underside of his jaw and then on the mouth. She kissed him again, trying to apologize without words for the things she couldn't say. He caught her wrists and flipped her over on her back and kissed her back.

"John," she whispered. "I can't explain Caroline to you, but I can tell you about me, and how I feel about you. That will have to be enough for right now."

He rubbed his face against hers, caught her lip between his teeth and kissed her, breathed into her. "You're what I want," he said, and then he pulled away from her. "You, and a shower." He caught her wrist and drew her along with him.

The tub was ancient, huge, a luxury boat with paws for feet. An awkward shoulder-height shower arrangement had been added in the sixties, but this bathroom was the first thing John had remodeled after his aunt died. He kept the tub, updated the shower hardware, and added a pale linen curtain that could be drawn around the entire circumference.

They stayed there until the hot water was gone and they were both exhausted and Angie was as soft and loose and open as an overblown rose. John wrapped her in towels and rubbed her dry and then tucked her into bed next to him. She was almost asleep, breathing deeply, when she suddenly roused herself enough to roll out of the towel and drop it by the side of the bed.

"Skin," she mumbled. She pressed herself against him, and slipped away into sleep. John stayed awake for much longer, every sense focused on her textures and smells and the sight of her. He had brushed his teeth and lost her taste: salt sea, milky sweet. He thought of spreading her open with his hands, taking his fill, swallowing her whole, and then pushing himself, all of himself, inside her while she whispered in his ear and undulated around him, hair like floating seaweed, her body suckling insistently, come and come and come. When he woke she would be next to him. Angie in the night. Angie in the morning. He let himself relax and slip down, follow her down and down into sleep.

The plan was, Angie would leave first and walk back to Ivy House while John went his usual route to campus. Standing in the kitchen with a cup of coffee, she listened to him talk about the day ahead, things that might happen when Caroline came back, how he would deal with each possibility. She was oddly calm, at ease with him and herself, though the potential for disaster was tremendous.

She was putting on her shoes when John said, "You know what I said about difficult women?"

"That you're drawn to them, sure."

He said, "You're worth whatever trouble comes my way."

She relaxed a little, and then happiness made her sloppy and she said what she was thinking. "Not that there's any such thing as an easy woman."

"Sure there is," John said, and a small line appeared between his brows. Normally Angie liked arguing with him about this kind of thing, but it would be foolish to let the conversation move in that direction just now.

"Okay," she said.

"I would call Rivera . . . not easy, but straightforward. You don't have to guess what she's thinking."

"Hmmmm," Angie said.

"I don't know Jude Parris very well, but I'd say the same of her."

"I better get gone," Angie said, but she could see that it was hopeless, because he was pacing now.

"Even Meg, if you think about it—"

Let it go, Angie prayed. *Let it go, let it go.*

"Of course all three of them are—well, maybe not all three are lesbians, but almost."

She waited, breathless, to see if he could dig himself out.

"Okay, so that's a generalization that deserves to be shot down," John said, as if she had objected aloud. "But there's something there. Maybe it's just that women who are openly gay don't worry about impressing men. Meg sure wasn't worried about what the men at the table thought of her last night."

"Wow," Angie said. "Look at the time, it's getting—"

"Though she went over the line when she got going about Miss Zula," John finished.

"—late," Angie said. She took an imaginary sip from her empty cup. When she looked up, John was watching her.

"Come on," he said slowly. "You don't buy into that garbage Meg was spouting."

"That Miss Zula is a lesbian?" Angie shrugged. "I don't know one way or the other, not for sure. Does it matter?"

John blinked at her. "Of course it doesn't matter," he said. "But it isn't true."

"And if it were true, would you be upset if we pursued the subject with her?"

"The question is moot," John said. "Because she isn't."

Angie closed her eyes briefly, and then opened them. "This is something we have to talk about," she said. "But not just now. We don't have time."

John said, "There are things you don't know."

"I forgot how stubborn you can be when you get your teeth into a subject that interests you." Angie tried to grin, and failed.

"Nice try, Mangiamele."

"Okay," she said. "Sure, there's a lot we don't know. We've only been working on this for a month. So what exactly is it you're talking about?"

"There are family tragedies I'm not sure Miss Zula would want you digging around in."

Angie said, "That's between Miss Zula and Tied to the Tracks—as you pointed out last night. So far she hasn't refused to answer any question we've asked."

"Is that so?" John said, looking more than a little agitated. "So, how much has she told you about her mother and her brother?" And, seeing her expression, he said: "That's what I thought."

"We haven't really pursued the subject," Angie said, feeling suddenly defensive and intrigued, too. "But why don't you go ahead and tell me this big secret. Unless you don't trust me with it."

He shot her a disgusted look. "You know that's not the issue."

"Could have fooled me," Angie said. "Look, we should leave this—"

He cut her off with a shake of the head. "Listen. The reason Anabel Spate moved to Savannah had nothing to do with Zula," said John. "Or only indirectly. What happened was, she got on a train one summer day and without telling anybody went up to Oberlin. Abe Bragg was there, on leave, waiting for her. And they got married by a Catholic priest."

Angie tried to make sense of the words. "Anabel Spate and Abe Bragg?"

"I don't know the details of what happened next, except that Miss Louisa brought enough pressure to bear that the marriage was annulled within the week. The next time Abe came home on leave he married Lavinia, and then he was gone again. After that I don't think he was back here more than three times before he was killed in action."

"Christ," Angie said.

"I told you, it's explosive stuff."

"What in the hell could his mother have said to him?"

"Your guess is probably better than mine. It must have been pretty ugly, the whole thing, but at least Abe didn't have to stick around and face the consequences."

"So Anabel had to handle it on her own."

"There wasn't much to handle, Angie. We are talking about Georgia in the fifties. I can't claim that things are perfect now, but back then, black on white? It must have been hell for her. Of course she couldn't stay. She moved to Savannah and made a name for herself as an activist."

"That's what Jude was talking about last night."

"Part of it," John agreed.

Angie closed her eyes and tried to put it all together. She saw Miss Anabel's crowded parlor, the pictures on the wall. There had been friends and family and students, but she couldn't recall Abe Bragg among them, and she thought she would have noticed. She said as much to John.

"Do you have any photos of me hanging on your walls at home?" John said, and Angie had to give him that point, though there was something else, something so small and quiet that she had to close her eyes to try to make sense of it. She saw Miss Zula in Anabel's parlor and the tenderness in her expression when she touched the older woman's hand, dark skin against the almost translucent white. The fragile skin of a true redhead, something she had seen in another photograph, not so long ago.

And it came to her: Abe Bragg in civilian clothes and the young woman standing in front of him, the way the camera had caught the movement of her hand as she lifted it to touch his fingers where they rested on her shoulder. White on black. Anabel Spate, Abe Bragg.

"You don't believe me," John said.

"Oh, I believe you," Angie said. "I believe you about Anabel and Abe."

He threw up his hands. "What does that mean? Miss Anabel isn't a lesbian, but Miss Zula—" He broke off and his expression stilled.

He said, "You think Miss Zula was in love with her brother's wife. The brother who abandoned his wife when she needed him most. You think Miss Zula is—"

"Harvey Carson," Angie finished for him. "Miss Zula buttoned herself."

"Wait," John said. "You can't draw conclusions on such—" He stopped. "Shit." He ran a hand through his hair. "That's a trick she teaches in every introduction to writing class—switching genders in a story you want to tell to get some distance from it."

Angie felt a huge wave of relief, and of appreciation, too, that he had taken this jump, though she could see what it cost him.

"If it is true, is that so horrible?" she asked, more gently. "Maybe she decided to go ahead with the documentary because she's ready to . . . to . . ." She couldn't make herself use the cliché, and so she stopped.

He said, "This is what you wanted to talk to me about, that night after the train."

She nodded. "I saw a connection, and Tony saw it too. I wanted to ask you about it, what you thought."

"I'll tell you what I think. I think, if it's true and you're right—and if Miss Zula does want the story told—that things are going to get really messy. In every way. At every level. I think the board of regents is going to look for somebody to blame, and it's most likely to be me. I think we're in for a couple years of major problems. Christ, Angie," he said, pushing out a breath. "Is it really necessary?"

Angie looked at his face, at the expression that was half-angry, half-desperate, and she felt those same things rising up in herself. Anger that he should ask such a question, and desperate for a way out of this. "Is what necessary? The documentary? I think you know the answer to that."

He ducked his head and looked at his shoes. "I'm wondering if you need to go into this whole business. Do you have to set out to prove that every woman who never married is a lesbian?"

"You jerk," Angie said, her voice wobbling and cracking, but that was better than shouting, certainly, wasn't it? The look on his face said it wasn't, but she couldn't keep the words from spilling out anyway. "That is the most ignorant thing I've ever heard you say, and the most insulting, to me as an individual and as a professional, to Rivera, to Miss Zula, to—"

John had the good sense to look guilty, but he didn't sound that way. "I didn't mean it like that, and you know it. You aren't some third-rate shock journalist."

"You're right, we're not. That's not what we do. Miss Zula knows that. I assumed you did, too."

John looked as miserable as she felt, but they stood on opposite sides of the kitchen and neither of them moved.

He said, "I'm just suggesting you don't need to go looking for a scandal. I'm saying that not everything has to be about sex."

"It is not about sex," Angie said. "It's about love. And what you *are* suggesting is that we look the other way." She heard herself slide over into the realm of too far, too much but was unable to stop it. "You don't like messy, John, you never did. You want pretty and presentable, but that's not us. That's not me. It wasn't me five years ago and it isn't me now, and guess what, it isn't—"

She stopped herself. All the color had left his face, but his eyes were unnaturally bright. "Go on."

Angie shook her head.

"Go on," he said calmly. "Say it."

"I don't know what I was going to say," she lied, near tears.

He was looking at her steadily, his expression unreadable. Angie turned and left, and he said not one word to stop her.

The screen door had just slammed behind her when Angie saw a car pulling up to John's garage. It was beautiful and sleek and expensive, as was the older woman who was getting out of it. She saw Angie and raised a hand to wave, her perfectly made-up face breaking into a genuine smile. As if Lucy Ogilvie saw nothing odd in the fact that her son's old girlfriend was coming out of his door early on the morning of the day before he was supposed to be marrying somebody else.

"Why, Angeline, is that you? Love becomes you, sugar. You are all aglow. Now come here and give me a hug."

John stood at the kitchen window with the phone in his hand listening to it ring.

"Chair's office."

"She's here. I'm looking at Mama and Angie at this very moment, and I don't think they're talking about me getting married tomorrow."

Rob drew in a sharp breath. "Okay, let me explain."

"You caved."

"I caved. You know Mama, she's half bloodhound when it comes to affairs of the heart. But listen, she was delighted to hear that the wedding's off. She was never so crazy about Caroline."

"Rob, the wedding isn't off, not officially. Not yet." He almost said, *not for sure,* and stopped himself.

There was a small silence on the other end of the line. Finally Rob said, "She might be a help, if you let her. Things could be worse."

"It could also be a hell of a lot better," John said, and hung up the phone. Angie had managed to extract herself and disappear, and now his mother was coming toward the porch. His mother, his beautiful, impossible mother, looked up at him standing in the window and threw him a kiss.

· EIGHTEEN ·

Louisa McCleod Bragg. 1890, Daytona, Florida–1953, Ogilvie, Georgia. Graduated 1910 magna cum laude, Bethune-Cookman College, an institution founded by her aunt Mary McCleod Bethune. Teacher, Ogilvie Colored School, 1910–1945. Married Martin Bragg 1920. There were three children of this marriage: Abraham (1925–1952), Zula (1930–); Maddie (1932–). Mrs. Bragg was arrested twice, in 1950 and 1951, for refusing to leave the polling place when the election board denied her the right to vote. Memberships: Mount Olive African Methodist Episcopal Church (President, Ladies' Society, 1927–1953; President, Missionary Works, 1926–1953); southeast Georgia chapter NAACP (secretary, 1950–1953); Delta Sigma Theta; Jack and Jill. *Profiles in Leadership: The Civil Rights Struggle in Ogilvie*

You're late," Tony said. "Hey, I don't think I've ever said those words before, but there is a certain ring to them." He deepened his voice to announcer mode: "Angeline Mangiamele, you are late."

"So I am," Angie said, falling into her chair. She avoided Rivera's gaze and opened her logbook. "Shall we get started?"

"No," Rivera said.

Angie looked up, closed her eyes in supplication, and opened them again to see that Rivera was unmoved.

"You've been crying," Rivera said. "Spill it, Mangiamele."

Angie considered. She saw that Rivera was perfectly serious, that Tony would go along with whatever Rivera wanted, and that Markus was sitting at rapt attention, not understanding exactly what was happening but content to wait and see; his fascination with their odd northern ways had yet to give way to less charitable reactions. She wondered what Markus would do if she just told him what she suspected about his missing favorite aunt.

Maybe he would get angry, or maybe, Angie thought wearily, he wouldn't be surprised at all. Markus was a sharp kid and saw a lot.

She said, "I have some background information on Miss Zula's brother that we should talk about."

Rivera looked disapproving and disappointed, but her expression shifted as Angie told them what she knew.

"Now, that's interesting," she said, almost reluctantly. "Anabel Spate and Abe Bragg." To Markus Tony said, "You heard any of this story before?"

Markus shook his head. "That's, like, fifty years ago. All I know is that Miss Zula had a brother who died in a war."

"But it sounds believable?" Rivera asked him.

"Sure." Markus shrugged. "People get up to pretty much everything down here, like they do everywhere."

"But how do we get the details?" Angie said. "This is one subject I can't just ask about, and I doubt they ran the story in the *Bugle*. 'Miscegenation in Ogilvie, Locals Speak Out'—I don't think we'll find that in the library anywhere."

"You could at least look up what there is to know about Abe Bragg," Markus said. "You've got all those town history books sitting in the next room."

Angie's cell phone began to ring. She switched it off and tossed it back into her purse. "So we do. Let's have a look."

John used the private door, the one he had started to think of as the better-keep-clear-of-Patty-Cake door to let himself into his office, and then was disappointed to see that Rob wasn't at his desk. Not that he intended to do his brother any physical harm over this newest complication. Not here, not now. Right now, at this moment, he needed to talk to Angie, because no matter how much went wrong today—and it looked as if some records were going to be broken—the one thing he had to do was fix things with her. On the walk in he had used the time to recite his sins to himself, and then he had tried to call her. He had been trying every ten minutes, without success.

He dropped into his desk chair, dialed again, and then hung up without leaving a message. He was thinking about going to see her in the editing suite when Patty-Cake knocked on his door and came in without waiting for permission.

"What's up?"

Patty-Cake without her blinding smile was an unsettling phenomenon, because of course she meant that to be the case. She said, "You've got messages," and put a short stack of pink slips on his desk directly in front of him. "The first one is the most important."

In her rounded hand she had written, *Caroline 9:15; will call again at noon.*

John felt a flush running up his spine, nerves prickling and jumping.

"It's eleven now."

"My mother just got in this morning." It took considerable effort to keep his tone even, but this was a game he understood, and could play. She was angry for whatever reasons—most probably because he had put a crimp in the way she used the photocopy machine to extract tribute—but he had offered her real currency to soothe the pain: news of Lucy Ogilvie. Patty-Cake would bank it, but first she would ask questions, lots of them, all cloaked as compliments. *How is your mama?* And, *My, it must be two years since she's been back,* and *I'll bet she's got the prettiest dress for the wedding from someplace fancy, Paris or London.*

But Patty-Cake wasn't going for it, against all expectations. Instead she stood there with deep lines bracketing her mouth. *I-disapprove* lines; *I-am-disappointed* lines; *I-know-you're-up-to-no-good* lines. He was about to throw all common sense to the wind and tell Patty-Cake Walker exactly what he thought of her, but then Rob was there, moving her toward the door in a bubble he created with his soothing patter.

"That was close," he said in a theatrical whisper when he had shut her out.

"You're right," John said. "I was on the verge of . . . something. Something not good."

"A lawsuit," Rob said. "Our Patty-Cake is a whiz at filing complaints. There are six of them in the last five years that I know of, and probably more I don't."

"Oh, great," John said. "Patty-Cake Walker is going to sue me for breach of promise."

"Or harassment or chilly climate in the workplace or something else along those lines. But let me see if I can turn her around, okay? No need to go looking for a defense lawyer just yet."

"You are my lawyer," John said. "Or you would be if you'd just take the damn Georgia bar." He looked at the telephone message again, tapped it with one finger. "Did you hear about this?"

"I was there when she answered the phone," Rob said. "If it's any use to you, Patty-Cake didn't get anything substantial out of Caroline, though she tried. Look, you need something to take your mind off the telephone, and I've got just the thing: the budget."

John sat down, his hands flat on the desk. After a moment, he nodded.

There were six different books dealing with Ogilvie's history, four of them self-published, one put out by the Coastal Georgia Genealogical Society, and a biography of Joshua Ogilvie that looked to be a worked-over doctoral dissertation published by a university press. Angie took the thickest of them, *Ogilvie Past and Present,* Rivera took *Ogilvie Goes to the Wars,* and Tony picked *Profiles in Leadership: The Civil Rights Struggle in Ogilvie.* Markus made himself ready to take notes, looking as eager as a cub reporter in a 1950s newspaper caper.

Fifteen minutes later Rivera looked up. "Here's something."

Tony sneezed three times. "Damn dust. Go ahead, read it."

Rivera said, "It's just about what you'd expect. Born 1925, first child of, blah, blah, blah, attended Oberlin on a full scholarship—"

"That had to be a huge deal," said Tony.

"Highest honors, gave up law school when his father died and came back here to teach at the Ogilvie Colored School." Her eyes were scanning the page. "Then he goes and enlists in the Air Force all of a sudden, 1948. Why would he do that?"

"We learned about that," said Markus. "A lot of black men from the South enlisted after President Truman ended discrimination in the armed forces. What?" he said to Tony, who was gawking. "Catholic school is big on history, so sue me."

"Go on, Rivera," Angie said, not looking up from her notes.

"Earned his pilot's wings . . . served in Japan and Okinawa. Korea in

1950. He was killed in action when his F-86 Sabre was shot down on October 25, 1952.'"

"That's it?" Tony said.

"No, I'm getting to the good part. 'Captain Bragg married twice. His second wife, Lavinia Smithson Bragg, bore him twin sons (Martin and Joseph) in 1949. His third son, Calvin, was born while he was serving in Korea.'"

"Okay, so that's corroboration," said Tony. "He married twice. Now I've got an idea. Call me crazy, but rather than shift through all these old books, couldn't we just go call on Miss Maddie? She'd tell us if we ask, you know she would."

"You think we can ask her about Anabel Spate?" Rivera said. "How exactly will we put that question, do you think? Hey, Miss Maddie, tell us about your brother marrying a white woman and then abandoning her, will you?"

"See?" said Tony to Markus. "It's Rivera's grace and sensitivity that get us through the hard parts."

"Bite me, Dr. Phil."

"You could pull it off, Rivera," Angie said. "With Miss Maddie, you could."

Markus said, "Why not just ask Miss Zula?"

"She's out of town," said Angie. "Savannah." *And that we might not pull off*, she could have said, but didn't.

They did need to go see Miss Maddie, but everything in Angie resisted the idea of venturing out into the heat; she was tired and tense, wound up and ill at ease; she wanted to go find John—whether to throttle him or climb on top of him, she wasn't quite sure. She said, "We really need to get on with this—" She lifted her chin toward the tapes stacked up on the table.

On his way out Tony stooped and whispered in her ear. "The couch is comfortable if you need to get some sleep while we're gone. You look like you could use it."

The lopsided budget John had inherited from his predecessor was the exactly the distraction he needed: numbers didn't shimmy sideways once you got hold of them, and problems could be solved. The whole process was soothing, almost as good as an hour on the river, but without the sweat. He had just said as much to Rob when there was a knock at the door and the elder four Rose sisters came in, with Patty-Cake bringing up the rear.

John said, "You've got to be joking."

Patty-Cake held herself very erect, her mouth pursed. "I told them that Caroline would be calling."

Rob started to say something, but he let it go when John held up a hand to stop him.

"So what is it you plan to do, may I ask? Hijack the conversation, or monitor it, or what?"

Connie made a clucking sound with her tongue. "Don't be silly, John. We're just worried about her."

"That doesn't answer his question, though," said Eunice. "I told you he'd be put out, and he's got every right."

"Well, excuse me for being worried about my baby sister," said Harriet. Of the four of them, she looked the angriest, peevish and defensive. Pearl put an arm around her shoulders.

"John, this is hard for us, too." Connie said. "Mama's on her way back home from the lake with Father Bruce, and what will we tell her if Caroline hasn't come back by then?"

"We do need to talk to her," Eunice said, her tone apologetic.

They went on like this for a while, a Greek chorus of woe and worry, while Patty-Cake stood with her arms crossed, watching John. He gave her a look he hoped she understood. It said, *I'm going to find a way to fire you for this.* She gave him one back that said, *Bring it on.*

Then the phone rang. John punched the line button and picked it up.

"John Grant."

"Sugar, where do you keep the gin? I know it's just past noon, but Sam and I—"

"Mama," John said, "I'm waiting for an important phone call. Can I get back to you?"

"All I need to know—"

"None in the house," John said. If he mentioned gin in front of this audience the whole town would be talking about Lucy Ogilvie's problem with alcohol before the day was out.

"Well, then, we'll just go down to the market and stock up—"

"Tell your mama we said hey," Harriet said in a stage whisper that could be heard a hundred yards away.

"Who is that talking, John?"

"Caroline's sisters are here," John said. "Waiting for her to call. They send their regards."

"Oh, I see." There was a pause. "I swear, don't you get yourself in the strangest situations? I was just saying to Angie this morning—"

"Okay, then, see you later, Mama, the other line is ringing."

"Now hold on, sugar. Is your baby brother there?"

"Sure," John said, shooting Rob a warning look. "He'll pick up in the other office."

Rob made a face and headed out. John would have liked to keep his brother close by, but there was no denying Lucy. The five women in front of him, all meticulously groomed and expensively dressed, were supposed to be his family, considered him family already, and thus were his responsibility. A ripple of irritation at them and Caroline ran down his spine, and he realized he had broken into a sweat, although the air-conditioning was on high.

Connie was saying, "We won't take long, we just want to know—" when the phone rang again.

"John Grant."

"Hey." Caroline's voice came over the line, clear and calm. He looked at her sisters and aunt and thought of an examination board, a judge's circle, a firing squad.

"Hey to you, too," he said, leaning back in his chair. "Caroline, right off, I want you to know all your sisters are standing right here waiting to talk to you. I think Harriet is about to chew her own knuckle off, she's in such a state."

Caroline made a small, hard sound. "Patty-Cake called them."

"You guessed it."

"I should have known. Put me on speakerphone, will you? So I can take care of this."

He pushed the button, put the handset down, and crossed his arms. The Rose sisters came forward, Harriet and Pearl dropping into chairs.

"Caroline, baby, where are you?" said Connie. "We've been worried out of our minds."

"You are getting married *tomorrow*," Harriet said. "There's a rehearsal and a dinner *tonight*."

"I'm on my way home right now," Caroline said. "I'll be there in a few hours."

"But where have you been?" Harriet burst out. "I must have left fifty messages on your cell phone—"

"I needed to work through some things," Caroline interrupted. "I'm fine now. I feel much better, really I do."

Pearl said, "So the wedding is still on?"

Caroline said, "Did somebody tell you otherwise?"

"Well, no," said Pearl, shooting her sisters a *help-me* look, "but—"

"Did John say the wedding was off?" Caroline's usual deferential tone was gone.

"No," Eunice said. "Nobody said any such thing." She met John's gaze and he tried not to look panicked.

"Except Patty-Cake," corrected Connie. At that moment John realized that Patty-Cake was gone. If nothing else, she had a keen sense of self-preservation.

Harriet said, "She's been telling us you weren't coming back, you ran away because of something John did."

"Well, Patty-Cake is wrong, as usual," Caroline said shortly. "Is she there? I'll tell her so myself."

"She was here—" Connie said, looking around.

"She lit out," said Harriet.

"So you're not canceling," said Eunice. "Just to be clear, you're not calling things off?"

"I am not calling things off," Caroline said.

"What about John?" asked Harriet, trying not to look at him directly. "Is he calling things off?"

"Nothing has been called off," said Caroline, her voice so clear and commanding that John wondered for a moment if it was really her, or if she had hired someone to make this phone call. Whoever was talking, he was glad that person was willing to spare him the lie Harriet wanted to hear.

Caroline said, "I'll see y'all at Thomasina's at seven for the rehearsal dinner, okay?"

"Um," said Eunice, "so you won't be at the rehearsal itself?"

"No," said Caroline, "and neither will you. We don't need to rehearse this wedding, we've done it four times already. Let's just meet at the restaurant, okay? I'd like to spend some time with Mama when I get home, and then I'll bring her and Uncle Bruce to Thomasina's."

There was a shocked silence, in which the four older Rose girls sent one another looks that needed no translations.

"Sugar, I have to say, you're scaring me a little bit." Pearl sent John a pleading look. "You don't sound like yourself."

"I'm sorry that I scared you," Caroline said, more calmly. "I really am sorry for the trouble I've caused. But I'm asking y'all to help me now, and trust me. Will you do that?"

"Why, of course we will," said Harriet, sounding a little shocked. "We'd do anything for you."

"Anything," echoed Connie and Pearl.

Eunice said, "I expect you want to talk to John alone, so we'll just—"

"Wait," said Harriet. "About your dress—"

"—go," said Eunice firmly, taking Harriet by the elbow.

"We'll see you at Thomasina's," said Connie, sounding doubtful.

"See you later, honey," Pearl said. She gave John one last, hard look, and then she closed the door behind her.

"I hate speakerphones," said Caroline when he had her on the handset again. And then: "Could you ask Rob to make sure Patty-Cake is in plain sight? I really don't want her listening in."

"Rob is dealing with Lucy on the other line," John said. "But I saw Patty-Cake at her desk when your sisters went out. I think we're okay."

Very quietly Caroline said, "Your mama is going to be so angry with me."

"No she won't. Caroline," he said, "right now my mother is the least of our worries. You want to tell me what's going on? Because I'm sure confused."

He could hear the sound of highway traffic and people's voices in the background. A rest stop on the highway, a hundred miles away or a thousand, far enough that it was hard to get any real sense of her as she tried to pull words out the void.

Finally she said, "I've been a coward, and it's caused you a lot of grief."

"Caroline," John said, hoping he sounded calmer than he felt. "Save the *mea culpa* for Father Bruce, and tell me what the hell is going on. Just say it, whatever it is, and we'll work it out."

"I don't want to get married," Caroline said.

John heard himself make a sound like a balloon deflating. It was what he had been hoping for and dreading. He supposed he should ask a lot of questions, sound hurt or outraged, demand explanations, but nothing came to mind. He felt like a man who has spent a great deal of time and energy planning a jailbreak, only to find that the doors had been unlocked the whole time.

She was saying, "I know I owe you a long explanation and we need to talk this through in detail, but right now I'm hoping we can work together to make this as easy as possible—" Her voice trembled, and she stopped. "I'm really sorry. I really am, but this can't be much of surprise, after all. Are you okay?"

"I took a letter up to the retreat house, the same day we dropped you off there. I'm assuming you didn't get it."

Caroline drew in a sharp breath. "It must have come after I left. They probably forwarded it home to Old Roses. Do you want to tell me about it now?

"Hell no," John said, and he felt himself flush with embarrassment and irritation.

"That's okay," Caroline said. "I can pretty much guess what it said. So we're in agreement, we're not getting married tomorrow?"

John cleared his throat. "Yes, we're in agreement. What comes next?"

"The hard part. I have to talk to Mama and Father Bruce before I—before we—make any announcements. I know I'm asking a lot, but could you keep this quiet until this evening? We could tell the families at the dinner, when we've got everyone together."

"You've thought this through," John said, feeling only vaguely more charitable toward her.

"I've had some time," she said. "Before I go, I wanted to ask, how is Miss Zula? Are things going along okay with the documentary?" Her tone had shifted, and she spoke in a rush. "Tony and Angie and Rivera, are they getting the help they need?"

"They seem to be," John said slowly, suddenly on guard again, trying to make sense of the change in subject. Maybe she did know about Angie; maybe she was going to slam him with that after all, and then he would have to find the words to explain how all this had come to pass.

She was saying, "Because Miss Zula did ask me to work with them, and then I just disappeared."

"As far as I know everything is going fine," John said. "I can't say I'm very comfortable with some of the topics they're pursuing—"

"Like what?" She sounded more than interested; she sounded as if she needed to hear more.

"Well, Angie and Rivera came up with the theory that Miss Zula . . ." He paused. "It will sound crazy."

"John, right now not much could surprise me," Caroline said. "Go ahead."

"They think Miss Zula has had a lifelong affection for Anabel Spate." There was a short pause. "Caroline?"

"They want to out Miss Zula?"

John's voice caught. "Are you telling me that Miss Zula has been in love with her brother's first wife for what, fifty years? She told you this?"

"Of course not," Caroline said. "Miss Zula would never tell me something so personal."

"She wouldn't tell you, but she would tell a documentary film company?"

"My sense is, she's ready to have the story told."

"That seems like a stretch to me."

"You don't know her as well as I do. And there's something else. She's got some kind of wager going with Miss Maddie and it has to do with Tied to the Tracks. My guess is that it has to do with how long it takes Angie and Rivera to figure out the mystery on their own."

John was silent for a moment. "I still don't see how you come to the conclusion that Miss Zula and Miss Anabel . . ." He stopped, because Caroline had hiccupped a laugh.

"I've seen Miss Zula with Miss Anabel many times, John, and I'm not blind. She looks at Anabel the way you look at Angie."

For a long moment John thought he'd lost his voice for good. Then Caroline said, "John, don't worry. I am fine with this. With all of it. Miss Zula and Tied to the Tracks will work things out between them, and you and Angie—you'll work that out, too. I'll see you this evening, okay?"

And then she was gone. John still held the cool plastic of the receiver against his ear. It was as empty as a seashell, filled with nothing but echoes.

· NINETEEN ·

I have read all Miss Zula's stories and books and essays, and for years I have been trying to get a discussion group going so we could talk to her about them, but she will have none of it. I am surprised she ever agreed to this documentary business, she is such a private person. The only way I can explain it to myself is, there must be some story she wants told she can't tell herself.

Your name: Annie Lord. I am the head librarian at the Ogilvie Free Library, where this memory book was first kept and where it should still be, in my opinion.

A ngie did fall asleep on the couch in the reception area, but first she locked the door so that no one could come into the editing suite and surprise her. When she woke it was because the phone was ringing. She picked it up just to stop the noise.

John said, "Your cell phone is still off, and I'm an idiot."

"Okay," Angie said, her heart racing already just at the sound of his voice, which made her something of an idiot, too, though she wasn't going to admit that to him just now.

"I'm sorry."

"I'm listening."

"Christ, you're a tough audience, Mangiamele."

"Whine, whine, whine," Angie said, smiling into the phone. "Give it up, Harvey."

"Okay, here it is: I reacted badly this morning."

"You were a jerk."

"And insensitive. And wrong."

"Wrong?"

"Well, wrong in the way I handled the subject. I'll keep my nose out of your business from now on. It's between you and Miss Zula."

Angie said, "This is very suspicious. Why are you capitulating so easily?"

"Maybe I'm learning," he said.

"Maybe you are." Now she was grinning so that her cheeks began to hurt. "So, is that the only reason you called?"

He cleared his throat. "No. I just talked to Caroline. She's on her way home."

Angie sat very still while he told her about his phone conversation with the woman he was—as far as everybody in Ogilvie still knew—going to marry tomorrow.

"So dinner tonight at Thomasina's, and all will be made clear?"

"That's the plan. I can't see how this is going to work, but I have to go along with her, for now at least. And there's something else. She knows about you. You and me, I mean."

"You told her?"

"No, but she knew anyway. She said she saw it on my face when I look at you. She wasn't unhappy about it."

She said, "Are you unhappy about her not being unhappy?"

"Angie, I have no idea how I feel about anything. Except you."

She closed her eyes and tried to think of Rivera, what she could say to John and what she should not, and how much worse it would be down the line when he found out the things she had been thinking but not sharing.

"What are you thinking?"

Angie imagined Caroline Rose getting up in front of Ogilvie's entire Catholic population to announce the wedding was off because she was moving to New Jersey to live in sin with a woman. It was such an absurd idea that she hiccupped a short laugh. And, of course, she couldn't say who Caroline loved with any certainty. "That I'd rather not be there tomorrow when Caroline makes her big announcement. Whatever it is."

"Can't you leave the videotaping to Rivera and Tony?"

"Do we need to be there at all?" Angie asked.

He said, "I'll ask Caroline about that after supper, and then I'll call you later. Can you wait up to hear from me?"

Angie said, "I doubt I'll have much choice about it."

You will not believe this," Tony said when Angie got back to Ivy House a little past five. "I still don't believe it, and I'm looking at it."

He and Rivera were sitting at the kitchen table. Between them a manuscript, its pages slightly yellowed around the edges, typewritten rather than computer generated.

"What is that?"

Rivera put her hands flat on the table and bowed her head as if she were praying. "When we got to Magnolia House, we sat down with Miss Maddie and had some lemonade," she said. "And so I asked her about Abe and Anabel Spate."

"And?" Angie said, impatiently. "Come on, you mopes. It can't be that bad."

"It's that good," said Tony. "As soon as the question was out of Rivera's mouth, Miss Maddie got up and took this out of a desk drawer and handed it to her." He put his hand on the manuscript.

Apparently Maddie and Zula had been waiting for the question of Abe to come up ever since Tied to the Tracks first came to Ogilvie. According to Tony, Miss Maddie looked almost relieved.

"It's Miss Maddie's autobiography. Written in 1980, never submitted, never published." Rivera picked up the manuscript and came across the kitchen to put it in Angie's hands. She promptly slid to the floor, where she sat, her back against the wall.

"According to Miss Maddie, we can use whatever parts of it we see fit. As narration, if that seems right."

"What will Miss Zula have to say about that?" Angie asked. It was a moot question, in some ways; the only question, in others.

"Miss Zula knows about the autobiography."

"That it exists, or that we have it?"

"Both." Rivera's voice cracked.

"So what's in it?" Angie's voice sounded thin and far away, but that was because her heart was beating so hard.

"Everything," said Tony. "And then some."

It was ten o'clock before Angie even thought about John. All evening they had been sitting reading parts of the manuscript out loud to each other, sometimes just to hear the rhythm of the words, other times because the story dragged them along as surely as dogs on a leash.

"Why hasn't she ever published anything?" said Tony, more than once. "She writes as well as her sister."

At some point Angie had dug out her binder and started to take notes. They discussed strategy at first, how to bring Miss Zula into the conversation about the autobiography and how to handle the information it revealed.

"Voice-over narration," said Rivera. "It's the only way to do this." Tony liked Anthea Bragg's voice, which was low and a little husky; Rivera thought her sister would be a better choice.

There was an energy in the room, words sparking in the air.

"Do you think Maddie would have held it back and never given this to us if we hadn't raised the subject of Abe and Anabel?" Tony asked, when they had settled down a little.

"I'll bet it was Zula holding it back," Rivera said. "It was a test, and we didn't even know it until we passed and the gates opened."

"It was a bet," Angie said. She sat up straight. "She and Maddie had some kind of bet. Zula lost and she had to let Maddie give us the manuscript."

That sounded exactly right, but what were they betting on? Angie looked at a quote she had copied down from the manuscript: *Not every woman is suited to motherhood. Our mother was one such woman.* "Without Maddie's manuscript, whatever we put together would be only part of the story. Miss Zula knows that, but she would have let it happen."

"It's going to be an interesting discussion," Tony said. "But it will have to wait until tomorrow. I'm hungry. Anybody want to go out while we can still get dinner someplace?"

"Thomasina's," said Angie, bolting up from her chair.

"Thomasina's stops serving at ten," Tony said, looking at her with some alarm. "It's quarter after."

Angie closed her eyes. "Tony, this is going to sound so rude, but could you go away? I need to talk to Rivera. Right now."

"'S okay," he said, pushing back from the table. "I'll head on down to the Hound Dog and dine on Vienna Sausages."

The doorbell rang.

"Too late," Angie said. And to Rivera: "I'm really sorry, I wanted to tell you about this before. Caroline is back."

Rivera's face lit up, with excitement and with hope.

Tony looked at her with a new understanding. He said, "Oh."

The doorbell rang again, and Angie went to get it.

The first thing to be thankful for, John realized when he got to Thomasina's just before six, was the fact that the private room they had reserved for the rehearsal dinner really was private, isolated on the second floor, above the main dining room. The second good thing was the fact that Rob and Kai were right behind him, because otherwise he might have bolted when he saw Lucy Ogilvie already established at a table, deep in conversation with Harriet Darling.

John took a deep breath and raised his voice in what he hoped was friendly greeting. "Mama, don't you look pretty this evening."

She got up and came toward her sons, both hands outstretched so that the jewels on them caught light and shot it out again. "Now, boys," she said, "how could I stay away, with Caroline going to all that trouble to make sure I was invited?" She went up on tiptoe to kiss John on the cheek, and whispered in his ear.

"Just say the word, sugar, and I'll go, if you really want me to. But I do hope you'll let me stay for all the fun."

This was pure Lucy, endearing and infuriating all at once, and John laughed. He said, "Of course you have to stay, Mama. I wouldn't have it any other way."

"Liar." She winked at him and hooked arms with Rob and Kai. "Come on, children, let's you and me go find a drink. Here come the rest of the Rose girls, and we don't want to be in the way, do we?"

John took a deep, steadying breath and turned just in time to greet the four elder Rose girls as they came up the stairs, all of them looking slightly frazzled. Eunice took his hands and kissed his cheek and said, "I hope you don't mind, John, but our husbands are all over at the hospital playing poker with Tab."

"What Eunice is trying not to say," Connie added, throwing her sister a fierce look, "is that we have an uprising on our hands. The husbands smell trouble and they have closed ranks because they don't want any part of it."

John tried to look surprised, but knew he had failed, because Pearl was scowling at him. "Oh, sure. Go ahead and laugh, but I warn you, worse is to come. Everybody is going crazy, your fiancée included."

She marched off with Eunice trailing after her; Connie headed toward Kai, which might be a disaster in the making but there was nothing John could do about it just now, because Caroline was coming up the stairs with her mother on one side and Father Bruce on the other.

She looked up and caught John's eye and smiled, a little tentatively, a little slowly, but what that might mean, he had no idea. What he did know with complete surety was that he didn't want to be here, and that she didn't, either. John went forward and kissed Caroline on the cheek without saying anything at all, and then he took Miss Junie by the hands and kissed her, too.

She regarded him for a moment with her solemn, gray-blue gaze and then put her hands on his face, gently, as though he were one of her grandsons and in need of comfort. "My poor baby," she crooned. "You poor, poor man. I am so sorry, I truly am. Lucy, darling, come on over here and give me a kiss. I want you to sit right next to me, will you? I'll need your support through this."

It was Harriet who started it, by simple virtue of the fact that she was always the sister to say out loud what the others were thinking. No sooner had the ten of them sat down at the elaborately set table than Harriet popped up again. "I don't care," she said to Pearl in a harsh whisper. And then, tugging at the jacket of her suit, she cleared her throat. "We all know why we're here. I say forget the food and let's get the talk over with. Caroline, John, tell us what's going on before I lose my mind and start throwing things. Mama, don't look at me that way. I know it's not ladylike, but really." And Harriet sat down again, picked up her wineglass, and put it down hastily when she realized it was still empty.

Caroline caught John's gaze and shook her head slightly. Her eyes were bright and her color high, and John was struck by how pretty she looked.

"Go ahead, Caroline Mae," said Father Bruce, touching her elbow. "It's best to be direct in matters like these."

"Yes, dear," said Miss Junie. "Go ahead."

"Thank you," Caroline said, floating along on a cushion of flawless manners. John wondered if she realized that there was a muscle twitching in her cheek. She said: "I want you all to know that I am sorry for my behavior this past week. I realize I have caused you considerable worry and trouble."

She paused, looked at John, and smiled a little. "John, I don't know if I can ever explain to you how much your patience and understanding has helped me through this difficult decision." Then she took a very deep breath and said, "I have spoken to Mama and Father Bruce about this, and John knows some of it. Now I want y'all to know that none of this has anything to do with him. He's not at fault, in any way. I want y'all to accept that, and I expect you to make other people accept it, too. Do you understand me, Harriet?"

"Well, of course I do," Harriet said peevishly. "Go on, would you, sugar?"

Caroline nodded. "What I have to tell you is this: I am resigning my position at the university effective immediately. I don't like being a professor. I never did. I haven't had any real interest in the research I do for a long time, and I'm only a mediocre teacher."

"Why, that's not—" Connie began, and stopped dead because her mother was sending her a disapproving look. John assumed his own expression was a lot like the ones he was seeing around the table, disbelief and shock and confusion. Kai was the only person who seemed unfazed, and she had tilted her head to one side in a way that meant she was waiting for more data to process.

The things that ran through John's mind were disjointed, disturbing, but unstoppable: *That's the last thing I expected;* and *This will make a mess of the fall schedule;* and *Patty-Cake will implode;* and finally, the realization that he would miss Caroline, who had been a friend first, and someone he liked working with.

"Why, baby," Eunice said very slowly, as she might speak to someone who has had a blow to the head. "That's your business. Nobody's going to think any less of you if you decide you don't want to work. John can support you." She sent him a questioning glance, which he studiously overlooked.

"I'm not finished," Caroline said sharply. Connie and Pearl were just across from John, and he saw the alarm in their faces. His own mother was all glittering eyes. Caroline said, "I am going to be moving away from Ogilvie, and I won't be coming back—"

"Oh, Lord," said Connie, closing her eyes. "You're going into the convent, aren't you. I knew it."

"—except for visits now and then," Caroline finished, shooting Connie an exasperated look. "No, I am not going into the convent. I wouldn't make a very good nun, Father Bruce and I are agreed on that, aren't we?"

She turned to her uncle and he bobbed his head. "No convent for our Caroline," he said.

"Well, color me confused," Harriet said, throwing up her hands. "You don't want to be a professor, you don't want to go into the convent, you don't want to live in Ogilvie—" She broke off and turned toward John.

"John won't be going with me," Caroline said, before Harriet could ask the question.

"Are we talking about a long-distance marriage?" Connie asked, her color rising along with her voice.

"No," Caroline said. She turned to her mother as if to ask for help, but Harriet was on her feet.

"So the wedding is off! I knew it. How could you lie to us, Caroline? Now we'll have to face all those people tomorrow and we'll never live it down—"

"Now, Harriet, hush." Miss Junie's voice, sharp and sure, cut Harriet off as neatly as a chainsaw. "You have to let your sister finish."

"I don't think I care to hear any more," Harriet said with all the defiance she could muster. Then she crossed her arms and sat down again.

Caroline said, "I'm hoping we can turn the wedding into a going-away party, but there's something else I've got to say before we talk about that. And, please, if you love me, don't interrupt.

"I've been pretending for all these years that I'm something that I'm not. I'm not like y'all. I wouldn't be happy doing what y'all do, career and kids and softball on Friday nights, Junior League, the Jubilee committee. If I try to make myself fit into that mold, I'll be miserable, and I'll make John miserable."

"But John loves you!" Pearl wailed, and burst into noisy tears. Caroline's own face was bright red and her eyes were swimming, but she was resolute and sure and she didn't flinch, answering questions that came flying at her with tremendous calm until her mother got the upper hand by raising her voice.

"Girls!" Miss Junie said sharply. "Where are your manners?"

Caroline leaned down and pressed a kiss to her mother's forehead. Then she straightened and smiled. She said, "I'm very happy to tell y'all that I've enrolled in the two-year program at the Culinary Institute in Hyde Park, New York, and I'll be moving up there as soon as I can pack my things. I am going to be a chef."

When the doorbell rang, Angie went to let John in.

"You look like you just ran a marathon," she said, and then he pulled her up against him and kissed her, hard and quick, and let her go so suddenly that she nearly lost her balance.

"That's just about how I feel," he agreed.

From the kitchen Tony called, "Anybody know where the van keys went?"

John took Angie by the wrist and pulled her toward the door. "Come on," he said. "Let's go for a walk."

They circled the house and headed down toward the river, Angie asking questions and John ignoring them until they were almost to the bank. John flung himself down on the grass, and she followed him, ill at ease, reluctant. She looked toward the house. There was a light burning in Rivera's window.

"You won't believe it," John said. "I still don't believe it."

"Try me."

He was staring into the sky, bright with stars and a moon that was close to full. "The main points: Caroline called off the wedding. She's resigning her faculty position and she's leaving Ogilvie for good. All because she realized, at the age of thirty-five, that what she really wants is to be a chef."

Angie sat very still, trying to string the words he had produced into something recognizable. "A chef?"

"She's going to cooking school."

"Oh."

"My reaction pretty much exactly," John said.

"So," Angie said, "as far as anybody knows, this is all her decision and you're—what? Deserted and heartbroken?"

He frowned. "I hadn't thought about it that way, but yeah, I suppose that's the way this will play."

Angie didn't need to ask how that sat with him, because it was clear he didn't know himself. She could see him running the scenario through in his head. Would he mind, if all of Ogilvie thought Caroline Rose had dumped him? The answer to that, she was pretty sure, had to do with Caroline's reasons. Or at least what people believed about her reasons.

John said. "You should have seen the look on Harriet's face. If Caroline had announced she was a closet Hare Krishna and was moving to a commune in Siberia, I don't think she could have been more shocked. I just came from a three-hour Rose family discussion that had to be heard to be believed." He turned his head toward her abruptly.

"You spent a lot of time with Caroline in the last weeks. Did you have any inkling of this?"

"That Caroline wanted to give up everything to go to cooking school?" Angie shook her head. "Not the first clue. Did they try to talk her out of it?"

"Oh, yeah. Harriet and Pearl leading the charge, Eunice hanging back like the voice of reason she has always been, Caroline trying to make everybody happy and doing just the opposite."

"And Miss Junie?"

He shrugged. "Miss Junie did what she always does. To anybody who doesn't know how she works, it looks like she's staying neutral. But believe me, if she wanted to put a stop to the discussion, she could do it. Harriet and Pearl will do her fighting for her, and the sad thing is, none of them really see that for what it is."

"But the wedding is off?"

He nodded. Angie watched his eyes as he talked about what was going to happen. Caroline had wanted to call all the wedding guests and tell them that what they'd be attending tomorrow would be a going-away party instead of a marriage ceremony; Harriet, Connie, and Pearl had lobbied for a tactical delay. If she spent one more night thinking through the long-term repercussions of her choices, they would surrender their worries and doubts and support her decision. What they were hoping, John said, was that she would come to her senses overnight and wake up eager to get into her wedding dress.

"And they all just assumed you'd go along with whatever she decided, one way or the other?"

His mouth jerked at the corner. "Kai pointed that out, but nobody listened. Later Caroline took me aside and said I didn't need to worry, there would be no more changes to her plans, no matter what her sisters were hoping for."

John put back his head and laughed up into the sky. "I am such an idiot," he said. He sounded relieved and bitter and confused; he sounded angry. He was blaming himself, but for what? How badly he had misread Caroline? Or maybe he realized, on some level, that she hadn't been telling the whole truth.

"You're not the idiot," Angie said. "Caroline lied to you."

He was looking at her, silent, appraising. "It takes two to lie, Marge. One to lie, and one to listen."

"If you're going to start quoting Homer Simpson, I'll concede right now." Angie's voice came sharp and unpleasant, and she got up to move away but he caught her by the shirttail.

"Hey," John said softly. "Hey. Settle down."

She made herself do just that. She lay down next to him on the cool grass and took stock. His arms were solid and strong around her, his breathing was even. Her choices were to stay like this and let him come to a peaceful place with the situation Caroline had handed him, or she could go find Rivera and get the rest of the story. Because she had come to the end of her own patience.

He was saying, "So here's the deal. I have to show up tomorrow at Old Roses at ten o'clock. Caroline asked me to stand there with her and her family when she makes her announcement."

"Where is she now?" Angie asked.

He turned his head to her. "She went back to Old Roses. Where else would she be?"

Angie sat up and looked toward Ivy House. The screened porch was dark, but the door to the kitchen was open, a perfect rectangle of blinding white light, and framed in its middle was Caroline.

John said, "Or maybe not. What is she doing here?"

It wasn't really a question, and Angie said nothing at all. They watched two tall, slender figures moving past the rectangle of light, forward and back, like uncertain dancers; like lovers circling each other. They never touched, and that somehow made it all the more clear that they meant to, but could not quite.

The whole world seemed to have gone very still. Beside her, Angie could almost feel John's heart beating. He said, "Angie. Why is she here?"

"You should ask her that," Angie said, and felt his hand on her arm, his grip strong and unrelenting.

"Angie."

"She didn't tell you the whole truth, John. All that stuff about wanting to quit academics and leave Ogilvie and become a chef, I don't doubt that's all true, but she left out the part where she fell in love with somebody else."

His voice came cool and from far away. He said, "I don't believe it."

Miserable, Angie nodded. "You're right. You shouldn't take my word for it. Nobody has said anything to me directly, not Rivera or Caroline. But—"

"You've seen how they look at each other." He stood up abruptly and shook himself like a dog. When he looked at her she couldn't make out his expression; she didn't recognize him at all. He started to walk away and she called after him.

"Is it me you should be mad at, John?"

"You'll do for a start," he said, without turning around.

She watched him walk around the house and disappear into the night shadows.

When she could make herself go back into the house, Angie found that Caroline had left, too. She turned off all the lights one by one and then made her way upstairs by touch. Rivera's bedroom door was open and she was sitting on the edge of the bed, her hands folded in her lap. The lamp on the dresser was on, but her face was lost in shadow.

Angie stood in the hall until Rivera raised her head and looked at her directly.

"That bad, huh?" Angie said.

"Worse," Rivera said. "You've been so good, never asking. I know you've been worried and you must have been confused."

"I'm still confused," Angie said.

"Me too. Remind me never to get involved with Catholic girls, would you?"

"Ah." Angie closed her eyes. "I wasn't sure."

"Neither is Caroline. She's not ready to come out to her family; she's not sure she ever will be, but hey. I'm supposed to be satisfied with the fact that she's getting out of Ogilvie. Apparently, mastering the perfect Béarnaise sauce will be enough of a challenge for Caroline Rose."

"And you fit into this where?"

"I wish I knew. I wish she knew."

"That stinks," Angie said.

"Yeah, well." Rivera drew in a long breath. "What about you?"

"The other shoe just dropped for John. He didn't take it well. I don't know what's going to happen now."

"Right now I'd be happy not to know a lot of things," Rivera said. And then she got up and closed the door in Angie's face.

TWENTY ·

Mrs. June Callahan Rose
requests the honor of your presence
at the marriage of her daughter

Caroline Mae Rose

and

John Ogilvie Grant

And to the reception and luncheon immediately following

Saturday, 8 July
11 in the morning
The Gardens at Old Roses
Ogilvie, Georgia

R.S.V.P.

In the morning Angie found out, to her surprise and considerable horror, that Tony and Rivera were going ahead with the videotaping of the Rose-Grant wedding.

"Nobody canceled, as far as I know," Tony said as he took stock of his camera bag. "Anybody call you to cancel, Riv?"

"Nope," Rivera said. She managed a grim smile. "We can handle this without you, if you'd rather not." She was wearing black slacks and a short-sleeved white shirt, their standard costume for such gigs. She looked rested and calm and without a care in the world, which frightened Angie and irritated her even more.

"You'll have to," Angie said. "I'm going into the editing suite to work on the logging."

"Well, good," said Tony. "Because there was a message for you on the machine from Patty-Cake. You've got a special-delivery envelope in your mailbox in the department. Not that we won't miss you at the wedding of the season, understand."

It should have felt good to slam the door on the way out, but it only made her headache worse.

In Angie's experience the English department, pretty much deserted during the week, was more like a mausoleum on the weekends. This suited Angie, who had almost perfected her schedule to the point that, if she was careful, she could avoid Patty-Cake completely. Of course there was no avoiding e-mail, and the continuous flow of tack-like little notes about her many transgressions. Angie had begun to cut paper dolls out of them and was constructing a collage on one wall of the bigger editing room.

Today there was next to no chance Patty-Cake would be in the department, and so Angie took the direct route to the main office, used her key to get to the mailboxes, and found the special-delivery letter. It had been mailed from a Savannah post office box, and while it looked very official and serious, with its multitude of rubber stamps and stickers, there was no clue at all as to who had sent it. Angie opened it on the spot.

The DVD box was of the plain vanilla variety. On the DVD itself there were two words in plain block print, written with a Sharpie: WATCH ME. A little shiver went up Angie's spine as she tucked the case into her work bag and headed to the staircase that would take her to the editing suite, where she intended to hide all day long.

She let herself in and reached for the light switches with her free hand. The reception room sprang to life, and with that John Grant jumped up from the couch, startled and wild eyed, hair standing on end.

"Shit!" Angie dropped her bag and most of what was inside it spilled across the floor. The door closed behind her with a soft click and she jumped again.

"Christ," John said. "You scared me half to death."

Angie swallowed hard. "Then I'll go out and come in again."

"Very funny." He scowled at her. "What are you doing here?"

"I work here," Angie said. "What's your excuse?"

John followed her into the kitchenette and raised his voice to be heard over the noise of water running into the empty coffee carafe.

"Why aren't you at Old Roses?"

"I don't have any business at Old Roses," Angie said, looking at him over her shoulder. He looked thoroughly rumpled: his eyes were slightly blood-shot, he needed to shave, and he smelled like the Hound Dog on a busy night. "You do, though. You'll make quite a splash, showing up like that."

"I couldn't go home," John said. "I was afraid Caroline would come look-ing for me."

After a full minute had passed she finally gave in and looked up at him. He was leaning in the doorway, his arms crossed, one eye closed and the other narrowed.

He said, "How long did you know, and not tell me?"

"Oh, so you're in the mood to talk now?" Angie said. "Well, I'm not. Go to your wedding, John. I've got work to do."

"I'm not getting married today, and you know it."

"I don't know anything," Angie said. She marched back to the reception area, leaned down to her bag, and snatched the DVD case out of the mess. "And if I did, you wouldn't believe me anyway."

He had the good grace to flush at that. "You don't think I have the right to be upset?"

"Sure," she said, "but not with me."

He followed her down the hall and into one of the smaller editing suites. He said, "There is such a thing as a sin of omission."

"Listen to him." She flipped the DVD out of its case and slid it into the slot. "Since when did you join the Vatican Council?"

"I just want to know," he said. The line between his brows was deep enough to lose a penny in. "Since when has Caroline been involved with . . ." His voice faded.

"Her name is Rivera," Angie said. "And I didn't say anything because I had nothing concrete to tell you. All I had were a few . . . observations that I couldn't present to you, because I knew—" She hesitated.

"What?"

"That you'd react like this. I still don't know any more than you do, which brings me to a crucial question. Why aren't you directing these ques-tions to Caroline?"

"I'm sorry that things have come to this point," said a voice from the computer's speakers. "But you give me no choice."

"The hell?" said John, and Angie sat down heavily on the chair in front of the computer. Patty-Cake Walker was looking back at her. Her expression, self-satisfied, prim, superior, told the whole story before the bright orange mouth opened again.

She was saying, "I simply won't allow you to interfere with the happiness of the people I love best in the world. John Grant and Caroline Rose were made for each other, and they deserve a perfect wedding day. All I'm doing is making sure you're not around to cause more trouble."

Angie punched the pause button, leaving Patty-Cake with her mouth contorted and her eyes half-open. She looked at John and he looked at her and they bolted. He got to the exit first, grabbed for the doorknob.

"Fuck," he said.

"Well, no," Angie said. "That's just the problem. Patty-Cake thinks we're doing too much fucking."

When they got back to the computer Patty-Cake was still waiting patiently in suspended animation. Angie punched the play button.

"I know about that nasty business on the afternoon of the Jubilee, when you went to so much trouble to seduce John . . ." Patty-Cake said.

"See?" said Angie.

John threw up his hands. "How does she know about that?"

"Win Walker," Angie said. "And an unfortunate condom sighting."

". . . I know a lot of things, and I'm making it my business to put an end to all your scheming. As anybody in the English department can tell you, it's not wise to trifle with me, and you're about to learn that lesson the hard way.

"Let me spare you some trouble. The phone lines and the Internet connections to this part of the building have been turned off. I understand these rooms were constructed with soundproofing and without windows for technical reasons. I expect that's why there's no cell phone reception. You'll find a sack of groceries in the front closet and the plumbing is working just fine. If you get bored I suggest you turn on the television, which is working. On channel twelve you'll find a live broadcast of John's wedding to Caroline. I'm sure you won't want to miss that." She smiled broadly, and Angie was glad to see a smear of lipstick on one of her incisors. "Tomorrow morning, once they have left on their honeymoon, I'll open the door."

The screen went blank. Angie turned to John, who was wobbling on his feet. He looked vaguely green.

"Honeymoon?"

"Montreal," he said.

"How elegant." Angie said. "If you're going to throw up, please don't do it here."

In the plastic cubicle that served as a shower, John stood for a half hour with his head bent until the last of the nausea left him. Then he wiped himself down with a fistful of paper towels, got back into clothes that deserved to be burned, and went to find Angie.

She was in the bigger editing room, working in front of a monitor. Her gaze shifted from the screen to the paper in front of her and back again, her pen moving steadily. Once in a while her left hand reached out to touch a control that stopped the flow of film, and then to start it again. For a few minutes John listened to Miss Zula talking to her sister about whether it was 1960 or 1961 that Martin Luther King Jr. had stopped in Ogilvie and preached a sermon, and then he called her name.

She looked up, startled and confused and irritated, and John felt his throat closing on all the things he had wanted to say to her. Instead something completely different came out.

"It's half past ten," he said. "Can I turn on the television?"

Angie looked at the set, suspended from a ceiling mount in the corner. "If you're dead set on watching Caroline get stood up, be my guest."

He found a chair and the remote and then sat for a long minute, unable to push the power button. Not a half mile from here some hundred people were converging on Old Roses. Behind the scenes another dozen people would be hysterical, because the groom—probably some of them were still thinking of him that way—was missing. No doubt the Rose girls had sent their husbands and older sons out to look for him, and some of them would come to this very building. Possibly one or more of them was upstairs right now, knocking on his office door. They would be in touch by cell phone, this search posse, and in between calls they would be speculating on where he might be, and with whom, and what punishment he deserved for what he was about to do to Caroline. The fact that she was about to dump him would not enter into it at all; they would want his head on a platter.

John realized he had said that last bit out loud.

"Well, first," Angie said, "it's not like it's your fault. We've got Patty-Cake on DVD. That should make it clear that you were stuck here against your will."

"But not why I was here in the first place," John said.

"Second," Angie went on, as if he hadn't spoken at all. "Second, she's about to dump you in front of everybody anyway. Look at it like this, all you've done is to steal her thunder."

He thought for a while, weighing the things he might say, the places this conversation might go. Once the disaster unfolding on the screen in front of them had played itself out, he would pursue one or more of those lines of discussion, but right now there was nothing to do but watch and wait.

"This is going to backfire on Patty-Cake, you know that," he said.

"I'm counting on it," Angie said. "What I can't decide is, should I wait for the full force of public humiliation to wash over her before I kill her, or just indulge my fantasies straight off."

John felt himself flush and stir, and what a mess he was: Angie Mangiamele said the word *fantasies* and he felt himself stirring. "That's a question worthy of some deliberation," he said, and turned the television to channel 12.

He was disappointed when Angie left the room; he was about to go find her to admit he needed her with him through this when she came back with a tray: coffee, milk, a few apples, and a pile of diet bars, the kind made of sawdust and fake chocolate, kept afloat by marketing and Orwellian names: Choco-Mint Extravaganza and Orgasmic Orange.

"Patty-Cake strikes again," she said. "You can take this as a commentary on my figure." And then, as she pulled up a chair to sit next to him, she did a double take at the television screen.

"Who the hell," she said in a conversational tone, "is behind that camera?"

It certainly wasn't Patty-Cake, who had stuck her microphone in Button Ogilvie's face and was asking about her dress, and was that Dior? Patty-Cake herself was in a sheath of electric blue that showed off her cleavage and the exact shape of an obviously enhanced derriere and tilted her slightly forward, so that she looked like an exotic breed of chicken, which John pointed out because it was true, and because he desperately wanted to make Angie smile.

"The feathers on her hat complete the image," she agreed.

There was some work to be done with Angie, John knew that; maybe being stuck here would be a good thing, in the end. Neither one of them would be able to bolt off when the discussion got rough, as it was bound to.

"John?" Angie said. "Do you know who's behind that video camera?"

He said, "My guess is, Will Sloan. He's got the public-access TV station all tied up these days."

Tony walked past Patty-Cake and her cameraman and shot them an incredulous look. Angie snorted a laugh.

"This will be the best-documented no-show wedding in Ogilvie history," John said. Then he realized that if Tony was there, Rivera must be, too. He thought about that, wondered if he should raise the subject, and decided there weren't words enough in the language to sort out how he was feeling about Rivera.

Patty-Cake was running in tiny little steps to catch up with Kai and— John gulped as he saw this—his mother and stepfather. OP-TV wasn't alone in wanting to talk to Lucy, who had her usual small crowd of admirers trailing along.

"Sam looks a little thunderstruck," Angie said.

"Lucy Ogilvie in her element is more than most men can handle."

"Lucy!" Patty-Cake was calling. "Lucy, won't you spare a few words for *Girl Talk?*"

Apparently Lucy would not; she never slowed down, though she did throw Patty-Cake and her viewers her own version of the royal wave.

"She's going to sit with Miss Zula," Angie said.

John had successfully avoided the idea of Miss Zula for the last day or so, but there she was on the screen with her sister and a half dozen other Bragg relatives. For the first time he was actually glad to be locked in the editing suite.

Angie glanced at him, and he had the sense he was reading his thoughts. She said, "I'm sorry this happened to you. I'm sorry for Caroline, too. But mostly I'm sorry for Rivera. You're not the only one Caroline disappointed last night, you know."

That caught him off guard. He said, "Caroline dumped Rivera?"

Angie shot him a sour glance. "You can't dump somebody unless you're already with them. That make you feel better?"

It should, but it didn't. He thought of telling Angie so, but there was something small and hard in his gut that clenched when he thought of having to apologize again, of always being wrong.

Without looking at him, Angie said, "Caroline has done a pretty good job of misleading everybody, including herself. She's still at it, too."

And just that easily all the aggravation and anger left him, as though she had stuck a tap in his head at exactly the right spot and drained it out of him. He was overcome by surprise and a deep sense of awe, that Angie should understand so easily, and offer him so much.

Her hand was resting on the arm of her chair. It would be a small matter to touch her, take her hand, try to bridge the gap. But they hadn't come that far yet, and John kept thinking of Fran Mangiamele on the phone: *You pushed her too hard you went too fast you wanted too much.*

On the screen Patty-Cake was saying, "Notice how the ribbons on the flower arrangements echo the color scheme of the garden itself, an elegant touch in line with the bride's superior sense of style." Rob appeared behind her, looking grim, and went straight to the house.

This much even Patty-Cake couldn't ignore. She said, "Of course, even the best-organized wedding will run into a bump or two. The trick is to be prepared for every eventuality."

It was eleven o'clock, and the camera slid away from Patty-Cake's face, now sporting a fine line of perspiration along the upper lip, and fixed on the house, where French doors had opened and a crowd of people could be seen poised to come out onto the gallery. A murmuring rose among the wedding guests, and the camera panned across them jerkily. John took in the familiar faces of his own cousins, friends he had grown up with, the few colleagues he had invited. All of them wondering where exactly he was, and if it was really possible that John Grant, steady, responsible, proper John Grant, could be missing in action from his own wedding. Most of his people would give him the benefit of the doubt, but Caroline's were another matter. Especially if Patty-Cake started talking, something that might just happen if she lost the last bit of common sense she stilled called her own. Somewhere a child began to cry, and John wasn't far from joining in.

Patty-Cake was talking to the cameraman in a harsh whisper and the picture lurched back in her direction, providing an excellent view of one heavily mascaraed eye, one flaring nostril, and half an angry scowl. Then it swung away again, as if pushed. Will, who seemed to have no real feel for camera work, somehow found Rivera. She was standing against the wall of the house, her camera cradled in her arms, her face drawn.

Angie said, "After I kill Patty-Cake, I may just go looking for Caroline."

Caroline, who had just come out onto the gallery, bracketed by her family on all sides. Mother and uncle, sisters and brothers-in-law, nephews. She was wearing a suit in a delicate shade of pink and a silky white blouse with a scooped neck. There was a single rose on her lapel that matched the color in her cheeks almost exactly, and her eyes were so bright that John wondered if she had been drinking.

"That must be her going-away outfit," Angie said. It wasn't really a question, which was just as well, because John couldn't have said one way or the other. All he knew for sure was that Caroline wasn't wearing a wedding dress. That was such a relief that for a moment he couldn't talk at all.

The camera was on Patty-Cake again, who looked suddenly ten years older, and angry. She batted at it openly and it tilted.

"John's not here," somebody said, very distinctly from behind the camera. "John Grant is not here."

Then Caroline raised her voice and spoke, her tone sure and easy. This strange new Caroline, confident, unshakable. "Y'all must be wondering what exactly is going on," she said. "So come on over here and let me explain."

There was a scuffle and then the screen shifted: to the sky, a clear deep blue, to the grass, and then nothing.

"She turned it off," Angie said. "That bitch. She turned the camera off."

Sometime later, when the television had sparked to life again with a rerun of a local beauty contest, Angie roused herself. John was sitting slumped in his chair, his chin on his chest.

"I've got this idea that Patty-Cake may not come unlock the door tomorrow after all."

"You think?" John said. "What about Tony, or Rivera?"

"Possible," Angie said. "But unlikely."

He didn't seem upset by the idea that they might be here all weekend; he didn't seem happy or angry or anything at all. He had a right to a little shock, Angie thought. She had no idea how she would react if she knew all of Hoboken was out looking for her with malice on their minds for something she hadn't even done.

She said, "Last year I totaled my father's car. Some idiot ran me off the Parkway and I ran into a construction site at about sixty miles an hour. The airbag went off. Have you ever had an airbag go off?"

He shook his head.

"You get slammed with what feels like a full-body punching bag moving about three hundred miles an hour."

John looked thoughtful. "You're right," he said. "That's just about what this feels like." He finally turned his head toward her. "You didn't get hurt?"

"Nah. Just some scrapes."

He leaned forward in his chair, put his elbows on his knees. Angie, who had been sure last night that she would be angry at him for the rest of her life, looked at the back of his neck and knew she was bound to give in. For better or worse, she was stuck with the guy. She put her hand on him, felt the curve of his spine and the heat of him. He shuddered.

He said, "I don't suppose there's any alcohol around here."

"That's an excellent question," Angie said. "Let's go see if we can find Tony's stash."

They piled the provisions on the coffee table in the reception area. In addition to Patty-Cake's contribution of apples and diet bars, they had a bag of potato chips, a half-empty box of stale doughnuts, and in the refrigerator they found milk, cranberry juice, and an assortment of Mexican and Chinese leftovers.

"Not even any fermenting juice," John said.

"Oh," Angie said, and dashed off. John followed her to the kitchen, where she opened the refrigerator again, empty now of everything but film, and then peered into the freezer compartment.

"Voilà." She pulled out a bottle of vodka that was almost full, and turned to hold it up. John found himself close enough to feel her breath on his face.

Her smile faded away and they stood there a moment in the open door of the refrigerator, unwilling, unable to move.

"Déjà vu," Angie said finally, her voice rough.

"All over again." John ducked his head and kissed her. An easy kiss, a question she could answer without much discussion. Angie kissed him back, tasting of apple and coffee, and then put her forehead against his shoulder and shook her head. He pushed a coil of hair behind her ear and stepped back.

Angie said, "You don't have to get me drunk, you know. It won't make a difference one way or the other."

They had spread out their odd picnic on the floor of the reception room with the vodka bottle right in the middle, where both of them could keep an eye on it.

"You're the one who's pouring," John reminded her. "Maybe you should stop."

She frowned elaborately, her whole face contorting. Mouth and brows and cheeks disapproving, but she looked at the plastic glass that still held a swallow of vodka, and put it down on the table.

"Spoilsport."

"So tell me," John said, "what do you think Caroline said, after Patty-Cake turned the camera off?"

Angie looked at him hard, and he saw that she really wasn't drunk at all, nor was she as angry as she had been. On the other hand, it wouldn't take much to push her right back to that place. His own anger had disappeared sometime during the broadcast from Old Roses, and in its place was a void, waiting to be filled.

"Because," John said, moving ahead carefully, "I've been thinking about this whole thing, and I've come to some conclusions."

"Let me guess. A vast left-wing lesbian conspiracy has kidnapped and brainwashed your girlfriend. The one you didn't want to marry anyway."

"I guess I deserve that," John said. "But it is insulting."

"Exactly," Angie said. And then: "So go ahead, tell me your conclusions."

He thought for a moment, considered retreating, and understood it would be the worst course of action, the one thing certain to alienate her, possibly past the point of recovery.

"I can see that Caroline has changed, I guess is the word. She stood up to her mother and her sisters. I didn't think I'd ever see that happen, but she did." He focused on a spot on the wall, because to look at Angie was to lose his resolve. "I'm willing to accept the idea that Caroline decided to back out of the wedding because she realized she can't make that kind of commitment to any man."

"But?"

"Maybe she is in love with Rivera and she's already announced it to the world while we sit here eating stale doughnuts."

"That's doubtful," Angie conceded.

"But maybe—and this is another maybe, Angie, but I've got to say it—maybe she's not."

"Not in love with Rivera?"

"Maybe she's not gay, or if she is, maybe she's decided Rivera isn't the person she needs in her life. Or maybe—and I'll admit to you that this seems the most likely situation to me—maybe Caroline has decided that she likes women but wants to be celibate. There's a reason her sisters were worried when she ran off to the retreat house, you know. They've always half expected she'd end up a nun. So she might decide to live as a celibate, and whether or not that's right or good or healthy, whether it's fair to Rivera or herself or not, it's her decision."

His voice grew rough as he spoke and was almost hoarse at the end, just as Angie's expression had gone from very still to stone. She wasn't looking at him, but at her own hands, locked around her glass. John took short, shallow breaths and waited for her to scream at him or laugh at him or tell him exactly what an idiot he was being.

Vodka, Angie was thinking, *is not my drink*. Her head hurt, and she was noticing a very odd side effect: all her good anger, carefully fed and flamed and tended over the course of a long and sleepless night, was seeping out of her like gas from an old balloon. John went on and on saying things that sounded sensible and fair, but when added up together meant that Rivera was going to be miserable, and that maybe even Caroline was doomed to be miserable, and there wasn't anything anybody could do about it except Caroline herself.

Angie tried to throw the anger switch, and found she couldn't. Because he was right, and that irked her but she couldn't be angry about it.

She said, "So you don't care if Caroline dumped you because she likes women. If she just stood up and told all of Ogilvie, you don't give a damn."

He blinked at that but before she could work up any indignation he found a way to steal that, too.

"Well, shit, Angie," he said wearily. "Of course it's going to hurt like hell. You think it's easy admitting that I didn't notice there was something missing? I'll take heat for this for a long time."

She leaned forward. "So why didn't you notice?" It was as close as she could come, as she would ever come, to asking him about sex with Caroline. If he didn't answer her, she wouldn't be surprised.

He blew out a breath and closed his eyes. "I've been asking myself that pretty much nonstop since last night, as soon as I saw her there in the doorway talking to Rivera. Right before I made an ass of myself to you and walked away."

"Sweet talk won't get you anywhere just now," Angie said. "So did you come to any conclusions?"

He put his chin on his chest. "One possibility. You won't like it."

"Try me."

"Caroline," he said evenly, "isn't you."

"Oh, please." Angie wanted to lean over and slap him, but she also wanted to lean over and run her hands over his body; she was a weak human being, unable even to keep herself from smiling.

John was looking at her in a calculating way. "You know what I'm trying to say. I spent five years dating women who weren't enough like you to keep my interest, and it got to the point that I just gave up. I came to the conclusion that something was always going to feel slightly off."

"That'll do for a start," Angie said. "But you're not off the hook yet, Harvey."

He gave her a half smile. "Does this mean you're not mad at me anymore?"

"Don't rush it," Angie said, taking the last swallow of vodka in her glass. "Let me think."

He reached across the litter of their meal, took her wrists in his hands, and pulled her face to his. "Can you think while I do this?"

"I do my best thinking when I'm lying down," Angie said, when the kiss broke. "Or sitting in a chair. Your call. What?" she said, alarmed by the look on his face.

"I don't think I have any condoms." He got up and patted his pockets, found his wallet, pulled it out. He looked as frantic as Angie felt as he tried to open it. The wallet flipped out of his hands, spitting out a shower of credit cards and bits of paper and business cards that flew over the floor. Angie caught a flash of foil and went diving after it, came up with a half piece of gum still in its wrapper.

"Shit," John was saying. "Shit, shit, shit."

Angie flung herself down on the couch and the cushions crackled suspiciously. John heard it, too.

"Didn't you tell me Tony brings women here sometimes?" John asked. And then they were both taking the couch apart. Among candy bar wrappers and store receipts and note cards covered with Tony's scrawling handwriting there was a long streamer, bright blue foil squares each containing a ribbed circle. Six of them.

John reached for her, grinning. "I'll die trying, I promise you that."

Somewhere among the wreckage on the floor, Angie remembered, there was a carton of juice. She was thirsty enough to go look for it, so she began to disentangle herself from John. Her sweaty skin peeled away from the leather cushions with a vaguely obscene sound, and he cracked one eye at her.

"Who," Angie said, "puts a leather couch in an editing suite reception room?"

John's hand moved up her back, his thumb questing. "Hey. I may have my faults, but when it comes to negotiating with university autocrats, I am without peer. First class all the way for the new film program."

"You're responsible for this couch?" Angie grinned. "Did they hire you for your skills as an interior decorator?"

"No, they hired me as chair of the English department," John said, yawning, but his hands seemed completely awake and interested in exploring. She knocked them away.

"Explain."

He cocked his head at her. "They made me an offer, I made them a counteroffer, you know how it goes."

"You asked for a leather couch in the editing suite."

"God, you're dense sometimes." He pulled her closer and kissed her. "I told them the department needed to add a film studies curriculum. I made it a condition of my hire. I was right, they didn't fight it."

"Explain the couch."

He laughed at that. "What's to explain? I negotiated a budget for production facilities. I made some calls and had it designed. They started what, last January, finished in June. Money does make some things easier."

Angie thought about that for a minute. "But you don't have any film faculty."

"We're going to be searching this year," John said. "Two faculty positions, one administrative to run this place."

They would be looking for a new medievalist, too, Angie knew, but now was not the time to be thinking about Caroline Rose.

He said, "You interested?" His tone was perfectly easy, as if he had an endless supply of good things in his pocket, things that were hers for the asking; things he wanted her to have.

Angie sat up and scooted away before he could stop her. "I might teach one course in the fall for you, but that's it." She looked at him over her shoulder as she began to shift through the stuff on the floor. "You'll have five hundred applications, you won't miss mine. Here"—she tossed him a takeout carton—"the last of the dim sum. *Mangia*, Harvey, you've got to keep up your strength."

He was starting to say something, trying to draw her back into this discussion: the wheres and whys and hows; whether they could live together; if they'd survive living apart; what the costs would be, the dangers, the sacrifices; what she was willing to risk. He had already risked everything, but he would never remind her of that, and she was thankful.

John said, "Come here."

She saw the juice carton and grabbed it, and caught sight of what it had been covering up: a small photograph, no more than three inches square, molded to the shape of John's wallet, slightly frayed at the edges, as if it had been often taken out and studied. A photograph of her. Five years younger, just out of graduate school, frightened, miserable, in love. She was sitting on a Long Island beach in a drizzle, on a Sunday afternoon in August. Rain or tears or both on her face, her hair a mass of blue spikes. She had been thinking about leaving John, about walking away from things she couldn't cope with, didn't understand; walking away before he had a chance to see her for what she was. As she had, that very night.

Now John was watching her look at the photograph. His expression was thoughtful, too, a little wary, hopeful.

Angie got up and went around the coffee table to sit on the edge of the leather couch. He took the photo from her and put it aside, cupped her face with his hand, and smiled at her.

She said, "John. What were we thinking?"

He shook his head. "We weren't thinking."

"I have some questions for Miss Zula."

"Later," John said, drawing her down to him. "Tomorrow, or maybe the day after."

TWENTY-ONE

You want my opinion, you should be making a documentary about how y'all talk a different language than we do down here. And I don't mean English, neither. I never have run into a Yankee who don't come down here with all kinds of crazy ideas about who we are and what we think and how we spend all our time figuring out how to make life hard for black people, but then never really listen when we try to say plain how things really are. You had best start large, if you really want to tell the story of Miss Zula's life, because all of Ogilvie had a hand in bringing her up, as she has had a hand in each of our lives.

Your name: Walker Winfield. If you're willing to listen to what I have got to say, stop by and see me anytime.

Sunday morning Angie was trying to make some order out of the mess in the reception area while John slept. She was folding his trousers when his cell phone fell out of the pocket and gave a soft beep.

She picked it up and looked at the display screen. It was the battery that was beeping, down to its last half bar of life. The reception bars, on the other hand, were all there: five of them. The ringer was off, but the tiny envelope that indicated waiting voice mail was glowing. The number next to it had a certain symmetry that Angie had to appreciate: eighty-eight. He had eighty-eight messages, from the woman he had left at the altar, her family, his own, curious neighbors, relatives, colleagues, most probably one or all of the people who wrote for the *Bugle*. Messages that would be distraught and angry and colorful in a variety of ways. If this were her phone, if these messages had been left for her, she would have deleted them all, without ever listening to a single one. But John would listen; that was one difference between them, and nothing she could be proud of.

John woke up when she kissed his cheek. He turned his head toward her, mumbling, "Where did you go?" His arm came up and pulled her in.

"Just tidying up," Angie said. She held up his phone for him to see, and watched him wake up, fast. "This is a satellite phone. We could have got out of here yesterday, and you knew it."

He didn't avoid her gaze, made no apologies. "I suspected, but I didn't look."

"Ah. Plausible deniability?"

"That was my plan, pretty much. You mad?"

His eyes were very blue, and his expression only vaguely contrite.

"Nah. So, you want to get out of here?"

He stretched, yawned, stretched again. Peeked at her with one eye cracked open. "How many condoms left?"

She smacked him. "Are you going to call the police on Patty-Cake?"

"Do you want me to?"

She shrugged. "On the one hand, I'd certainly like to see Win Walker's face if he has to arrest her. On the other—I think you could be more creative than the police would be."

"You're right," John said. "I have a few unorthodox ideas for dealing with Patty-Cake. But that comes later. First I have to talk to Caroline, and then we have to get out of here."

Angie found she didn't want to listen to any conversations John might need to have. She took a shower, washed plastic cups, made coffee, cleaned up in the conference room. Thinking, as she did, of all the things that might be going wrong out there in the light of day, where people were no doubt still looking for John, and Rivera, if no one else, was beginning to wonder about her. Suddenly the idea of another twenty-four hours locked in these rooms with John seemed very attractive.

When he came to find her she told him so. She said, "I'd actually like to show you some of our footage, especially the stuff we shot in Savannah. I'm thinking it might be pretty effective to use it layered with passages from Miss Maddie's autobiography— Oh. Um, I never did get around to telling you about that."

He looked more intrigued than concerned. "Miss Maddie wrote an autobiography?"

As Angie explained, John studied the floor. There was nothing frightening in that, especially, but she wished she had not brought up the subject of work so soon. The day ahead of them would be hard enough.

John raised his head and looked at her, his expression thoughtful, alert, almost severe in its sincerity. He said, "I know how important this is, I do. But just for today, can we forget work?"

She walked up to him and put her face to his shoulder and her arms around his waist. And nodded, because she didn't trust herself to talk.

"Hey," he said gently, rubbing her back. "Did I manage to say the right thing?"

She nodded again, cleared her throat, and leaned back to look at him. "Thank you."

"Why, you're welcome, darlin'. Do you want to know about Caroline?"

"Not especially," Angie said. "But you better tell me anyway."

"It was Miss Junie on the phone. Caroline was out running."

"Running."

"After early mass, according to her mama."

Angie said, "So, did Miss Junie take you apart?"

"Oddly enough, no," John said. "Miss Junie said, and I quote: 'We had a lovely going-away party, I'm so sorry you had to miss it.' She still sees me as the injured party."

"You did tell her why you weren't there?"

"Sure. Later today the Rose girls will be paying Patty-Cake a visit, you can be sure of that. Whatever vitriol was headed my way has been effectively diverted."

"You are *bad*," Angie said, laughing.

"Listen." He lifted his head. "Here comes Rob."

From the other side of the door came the sound of muffled voices and something being dragged along the floor. Angie was just starting to realize that she wasn't hearing Rob Grant's voice when a key turned in the lock and the door swung open.

". . . hell if I know," Tony was saying.

His head was turned away so he didn't see Angie and John standing there, but Harriet Rose Darling did. Her eyes went very large and very round, and the color drained out of her face.

"What?" said Tony, and turned. He blinked.

"Hey, Ang," he said. "John. Great minds, and all that." He managed a half grin.

Harriet said, "John Grant, what are you doing here with Angie?"

"The same thing you were going to do here with Tony," Angie said. "If I'm busted, so are you."

Harriet flushed, her mouth in a perfect circle, but Tony put himself in front of her before she could say anything more. "We'll have to go to plan B. See y'all later." He pulled the door shut and opened it again immediately, ducking his head apologetically. "Uh, there's something here I need to—"

Angie grabbed the remaining condoms off the coffee table and handed them over without a word. Tony wiggled his eyebrows at John, and closed the door again.

Angie said, "Well, that explains a few things."

"And confuses others." John snorted, and then they were laughing so hard, they had to hold on to each other. They were still laughing when a hesitant knock at the door interrupted them. John opened it. Rob and Kai were standing in the hall, looking at a high-backed wooden chair. The one, Angie assumed, that Patty-Cake had wedged under the doorknob.

Rob said, "How hard did you try to get out, anyway?"

"I am not an attorney, but I advise you anyway, don't answer." Kai held up a large white paper box. "We brought breakfast from the bakery."

"I trust y'all have coffee," said Lucy, swooping in. "Don't make a face, John, and don't blame your brother. I wasn't about to be left out. A boy needs his mama at a time like this, I don't care how old he is."

John looked remarkably sanguine at the unexpected sight of his mother. "I'm thirty-six, Mama, which means you must be—"

"Now, don't be fresh," Lucy said, frowning at him. She came over to Angie and hugged her. "Sit down and eat something, sugar. John, you look like a bum."

"Why, thank you, Mama," John said dryly. He lifted the lid of the bakery box and peered inside. "Speaking of bums, where is Sam?"

"Stop," Lucy said. "I'm not going to let you rile me, not this morning. I sent Sam home. This kind of family melodrama gives him hives."

"And he was getting on your nerves," Kai volunteered.

"That too." Lucy winked at John. "Y'all missed one hell of a party yesterday."

"So Miss Junie tells me." He turned to his brother. "How did Caroline seem to you?"

"Transformed," Rob said. "She wouldn't let anybody leave. Insisted they all stay and have a good time. I know I did. Or I would have, if I hadn't been worried about you."

Lucy and Kai laughed at Rob openly, until he held up his hands to ask for mercy.

Angie said, "Will somebody please give me the highlights?"

John was glad to see Angie relax as Lucy and Kai worked together, the oddest relay team imaginable, to reconstruct the non-wedding of the season at Old Roses. She was leaning against him, her skin cool against his, and John was sorry that she had found his phone, even sorrier that Tony had showed up to reclaim his condoms. They'd have to stop at the drugstore on the way home.

"Now, my personal favorite part would have to be when Patty-Cake fainted dead away," Lucy was saying. "Just as Caroline said she was moving north to start cooking school, Patty-Cake went down for the count."

"I think Tony got that on video," Rob said. "You'll be able to see it for yourself."

"I'm looking forward to it," John said. "Almost as much as I am to her resignation."

"So now what will you two do?" Kai said cheerfully, looking from John to Angie and back again. "Everybody thinks you ran away together, of course. "

Angie said, "Oh, great." John could feel her tense, humming like an electric current where their arms touched.

Lucy leaned over and squeezed her hand. "Sugar, I have been coping with Ogilvie gossips for all of my life, and my best advice is this: Don't disappoint them."

Rob groaned, but Lucy ignored him. "If they want to believe you two have run off together, then run off. It will make them happy and stop the talk quicker than trying to convince them otherwise. Beyond that, everybody loves a happy ending, and you two certainly deserve one."

"Unless you do not want to be together," Kai said, equably. "In which case, such a solution would be counterproductive."

Angie took a deep breath, while John found he could hardly breathe at all, wondering what was about to go wrong. She sat up very straight, took one of John's hands between her own, and squeezed it. "That may be the most unorthodox bit of advice I've ever heard," she said. "But it makes sense to me."

"It does?" John heard his voice crack. "What about not being rushed, and needing time, and all the rest of the stuff your mother told me?"

She drew in a shaky breath and smiled. "John, you've been hanging in my closet for five years," she said. "If you're ready to come on out, so am I."

Lucy put a hand to her throat, a delicate, desperate gesture. She said, "Closet?"

"It's not what you think, Mama," John said, laughing. "Not at all."

Angie kissed John good-bye and went back to Ivy House on her own, because, she told him, she was worried about Rivera. It happened to be true, but it wasn't the whole truth. John, who had developed the beginnings of an insight into the way she thought and the things she needed, kissed her soundly and then whispered into her ear so that nobody else could hear.

"Take whatever time you need," he said. "You call me when you're ready."

All the way back to Ivy House, Angie thought about the strange state of being *ready*, about being willing to take the next step, prepared for almost anything. To call John Grant on the phone and tell him he could come and get her now. There were some hard discussions ahead of them, decisions to be made that wouldn't be easy, but even that didn't scare her anymore. The only thing with the power to frighten her was the thought of Rivera. Rivera, who was like a sister to her, who had helped her through so much, was alone at Ivy House, coping by herself with a broken heart.

But maybe not. There seemed to be some kind of party going on at Ivy House. There was music loud enough to be heard on the street, and when Angie opened the door, the sound of women's voices raised in laughter and talk was clear.

She found them on the screened porch. Rivera and Jude, Miss Zula and

Miss Maddie, and in a corner of the old striped couch, with her bare feet tucked under her, Caroline Rose, laughing, her color high and her eyes bright.

"Miss Junie thinks you're out running," Angie said to her.

"This is where I ran to," Caroline said. "I just stopped by to say hello."

To Angie Miss Zula said, "Girl, we thought you'd never show up."

"Where have you got John hid away?" said Jude Parris.

"Don't you be thinking about John Grant," said Miss Zula. "Now that he's good and settled."

"That's not what I want him for," said Jude. "I want to talk to him about applying for one of the new film positions."

"He would have been there yesterday," Angie said, mostly to Caroline. "But Patty-Cake got in the way."

"Mama told me. Now she's so mad at Patty-Cake it takes some of the pressure off me. And she's just about ready to canonize John for putting up with me for so long anyway."

Rivera had been sitting quietly through all this, smiling broadly at everything and everybody. Angie said, "Rivera, aren't you going to say anything to me at all?"

And then Rivera was there, her strong arms reassuring and welcoming, her smile unforced and full of promise. "Sure I do," said Rivera. "Good things come to those who don't panic."

"Girls, sit down," said Miss Maddie. "Jude, give Angie a glass of wine."

"Wine would be nice," Angie said. "Some answers would be even better." She looked right at Miss Zula when she said this, and for once got a look in return that was completely open.

"You'll get those, too," Miss Zula said. "Today, Angeline Mangiamele, you'll get just about anything you can bring yourself to ask for."

· EPILOGUE ·

Ogilvie Bugle

NEWS ABOUT TOWN

OP-TV public access television is looking for folks who want to develop innovative ideas for new programming. If you've been watching since Tony Russo took over as director, you'll have a sense of what they're looking for, such as Kai Watanabe's program on philosophy and religion. This week she will be talking to Win Walker and Walker Winfield on definitions of God and goodness. There's a rumor that Markus Holmes has convinced Miss Zula Bragg and Mrs. Button Ogilvie to debate their views on Ogilvie's past, on his new program called *Stories and Histories*. Anybody interested in learning more about video filming and television production is welcome to attend an introductory evening, to be held at Ogilvie College, where Tony is director of the Film and Video Production Center.

Patty-Cake Walker has recently received her Georgia State certification as a dental hygienist. You'll find her at Dr. Tab Darling's office five days a week. Come by and let her polish up your smile.

Miss Junie Rose tells us that our own Caroline Rose is at the top of her class at the Culinary Institute in Hyde Park, New York. Once she's finished with her studies, Caroline intends to open a new restaurant called Southern Comfort in Hoboken, New Jersey.

If you've been following our coverage you'll know that *Zula*, the documentary that premiered at the college's 150-year anniversary celebration this past June, has received prizes and honors at film festivals from California to France. Tied to the Tracks has begun work on a new documentary on the North-South cultural divide, with funding from the NEA and other organizations. If you've got stories to share, please contact the Tied to the Tracks branch office on Main Street, make an entry in the new memory book at the Piggy Wiggly, or stop by John and Angie's. They'd be pleased to see you, anytime.

Author's Note and Acknowledgments

Zula Bragg is an entirely fictional character, and so is everybody else in this novel. Thus: any resemblance to persons living or dead is entirely coincidental, and the figment of somebody else's imagination.

There is no Ogilvie College nor is there a town called Ogilvie in Georgia. I have put my imaginary Ogilvie southeast of Savannah on a railway line that is mostly fictional. The Seaboard Coast Line once existed, but in 1986 it was subsumed into the less poetically named CSX Transportation, and diverted.

All reference works quoted here also are fictional, and of my creation alone, but *Farscape*, Rivera's and Angie's favorite sci-fi television program, is indeed real.

Lots of people lent a hand with this, many of them born-and-bred southerners; others who came to the South by choice or chance. These include Bruce Beasley, Penny Chambers, Thor Hansen, and Suzanne Paola. I'm especially thankful for the thoughtful reading of early and not-so-early drafts by Pokey Bolton, Cheryll Greenwood Kinsley, and Ruth Czirr. Ruth was tremendously helpful in sorting through some of the complexities of southern small-town customs and social structures. Joy Johannessen provided much-needed and very welcome editorial commentary and a new perspective, which were immensely helpful. Joe Vassallo answered a lot of questions about documentary film production with great clarity and patience. As always, mistakes are not to be laid at anybody's doorstep but my own.

Thanks especially to Jill Grinberg, for thoughtful feedback and encouragement when it was most needed, to Leona Nevler, who fell for Ogilvie just as hard as I did, and to Bill and Elisabeth, whose faith in me seems to have no bounds.